POWER AWRY

WILD HERITANCE, BOOK 2

S. LYNN HELTON

Copyright © 2019 S. Lynn Helton
Cover by R. M. Helton

ISBN (Paperback): 978-1-7326763-4-3
ISBN (eBook): 978-1-7326763-5-0

Scripturio Books
www.ScripturioBooks.com
24.04.05

DEDICATION

To my husband, my love, first reader and
amazing source of all sorts of great ideas!

ACKNOWLEDGMENTS

Thank you as always to my beta readers, for insights,
feedback and great suggestions to help improve the story.

CHAPTER 1

"Fire?"

Namid nodded and grinned at Thes. "Yes. I can do more than just move heavy rocks around to help rebuild the Keep." Close to four weeks Namid had spent, so far, back in the devastated city of Rhadanthus, helping rebuild Shadow Keep, home to the Shadowers, the city's select guild of rogues. Or rather the remnants of that guild.

Thes returned her grin, the expression almost hidden in his gray tangle of beard. "So what I'm hearin' is that we could be makin' more use o' that magic o' yours."

Namid sighed and brushed her sweaty bangs off her forehead in the unaccustomed heat of the early winter day. The bangs flopped right back into her eyes. She should cut them. A single long braid contained the rest of her black hair, but the bangs had gotten rather shaggy. She would not be surprised to learn that the few others who still called the city home had set aside appearances, as she had, until they could rebuild shelters for winter.

"Those of us who use it call it Power, Thes. And do you want to hear the rest before you find yet more for me to do?" Namid said as she stepped over some of the scattered debris from the destruction of the city the past autumn.

Thes paused and faced her, of a height with her to look her straight in the eyes. "O' course I'll be askin' you t' use your ma— Power t' help as much as you can. This weather won't last. We all know it. And the Shadowers need better shelter if we're t' last the winter."

Namid nodded. "I know. I'm just tired, I suppose."

Thes patted her shoulder. "We're the only two left who are anythin' like leaders in the Shadowers. Makes it rough. But a good leader takes the time for bit o' rest now and then. Makes sure the rest o' them know they should, too."

"So this is rest, is it?" Namid said, with a grin for the man who was probably over two score years her elder.

"Well, it's not haulin' the rocks around, is it?"

They resumed walking, headed to something Thes had said he wanted to show her. And Namid continued telling him about the events of the previous autumn in which she had been entangled… Enric's quest to restore Akavos, the broken sword of Power, and how that connected to the end of the god Sesaisyd and his Dark Priests in their city of Corentris, including the man known variously as the priest Chendrukhar, mage of Rhadanthus, or Myung or Wesh. She avoided mentioning that she had learned that the gods were not really divine beings, but rather only ancient, Power-grabbing mages. That knowledge had come from Sesaisyd himself and she felt uncomfortable sharing it.

The end of her tale coincided with their arrival at the center of Rhadanthus. Or rather the destruction that marked the center of the city.

Namid felt Thes' gaze on her as she took in the sight.

They stood near the edge of what had been the temple circle, the literal center of Rhadanthus. Here the destruction took a different shape from elsewhere in the city. Here, instead of melted structures from the killing fog Sy'shythys, everything looked like it had been blasted up and away from a depression in the middle.

Namid scrutinized it, then looked all around her. Beyond a distinct edge, the destruction consisted of melted buildings, rather than thrown ones, with not a single building intact.

"They lied… those false Warders I told you about from last autumn," Namid murmured. "Sy'shythys *did* encompass the whole city."

Thes nodded. "And this," he said and waved an arm at the area of differing destruction. "What do you make o' this?"

"It matches where the Power blasted upward when Aah— when Aahmes broke the sword…" Namid said, stumbling over the former Shadower's name as she usually did when she spoke of him. At least she no longer looked for him more than half a dozen times a day. Or so.

Thes stared at the destruction, giving her time to regain her composure. "You miss him."

Namid nodded. "And Dar…. My brothers…." Namid pulled herself away from those thoughts and studied the devastation before them.

"Incredible," she murmured. "Looks like not only Sy'shythys but any Power that affected Corentris also hit Rhadanthus."

"Probably good it's all buried and gone now," Thes said. "It is, right?"

"Definitely," Namid said with a firm nod. She pointed to a line of lighter-colored stones embedded in the far wall of the hole. It lay more than a pace lower than the rubble that clearly came from familiar buildings of Rhadanthus. "What's that line, do you think?"

Thes peered at it. "Probably just more broken bricks and worked stone," he said. "Nothin' like from any o' the buildin's that stood here. Maybe our city was built atop older broken buildin's."

"Maybe." Namid studied the line a little longer. It did not look very thick, certainly not enough to be the rubble from entire buildings, she thought. With a shrug, she headed back to Shadow Keep and Thes kept pace with her.

About halfway back, Namid slowed to look around. "We're near where that jeweler used to have his shop…."

Thes gave her a questioning look. "Jeweler?"

"Uh, that goldsmith who would allow himself to be persuaded to make copies of signets and seals. His words. For a price, of course," Namid said.

"Oh, aye. But I think he turned the business over t' his nephew a couple years back."

"Do you know if he survived?"

Thes shrugged. "Hard t' say. So many survivors left runnin' as fast as they could. What would you be needin' a signet or seal for?"

"Oh, I don't need either of those." Namid pulled a small wood box from a pouch secured to her belt and held it out to Thes. "This is what was in that parchment you gave me a couple of weeks ago. That Dar left with you for me."

Thes opened it and studied the impression of the key in the clay inside—one half in the top and the other in the bottom of the box—with its distinctive, roughly star-shaped bow. He whistled, then spoke in a near-whisper. "Exactly the shape o' the Star o' Corentris…."

"Yes," Namid said, keeping her voice as quiet as Thes'. "I thought of trying to melt some metal and pour it in myself, to make a copy. See, there's even a hole in the end. But I've not ever done something like that. So, I thought I'd see if I could talk with someone who might know more of that sort of thing."

Still whispering, Thes glanced to the east where the three towers of the dead mage's stronghold outside the city were just visible over the city walls. "Thinkin' it's the key t' Chendrukhar's hold? Never been much for the copyin' m'self. Would rather pick any lock I'd be needin' t' open. Probably not wise for a mage's place, though. Maybe one o' the other Shadowers knows about the copyin'. I can check around, unless you want t'...."

Namid shook her head. "My thanks. Doesn't have to be me. Just keep it quiet about what we think the key goes to."

"O' course."

~ ~ ~

After the evening meal, a woman, a young Shadower that Namid recognized but did not know well, approached her and gave her a diffident bow. They had the Keep's unroofed main level mostly to themselves as most of the Shadowers had already settled in the underground rooms for the night.

"Leader," said the woman, shifting her feet around. "Leader Thes told me I should come see you.... Have I done something wrong?"

Namid guessed the woman had to be close to her own years, but the way she acted made her seem much younger. She seemed terrified of Namid and avoided meeting her gaze.

"Have you?" Namid said in a gently teasing tone.

The woman gave her a frightened glance, then stared at the floor. "N-no, I don't think so."

All right, no teasing.

Namid sighed. The Shadowers seemed all too serious these days. She missed the jokes and banter. Still, with all that had happened, it was probably to be expected.

"Call me Namid, not 'Leader'," she said. "I keep telling everyone that. Sit, please. I remember you, but not your name...."

"I-I'm Vayaza, Lea— uh, Namid."

Namid nodded. "Well, then, Vayaza. Thes sent you to me because I have need of a specific skill, one I'm hoping you have."

Vayaza glanced at her and looked away again when she saw that Namid watched her. But Namid caught a hint of interest in Vayaza's expression.

"I-I don't know what help I can be," she said. "I passed my Trial just the past summer."

"Ah. Congratulations and welcome, then," Namid said. "What I need is someone who knows about making a copy of a key."

Vayaza gave her a quick, genuine grin. "Oh, aye, that I can do! But we don't have what we need to do it anymore. No clay to make the impression, no metal to melt…. How would we even melt it?"

"I can melt the metal," Namid said.

Vayaza's eyes widened. She gulped and nodded.

"As for the rest," Namid continued, "perhaps we can scrounge up enough metal, maybe from the horses' tack or something else the Shadowers brought back from Wesh's camp. Maybe we can even find some melted chunks within the city, in the midst of the melted stones. And I already have the impression, so…."

"So we're already halfway there." Vayaza shared a grin with her. "I'm happy to help with this. I've missed these parts of being a Shadower." She lowered her voice and glanced around. "To be truthful, I'm tired of moving rocks."

Namid nodded. "To be truthful, I am too. But I don't want to find myself sleeping in a snowdrift in a few weeks."

Vayaza actually chuckled at that. "True. I'll poke around and see what I can come up with for metal. Just one key?"

"If we can find the metal to make two, that would be good. But at least the one."

Vayaza nodded. "Could I see the impression? Give me an idea how much metal we'd be needing."

With a nod, Namid pulled the small box from her pouch and handed it to Vayaza.

The younger Shadower opened the box with care and studied the impression within. She touched a finger to the clay and frowned.

"Something wrong?" Namid said.

"We can't use this as it is," Vayaza said. "The clay is very dry, which is good for a start. And it's a kind of clay that hardly shrinks at all. Also good. But if we pour the hot metal into it as it is, the key will come out very rough. Maybe so much so that it won't even work in the lock."

"So it's useless?"

Vayaza shook her head. "I didn't say that. We just have some extra work. We need to fire the clay for the mold to work. And I must warn you, even then it will probably crack after just one key. I don't think we'll be getting two from it."

Namid studied the box in Vayaza's hands while she considered that. "Well, if we can only get the one, that'll have to do. So how do we fire the clay?"

"If you can melt metal, you can heat the clay enough to fire it. But it has to be heated slowly or it'll break before it's finished."

"How long, then?"

"Most of a day, just for the heating. And then about the same number of candle-marks to cool. It can't cool down too fast either."

Vayaza closed the box and returned it to Namid, who tucked it away again.

"And we must do this?" Namid said.

Vayaza nodded. "To have the best result, yes."

"All right, then. I'll pick a day soon and find a place to do this, then grab you to help."

"I was hoping you'd say that. I could *really* use a break from rebuilding." Vayaza grinned and took her leave.

Namid watched her join a small group across the room. It looked like they teased her before they all settled along the wall and passed around a jug.

Namid wondered if the fear and diffidence were because she—along with Thes, of course—was the only remaining leader from before Sy'shythys or if it was because of the Power. She had tried to keep her use of Power reserved, tried to use it without being too obvious about it. But she suspected that was the source of Vayaza's manner.

Not much to be done about it.

Namid stretched and yawned and headed off to one of the crowded underground rooms to grab one of the mats they were all using to sleep on. The time to get up and continue rebuilding would come all too soon.

~ ~ ~

Near midday a few days later, what seemed an excess of activity among the Shadowers disturbed Namid's concentration in the Power. She had been trying to devise a solution to the holes between the irregularly shaped rocks the Shadowers were using to recreate the Keep's walls. The rebuilt parts of Shadow Keep still had so many gaps as to make the interior almost as cold as not having any shelter at all. And none of the Shadowers—including her—knew much of anything about how to build walls, especially with the limited materials to be had in the ruined city.

Shadowers learned a number of skills, but stonework was *not* one of them.

They *had* considered trying to fill the holes with thick mud and letting it dry. But while Namid could use the Power to dig up dirt, the two working wells were providing only enough water for the people and horses in the city. And the small river that ran through Rhadanthus was dry, as normal for the season. They had no spare water to make mud.

So Namid had been trying to use her Power to fuse rocks together much as Haeith had fused dirt for a ramp the previous autumn. Her idea was to either fuse a bunch of little rocks within the holes to fill them or somehow bring the edges of the bigger rocks together to close the holes.

It had not been going well.

Nearly every attempt resulted in the opposite effect and blasted apart whatever rocks she was working with, no matter how large or small. Or worse, blasted apart a section of rebuilt wall. And the Power often slid away from her without warning, usually giving her a much larger burst. Not even counting the times she could not seem to grasp it well enough at all to do anything needing finesse.

She almost felt like she had when she was first learning to use her Power... inadequate and unprepared. She held more than enough Power, with the half of Sesaisyd's Power that had come to her at his death blended with her own Power. But it had become slippery and shifty. With a sigh, she dropped the latest handful of broken rocks.

She stretched stiff muscles and watched the other Shadowers' activity from her spot many paces away. After the first couple times she accidentally blasted apart the rocks, she had taken herself far away from the others for working on this rock-fusing idea.

A number of Shadowers seemed upset, but she saw nothing obviously wrong. She sent a thin wave of Power out into the surrounding city, stretching her senses, but sensed nothing amiss there either.

At least *that* worked as it had before.

With a groan—she had sat too still for too long—she levered herself to her feet and walked over to find Thes in the center of the activity. The look he gave her told her something was wrong. But most likely more an annoyance than a threat of some kind, she decided from his expression.

She held up a hand for him to wait and grabbed something to eat from what had been set out for the midday meal. Then she joined Thes at one of the few tables they had, all constructed from the wagons they had brought with them from Wesh's bandit camp and the few wooden scraps the Shadowers found in the city.

"What's all the fuss?" Namid said around a bite of food. "I haven't sensed anything with the Power."

Thes frowned and narrowed his eyes at her statement.

"Seems we've got ourselves a thief—"

Namid laughed, unable to help herself. Thes glowered at her, then grinned, at least seeing the humor of someone stealing from a guild of thieves.

"Wasn't so sure at first," he said when Namid's laughter quieted. "Started near a week ago, maybe more. Hard t' be sure. Whoever's doin' it's good. Leaves no obvious gaps in our stores."

"Are we sure it's someone stealing? Maybe some Shadower's been taking some things to help out a friend in the city."

Thes looked thoughtful. "Suppose it could be…."

"What's missing?"

"Can't be sayin' exactly. But some food. And some o' the clothin' that we kept stashed for use as guises before."

"I'm sure Keizha can at least tell us which clothing is missing," Namid said.

"Oh, aye. She told me a warm cloak and a couple of the plainest tunics and trousers. Brown-gray, she said. Big enough for an adult. A dagger."

Namid considered the information for a couple more bites of food. "Is there anything left in the city worth stealing? Anyone left worth stealing from? That almost sounds like someone planning some pilferage."

"Aye, that it does. Except for the missin' food." Thes shook his head. "But we don't know that one person alone took all the missin' things. Could be more than one. I was wonderin', could you perhaps take a bit o' a look, with your mag— Power? Maybe you'd notice somethin'?"

Namid nodded. "I can try. I don't know that the Power will show me anything you haven't already noticed, but I'll take a look."

"My thanks." He placed a hand on her arm. "And after, maybe you should do some restin' before you go back t' the rocks. You're not lookin' so good."

Namid gave him a wry grin. "Why, thank you for pointing that out."

Thes chuckled. "Off t' deal with the next problem." He left her to her meal.

As she finished her last bite, Namid took the stairs to the underground rooms. This level consisted of four rooms: the larger room that used to house all the apprentices sometime before Namid became a Shadower, the two rooms where Keizha stored odds and ends the Shadowers had gathered over the years and the storeroom that held the bulk of the Shadowers' foodstuffs. A short hall that began at the bottom of the staircase connected all the rooms.

"Keizha," Namid called.

When the older Shadower did not answer, Namid eased into her two rooms. Keizha was not there, probably occupied up above like the rest of the Shadowers.

Namid set a thin shell of Power around herself—twice, as the first one slid apart immediately—with tendrils that extended outward, then she drifted through the two rooms. Keizha kept all the clothing and random items stacked in neat piles in her own system of organization. Tucked far back in the smaller room was her bed and a small trunk for her personal items.

Namid sensed nothing through the Power. And certainly noticed nothing missing. But then only Keizha knew everything stored in the place.

Namid checked the storeroom next. Again, she would not have known by looking that anything was missing. It looked like they had a good amount of food. Enough to make it through the winter, she hoped. She again sensed nothing through the Power.

For thoroughness, she decided to look in the last room, too, although it almost always had someone in it. That was the room in which most of the Shadowers had been sleeping until they completed the main level ceiling enough to—hopefully—block any snowfall. Namid still worried about the many gaps between the larger stones in the walls, too.

Namid paused in the doorway and looked around. For once, no Shadower lingered in the room. But a lot of bedding still lay scattered on the floor. As she paced through the room, she remembered the secret passage Aahmes had used, the duplicate of which he had shown her and their companions in Corentris the past autumn.

Namid sent out a slightly greater amount of Power, reaching toward the section of the floor where she thought the door had been in the duplicate Keep. She was off by less than a pace.

She pushed aside the bedding that partially covered that area and studied the floor through the Power.

Yes, it looked like this one would work the way the one in Corentris had. She started to turn... almost glanced over her shoulder to share a grin with Aahmes, as she would have before. With a grimace, she stopped herself.

She reached out with the smallest tendril of Power and tapped the edge of the rock that she sensed formed the door. Without a sound, the door took shape in the floor. She lifted it without trouble.

She looked down into a tunnel she remembered. It looked like the duplicate she had seen in Corentris, complete with hand-holds and foot-holds sticking out from one of the brick walls.

Namid studied the tunnel from the lip of the trapdoor. From her vantage, the rock floor looked clean, no dirt or dust to show footprints. She did not know if it had always been that way. She closed the trapdoor again and watched it blend into the floor, then hunted down Thes.

Together, the two Shadowers studied the tunnel visible through the trapdoor as Namid had on her own.

"Thinkin' you should check it further?" Thes said.

"Possibly," Namid said. "I'm interested in seeing if it comes out the same place as the duplicate did in

Corentris."

"And what of the other direction?"

Namid shrugged. "I know nothing of what might be that way. Might be good to find out. Or... I could just block the door with Power. No one's likely to get through that."

Thes nodded. "Though we don't know that our thief is even usin' this way to get in."

"True enough."

Thes closed the trapdoor and watched it become one with the floor.

"Nice trick," he said and smiled at Namid. "Just let me know before you go explorin'. In case I need t' send someone t' find you when you get lost."

Namid chuckled. "I won't get lost."

CHAPTER 2

Namid fiercely squelched the thought that she might be lost and peered around. Momentarily misplaced, she decided. Temporarily wandering randomly.

But truly, she had not expected to find a whole maze of tunnels beneath the city, although there had been something similar beneath Corentris. With that city duplicating Rhadanthus, she probably should have expected the maze.

But she had not yet found anyplace in these tunnels that duplicated any of the specific areas she remembered from Corentris.

Curious.

Namid sent her small orb of glowing Power a pace in front of her and continued along the current tunnel, stepping around and over uneven sections and minor rockfalls. She had been traversing these passages for close to two candle-marks, but she felt little concern yet about finding her way out. She did wonder however, with some misgiving, just how extensive these passages were. And why hadn't she heard of them through the Shadowers?

As she walked, she sent tendrils of Power through the

walls on either side, trying to learn something that way. So far, she had learned nothing.

Another twenty or so paces brought her to a branch. Her current tunnel split into two that headed off in slightly different directions.

She sent her glowing orb down first one, then the other, but saw no real difference between the two, at least as far as she could see the orb.

She slid down the wall to sit and drank from her waterskin. At least she had brought water with her. She leaned back with her eyes closed and reached out as far as she could along each passage with the Power.

At the edge of her reach with Power—without drawing from surrounding Power anyway—she sensed something. A sort of Power barrier.

Why had she not noticed it before?

She gave that some thought and realized that every time she had previously sent out her Power, when on the surface, she had not directed her attention down into the ground at all. Something to remember for the future.

She took another drink of water and headed toward the Power she had discovered.

She found its location obvious when she arrived. She stepped out of the narrow tunnel into a large cavern. Sending the light orb to hover near the ceiling, she fed it more Power for more light. The cavern reached twenty or more paces across, roughly oval-shaped. Namid saw several dark recesses along the walls, she assumed openings that led to more tunnels. The rocks of the walls, floor and ceiling looked no different from what she had seen in the tunnels, pale gray and rough to the touch. But the Power that had drawn her here surrounded her and permeated the walls, floor and ceiling.

What could the Power be for? And who had done this? The feel of the Power was somewhat familiar. But Namid felt certain it had not been set by anyone she knew. Perhaps some Power she had touched before somewhere?

But where? The memory would not come. The Power had an impression of age to it. Some long-forgotten mage, she decided.

She had no trouble maintaining and controlling her light orb, so the Power in the rocks around her did not prevent the use of Power. She wandered around, absently pulling her light orb with her to study the place. She found random scorch marks on some parts of the floor and walls.

Namid sent a few tendrils of Power out and they stopped abruptly at the walls. The same for the floor and ceiling.

A place that Power could not get out of?

She reached to draw in Power from her surroundings. It came through walls, floor and ceiling without trouble. She gathered more and smiled with delight at the heady rush of filling herself with the Power.

Then she threw it back out. Raw Power flew out in all directions. It hit the walls, ceiling and floor... and dissipated. No damage to them, and it did not go through.

"A room strengthened with Power to contain anything within," she muttered. "A place to work with Power? Or to hold someone with Power?"

Well, probably not the latter, with all those openings, she decided. She would have to return here and try some things she had thought of with the Power, things she dared not try elsewhere because they could be too dangerous to anyone else anywhere nearby.

Namid drew more Power to herself then sent it flying out again. But this time, she felt a strange twist. And the Power spun out of control around her.

As she scrambled to build a protection of Power around herself, the loose Power exploded around her and pelted her with tiny Powerful shards, much like when Sesaisyd's Power had come to her. The shards stung. But she found no visible harm when she examined her arms and hands, the only skin other than her face not covered by clothing. And her clothes showed no damage from the shards of Power.

In the next breath-of-time, the Power dissipated.

Namid staggered under a wave of exhaustion that washed over her. She sat abruptly, wincing at a sudden burning sensation in her back, in her scars from the Dark Priests' whips. Since the previous autumn the scars sometimes hurt again, after years of only minor stiffness.

A sound like rock on rock caught her attention. She froze and listened, pushing aside her concerns over the pain. She dimmed her light orb so that she could still see but likely no one else could. Being able to see well in light too dim for most people had come in handy before. And she waited.

She had the sudden sensation of being watched. Gingerly she drew on her Power, gathering it together in preparation for use. No pain, this time, but some Power slipped away, like water sliding through her fingers. Still she held enough. She also drew a dagger. She sent the Power out, this time directed toward all the openings.

Nothing.

With a sigh, Namid clambered to her feet and made her way to the closest wall. From there, she sidled toward where she thought the sound had come from.

She felt nothing through the Power, so she peered into the tunnel. Maybe a scuff mark on the rock floor. But who knew how long that might have been there.

Namid quenched her light orb and sat right next to the opening, inside the large cavern, for close to a quarter candle-mark. She heard nothing further.

So she formed a light orb again, still keeping it dim. And waited a bit longer.

Still nothing.

She took a long drink of water and looked around the cavern, wondering how she would best get back to the trapdoor in the Keep's lower level, her entry point into this maze.

A hint of light from her right attracted her attention.

But when she turned to see it more clearly, it disappeared. She felt the faintest trace of Power, though.

What might have triggered some Power?

She grinned as she suspected she knew. Again she concentrated on thoughts of the best way back to the trapdoor, and this time saw a faint glow come from one of the tunnels. The glow lingered as she approached that tunnel, then faded away when she stood a pace from the opening.

With a shrug, she headed into the tunnel. Reasonable to assume that long-gone mage might have left something to help with finding the way around. She hoped she was right.

~ ~ ~

"About time for you t' be returnin'," Thes said when Namid climbed through the trapdoor. "Close t' four candle-marks…. Did you find out anythin'?"

Namid shrugged and closed the trapdoor behind her. "Yes and no. I followed the tunnel toward the other entrance that I knew about but didn't get that far. The tunnel had collapsed and is now blocked. So, I followed it the other way. Did you know there's a whole maze down there?"

Thes shrugged. "Not 'know'. There've been stories from before I became a Shadower. People have looked. But no one could find anythin'. No entrances. Nothin'."

"I still only know of this one entrance." Namid waved her hand at the hidden trapdoor. "But there are a lot of tunnels down there. Caverns, too."

Thes looked thoughtful. "Do we need t' have someone guardin' this trapdoor, then? Did you find any signs that our possible-thief is gettin' in through here?"

Namid shook her head. "Can't tell if it's been used recently. But I'll seal it with Power, just in case."

Thes nodded and watched, his expression curious, as

she did so.

"Thought most o' this mag— Power stuff would be a mite flashier," he said as he followed her toward the stairs.

Namid chuckled. "Thes, you can keep calling it magic. And I'll call it Power. We'll both know what we're talking about."

"Aye."

"I could be much flashier, if you'd like," Namid said. "I just usually try to be inconspicuous, though."

"Good for a Shadower," Thes said with a grin. "Oh, almost forgot t' tell you… Vayaza's lookin' for you."

Leaving Thes, Namid found Vayaza taking a turn in the kitchen area. She greeted Namid with a smile.

"I've found something I think'll work," she said. "I'm almost done here."

"Meet me outside when you are." Namid snatched a piece of bread on her way out.

She waited less than a quarter candle-mark for Vayaza to join her. While she waited, she studied her surroundings. She had that sensation of being watched again. But she spotted no one. When Vayaza joined her, Namid held up a hand to forestall talk and led the way to the makeshift stables the Shadowers had constructed.

No one was there, so close to time for the evening meal, and Namid led the other Shadower in among the horses before stopping.

To Vayaza's delight, Namid created a dim glowing orb.

"Have you found some suitable metal?" Namid said. "I'd hate to have to take apart some of the tack." She kept her voice quiet, in case her sense of being watched was more than just a feeling. With the horses all around them, likely no one would be able to see what they were doing.

Vayaza smiled and pulled something from her pocket. She opened her hand to show Namid the several small lumps of metal she held.

"These should do well," Vayaza said, also speaking quietly.

"Good. Do we need anything else?"

"I've got a fired clay cup that will work well enough. Although I think Keizha won't want to put it back in her stores after we're done. And I found some tongs to use to lift the cup to pour the metal. This'll be crude, you know."

Namid nodded. "How soon can we do this?"

"It's been days since we fired the mold. I think it should have cooled long enough now… so as soon as you want. Tonight, even. We can use one of the small ruins nearby, if you don't want to do this in the Keep."

Namid nodded again. "That'll be perfect."

They agreed to meet again after the evening meal.

~ ~ ~

Namid and Vayaza crouched in a corner of one of the small ruined buildings near Shadow Keep. It offered no true shelter from the cold but kept them invisible to anyone standing any more than about a pace from them. One of Namid's small light orbs hovered close over their heads. Vayaza used the tongs to hold the cup. She dropped the metal bits she had collected into it. The mold sat between them on the ground, the two halves tied tightly together.

"Do you need me to do anything special for the magic?" Vayaza said.

"No. Just tell me when to stop."

Vayaza nodded.

Namid drew on her Power reserve and hoped her control would not slip during this. Concentrating, blocking out her awareness of the cold, she sent a tendril of Power into the cup and touched the metal bits with a thought of heat.

A small blue-white flame jumped up from the metal and startled Vayaza, but Namid clamped down on it and it sank back into the cup. Namid spared a moment to wonder at the color. Before the past autumn, any fire she had produced with Power always looked like normal flame. Maybe something to do with her heritage of Power from Sesaisyd. She set aside those thoughts and brought her attention back to what she and Vayaza were doing.

They both peered into the cup to watch the metal bits melt from the Power, the heat Namid slowly poured into them.

After several long breaths-of-time, Vayaza said, "Enough."

Namid sat back to watch.

Vayaza swirled the metal around the cup, then carefully poured it into the mold of the key. When the metal filled the mold, she set the cup aside an armlength away.

So neither of them would accidentally touch it, Namid assumed.

"And now we wait," Vayaza said, with a shiver.

"Maybe I can use Power to cool it, too. So we can get back to the Keep sooner," Namid said.

"I'd like that."

So again, Namid sent a tendril of Power into the metal. She found it harder to cool it, but still managed to speed the process. When Namid had the metal and mold completely cooled, Vayaza untied the mold to remove the key. As she separated the two halves several pieces of the mold broke off. But the key looked good.

"A little rough in spots," Namid said.

"Easily taken care of," Vayaza said as they gathered everything up. They hurried back to the Keep amid wind and falling snow. Vayaza kept the key to file down the rough spots, with the promise to return it to Namid first thing in the morning.

The next morning, the sun shone again. Some snow lay on the ground, with ice beneath. The Shadowers worked to stuff the remaining holes in their reconstructed Keep with anything they could spare that might help keep out the wind, but spent most of their time in the warmer underground rooms. Everyone there at the same time made it crowded, but still better than spending much time on the ground level.

About mid-morning, Thes made his way through the crowd to find Namid.

"Grab your cloak. Maybe a second one, too. Let's go up top," he said.

On the Keep's ground level, Thes led Namid to the kitchen's fire, low this time of day but still giving off heat.

"We're most out o' usable rocks and such from close by t' rebuild with," Thes said. "O' course, your magic's been a great help movin' everythin' int' place, but any o' us truly can get more rocks from further out in the city, get them back here. Just that'll be takin' a few days most likely, 'til we have enough for you to be workin' on again...." He stared at the floor, lost in thought, while Namid waited and wondered about his point.

"You got that key made, didn't you?"

At Namid's nod, he continued. "Would you go scout out the mage's stronghold? See if there's anythin' there we can use? That's somethin' none o' the rest o' us can safely do...."

"Make sure there are no Power traps for the unwary?"

Thes grinned and nodded. "If you find anythin' there we can use, then a bunch o' us can go over there and clean the place out."

"No one's seen any signs of life over there?"

"Not a one."

"All right, then." Namid wrapped her cloak more tightly around herself and headed toward the door.

"No need t' be goin' right this breath-o'-time," Thes called after her.

Namid glanced back at him. "Might as well. Better than huddling with everyone else, trying to figure out how to get all those holes filled before a real storm."

Thes chuckled. "Aye, you have the right o' that. Be wary."

"Of course."

~ ~ ~

As Namid approached Chendrukhar's stronghold outside Rhadanthus' walls, she studied the three towers and their surrounding wall. The place looked unchanged, clearly untouched by Sy'shythys the previous autumn. With the mage dead, Namid wondered if any of his Power still clung to his home. From this distance, she did not sense any.

She still had seen no sign that anyone was inside by the time she reached the stronghold's closed double gate. Two squat towers flanked the gate and reached above it a couple of paces. Namid tried the gate, and found it locked, as she had expected.

She again felt that sense of being watched and took her time scanning the surrounding land, sending out tendrils of Power, too. She saw and sensed nothing out of the ordinary. The sun had enough warmth that much of the light snow that had fallen had already melted, except in patches shaded by tall grass clumps or low bushes.

With a shrug, Namid turned back to the gate. But she kept a thin aura of Power extended around her, to help sense anything untoward.

Namid pulled out the key that Vayaza had returned to her early that morning. Vayaza had done an excellent job of smoothing the rough edges. Namid tried the key in the gate.

It fit beautifully and turned with only a little more effort than she expected. She pushed the gate open.

Namid caught a glimpse of an empty courtyard when something—a hint of Power, a whisper of sound—warned her of the attack.

She turned enough to wrench herself away from the hand that tried to grasp her but felt the hot, burning pain in her side that meant the attacker's blade had found her.

She jerked away, desperate to get some distance from

her assailant. The motion took her into the courtyard. Quick twists of her wrists dropped her stilettos into her hands from their sheaths within her armguards.

She spun to face her attacker, and froze.

"Aahmes?"

CHAPTER 3

Namid's stunned hesitation almost cost her dearly.

Without a word, Aahmes lunged for her, reaching to grab her again, dagger held ready to strike. She narrowly evaded his grip and slashed at him as she again put some distance between them.

Still, he sliced her again, across her forearm this time.

"How?" she said, her thoughts in confusion.

How was this possible? How could he be here?

As Aahmes' blade almost caught her again, she smothered her bewilderment. She needed to concentrate on the fight.

She was only just keeping away from his blade, his grasp. His attacks came as fast as she had ever seen, his deadly intent quite clear.

But his expression puzzled her, a mix of determination and… sorrow?

Aahmes tried to close with her and she discouraged that with both stilettos, drawing blood from slashes to his forearms.

Still he came after her.

Why was he attacking her?

She twisted to evade him again and gasped at the pain that shot through her side with the motion.

His dagger caught her in the shoulder. At this new shock of pain, she lost her grip on the stiletto she held in that hand.

Namid spun and attacked with her other blade, hoping to open some room between them.

Might this not really be Aahmes? Might someone else know of Wesh's ability to steal the Power and likeness of another?

She could almost hear Wesh's voice again from the previous autumn, listing the people whose Power, knowledge and essences he had stolen, allowing him to replace them. If her attacker was *not* Aahmes, he certainly seemed to have Aahmes' knowledge.

Could one of the other Dark Priests have escaped the destruction of Corentris with the knowledge to do what Wesh had done?

Distracted too much by her questions, Namid slipped on a spot of ice and hit the paved ground of the courtyard hard. She tried to roll away.

Aahmes slammed a foot down at her hand. She jerked back so he narrowly missed crushing her fingers. She stabbed at his leg and almost lost her blade when it caught in the heavy leather of his boot.

She scrambled back to her feet as he reached again to grab her. This time, he was the one who slipped. But his blade drew a bloody line down her leg as he fell.

Namid scuttled away from him and dashed for the gate.

He hurled a blast of Power and slammed it shut in her face.

With a snarl, she whirled to face him. So that was how it was going to be?

Fueled by her anger, her answering bolt of Power became a blue-white fiery blast that slammed into him. He blocked it somehow, kept it from burning him, but it still knocked him back several steps.

She stalked toward him.

"Wait!" he shouted. "I was wrong!"

He dropped his dagger and backed up, holding his hands out, empty.

Namid stopped. She did not want to be too far from the gate if this turned out to be a ploy of some kind.

She glared at him. "Oh?"

Aahmes propped himself up with his hands on his thighs, his breathing labored. And Namid studied him, looking for any sign that he was not who he seemed, the man she knew who so closely matched her in physical appearance: faces of similar shape, lean builds, straight black hair, red-brown skin. There were a few differences between them as there had been before. Namid's hair reached below her waist, when not in its customary braid, while Aahmes wore his at shoulder length. And she stood about half a head shorter than he did.

A partially healed wound ran along his jaw and he looked haggard. His clothes looked like the ones that Thes had told her were missing from Shadow Keep.

He looked like the Aahmes she knew.

"What do you mean 'wrong'?" Namid said.

Now that she was no longer fighting, the pain from her wounds tore through her. She hoped she was not bleeding too badly, but feared to look away from Aahmes, even just a glance, to see.

She also feared that if she looked away, he would vanish, like her visions of him several weeks earlier, after she thought he had been killed in Corentris.

She backed toward the gate.

Aahmes sank down to sit on the cold ground. "I was sure you were Wesh… that Wesh was you. When I saw you use the key to this place to open the gate—"

"Wesh? What?! He's dead. I killed him in Corentris. You were there!"

"I feared that you hadn't. Killed him. That he had instead taken you, your Power, as he bragged about how he took those others. That he'd become you…."

Namid shook her head as she tried to make sense of Aahmes' words, and also her whirling jumble of feelings. She had never known that she could be elated, relieved and angry all at the same time.

She shook her head again, and almost lost her balance as the motion made her dizzy.

"You think I'm Wesh?" she said.

"I'd suspected it. But not anymore."

"Why not?"

"Even if he had stolen your knowledge, your likeness, there's no way that Wesh could fight like you. Even with the knowledge, he wouldn't have experienced the many practice bouts, the real scuffles that you've had. That we've had. He might've known how to fight with daggers, but still wouldn't fight like you."

And that's how she knew this was really Aahmes, Namid realized. No one else fought like him. She sheathed her stiletto as she backed into the gate.

"But how can you even be here?" she shrieked. "I thought you died. We all thought that." And her anger flared. "It's you I've felt watching me! Why couldn't you tell me you still lived?!"

Aahmes just shook his head.

Namid glared at him, then stalked forward to retrieve her dropped stiletto. She almost fell when she bent to grab it.

"You'd better get back to the Shadowers, get Elnathan to Heal you," Aahmes said.

"You're coming, too," Namid said and picked up his dagger.

He nodded and stood with some difficulty. Namid urged him out the gate and closed and locked it behind them.

Then came the long walk back to Shadow Keep, neither of them steady and Aahmes limping badly. Their injuries caught up to both of them as the intensity of battle faded. Namid grudgingly accepted Aahmes' help, and helped support him in turn, so they could make the trek back.

Neither spoke.

By the time they reached the Keep, they both stumbled more than walked. Namid could not move the arm with the deep shoulder wound and her side hurt so much she could barely remain upright.

They left a faint trail of blood through the streets, but no one was about to notice.

At the Keep door, Namid fumbled it open and staggered through. Aahmes stumbled through too and fell to his knees next to her. Their entrance startled the young apprentice who was the only one on the main level. The boy ran for the stairs, yelling for Thes.

Namid was aware of loud voices, a lot of voices, people fussing, and someone lifting her. Pain shot through her and she cried out. She heard Aahmes cursing.

And she woke on one of the too-thin mats the Shadowers were using for beds. For a breath-of-time she did not move. Someone had bound her wounds and she did not hurt as much as before. She hoped that meant Elnathan had Healed her. Maybe more than once, considering the severity of a couple of the cuts.

Namid turned her head, holding herself still otherwise, and saw that she lay on the mat she had been using to sleep in the smaller of Keizha's rooms. Across the room, Aahmes lay on another mat, covered with a blanket, either asleep or unconscious.

But he was still there.

He was really there!

She studied him and tried to sort through her muddled feelings. How could he have tried to kill her? His explanation made sense… but he should have been able to tell it was really her without all the bloodletting.

Shouldn't he?

Another part of her pointed out that he couldn't have,

with what he suspected.

And he was alive. And here! But he hadn't told her. How long had he watched her, followed her, while she mourned his death?

She frowned and turned away.

The sound of the door opening prompted her to turn back again. Aahmes was awake and she briefly met his gaze, then looked away.

Elnathan came into the room, followed by Thes, who closed the door behind them.

Elnathan checked first Namid, then Aahmes, and Healed them both further. Thes waited until Elnathan had left, then leaned against the closed door and studied the two of them.

"Who do we need t' be lookin' out for?" he said finally. "Was it someone o' the mage's? And how do you come t' be here at all?" He pointed to Aahmes.

Namid resisted the urge to look at Aahmes. "You don't need to look out for anyone," she said. "There's no danger to the city or the other Shadowers."

"Then what happened?"

"A… misunderstanding, you might say," Aahmes said in a quiet voice.

"Misunderstanding?!" Namid said as she raised herself up on an arm. She ignored the pain the motion caused her. "You tried to kill me!" she hissed.

Thes turned a hard look on Aahmes. "You did what?"

"Because of a misunderstanding," Aahmes said. "I was wrong. It's all settled now."

Namid snorted and glared at him.

Thes looked from one to the other. "If Elnathan hadn't said the two o' you need t' stay here for a bit, I'd be thinkin' you"—he pointed at Aahmes—"would be better doin' your recoverin' somewhere else. Far away."

"Stay here how long?" Namid said.

"Couple o' days, probably, Elnathan said," Thes said.

Namid shook her head and gave Aahmes a hard look.

"So I'm stuck in here with you."

"I'm unarmed," Aahmes said, his voice still quiet. "Nothing will happen."

"You're right nothing will happen," Namid snapped. She turned to Thes. "How long has it been already?"

"Just since this mornin'. And Elnathan said the two o' you'd be needin' more Healin' before you're up t' doin' much o' anythin' again." He turned to go. "Someone'll be bringin' you somethin' t' eat in a bit. The evenin' meal's almost ready."

After he had left, Namid shifted on her mat so she could see Aahmes without having to move further. He watched her in silence.

"Your stuff's there, if you want it." She nodded toward a worn pack tucked away under some shelves near Aahmes.

He followed the direction of her gaze. "You pulled my pack from the ruin of Corentris?"

She shrugged. "After I got us out, when I was trying to reach you with the Power, I touched our packs where we had hidden them. I was able to toss them out to the others."

Aahmes gazed at her, perhaps hearing all she did not say. "Thank you," he said and settled back on his mat.

She frowned, torn between the urge to hit him and the desire to touch him, have him hold her again. She stared at him until he looked away and they waited in silence for their meal.

~ ~ ~

Namid slept much of the next day, waking only when Elnathan Healed her again and to eat the meals she found by her mat. She did not see Aahmes awake during those times but did see empty dishes next to him twice. After Elnathan's Healings she could not keep her eyes open long enough to see how Aahmes was doing when Elnathan

Healed him. She suspected the Healer had something to do with that.

The second day after the fight, Namid felt much more alert. Following more Healing after the midday meal, Elnathan allowed Aahmes and Namid to get up and move around. Slowly. And he warned them, "You'll still be stiff, a little sore, and tire easily for another few days."

After Elnathan left them again, Namid sat on the edge of Keizha's bed and watched Aahmes try to ease some of the stiffness.

"So… how did you escape Corentris?" she said.

"Some of it I don't remember clearly." He glanced at her, then away.

"I thought you'd died," Namid said in a faint voice, her gaze on the floor. "I tried to find you. I reached with the Power… but I couldn't sense you."

She glanced at him. "Tell me what you *do* remember? How'd you survive?"

He raked his hair back out of his eyes with his fingers. A haunted expression crossed his face and he stared off into the distance. As she was about to withdraw her request, he broke his silence.

"What I remember is disjointed, but I think I've pieced together what happened. I remember the ceiling falling, rocks hitting me, driving me to the floor. I was having trouble breathing. I'd heard Haeith telling you how to get out of there, and I felt your pull on me, but something broke it. Someone, I should say. I sensed that Dark Priest nearby… Randoq. I think he was opposing you. Your thoughts touched me. I tried to respond, but after absorbing all that Power, I just felt raw. I couldn't control the Power for something that needed such finesse. I followed Haeith's instructions and threw myself out of there, even against Randoq's opposition. Somehow, I drew him with me, I think. I hadn't meant to."

Aahmes paused and closed his eyes. "I remember a battle of Power… just throwing raw Power… and trying to step away from Randoq. Then everything went black…."

He looked at her, his gray-brown eyes looking very dark. "I woke up lying near a road, hurting, battered, but alone. It was early morning and I didn't know how much time had passed. I followed the road to a village and sheltered there. They had a Healer and she Healed me some, although she couldn't do much. I was there for a few days…." Another haunted expression crossed his face but was gone so quickly Namid wondered if she had really seen it.

"As soon as I could… when I'd recovered enough to control the Power somewhat reliably again, I stepped back to where Corentris had been. I saw where it looked like someone had dug into the destruction. You?"

Namid nodded.

"But no one was there. And the Power remnants were too mixed, too chaotic, for me to tell who had been digging or where they, you, had gone. Or even when."

Aahmes sat on his mat, with a wince. "I returned to the village again, got some more Healing… then left." Again his expression grew haunted. "I used the swift travel to return to Rhadanthus. It still took me a while. I tried to sense you, many times, to contact you through the Power, but couldn't. Then I saw you here. But still, when I tried to reach you through the Power, it didn't feel like you…."

"And so you decided I wasn't really me?" Namid said with an edge to her voice.

"I suspected. As I told you, I was uncertain… until you pulled out that key. How would you have a key if you weren't Wesh?"

Namid studied him and reached out with her Power. She knew he was who he looked like, but his Power felt different from before… from before they had both absorbed Sesaisyd's Power, she realized.

"Dar left an impression of the key for me," Namid said. "With Thes. And maybe the difference is because of

Sesaisyd's Power…. Maybe that's why I couldn't find you either when Corentris fell."

Aahmes met her gaze and she felt the light touch of his Power. He nodded.

Thes opened the door and glanced at Aahmes, then beckoned to Namid.

"A breath-o'-time?" he said.

Namid rose carefully, pleased to find the stiffness and little lingering pain tolerable. She followed Thes into the short hall and into the storeroom. From there, they could still see Keizha's door. They both positioned themselves to have a clear view of it.

"What is it?" Namid said.

Thes nodded toward the closed door. "Can we trust him?"

Namid grinned as she remembered past conversations with Aahmes on the topic of trust, then sobered when she remembered Dar's last words.

After some consideration, she nodded. "I think so. As much as we all normally trust each other, anyway."

Thes gave her a quick grin.

"I don't think he's going to attack anyone again," Namid added.

Thes gave her an unreadable look, then nodded.

"Did you find anythin' in the mage's stronghold that we can use?"

"I didn't have the chance," Namid said. "But I'll go back as soon as—"

"I'm thinkin that needs to wait a bit," Thes broke in. "We've been gatherin' more materials while you've been recoverin' and I think we've got enough to be finishin' the main level. Might be Aahmes'd be a help on the rebuildin'. You did say he's got the magic, too…."

Namid nodded. "I did. And, yes, he should be able to help. And probably will be willing to." She folded her arms and rubbed them to get some warmth. "It's gotten colder."

"Aye, it has. And there's been a bit more snow. He'd

not be goin' anywhere anyway...." Thes gave her a piercing look. "Can you work with him? Or do we need t' be puttin' him t' work somewhere away from you?"

Namid smiled and patted Thes' arm. "Thank you for the thought. I can work with him. And with two of us, we might even get the main level livable before the first heavy storm drops on us."

CHAPTER 4

Aahmes and Namid struggled over several days to discover a way to fuse rocks together. To make the idea work, they finally had to mesh their Power. Neither could do it alone. And it was draining work, more than Namid thought it should be, made even worse by disjointed nightmares that disrupted her sleep.

This nearly constant use of their Power meant they exhausted themselves each day. Even so, they raced to finish, working their way around the Keep's walls to close the gaps between the bigger rocks before they might not be able to work because of storms.

Unable to shake a sliver of unease when she could not see Aahmes, Namid made certain to position herself so he was always in sight as they worked. They worked cordially enough together but spoke little and then mostly about things related to their task. That suited Namid, who ranged from anger over Aahmes' attack to wanting to be near him.

From time to time, as the task turned into days of work, Thes chased them away from the Keep, telling them to take some time away from the rocks. The first such time, Aahmes suggested perhaps they spar with their Power somewhere, to learn the extent and limits of their heritage of Power, much as they had sparred with blades years before. When Namid hesitated, he pointed out that they had no one else against whom they could hone their skills with the Power. They would still probably be exhausting themselves, but it was at least a different use of Power.

After Namid agreed, they decided to use the hidden cavern she had discovered under Rhadanthus. She learned Aahmes had also discovered it—only recently—probably only days before she had found it. With its barrier to keep Power from escaping, the cavern made the perfect place for them to throw Power without being seen or endangering others.

So, almost half the times that Thes chased them off from their rebuilding tasks, rather than truly resting, they retreated to the hidden cavern to test their Power against each other. And try to learn if they could coordinate its use for more than fusing rocks.

After close to two weeks, Aahmes and Namid finished the rock-fusing and Shadow Keep had a ground-level sheltered area. The Shadowers had been able to roof about half of the original ground-floor area before they ran out of usable wood. They had even sacrificed the tables and benches to help, since the roof was the more important need. And Aahmes and Namid had more time to slip away to the cavern and work with their Power.

~ ~ ~

Bolts of raw Power slammed into the Power shell Namid held around herself for defense. She flinched at the brighter ones and strengthened her defenses here and there. No problem. She drew from her Power reserve and hurled fiery bolts across the cavern.

"You call that fire?" Aahmes taunted.

He intensified his rain of raw Power, surrounding her with brilliant flashes, but came nowhere close to breaching her defense.

"Namid, throw the fire!" Aahmes said.

And the barrage intensified again.

"You want fire?" Namid snarled and yanked at her reserve. She hurled Power across the cavern and piled it into a great flaming storm. Faster it spun, hotter... blue-white flames scorched the ground beneath and the ceiling overhead as she poured more Power into it. Just like the previous autumn, except blue-white fire instead of yellow-orange... except for that, just like in Corentris....

Her control slipped.

"No...."

The raw Power barrage ceased as the whirling firestorm spun crazily, then thinned and stretched out away from her target, finally stretching out of existence, revealing Aahmes standing unscathed by the storm. Namid glared across the cavern at him. He shook his head and brushed his hair back with one hand.

"Better," Aahmes said and headed toward her, stepping gingerly on the fire-blackened ground. "And see, like I said, the firestorm didn't get through to me. We're that closely matched in Power."

Namid nodded. Yes, that closely matched in Power. She kicked at some small, loose rocks and studied the scorch mark she'd left on the ground, a good-sized ring around the spot where Aahmes had stood. "I know I said I have to be able to use that...."

Aahmes nodded slightly then studied her. "That's what you've told me."

"It's just— after Kalon and Jiro...." She frowned. Roughly ten weeks she had worked with the Power from Sesaisyd, off and on, and *still* her control slipped randomly... and not just that, sometimes the Power itself felt shifty.

"So, work on shaping Power attacks some other way,

instead," Aahmes said.

Namid shook her head. "Fire seems to be what I throw when I don't have time to prepare. I think I'd better get good at it *with* preparation."

And ten weeks was not that long, once she thought about it.

"Makes sense," Aahmes said. "But you've been pushing hard, almost without rest, since you got here. It'll come—"

"I just have this feeling that I need to get there as fast as possible," Namid said.

Aahmes studied her. "Why?"

Namid shrugged. "I wish I knew. I just think I… we… are going to need to be sure of our Power. We need to be confident of this Power heritage that came to us, need to work on controlling and learning to use it, learning its limits…."

Aahmes nodded, with a thoughtful look. "All right. But later? I'm hungry."

Namid glanced around the cavern to check for any damage other than the scorching from all the Power they had been flinging about. She found none.

Back at the Keep, they scrounged some food from the makeshift kitchen and claimed a spot on the floor in a corner of the large common room. The room doubled as a weapons training arena during the day and a dormitory for many of the Shadowers at night, those who preferred not to sleep in the underground rooms. The room had also become a shelter for hangers-on they had begun picking up from around the city.

With a quick look around at the others in the room, Aahmes leaned closer to Namid and spoke in a quiet voice that would not carry beyond the two of them.

"I've been thinking about us…."

Namid looked up sharply, startled. "Us?"

He grinned, with a hint of his old impertinence. "How we must be related."

"Oh." Namid nodded and took another bite to avoid

having to say anything.

"Aren't you wondering about that?"

She swallowed quickly. "Of course. So what do we do? Compare all our ancestors until we find someone we have in common?"

"Do you know a better way?"

Namid shrugged. "I had to learn my ancestors back several generations. I'll probably remember them all. But what about you?"

"As I remember, any meeting of clansfolk almost always included talk of how everyone was related, after greetings were exchanged. So I, too, learned about a number of ancestors and other relatives."

Namid nodded. "All right. Let's start with the parents, then…."

Close to a half candle-mark later, when Thes joined them, Aahmes and Namid had been unable yet to find any recent mutual ancestor in their respective family lines. Their discussion had taken them down some family branches, which also did not connect, and back nearly ten generations, at which point neither of them remembered the people with any certainty.

Thes plopped down on the floor next to Namid and glared at them both, drawing their attention away from their discussion.

"I've decided it's the two o' you I'm blamin'," Thes said and pointed at each of them in turn.

"I wasn't there," Namid said.

"I didn't do it," Aahmes said at the same time.

They shared a look and almost-smiles. Thes grinned, his mirth nearly hidden by his tangled gray beard.

"Aye, you two learned Dar's teachin's well," he said. "Never admit t' anythin', he used t' say. But it's still because o' you."

"What's that?" Namid said.

"All o' this," Thes said and waved his arms around at the room. "The two o' you are too good at puttin' the

Keep back together, with your magicks. And word's gettin' out. Seems we're the only thing like authority in the whole city. And now the few people who're still left in the city are comin' t' us t' take care o' things."

Namid exchanged glances with Aahmes.

"I hadn't thought of that aspect," Aahmes murmured.

Namid pictured the destruction she had seen in the city center. Along with the temples, every one of the former rulers' houses and buildings had been wiped away.

Namid nodded. "Seems we've set ourselves up for it," she said.

"Aye, that you have," Thes said. "Just as I said. So, what will you be doin' about it?" He folded his arms and gave them stern looks.

Namid glanced at Aahmes, then looked down at the floor and traced the pattern in the rock with a finger. "Not what I'd thought to do here."

Aahmes shook his head and leaned back to stare at the ceiling. "But let's see… Thes, you brought all the food and goods from Wesh's camp back with you…."

Thes nodded. "There's fewer non-Shadowers in the city now, than Shadowers," he said. "With what we had from before added t' what we got from Wesh, we should have food t' hold us 'til the caravans start comin' at the end o' winter, even sharin' with others in Rhadanthus—"

"And some of those goods can be used for trade when the caravans do come," Aahmes said.

"Sounds like you two plan to set up as city rulers," Namid said.

Thes chuckled. "Well, a person can think o' it, can't he?"

Aahmes glanced at Namid. "Maybe not such a bad idea," he said. "The Shadowers might be fewer in number than before, but they have all sorts of abilities that would be useful. And didn't a lot of the late-night talks run to how the Shadowers'd run the city, if they could? You could even be lord of the city, Thes—"

"Aw, now, who'd make me int' some sort o' lord?"

"I'd wager that Namid could."

Namid stared at him. "I… what?"

"What are you talkin' about, lad?" Thes said.

"Isn't that something the heir can do?" Aahmes said with a wicked grin. "Make new lords and such?"

Namid glared at him. "I don't know. And that's my brother Tal, anyway, not me. You know that. But if we were further north, *you* could just do it."

Aahmes grinned and shrugged.

"Now what's all this?" Thes said, looking from one to the other. "Seems I'm missin' somethin'."

Namid nodded. "Right. There's a bit more to tell you about what happened after we left Rhadanthus…."

So, after Aahmes grabbed a jug of wine and some cups, they told Thes about some of the things Namid had left out earlier. They told him that Aahmes was the last of one of the northern clans who had ruled there and Namid was a daughter of the Monarch of the Six Realms. As Namid had before, they left out, without even having to consult with each other, what they had learned about the gods.

When they had finished, Thes drained his cup and refilled it to the brim.

"I *knew* it was all your fault," he told them. He raised his cup in a salute to them and drank.

"So, that bein' said," Thes continued, "what're we goin' t' do about this city?"

"We?" Namid said.

"Aye. I'm figurin' you two are my court mages." Thes grinned.

Aahmes gaped at him and Namid chuckled. The two men joined in.

"Bein' serious, though," Thes said. "Your magicks can make the difference in helpin' keep Rhadanthus from dyin'. For now, for the winter, we're good – just keep on workin' on the Keep and get everythin' set with us in charge. But come winter's end, we'll be needin' some sort of inn or we'll lose the caravanners' trade. Got t' clear more of the wells and make sure the water's still good. And I think gettin' Carssi's Baths goin' again. Maybe help the non-Shadowers with gettin' their houses back up…."

"Sounds like you've thought this through," Aahmes said.

Thes grinned. "All that time workin' between Dar and the city rulers taught me a bit. And I'm plannin' on stayin' in Rhadanthus now. Might as well get it fixed up t' m' likin'."

They spent the afternoon discussing how to get things done, making plans and drawing the other Shadowers into the idea. By the evening meal, every Shadower had tasks to work on and all of them knew of the plans for the city.

After the meal, Thes shooed everyone away again to speak with Aahmes and Namid.

"One last task," he said. "I'm thinkin' has t' be just the two o' you… Chendrukhar's stronghold."

Aahmes and Namid exchanged looks.

"Is that what you were doing there?" Aahmes said to Namid.

"When you tried to kill me?" Namid said sharply. "Yes, I'd planned to scout the place."

"Worried about any Power Chendrukhar might've left?" Aahmes said.

Thes and Namid nodded.

"I'm thinkin' you two can handle any o' that," Thes said. "And we could likely use a lot from his place – him not needin' it any more. Even right down t' the stones it's built of. And the doors."

At Namid's surprised look, Thes grinned. "We're a mite short o' wood, right now. You might've noticed."

~ ~ ~

The next morning, Namid and Aahmes hiked through Rhadanthus' damaged streets, heading for the mage's stronghold. They followed much the same path that Namid had taken on her previous trip there.

Aahmes walked at Namid's side, a careful armlength away, with little care for the crisp, cold air and the layer of snow underfoot. Namid breathed on her hands to warm them as she gave him a sidelong look. And she slipped on an unseen patch of ice when her attention wandered.

From the corner of her eye, Namid saw Aahmes start to reach out to her, then hesitate and pull back, while scrutinizing the destruction around them. In the next breath-of-time she wondered if she had imagined the hesitation and the scrutiny as he steadied her to help her keep from falling. She gasped at a sudden stab of pain from the scars that crisscrossed her back.

"What is it?" Aahmes said and pulled back.

Namid shrugged and ducked her head. "The old scars… they've always been somewhat stiff, but now they hurt again from time to time."

"I thought you said Cameni Healed the wounds," Aahmes said and stepped around her so she would look at him.

Namid nodded. "And she did. But sometimes they still hurt for a bit." She stepped around him and continued walking. He kept pace with her.

"I don't remember you having any problems before that Randoq got to you again last autumn."

"Oh?" She gave him a long look. "And you were paying that kind of close attention to me before we fled Rhadanthus?"

Aahmes looked away and brushed his hair back with one hand.

Namid suppressed a smile. "No, they didn't bother me like this before last autumn," she said. "Some stiffness sometimes, but nothing more than that."

"Maybe full Healing was beyond Cameni's ability. She's good, but hadn't much training or experience, yet, right?"

"Maybe that's it."

Aahmes let the silence stretch between them before he spoke again, his voice lighter in tone.

"Did you notice the touch of wildness in that Power you threw at me in the mage's courtyard?"

Namid gave him a sharp look and shook her head. "You're saying I pulled Wild Power? I shouldn't be able— Isn't it out of reach again?"

Aahmes shrugged. "It felt like Wild Power, when I redirected it."

"You didn't just block it? You could control it too?"

"To some extent."

They stared at each other.

"We can still shape the Wild Power?" Namid whispered. "Something from Sesaisyd's legacy? Or can everyone still call it?"

Aahmes shrugged. "Maybe. I don't know. But I suspect we'd be able to combine the Wild Power we pull…."

Namid stared at him while the possibilities flooded her thoughts. She was not certain she liked the idea, but if they joined their Power….

Aahmes watched her expression change and grinned. "Yeah," he said.

At the city's East Gate, they paused before they went through. Aahmes chuckled as Namid again blew on her hands to try to warm them.

"What?" she demanded.

"You do know you can use the Power to ward off the cold?" Aahmes said.

Namid glared at him. "Well, sure, I can just make a fire. But that doesn't help while walking."

Aahmes shook his head. "Not what I mean. I can show you." He extended a hand toward her, then pulled up short and gave her an uncertain look.

"If you'd like," he added.

Namid shrugged. "Show me."

After a quick look around, Aahmes touched the back of her hand with his fingertips and wrapped a tendril of

Power around her, showing her how he used it to ward off the cold.

Namid smiled and stretched her fingers. "Much better."

Then Aahmes whisked the ward away. "Your turn." He gave her a look full of challenge.

Namid wrapped a tendril of her own Power around herself and attempted to duplicate what Aahmes had done. It worked. Mostly. Her nose still felt cold, and she frowned.

"Good for the first time," Aahmes said. "Keep working at it, you'll get it." And he headed out the gate toward the mage's stronghold.

Namid made a face at his back, then tried wrapping the tendril again. This time her ears stayed cold.

With a sigh, she followed Aahmes into the snowy countryside surrounding Rhadanthus.

CHAPTER 5

Several paces from the mage's hold, Namid and Aahmes slowed and studied it in the morning light. No movement, nor any sign of life. And no signs that anyone had been there since Namid's last visit, either.

"I remember hearing Chendrukhar had some kind of guardians," Aahmes said. "Guardians that weren't people."

Namid gave him a sidelong look. "You didn't see his 'guardians that weren't people' when you returned the Star?"

"I never entered his hold. I found another way to return that statue."

"Oh?" Namid invited him to explain further.

"Another time, I'll tell you. Let's do this."

Namid looked back at the gate and shivered, and not just from the cold. But the cold did not help. She breathed on her hands again as they approached the gate, then covered her ears to try to warm them.

Aahmes chuckled and again wrapped a tendril of his Power around her to ward off the cold, this time without touching her. "Practice, practice. Best way to learn this technique," he said.

"I just can't seem to make it cover all of me at the same time. I keep ending up with cold nose or ears or something."

He just gave her a bland look.

"I know," she grumbled. "Technique?"

Aahmes shrugged. "I'm not going to call it a *spell*. I'm not some magician who lives in a tower and casts *spells* while going around dressed in long, fancy robes." He waved a hand at the towers in front of them.

Namid chuckled at the image. "Well, you might end up with the living in a tower part. If this place is clear of Chendrukhar's Power, it might be a better place to set up the Shadowers than continuing work on the Keep over the winter."

Aahmes narrowed his eyes as he studied the towers and wall. "Might work," he said. "I wager Thes'd love living in this stronghold."

Namid nodded and unlocked the gate. Aahmes looked curiously at the key.

"The Star, huh?"

Namid shrugged and opened the gate. They both peered around the courtyard where the mage's three tall towers stood, connected by bridges at various levels.

Still no sign of anything alive, not even rats. Off to the left, by the outer wall, stood a large stable, empty of horses, but Namid glimpsed some bags of feed through the open double door. She did not remember the stable from her previous visit, but then her attention had been elsewhere. Perhaps she had just not noticed it.

Namid called up some of her Power and let it flow out into the stronghold. She touched on Aahmes' Power as he did much the same.

Namid got a much better feel for the layout of the place and found no signs of the strangeness she had experienced years earlier when she had been there as part of her Trial. She sensed two levels below ground to add to the many floors of the towers, although the towers themselves did not look nearly as tall as she remembered. Probably more of the mage's Power had created that effect.

"I think I sense small hints, remnants really, of his Power," Aahmes said. "But no overlying... spells." He grinned.

Namid nodded. "Possibly those are items holding Power. Still—"

"Vigilance is the word," Aahmes said.

They both held Power ready and used it to sweep the courtyard again before they stepped through the gate.

When nothing happened, Namid let out the breath she only then realized she had been holding. "Good so far."

Aahmes grinned. "I say we stay together so we both can look over any Power we find."

Namid nodded. "Down or up first?"

Aahmes frowned. "You've been where before?"

Namid studied the towers. "Parts of the two shorter ones.... I think. Maybe. The layout looks different from what I remember. I think he'd used Power to affect the inside structure for unwelcome guests."

Aahmes grinned and nodded.

They finished checking the main courtyard, then looked over the secondary one formed by a wall that joined the two shorter towers and extended out from them to the outer wall. After finding nothing of interest or concern, they locked the gate to the courtyard, and sealed it with their Power, too. No one would be able to try to enter without alerting them.

Namid remembered the setup of the ground floor of one of the shorter towers, so they looked through there first, using small orbs of Power they created for light. They found a kitchen area and a couple of rooms that she remembered the mage using for entertaining guests. Stairs led down from the kitchen to storerooms in two underground levels.

Mostly empty, those storerooms still held some

preserved foodstuffs that looked edible. Close to half of the lowest level held wine barrels, with tables and chairs scattered about the rest of that level and shelves with a variety of goods.

And here they found the first small touch of Power, some kind of concealment. A light touch of their own Power and it melted away to reveal a door in one wall. Namid opened it to a tunnel that extended off into darkness.

"Isn't Rhadanthus this direction?" Namid said.

"Yes."

"Something else to check out. But for now, let's just secure it."

Namid closed the door. A touch of Power secured it, keyed to just her and Aahmes.

They worked their way up inside the tower, noting the location of the one door Namid thought she recognized as leading to a bridge to another of the towers. They secured that door with their Power as they passed. The upper levels of the tower held guest rooms, sitting rooms and servants' quarters, all deserted and all looking like no one had been there in a while. They found no further touches of Power, either.

The top room of the tower held a large wood table and chairs. Several doors opened to a balcony that ran all the way around the tower.

Aahmes joined her at the waist-high wall that edged the balcony and looked down. "Interesting.... From the courtyard, didn't we see several bridges connecting the towers?"

Namid looked over the side and saw only two bridges, each extending from their tower to one of the other towers. "We seem to have lost some."

"Or missed the Power holding illusions of bridges."

"Or, from this vantage, the illusion hiding them."

As they had done in the courtyard, Namid and Aahmes let their Power flow out into the stronghold. Many long breaths-of-time later, they shared a look.

"And I thought Haeith was good with semblances," Namid said.

Aahmes nodded. "Nice mix of concealment and misdirection. Seems we've missed some doors."

"Yeah. Have to hunt them down. But let's look through the other towers, first. Maybe the bridges will be more obvious from the other ends."

Namid glanced at Rhadanthus and shook her head at the clear view of the city's devastation. Back inside, they descended to the door they had secured earlier.

"This is where things began to get truly strange when I came here for the Star," Namid said. "Chendrukhar had several different Powerful defenses designed to keep anyone from getting to his precious statue."

"I don't sense any Power now."

"Me neither. But I don't know what the reality will be. I'm fairly sure I saw only Power-affected things previously."

Aahmes nodded his understanding and they stepped through the door…

…Into a hallway that looked in no way unusual. It had no windows. To their left was another door, closed.

"When I was first here," Namid said, "Power initially concealed that door. And the end of this hall led to a fall to the courtyard. Or at least appeared to."

"So which way first?"

Namid pointed down the hall. She hoped that it really led to one of the other towers. The dim light from their orbs stretched enough into the hall to let them see the door at the far end. A few paces took them there.

"Still no sense of Power," Namid said. "The door wasn't here before."

Aahmes shrugged and opened the door to a small room set up like a simple sitting room, with several worn padded chairs and a few small tables scattered about. Across the room was another door.

After they poked around and found nothing of particular interest, they exited the room through the second door, to a landing on stairs going both up and down, curved to follow the tower's outer wall.

"Bottom to top again?" Aahmes said.

"Yes."

A few steps down the stairs, they both paused.

"Something…." Namid said.

Aahmes nodded toward a door on the landing below them. "There, I think. Or just before."

They both sent out tendrils of Power.

"A ward, maybe?" Namid said.

"Feels more like a sort of lock to me."

Namid considered that. "Think you're up to picking it?" she challenged.

Aahmes grinned at her and focused his Power. Namid felt a sort of twang through the Power. She gave Aahmes a questioning look and he shrugged.

"It might've worked. Or I just set off a trap."

"Great…."

They gathered Power around themselves, creating defensive shells, and edged down the stairs. Aahmes placed a hand on the door's handle and looked at her over his shoulder.

"Ready?"

"Sure."

Aahmes eased the door open. Namid caught a glimpse of cluttered tables, then Power surged out at her.

She and Aahmes threw themselves to one side, hugging the short wall next to the door and wrapping their own Power tightly around themselves. Namid staggered as the force of the blast almost knocked her from her feet, then Aahmes braced her against the wall.

Then the Power vanished.

Namid tried to catch her breath and noticed that Aahmes had placed himself between her and the Power. She looked into his eyes, so close to her own. For long breaths-of-time, they stood that way. Then Aahmes blinked and stepped back, running a hand through his hair.

"You all right?" he said, his gaze on the doorway, now lacking the door.

Namid took a shuddering breath and told her racing heart to calm. "Yeah. Startled... but yeah. You?"

"Good enough."

Together they eased up to the doorway and peered through. The tables and the clutter had been reduced to random debris. Tentatively Namid stepped forward, then jumped as she felt another surge of Power from somewhere ahead, behind the door across from her.

"Wager the same just happened in there, too?" Aahmes said with a grin.

Several more outbursts of Power shuddered through the tower, coming from below them.

"No wager," Namid said. "But I think we've taken care of the traps in this section anyway."

Aahmes wrapped another defensive shell around them as they continued their exploration. "Better make sure, anyway."

That level, and the ones below, each held two large rooms. And as they expected, they found that everything within had been reduced to debris, although the little bits still held faint residual Power of unidentifiable purpose. But nothing active. They found no more Power locks or traps.

"That's one way to take care of traps," Aahmes said as they climbed the stairs to the upper levels. There they found several plain bedrooms. Each held three or four beds and the same number of simple trunks.

"Student quarters," Aahmes said. "For the tyros."

Namid sent her Power out and grinned. "A hint of some kind of dampening in the walls.... Almost gone, now."

"Probably so they wouldn't practice on each other up here," Aahmes said. He gave the Power in the walls a nudge with his own and the remaining hint dissipated.

Namid chuckled.

The top room of the tower resembled that of the previous tower, except these furnishings were of a lesser quality.

"Good view of the countryside," Namid said, looking from the balcony toward the East Road, then between the other two towers to a stretch of the North Road. From the other side of the tower, they could see parts of the South Road as well.

"Easy to spot the caravans, when they come," Aahmes said. "Or anyone else."

Namid nodded and glanced at the sun. "We've some time before dusk…."

Aahmes nodded. "Let's check through that door on the bridge, then. Maybe it leads to the last tower."

"When I was here for the Star, it didn't," Namid said. "But likely what I encountered then wasn't the reality."

When they tested the door, they found it locked.

"It was locked before, too," Namid said.

The key Namid had used for the gate opened this lock, too. Aahmes slowly opened the door. Both he and Namid held Power ready to sense anything or defend from an attack.

They found themselves looking down another hall, this one with windows lining one wall.

"I recognize this from my Trial," Namid said. "Sort of. But I don't sense Power here, now. I'm sure there was some before."

Aahmes squinted at her. "Sometime you'll have to tell me about it. What you saw here during your Trial."

She smiled. "Sometime."

A few paces brought them to the door at the other end of the hall. When neither of them felt any worrisome Power, Namid opened it.

Beyond they found a small room, something like one Namid remembered. This room was furnished with a fancy rug, wall hangings, and a few chairs. In the center of the room, a spiral staircase led up through the ceiling about three paces above.

"I remember a room vaguely like this one…. But the staircase and furnishings weren't here," Namid said as she examined the walls.

Aahmes occupied himself similarly and they met at the far side of the room.

"No doors hidden by Power or any other means," Aahmes said.

Namid nodded, and they climbed the stairs to a room about half the size of the one below. There was a single door to the left. The room looked like an intimate dining room, with a small, circular table and four chairs. As in the room below, an ornate rug lay on the floor and colorful hangings decorated the walls.

Aahmes gave a low whistle. "With just the hangings in these two rooms, the Shadowers won't lack for money for a long time."

Namid nodded as she opened the door. She glanced within and smiled to herself. This *was* the way she had come… and it was still there.

As she and Aahmes eased inside the new room, Namid watched Aahmes—with a slight smile—for his reaction to the contents of the room. She laughed aloud at his look of astonishment when he spotted the silvery object atop the long, narrow table against the far wall.

Aahmes frowned at her merriment.

"Seems it's ours, now," he said as he lifted the silvery distorted-star statue that was the Star of Corentris.

"I sense no Power about it at all," Namid said.

He nodded and set it back on the table.

Namid spotted a door off to the right that she had not seen previously. No Power helped conceal it, but it blended into the wall so well that Power almost might have.

She glanced at Aahmes and he nodded, then secured

the door behind them with Power.

"Securing the Star, for now," he said at Namid's look. He joined her at the new door.

Beyond this door, they found a landing on stairs going both up and down. They headed down first, securing that door behind them, too.

The several floors in the lower portion of the tower were similar to the students' rooms they had seen in the previous tower, but much nicer, and fewer in number. And below these, they again found rooms that now only contained bits and pieces of things, all touched with Power.

After making sure no nasty Powerful surprises hid in the lower floors—Aahmes said they had probably already set them off with the others—they climbed the stairs to the upper levels.

Namid decided these must have been Chendrukhar's private rooms. The lavish decorations and furnishings looked undisturbed. The faint traces of Power she and Aahmes discovered only worked to preserve the mage's belongings. In the single fancy bedroom, they found two large wardrobes packed with clothing, both men's and women's, and two coffers of jewelry.

"Could've used these all these years for Shadower guises," Namid said, fingering a fine linen shirt.

Aahmes chuckled. "Wonder who his women were…."

"Might've just been him," Namid said. "Some of the people that he bragged that he took were women."

Aahmes nodded. "Wonder how many different people he actually was."

Namid shrugged and led the way back out of the room.

At the top of the tower, they found yet another single room, like the other towers, but this one held only a few small tables, several lush chairs, and two tall, wide bookcases that stood back to back in the center of the room. Two doors led out to the balcony that circled the tower, and large windows took up most of the rest of the walls.

Namid looked over the books in the bookcases. She did not recognize the languages of any of them.

"Namid," Aahmes called softly from the other side of the bookcases. She circled around them and stopped.

On one of the tables on that side of the room sat an open book with an unmarked cover of dark-red leather, thin spine upward so they could not see inside without lifting it. Aahmes gave a slight nod at the book.

"Yeah, I feel it, too," Namid said as she joined him. "I'm surprised we didn't feel this from outside."

She turned Power-enhanced senses to the walls and found a sort of blockage and defense fused into them, similar to the protection around the cavern they had been using beneath Rhadanthus, but to keep Power out. This Power had a different feel to it from the rest of the Power they had encountered in the stronghold. Older, more stable. Probably one to leave alone.

Namid brought her attention back to the room.

Aahmes stood with both hands held a handspan above the book, eyes closed. Namid moved closer but did not disturb his concentration.

"Well?" she said when he opened his eyes.

"Safe to pick up," he said and did so, revealing the items that had been hidden beneath: a folded piece of parchment, a ring, and a brooch in the form of a stylized hawk in flight.

Namid reached a hand toward them but stopped short of touching them. "No…."

Aahmes looked at her in concern. "What is it?"

"I know those. The ring and brooch…" Namid said in a quiet voice. "The ring is my father's signet ring. Well, a duplicate, really, for Tal. And Tal almost always wore that brooch, especially whenever he was out and about."

Aahmes lifted the parchment and slid the ring and brooch off onto the table. He opened the parchment and read it.

Namid reached out to the two pieces of jewelry with Power. No sense of Power about them, so she picked them up and examined them. Yes, the ring had the distinctive markings inside that meant it belonged to Tal. And the brooch was unmistakable.

"Look at this." Aahmes held the parchment out to her. "A letter of introduction to Lady Estaevi of Navele."

Namid took it and read it. "I didn't know my brothers had been sent on an official visit to Navele," she said.

"Look at the date," Aahmes said.

"Over thirteen years ago," Namid said. "Yeah, that fits what I remember. The handwriting and signature both look like my father's. Wonder why he didn't use a scribe for the letter. And the timing matches when I remember my brothers leaving on some journey. But what are this letter and Tal's ring and brooch doing here?"

Aahmes shrugged and flipped through the book he still held.

"I can't read any of this. I don't even recognize the language. You?"

Namid leaned close, very aware of the touch of his arm against hers, and peered at the book. "No, me neither." She touched the book's Power with her own. "Feels like some sort of holding Power on it, I think…. Maybe to keep the pages from falling apart. I *does* seem old."

Aahmes nodded absently and grabbed the parchment from her. He put it in the book to mark the page it had been open to. He closed the book and then gave it a surprised look as the sense of Power from it completely vanished.

He shared a look with Namid. "Handy, that." He tucked the book into his tunic.

"Think it's safe to remove it?" Namid said.

He grinned. "We'll find out." He glanced out a window at the westering sun and turned back to Namid. "I think leave the Power in the walls. It doesn't feel like Wesh's and I sense nothing other than defense in it."

Namid sent a small bolt of Power at one window. It splashed against the glass and dissipated without leaving even a mark.

She nodded. "Yes. Let's let Thes know about the towers and then we can decide what we want to do. And come back to track down the entrances to those other bridges."

She tucked the ring and brooch into a pouch at her waist, and they made their way back out, securing key doors behind them with Power.

When they reached the ground floor of the first tower, Aahmes turned toward the kitchen. "Let's see where that passage comes out in Rhadanthus. If it does."

They returned to the tunnel they had found. Aahmes secured the door behind them and they headed down the tunnel.

It was cool—although still warmer than outside—and close. Aahmes' head almost touched the ceiling. The tunnel seemed bored through rock, with smoothed walls, floor and ceiling, just wide enough for them to walk side by side. Namid was very aware of her hand brushing Aahmes' as they walked. She glanced at him sidelong and her face warmed when their gazes met.

Aahmes gave her one of his rakish grins, but when he spoke, sounded serious.

"You're going to try to find your brother, find out what happened, aren't you?"

Namid gave him a surprised look, then nodded as she realized the truth of what he said.

"I'd love to think he's back in Kilaadi now, with our parents. But somehow, I don't think so. I need to see, though."

"And if he's not there?"

Namid tapped the book that Aahmes had tucked in his tunic. "The letter said Navele."

"Where Haeith and Cameni are from," he said.

Namid nodded. "But I don't think this Lady Estaevi is

any relation to Cameni…."

And they walked again in silence for several paces.

"How soon?" Aahmes broke the silence.

"Probably not very," Namid said. "The winter storms will be getting worse now and we both know that's no time to be caught out in the lands nearby. I doubt I'll be able to leave Rhadanthus until spring."

Aahmes nodded.

Namid gave him a sidelong look and a smile. "Until then, I'll still need someone to throw Power at for practice."

Aahmes chuckled. "I'll throw it right back at you."

Namid chuckled, too. "Of course."

They walked several paces in silence, then Aahmes tapped her on her shoulder. "If you're not leaving until spring, you'll have plenty of time to learn how to use the Power to ward off the cold," he said with a grin.

She sighed.

CHAPTER 6

After more than a candle-mark, Namid and Aahmes reached the end of the tunnel. It opened into the Power-walled cavern that Namid had discovered. They came out through one of the openings she had not yet investigated. Aahmes did not look surprised at the sight of the cavern.

"You knew the tunnel would lead here," Namid accused.

He shook his head. "Only suspected. I haven't explored all these tunnels. I just sheltered in them after I returned to Rhadanthus."

"And spied on me."

"Watched to try to learn if you were really you," he said.

"You could've spoken with me."

Aahmes shook his head with a sigh and raked his hair out of his face with one hand. "I didn't dare. If you really *were* Wesh, I thought the only chance I'd have to take you out was with a surprise attack. And sometime while you were alone so you—Wesh—wouldn't kill others to gain even more Power. If I'd talked to you, and you *were* him, that would have ruined any chance of surprise and Wesh

61

would have taken *me* out. And then you—Wesh— would've had *all* of Sesaisyd's Power." He turned away slightly and created another light orb, lighting more of the cavern.

Namid nodded. "All right. I can see that." Then she muttered, "Doesn't mean I like it."

"What?"

She waved a hand in the air. "Nothing. Really." She looked around the cavern. "I just wish we had time now to see where the other passages go. Maybe we should've done so earlier, instead of just focusing on throwing Power about in here."

Aahmes shrugged. "Most of the passages I *do* know go to cave-ins," he said. "But I found a couple that go outside."

"Let's go to the closest to Shadow Keep, then," Namid said. "I don't really want to climb up out of that trapdoor into the middle of a bunch of Shadowers."

Aahmes nodded and led the way down one of the other passages. It ended at a fall of rocks and dirt, that Aahmes said had not been there the last time he went through. They speculated about what might have caused the cave-in as they cleared a crawlway through. When they finished and emerged in the city, full night had fallen. And the wind had picked up.

"At least we're not far from the Keep," Namid said as they sealed the hole with Power, to hold it until they could return to do a better job of concealment. The tunnel had opened out in what used to be a collection of the poorer houses in Rhadanthus. Namid did not know the exact building that used to stand there but knew it had not been one that would have drawn any particular attention.

The two Shadowers hurried through the dark, empty streets, trying to beat the storm. They were cold and soaked with snow when they finally stumbled through the door into the Keep.

Thes met them there and called some of the junior

Shadowers to bring dry clothes and hot food and drink. Namid slipped behind one of several curtains that hung along one wall for just this purpose and changed out of her soaked clothes into dry ones. They were big on her, but she cared little at the moment. She joined Aahmes near the kitchen fire, where they spread their sodden clothes on the floor to dry. Thes brought them hot food and drink there.

"Beginnin' to think maybe the storm had caught the two o' you too far out and you'd had t' hole up somewhere," Thes said.

Aahmes shook his head while Namid took a drink of the mulled wine.

"We were almost back when it really got bad," Aahmes said.

Thes leaned closer. "And? What does the mage's stronghold have that we can be usin'?"

"The whole thing," Aahmes said. He told the older Shadower what he and Namid had found there and their thoughts about moving the Shadowers to the stronghold. Namid added some details, too, around bites of food.

Thes looked thoughtful when they had finished. After a few sips of his wine, he nodded.

"Sounds like the best plan," he said. "I'll be wantin' t' get us all over there soon as we can. If you say it's safe enough, we can get right on gettin' it set up the way we want."

"Give us a couple of days," Namid said. "Some things still have remnants of Power clinging to them. We should clear those before anyone else gets in there."

Thes nodded. "Aye, true enough. So after that, we'll get all o' us Shadowers moved in all nice and cozy. And then, if the two o' you can do it, set up the tunnel so anyone can find the way all the way here, t' the Keep. This storm's just the beginnin' o' the season and it'd be a mite easier if we all can just be usin' a tunnel t' go back and forth, since we'll still keep this place, too, for an in-town base."

Remembering digging with her Power through the

collapsed city of Corentris weeks ago, Namid nodded. "Shouldn't be too much trouble. We might have to do some digging to shorten the distance to travel...."

~Good idea,~ Aahmes said to her using thought-speech. *~Keep our fellows away from that cavern with the Power.~*

"A lot of those tunnels seem to wind and split off," she continued telling Thes. "But probably more mess than anything else."

Thes nodded and left them to finish their meal.

"When will you tell him about leaving?" Aahmes kept his voice low.

"I don't know. Not for a while, I think. Get things set up here, first."

Aahmes nodded and turned his attention to his food.

Namid followed his example, but also watched him out of the corner of her eye, wondering. He had seemed remote, but maybe just because she had been holding him at a distance after the attack? He was still friendlier than before they had left Rhadanthus with Enric, but not as close as she thought they had become during the past autumn. Had she done that? Or something else?

He caught her gaze and grinned at her. "A navn for your thoughts?" he said, referring to the gold coinage of the Six Lands of the Monarch.

"Oh, so you're throwing around gold, now?"

He shrugged, still grinning. "Probably can, with what we'll get out of the mage's hold."

"You're going to steal from the Shadowers?" Namid dropped her voice.

Aahmes' grin grew wider. "Call it a fee off the top."

Namid shook her head at him but returned his grin. "I suppose court mages do get some sort of payment...."

He nodded and clapped her on the shoulder as he rose. "Exactly. And I'm off to sleep. Tomorrow and its work will be here too soon."

Namid watched him as he walked off. His usual easy saunter was still marred by a slight limp, but it seemed to be improving.

"Mm, that *is* nice to look at, isn't it?"

Namid jumped and looked around at the older woman who stood nearby.

"Keizha!"

"No, don't be getting up. I'll just join you there."

Namid studied the older Shadower as she settled on the floor next to her. Keizha looked younger than her supposed years—how many, no one knew exactly—but Namid saw a few lines in the woman's golden-brown skin that she did not remember seeing before. Keizha wore her white hair smoothed back behind her ears but seemed to be letting it grow longer. She gave Namid a quick pat on the shoulder.

"Been hearin' that you and Oh-So-Fine over there are our very own mages," Keizha said.

Namid laughed at Keizha's name for Aahmes, while agreeing with it. To herself. "Seems so," she said.

"Good. Then since I've helped you oh-so-much with guises over the years, I figure I can move myself closer to the top of your no-doubt lengthy list of tasks. So as to get my stuff done sooner."

"I'm sure we can come to some arrangement," Namid said with a smile and a wink.

Keizha laughed. "That's my girl." She leaned close and lowered her voice. "Thes knows, but it's not common talk yet… I'm takin' over Carssi's Baths. Making the business my own."

Namid gave her a sharp look. "All aspects?"

Keizha laughed. "The look on your face. And no, dearie. The excitin', sensual side o' the previous business will only be around when it's closed for the regular business. And not involvin' anyone who doesn't want t' be involved. No one forced into that work. Otherwise, it'll be a nice, clean, high-class place for the benefit of all the citizens." She gave Namid a sidelong look.

Namid grinned. "Sounds like you've already got your

plan to entice customers. So how badly ruined is the place?"

"About as much as everywhere else. Need to get the water and heat system workin' again. And clean. And, of course, need the building rebuilt."

Namid nodded. "Thes has already said that's one of the places to rebuild sooner rather than later…." She stared into the fire as she considered all there was to do during the winter. She had obligations here. Spring would have to be soon enough to find out about Tal. Namid brought her attention back to Keizha.

"Right after we get a more secure shelter for the Shadowers, I think." She waved a hand at a small drift of snow forming and melting in one corner of the room.

"I'll take it." Keizha patted Namid again on the shoulder as she rose. "You watch out for that lad o' yours. He's got some shadow that hangs on him."

"I'm not sure I'd say he's mine," Namid muttered.

"I wouldn't say he's not," Keizha returned over her shoulder as she walked off. She took a seat next to Thes and they put their heads together. Namid wondered if they were talking about her and Aahmes.

With a sigh, Namid rose and returned her plate to the kitchen area, to the Shadower assigned to clean up for the evening. She checked her clothes – still too wet. So she found a place off to the side, hauled out one of the sleeping mats and rolled up in a blanket for the night.

She drifted off to worries about Tal and what might happen if she did not get to him in time – whatever that might mean. She woke to the remnants of nightmares of screams and blood. While she had endured similar dreams in the time after she had escaped the Dark Priests years ago, such dreams had not plagued her in several years. Probably a combination of fatigue and worry about what she did not know about Tal's situation, she decided.

~ ~ ~

Before they returned to the stronghold to clear it, Aahmes and Namid created a connecting tunnel directly to the trapdoor in Shadow Keep. The new tunnel bypassed their practice cavern—as they had begun calling it—to keep that area separate and secret. They still had access to the cavern from the trapdoor, but they concealed the tunnel that led there with Power, much as the trapdoor had been concealed, so that only they two could find the way there. As with the rock-fusing, they found the work went better when they meshed their Power.

Aahmes and Namid needed more than just a couple of days to clear the mage's stronghold. Much of what remained there held no traces of Power, so they gathered all of those items—except the furniture—into Guest Tower, as they called the tower where Chendrukhar had entertained. During one of their early trips between Shadow Keep and the towers, Namid and Aahmes slipped aside to their practice cavern and hid the Powerful book they had found, with the thought that the protections there would keep it best from unwelcome eyes. Namid kept the letter, brooch and ring with her, leaving a small scrap of parchment to mark the place the letter had in the book.

Thes brought Keizha and a few other Shadowers through the tunnel to Guest Tower to sort through everything collected there and decide what to keep and what to use for trade in the spring.

Aahmes dubbed the tower they thought had been for students Tyro Tower. The unidentifiable Power-touched bits and pieces Namid and Aahmes had found there, and in the tallest tower, they both agreed would be best melted down and otherwise destroyed if they could not be melted. The Power felt tainted and they agreed the best way to clear it was to change the purpose of the items, whatever they had been originally. That project alone took many long days.

They dug out enough of one blacksmith's shop in the

city to be able to use the forge there, then hauled everything over there that could be melted. Namid concentrated Powerful fire on the objects while Aahmes drew out any lingering Power that resisted the melting process. He formed light orbs with it and soon they were surrounded with scores of them.

The times when Namid called on her Power reserve and found the Power slippery and shifty, she stopped for a short rest, which seemed to solve the problem. Aahmes seemed grateful for those times of rest, too.

When they finished—left with a lump of indeterminate metal more than an armlength on each side—Aahmes dispersed the light orbs.

"Ever wonder where the Power goes?" Namid said.

Aahmes gave her a startled look. "Not really. I just assumed it joined up with the Power we can draw from our surroundings when we're not using the reserve we carry."

He sent out a tendril of his Power and Namid imitated him. After sensing the Power around them, they shrugged at one another.

"It didn't join my reserve," Aahmes said.

"Nor mine."

"Can't really tell if it's part of the surrounding Power now."

"I do get a sense that it didn't join the Wild Power."

Another shrug, and they headed back to the Keep, leaving the lump of metal to cool further.

~ ~ ~

"Any of the Shadowers know blacksmithing? Weaponsmithing?" Namid said as she stared at the still warm lump days later.

Aahmes shrugged. "Let's hand that part off to Thes."

Namid nodded, then stretched and groaned. "That was not fun. I hurt."

Aahmes grinned. "Better get to work on the Baths, then. A good soak in the hot water would help those aches."

Namid nodded. "Soon. We've still got the final tower."

Aahmes frowned and walked back toward the tunnel entrance. Namid matched his pace. The snow creaked and squeaked under their boots in the sharp cold.

"So far no one recognizes any of the languages of those books," Namid said.

"You haven't shown around the one Powerful one we stashed, have you?"

"Of course not. It's still in the cavern, nice and hidden."

Aahmes nodded. "Think Odasoro might know any of the languages?"

Namid tilted her head as she considered the question. By now, the troubadour had probably arrived in Kilaadi, capital of Paronia and the rest of the Monarch's lands.

"Possibly. Another thing to wait until spring, though. We're not getting any messages or travelers across the plains this winter." She gestured at some knee-deep snow drifts nearby.

"Another thing for Thes, then. Maybe he'll just move the books into whichever room he plans to use as an audience chamber. They certainly look impressive enough for the 'Lord of Rhadanthus'."

Namid slipped on some ice hidden beneath the snow but caught her balance without needing the hand Aahmes offered. "Is he calling himself that?"

"No. But I've heard it from some of the non-Shadowers. It'll probably catch on. You know, even just a season ago, if we'd told Thes he'd be Lord of Rhadanthus, he would have chased us out of town for being drunk."

Namid chuckled. "Probably would have."

~ ~ ~

The rest of that day, after Aahmes and Namid had double-checked the upper floors of the tallest tower for any remaining Powerful concerns, the other Shadowers worked to move everyone from the Keep to Tower Hold, as Thes had decided to label their new home.

Thes took over the areas of the tallest tower that had been the mage's private rooms. Most of the rest of the Shadowers moved into the rooms further down in that same tower that had likely belonged to the mage's more accomplished students or more-advanced underlings. The newest Shadowers took rooms in Tyro Tower. Until houses in the city could be rebuilt, Thes welcomed all the non-Shadowers into the Guest Tower rooms for the winter. They were very crowded there but sheltered from the storms, at least.

Thes had found a former locksmith among the newer Shadowers. With the limited materials at hand, the woman had still managed to make a few locks. These Thes had her place on the doors that Aahmes and Namid had finally uncovered that led from Guest Tower to bridges to the other towers, and on the trapdoor in Shadow Keep, from which Aahmes and Namid had removed the Power concealment so all the Shadowers could use it.

The evening after everyone moved into Tower Hold, they feasted on a plain but filling meal and celebrated the move with games, makeshift music and some boisterous dances.

Thes persuaded Keizha to join him in several dances in a row, to the delight of the rest of the Shadowers. Then he pulled Namid out to dance but gave way with a smile when Aahmes stepped up to partner her.

And so, the evening passed in the manner of those Namid remembered from before the Dark Priests had set the killing mist on Rhadanthus. Very late, the Shadowers split out from their city-dweller guests and took themselves to a room in Tyro Tower that they had made into a sort of gathering area. There they passed around skins of wine, drank toasts to Dar and the other Shadowers who had fallen to the killing mist, shared tall tales of past exploits and eventually drifted off into slumber.

One of the last ones awake, Namid gazed around with a smile. This was home.

Her eyes met Aahmes'. He sprawled in a chair on the far side of the room. He gave her a slight nod, like he agreed with her thoughts. Then he closed his eyes.

Namid shifted in her own chair. She debated going to the bed she had claimed in Thes' tower but decided she did not want to move. And she drifted off.

~ ~ ~

A nasty storm moved in overnight and lingered for almost two days, so most of the work halted for that time. When the winds and snow subsided, everyone fell into a pattern of returning to Rhadanthus for as long as daylight held to work on the things the city needed.

The passing weeks saw progress made. At Thes' request, Namid and Aahmes created ground-level outer doors where they had not existed before in both Tyro Tower and Lord Tower – as the Shadowers had dubbed the tallest tower. In the city proper, the Shadowers rebuilt Keizha's Baths as much as they could. It became a popular place to visit after a long day of rebuilding, even though it still lacked a roof, as they had no wood to spare. They hoped to trade for wood in the spring.

Namid noticed that whenever she and Aahmes were outside, whether in the city or in Tower Hold, Aahmes seemed to keep half his attention on the surroundings, pausing to look around every so often. The times Namid imitated him, she saw nothing of concern, only the other Shadowers and citizens of Rhadanthus working on rebuilding, just as they were.

Several people created makeshift shrines to the gods in

the old temple circle and worked to erect at least the walls for actual temples there again. Two families who had escaped the killing mist—to return to nothing left of the city—rebuilt and began running one inn and an accompanying stable. After much debate, the Shadowers dismantled Shadow Keep's roof and used the wood for the inn and stable – a more urgent need, they decided, especially since Tower Hold sheltered everyone. While not as fancy as before, the inn should still serve the anticipated caravanners well.

When the rebuilding slowed because of lack of usable materials, Aahmes and Namid took more time again to work with their Power in their hidden cavern. With practice, they learned to better mesh their Power and gained greater control over it. They discovered that their Power meshed best when they touched, clasped hands. And they confirmed that they, at least, still sensed the Wild Power and could work with it, although not without difficulty. Namid still randomly lost the thread of the Power, whether her own or the Wild Power, and its control slipped away from her.

Slowly, indications of returning spring began to appear.

CHAPTER 7

Namid perched on a half-melted stone a short distance from Shadow Keep, glad for a chance to be alone for a time. Who knew that being one of Lord Thes' mages would be so demanding? But they all, Shadowers and non, had gotten through the last many weeks of severe storms, not without squabbles, but intact.

The sun warmed her, although the air still felt cold. She rolled Tal's ring over and over in her hand. What had happened on her brothers' journey to Navele, and all the years until she had seen her two eldest brothers dead at the hands of the Dark Priests the past autumn?

She looked around absently at the devastation that still characterized most of Rhadanthus but smiled to herself, content in the moment. Although soon she would have to gather herself and begin the journey to Kilaadi. She frowned at the pang of sadness that swept through her at the thought of leaving. This place and these people had become home, and she had to admit she did not want to go. But she feared what might have happened or be happening to Tal. She had to try to find him.

A slight noise behind her, back toward the Keep,

caught her attention. She reached out with a tendril of Power… it was Aahmes. She raised a hand in greeting but did not turn around, instead continued to bask in the sun on her face.

"Hadn't expected to find you here," Aahmes said. He plopped down on a rock nearby and also turned his face to the sun.

Namid shrugged. "Just had a feeling I wanted to be away from Tower Hold."

Aahmes gave her a sharp look, then looked around. Namid followed his gaze but saw nothing other than the Keep behind them and the usual destruction of the city elsewhere. She settled back on her rock again.

"Last little bit of peace before heading out on another quest?" Aahmes said.

She looked at him through slit eyes. "Another quest? I don't think so."

"Oh? The princess sets out on a journey to find and rescue her lost brother and return him safely home? Sounds like one of Odasoro's quest tales to me."

Namid snorted. "I don't do quests."

Aahmes chuckled. "Could've fooled me." He tossed a few pebbles one by one out at a larger rock, hitting with each one. "It's probably safe enough from the winter storms to head to Kilaadi any time."

Namid stayed quiet, fighting her longing to just stay with the Shadowers and continue the work on Rhadanthus.

Aahmes reached over and tugged on her braid. "Namid?"

"Hey!" She pulled the braid back and swiveled around on her rock to face him.

He started to say something more, then jerked upright, his eyes unfocused. Then Namid felt something too and turned in the direction he faced, as if she could look through the distant city wall.

"Late storm?" she said. She had learned over the winter

that Aahmes could often feel one of the storms approaching candle-marks before it gave any visible indication.

"No. Worse!" Aahmes jumped off his perch, grabbing her hand on his way, tugging her after him. "Run!"

They stumbled over broken rocks as Aahmes took them away from Shadow Keep. Namid did not need to look back to know an immense bolt of Power flew toward them. She wrapped Power around them even as Aahmes did the same. Then the bolt struck the Keep.

A wave of Power from the impact flung them to the ground, rolled over them, and flung the nearby loose rocks away in a circle around the pile of rubble that marked what had been Shadow Keep.

They looked up to assess the damage. Namid reached out to see if she could get a sense of who sent the Power. It did not feel familiar.

"No one was in there, were they?"

Aahmes shook his head.

She clambered to her feet and glared at the destruction. "Good. Are you all right?"

Aahmes rose and nodded. "Bruises, I'm sure. You?"

"Bruised, like you. Well, you won the wager."

"I could've wished otherwise."

"It *was* your week for the 'we won't make it 'til the end of the week without being attacked' side of the wager."

He grinned. "Yeah."

They both peered in the direction the bolt had come from.

"Just the one, you think?" Namid said.

She watched as his gaze lost focus. She felt him reach out with Power and touch the ruined Keep.

"Uh-oh."

"What? Another one?"

"I recognize the Power," he said. He gave her a long look. "Belaraketh."

"What? Are you sure?" The so-called god? At one time,

the god who had held Aahmes' allegiance.

"Yeah. Let's move."

They started to hike through the rubble-strewn street and partially melted snow away from the ruin of the Keep, then pulled up short as a wiry man appeared in front of them. He stood taller than Namid, but not as tall as Aahmes. Namid got an impression of skin lighter than theirs and light-colored hair before the stranger attacked.

Hands palm to palm, she and Aahmes formed a meshed shell of Power around themselves. They strengthened it from within as the man pounded it with his Power.

"This him?" Namid yelled to be heard over the attack.

"Yeah. Want a formal introduction?" Aahmes yelled back.

Namid chuckled and drew on more of her Power. "Let's do our kind of introduction, instead."

Aahmes matched her grin and twined his Power with hers. Namid tried reaching for Wild Power, too. Where was it? Was Aahmes having this trouble, too? She feared to divert her attention to find out.

Struggling to ignore the Power slamming into their defensive shell, Namid strained to focus her intent, calling to the Wild Power. A long breath-of-time passed. Still no Wild Power, although Namid could feel it hovering at the edge of her senses.

So, working together as they had practiced, Namid and Aahmes formed bolts of their own Power and flung them at Belaraketh. The first few splashed on his defenses, so Namid sent the next sliding around his shield of Power and began to form the firestorm around him. Aahmes poured more of his Power into it, then the Wild Power flowed to Namid, to them both, as if there had been no trouble calling it. The firestorm enveloped the so-called god, whittling away at his defenses.

Without warning, bolts of Power slammed into their defenses from a different direction. Namid lost her hold on the firestorm and it dissipated. Aahmes turned so he stood back to back with her, so he could see their new enemy.

"Ilenii, I think," he shouted.

Namid glanced back at the slight woman with pale hair and skin, and fed more Power into their defenses. "That's her. Wonderful."

"Attack or defend?"

"Both? A mix like we've been working on?"

"Yeah."

They twined their Power again, with the Wild Power still, then split it and sent half to their defense. The rest shot straight up, through their Power shell without disturbing it, then split again to spill down on their two attackers, two silvery vortexes of Power that pounded the others' defenses, fracturing them, but not breaking through.

"Why?" Namid shouted at their attackers.

The two 'gods' sidled toward each other, working to hold against Namid and Aahmes' attack.

"Can't have you telling tales or taking Sesaisyd's place. Certainly not two replacing one. We have enough gods," Ilenii shouted back and launched another attack.

"Thought they hated each other," Aahmes yelled at Namid, from right next to her. She could barely hear him.

"They hate us more?" she yelled back.

"Great."

Aahmes made a slight twist to their Power defense and Ilenii's attack rebounded on her and knocked her flat. She struggled to rise, managing it with Belaraketh's help. They locked gazes, then sent something different at Aahmes and Namid.

Namid felt the new attack slip right through their defenses and start to tug on her reserve of Power, like it intended to rip it from her. The small tattoos on her wrist and forehead—from her time at Ilenii's temple—tingled unpleasantly, then began to burn. She felt Aahmes jerk, heard him curse, and wondered if he was under a similar attack. A sudden insight came to her and she looked inward to discover a tie through those tattoos to Ilenii – something that had probably been there from the instant she had accepted the marks in Ilenii's temple complex years earlier.

"No!" Namid grasped Aahmes' hands and reached toward his Power with hers. They meshed their Power, weaving it together as they had before. Then something changed.

With a snap that Namid felt all through her body, her Power blended with Aahmes'. A sudden surge nearly knocked them both from their feet and their Power flew at Belaraketh and Ilenii, and at Ilenii's link to Namid. The Power bowled Belaraketh and Ilenii over and threw them back several paces. Namid and Aahmes pounded them again and sent them further back. Before they could hit them a third time, the two 'gods' vanished.

Her ears ringing in the sudden silence, Namid threw out a thin tendril of Power, but only learned that Belaraketh and Ilenii did not hide under some semblance. They had truly left. She did not sense where they had gone. With a wordless snarl, she kicked at the snow at her feet, while at the same time carefully releasing the unused Power. She staggered then as a wave of dizziness washed over her. It eased quickly but left her feeling a little queasy.

"Unbelievable!" she raged.

"Namid?"

"Bide. I'm being angry right now." Namid sent a few small Power bolts into nearby snow drifts, then stood and glared at the last spot the two so-called gods had occupied.

She felt a light touch on one arm and looked at Aahmes.

"Feel better, now?"

"Some. But this is bad. Want to wager that all of them will be coming after us?"

"Judging from the history Sesaisyd shared with you

before he died, I wouldn't be surprised."

Namid nodded and frowned as she recalled the memories that the 'evil god' had shared with her. Memories that showed the gods were nothing more than a bunch of immensely Powerful, Power-hungry, back-biting mages, him included. They had lived an extraordinarily long time and enjoyed their status as gods and had jealously destroyed any they thought would challenge their Power. But they were no more gods than Aahmes and Namid.

"Think that Power-theft they tried is what Chendrukhar... Wesh... did to the real Myung?" Namid said.

"Close enough, I'd think. Let's move."

Namid nodded and they hiked through the rocks and snow, headed for an entrance to their Power-secured cavern. Namid shook her head at the destruction at the Keep as they passed. After they secured the entrance behind them and stepped into their cavern, she let out a long breath.

"Agreed," Aahmes said and slumped down on the floor.

As she joined him, Namid curled back the edge of her right leather armguard and examined the shiny red mark on her wrist where the tattoo had been. She gingerly touched the spot of the other tattoo at her hairline under her bangs. It felt smooth, like an old burn, but still tender. Aahmes leaned closer to look.

"Those were from Ilenii's temple, right? Did you do that?"

Namid nodded to the first, then shrugged. "I think she burned them off. Casting me out, so to speak. But we did sever a link she had with me through them. Maybe that's what did it."

Aahmes looked thoughtful and reached across with his left hand to touch a spot at the back of his right shoulder.

"They marked us at their temple complexes...."

"You, too?"

He nodded. "A small tattoo, like yours. They used that to anchor a link. And I'd wager they've been able to keep track of us through that." He turned slightly away from her and pulled the neck of his shirt to one side. "Is mine gone, too?"

"Yeah. Looks like this one, now." Namid held out her right wrist.

Aahmes settled his shirt. "Feels like both links are severed," he said. "Ilenii's and Belaraketh's."

Namid sent out a thin Power tendril to make sure, then nodded. "Looks like they're completely gone. And I'd guess those two probably were behind some of the weirdness during Enric's quest last autumn."

Aahmes nodded. "At least without a link to us, we should be harder to locate next time."

"Yeah. Next time…. Great news." Namid studied the new scar on her wrist. Yet another one to carry. "Did you suspect our Power would do that? Blend like that, I mean."

Aahmes brushed his hair back from his face and shook his head. "I hadn't even thought of it. But it makes sense, in a way. Sesaisyd's Power split when it came to us. It's probably not too surprising that us trying to use it together would make it blend like that."

Namid nodded and leaned back with her eyes half-closed, trying to banish the last remnant of the dizziness. "I'm not looking forward to telling Thes about the Keep."

Aahmes frowned. "Yeah."

Namid gave him a sidelong look. "So now we know at least some of the so-called gods are after us. Who next, do you think?"

Aahmes shrugged. "Dark Priests, if any are still active. Especially that one… fairly sure he got away…."

"Randoq," she named the one High Dark Priest they thought had almost certainly escaped destruction. "Yeah, much as I wish otherwise, I expect him to turn up again. And then there's Staehw…." What had happened to the

Prazny who had chased them across the Six Realms already? He seemed to have just vanished after they last saw him.

Aahmes laughed and caught her hand to pull her to her feet. "Pick one, huh?"

She laughed, too.

"Hold a breath-of-time."

Aahmes gave her a questioning look, then nodded his understanding when she pulled the Powerful book from its concealment in the cavern.

"I feel we should keep this with us," Namid said. "Will you keep it for now? I'll take it with me to Kilaadi to Odasoro to see if he can make anything of it."

Aahmes nodded and tucked the book in his tunic.

~ ~ ~

Back at Tower Hold, Namid and Aahmes encountered grim faces, starting with the Shadower who met them at the storeroom exit from the tunnel.

"Thes is asking after you," he told them from his spot in the chair next to the door. A Shadower always lingered near the door to keep the non-Shadowers from getting into the tunnel.

"That's where we're headed," Namid told the man. "Is he in Lord Tower."

"Think so." He frowned at them, then leaned back in his chair and turned his gaze away.

Aahmes and Namid exchanged looks.

"We youngsters are in trouble, I think," Aahmes whispered to Namid.

She gave him a slight grin and nodded. "Certainly feels that way."

All through the Hold, the Shadowers' expressions told them the same story: trouble. By the time they met Thes in the top room of Lord Tower, they both were more than a little on edge. Even more than the attack had left them.

Thes greeted them calmly enough and sent everyone else from the room.

Namid and Aahmes exchanged glances, then took the seats Thes indicated. Namid noticed Aahmes gripped the hilt of one of his daggers and realized she had also rested a hand on the hilt of one of her own daggers.

"You didna mention there'd be other mages comin' after you two," Thes said in a quiet voice.

"We just found it out ourselves," Namid said.

"Who are they?"

Namid exchanged a look with Aahmes, uncertain she wanted to share what they knew about the so-called gods.

Thes slammed his hand down on the table by his chair, which caused both Namid and Aahmes to jump.

"Out with it. Whatever it is has brought danger t' us all."

"Doubt they'll care about anyone but us," Aahmes said.

"They destroyed Shadow Keep!" Thes yelled. "We saw the attack from here. And heard it."

Namid flinched, and Aahmes looked at his feet. But his voice came clearly to her thoughts.

~I think we should tell him all of it.~

~I don't know,~ she responded the same way. *~Telling anyone their gods aren't really gods….~*

~They're already coming after us. Telling Thes what's going on isn't going to make that worse.~

~True.~

Aahmes looked up at the older Shadower and told him what they had learned from Sesaisyd, the truth about the so-called gods.

Then Namid and Aahmes both watched Thes for his reaction.

Thes stared at them for many long breaths-of-time, then looked away, but not before Namid saw his surprise give way to fear.

She gave Aahmes a nervous glance and wished the sinking feeling in her belly would go away. Thes gave a heavy sigh and his shoulders slumped.

"It's no secret we probably wouldn't have survived the winter if the two o' you hadn't been here to help," Thes said without turning back to them. He sighed again and slumped even further. "But you need t' leave. T'day."

"You're kicking us out," Namid said. She did not see how he could have approached it any other way, but it still hit her like a punch to the gut. Was she going to be driven away from every place she considered a home?

Thes turned back to them, an expression of misery on his face. "What can I do? If you were sayin' you'd be keepin' us all safe, we'd all know it was a lie. You have t' go."

Namid and Aahmes both stood.

"Of course we'll go," Namid said. She tried to keep the bitterness from her voice. She headed to the door, Aahmes close behind.

"I wouldn't tell others about the gods," Aahmes said.

"Aye, lad. That I won't."

Right before she closed the door behind them, Namid heard Thes say in a soft voice, "Watch yourselves."

They paused outside the door and shared distressed looks.

"Where will you go?" Namid said.

Aahmes shrugged and looked away, brushing his hair back from his face with one hand. "Wherever you're going is where I'm going. Because neither of us stands a chance on our own, I think. We're clearly more Powerful together."

Namid nodded. "Meet outside the gate then? In, say, a candle-mark?"

After Aahmes agreed, Namid hurried to her room and deliberately filled her thoughts with what to take. Deliberately did not think about having to leave.

Almost a candle-mark later, she walked through Tower Hold's gate, carrying and dragging packs that held mostly food, a few items of clothing and, of course, her family-heirloom sword that had been with her since she had left Kilaadi years earlier. Outside the gate, she found Aahmes' packs in a pile and his footprints in the snow, but no other sign of him.

Then the gate behind her opened and he came through, wrangling two heavy bags of feed from the stables. He let them fall next to his packs and dumped the tack he'd draped around himself.

"I'll call the horses. I let them roam outside the walls when I can," Aahmes said, and suited action to words, using Power to summon the horses from wherever they had wandered. "They'll be here shortly."

They spent the time sorting out the tack and securing some things better in their packs. Aahmes pulled the Powerful book from his tunic and held it out to Namid, but she just shook her head.

"Why don't you just hold on to that still," she said.

Aahmes nodded and tucked it securely in one of his packs. "So which way is best to travel to Kilaadi?"

Namid let the silence drag on while she considered. She would rather go any other direction, but since they had to leave….

"I think the North Road will be slightly better. Less time on the plains so less chance of a late blizzard catching us. We can find a road going east to Kilaadi, I think, maybe a week's ride north of here."

"You don't sound sure about this," Aahmes said, studying her expression. "About going to Kilaadi."

Namid nodded. "I believe I should. And I'm getting the feeling sooner rather than later." Then she shook her head. "I'm *not* looking forward to it."

After a quick look around, Aahmes gave her shoulder a squeeze. "I'll watch your back, of course."

She nodded and bit back a snarky comment about him stabbing her in the back. She turned to grab her pack, but he stopped her with a gentle touch to her arm. He turned her toward him—and she saw him give their surroundings another quick scrutiny—then he caught up her hands. She gave him a questioning look.

He met her eyes, then looked away, but tightened his grip.

"What?" She stepped closer to look up into his face.

He brought his gaze back to her and just looked at her for a breath-of-time, then spoke softly. "I'd hoped to find the right moment… but now with the 'gods'… and who knows what else…."

"What?" she repeated.

"I feel I need to redeem myself for Foroughi, for—"

Something knocked Aahmes into Namid and they both went down in the snow. Gathering Power and drawing daggers, they struggled to scramble to their feet, ready to face their adversaries.

Namid looked up… into the face of her horse.

She wondered if horses had a sense of humor and began to laugh at the thought. She fell back into the snow, and just laughed harder.

"Great timing, horse," Aahmes growled, but he grinned. He helped Namid to her feet and mock-glared at her as she continued to chuckle. He reached into a pouch and drew out something concealed in his hand. He held his closed hand out to her. "Here's this anyway."

"What's this?"

"Take it and see."

Namid held her hand out and he dropped something shiny in it, warm from his grip. She looked closer at the object she held: a small, finger-length dagger, much like the one the Star of Corentris had given her many years ago, the one that had turned out to be the blade of Akavos. This new tiny dagger had a narrower blade than the other but looked like it would fit the sheath she still wore as a necklace. It also looked sharp.

"And this," Aahmes said and held out a small, stoppered glass vial more than half full of a thick pale-orange liquid.

Namid gave Aahmes a questioning look.

He shrugged. "I didn't know where your other poison came from, the one you used to put on your wrist blade, but I had a chance to recover this one from the wreckage. It's not a fatal poison, just takes someone out for a time. Thought you'd maybe want to use it with that." He gestured to the tiny dagger. "The dagger's not Powerful or anything like that."

Namid touched it with a bit of her Power and saw the truth of what he said. And she discovered something else.

"You made this for me? I thought they hadn't gotten the smithy going again yet."

Aahmes shrugged but looked pleased with himself at the same time. "I can shape small things with Power. The dagger required some extra concentration... I haven't shaped metal in a long time."

"It's perfect." Namid opened the vial and dipped the dagger's blade into it, then slipped the tiny dagger into its necklace sheath. She closed the vial and tucked it safely in a pouch on her belt. "Thank you."

Aahmes nodded. "And we'd better get going...."

He selected a horse for himself from the small herd Thes had brought, along with everything else, from the bandit camp. Namid found her own horse among the others.

They tacked up their horses and loaded their gear, then Aahmes sent the other horses into the Tower Hold courtyard for Thes to deal with. He and Namid mounted and followed the curve of Rhadanthus' wall to reach the North Road, which would take them into the northern portion of Paronia and eventually to a road going east to Kilaadi.

By the time they stopped the first night, Namid estimated they had traveled close to eight leagues from Rhadanthus, a good distance in the slushy snow. That night, nightmares again haunted her and at one point she lurched up out of her restless sleep, her neck burning with pain. The hand she put to her neck came away bloody.

She stared at it in disbelief. Was she still dreaming? She gingerly touched her neck with her other hand. She felt no wound, and this hand came away clean as the pain began to fade.

Aahmes made a sound then, drawing her attention. He still slept but seemed caught in some unpleasant dream. As she watched, though, he quickly settled back into calm sleep.

Namid reached out with tendrils of Power but sensed nothing amiss, and no attack. The defensive shell of Power that she and Aahmes had put around their camp still held. She took another look at her bloody hand, but the blood was gone.

As sleep claimed her again, she wondered what was going on.

CHAPTER 8

For the most part as they traveled through the slushy and sometimes deep snow that marked the near end of winter, Aahmes and Namid avoided towns they came across. They had enough provisions to last for a while, so no pressing need to stop. They rode mostly in silence, but sometimes reminisced about amusing happenings with the Shadowers. When they both were in a talkative mood, they again compared all of their relatives that they remembered and still found not a single one in common.

Much of the time when they were not riding, they worked to hone their control of their Power and their ability to work together. The more they worked with the Wild Power, when they could call it, the easier they found it to control. And almost imperceptibly, they found it easier to sense nearby Wild Power and call it... mostly.

More than a week of hard travel brought Aahmes and Namid far enough north that Namid directed them onto the next road going east. They had left the plains behind them and now traveled across hillocks with scattered clumps of trees.

As they traveled, winter began its retreat and they met

the resulting muddy roads, which kept their travel slow. Namid did not mind. Her reluctance to return to Kilaadi had grown and she welcomed the extra time to convince herself of the worth of the trip. She seemed to need a lot of convincing.

"Ugh," Namid muttered as she tried to brush the splatters off her knee. "I'm sick of the mud."

"We could find a little village and hole up there until the roads are better," Aahmes said. "Now that the links to Ilenii and Belaraketh are broken, we might be safe enough stopping for a while someplace out of the way." He moved his horse closer and their legs brushed as they rode. Namid smiled to herself at the warmth even that slight touch sent through her.

"Stopping for a day or two would be nice, but I don't want to delay longer. At least the road here is drier, for once."

"Race to the top of that hill, then?"

Namid looked around. She saw no other travelers on the road, not that she expected any. "Sure."

Aahmes waited for her to indicate she was ready, and they were off.

The hill stood far enough away on the drier stretch of road to give the horses a good run without exhausting them. The sun felt warm for spring and Namid found it wonderful to just enjoy the day for a time.

Namid had learned that Aahmes produced fierce devotion from the horses he rode and tended, enough to inspire them to some amazing feats. Apparently, he had practically grown up on horseback. So, she was not at all surprised that he reached the hilltop before she did, despite her horse's efforts. But then he pulled his horse up sharply.

"What's that?"

Namid joined him and peered down the road. In the shadows of a thicker copse of trees ahead there seemed to be something lying across the road.

"Fallen tree? Or brigand ambush?" Aahmes said.

"Or both. Straight through or around?"

Aahmes shrugged. "I'd say around. Might mess with their plans."

Namid nodded and they guided their horses off the road into the trees. They still traveled roughly the same direction as before.

Namid felt Aahmes send out a wisp of Power. She sent one out as well.

"I can't tell if there's anyone there," Namid said in a quiet voice. "But I just have the feeling that they are."

Aahmes nodded. "I also feel that someone's got some use of Power, but only a little. Maybe more than one. But I can't pinpoint anyone or anything. I do have the same feeling, though, that there are several lurking."

Namid studied the ground. Not a lot of low growth under the pines and few rocks. "Run for it?"

"I think so. Follow me."

And Aahmes' horse charged ahead. Namid kept hers close behind as they wound through the trees. Shouts broke out around them and she caught glimpses of shapes following, trying to catch up.

Motion to the side caught her attention, but too late. A man dropped from one of the trees to hit Aahmes and knock him off his horse. The two men rolled across the ground. Aahmes' horse stopped a short distance away. With no time to turn, Namid jumped her horse over the grappling men. She slid off and ran back toward them as she drew her daggers.

Someone grabbed her arm. She spun to break the grip then lunged for the brigand, daggers ready. Her opponent wielded a single long dagger, almost a short sword. He came for her again, and when she ducked away, grabbed her long braid.

Namid grinned when he howled in pain as the needles she had secreted in her hair stabbed deep into his hand with his grip. He let go. She laughed and swiped at him with both daggers at the same time. He blocked one with his own but took a cut in his arm from the other.

Namid worried where the man's accomplices were and tried to catch a look around. She almost took a cut to her face for her troubles, so she focused on the man in front of her. He pulled out a second dagger.

Namid heard a gasp of pain from Aahmes somewhere behind her. She dared not take her eyes from her assailant, who again lunged for her, his blades reaching for her.

She ducked and twisted and tried to glance over a shoulder to see how Aahmes fared. Her opponent seemed intent on preventing her. Then Aahmes screamed and suddenly she was done with this game.

Without a care for whomever might feel it, she called up her Power. She leashed it only long enough to shout a warning to their attackers.

"Run now."

When they did not run, she released her hold on the Power, keeping only enough control to hold it away from Aahmes, herself, and their horses. The Power exploded out around her with the look but not the substance of blue-white flames. Then Wild Power rushed to her, through her, and turned the flames from something intended to knock the brigands senseless into something deadlier.

The flames rolled over their attackers. They incandesced, held rigid by the Power, then crumbled into dust, leaving clothes and gear to fall to the ground.

Namid stared, stunned, at what she had done. She hadn't meant such destruction.

Pulling her attention away from what had just occurred, Namid looked for Aahmes and spotted him a few paces away, lying crumpled in a spreading pool of his own blood. A single bloodied sword lay next to him and next to the dust that had been his attacker. With a shudder, Namid drew her gaze from the dust and studied Aahmes. He already looked wan from blood loss.

She grabbed a tunic no longer needed by its owner and tried to use it to stem the flow of blood from the wound in his right side. It seemed to help some, so she tore strips from the other clothes scattered about and tied the wad of fabric tightly in place. She called up the Power again while calling on memories of what it had felt like when Cameni Healed her the previous autumn. She tried to use her Power to Heal Aahmes.

More Power than she had expected flowed out from her and the blood flow seemed less. But that was all. She just did not have the ability to Heal. She had to find him a real Healer.

And soon.

Namid used more Power to help steady Aahmes—he was, at best, half-conscious—and managed to get him onto his horse. She tied him there and wrapped a thread of Power around him to help keep him there. Without thinking about why, she snatched the sword that had lain next to him – presumably the sword that had caused his injury. She wiped the blood from it with a strip of cloth she had not used on Aahmes then stuffed the sword in a pack. She mounted her horse, grabbed the reins of Aahmes' horse and returned to the road. She continued riding the direction they had been going as fast as she dared. During all of this, Aahmes only groaned a few times, and seemed little aware of her actions.

For several candle-marks Namid pushed the horses, even bolstering them with bits of Power to keep them going. By early evening, she was forced to acknowledge that she would have to let them rest and so stopped for a while beside a small stream. She rubbed down the horses and fed them some of the grain they carried but left them saddled and ready to go. She grabbed some dried meat from her pack and ate, although she had no appetite. Aahmes was unconscious and still bleeding, although not as much as he had been at first. Namid did not know if that was a good or bad sign, but his color seemed worse.

While the horses ate and drank, she paced, fretted at the lost time and wondered just how far away the nearest village might be. From the state of the road, it saw a fair amount of traffic, so she assumed she should come to a village along it. She looked at the horses critically and realized that she dared not push them any harder. If she lost one or both of them, Aahmes would certainly be doomed.

Well, there was something that she *could* do. She had done it once to get them all out of the collapsing caverns of Corentris, so she imagined she should be able to use it for two people and two horses.

She hoped.

Namid cast a bit of Power out into the evening and followed the road ahead as far as she could. No sign of any town, but she did find a distinctive spot that held a small, roadside shrine to some local spirit. Keeping the image of that place firmly in mind, she grabbed the horses' reins, gathered Power and stepped. A slight tug on the reins caused her to worry that something had gone wrong, that she could not bring the horses with her, but then they all stood by the small shrine. She saw that more mud than had been there before now caked the horses' hooves. Maybe the mud had caused the tugging? She led them to firmer ground for the next step.

A couple of deep breaths to steady herself and a glance to see how Aahmes was doing, and again, she looked down the road for a place to step to. This step, she felt no alarming tugging.

After the fifth search-and-step, she fought to stay upright, half-blind with exhaustion and pain from the scars on her back. But she stood just outside a small village, the only one she had been able to find. It was full dark by then and many of the buildings in the village showed light at their windows. Namid stumbled forward and hoped she met someone before she fell flat.

Apparently, fortune favored her. As she drew even with

the door of the first building an older man stepped out and almost collided with her. When he saw her, he jumped back with an agility that surprised her. He as quickly stepped forward again to take the horses' reins.

"Here lass, let me help you."

"A Healer?" Namid croaked, her throat dry.

He peered in her face, then looked back at the horses and his eyes widened.

He whirled toward the building he had just exited.

"Chall, Nolan, Tarn, to me!" he shouted in a voice loud enough to carry all the way to the other side of the village.

Two young men and an older boy came running from the building. People also poured out of the neighboring buildings. Namid concentrated on remaining on her feet as the older man ordered everyone about.

"Tarn, run as fast as you ever have and bring Mehratar." The boy took off down the street. "Chall, Nolan, get this man off his horse and inside. Carefully! Watch his side there." Namid started to protest and the man shushed her gently. "Don't you worry. M'boys have experience moving those as are hurt. Lucky, you getting here when you did. Mehratar had plans to leave for the next village on his circuit tomorrow or the next day."

He looked at her closely then. "Did you take hurt, too?"

Namid managed to shake her head, but speech was beyond her at that point.

"For shame, Garai!" A large woman scolded the man as she hurried up to them. "At least let the lass sit down afore she falls down. Come along, m'dear. We'll take care of you."

Namid pulled away from the gentle hand the woman laid on her arm and reached out toward Aahmes as the villagers carried him into the first building. "No…."

"Let her stay with her kin, Etha," Garai said. "You can just bring everything she'll need to my place."

The woman glared at him, hands on her hips. Then she

gave an abrupt nod and turned back toward one of the other buildings. Namid's legs chose that moment to buckle, but Garai caught her and easily picked her up. He handed the horses' reins to someone, with quick instructions for the horses' care, then headed back toward the first building.

"You're just a slip of a thing," he commented. "Let's get you inside."

He carried Namid inside, through the front room and into a bedroom. Chall and Nolan were carefully laying Aahmes on the bed as they entered.

Garai set Namid on the room's single chair, worn but padded, and tucked a blanket around her. "You just sit there, lass. Anything you need, we'll get for you. And don't you worry. Mehratar's the best Healer around. He should be here any time now."

Before too long, the woman Etha slipped into the room with another blanket for Namid and a mug of hot tea.

"Now drink that down," Etha instructed her. "One of the others will be along with food for you shortly."

Namid nodded her thanks but kept her gaze on Aahmes. He had not made a sound when they carried him in and now he lay motionless where they had placed him. She sent a small burst of Power to bolster him, unable to do anything else. The action almost knocked her out.

Namid heard a small commotion in the outer room and a man she had not seen before stepped into the bedroom. She guessed he likely had ten years more than she, maybe even a few years more than that. His skin was light brown, lighter than her own and lighter than the others Namid had seen so far in this village. At first glance, he seemed dressed simply, like the villagers. But then Namid realized his shirt and trousers were made of the finest linen. He had deep brown hair, worn shorter than Aahmes', brown eyes that were even lighter than her own, and a neatly trimmed mustache.

He went straight to Aahmes and began to peel away her makeshift bandaging. She doubted he had even noticed her. But when Aahmes groaned and she made a small sound of dismay, he looked at her.

"You brought him to the right place, and got him here in time," he told her.

The smile he gave her reassured her even more, and for a breath-of-time, she had the impression that she held all of his intense attention. It was a heady, but disconcerting sensation. He radiated a sense of calm competence that put her at ease and she also felt a sense of disciplined Power from him. After the Healer turned back to Aahmes, Namid let out the breath she had not realized she had been holding.

The Healer stripped away the last of Aahmes' bandages then cut away his shirt.

Namid sipped her tea and watched.

One of the young men—Namid did not know whether Chall or Nolan—brought a large basin of water and several clean cloths. A young woman who looked like she might be the young man's sister followed. She wet the cloths and helped the Healer clean around Aahmes' wound.

Namid felt a light touch of Power, but directed at her, not Aahmes. The Healer straightened and gave her a stern look.

"Release the link to your friend here, before you seriously harm yourself," he said. "It was capably done, but I've got him now."

Namid startled. A quick check and she saw the link he spoke of. She must have made it when she tried to Heal Aahmes. She dissolved it and felt somewhat better right away.

The Healer smiled again, and gave her a nod, then turned back to Aahmes. Namid felt the Power gathering as he began to work on the Healing.

Sometime later, someone brought Namid a bowl of stew. She had just finished eating when the Healer looked up again. His assistant gathered the bloody cloths and the water basin and left.

The Healer stepped around the bed and crouched down in front of Namid, his attention entirely on her again. He took one of her hands and held it between both of his. His soothing, Healing Power flowed through her from his touch.

"He needs rest, but he'll be fine," the Healer said with that reassuring smile. "I'm Mehratar. Did you take any injury?"

Namid shook her head.

"What happened? Can you speak?"

"Y-yes." Namid's voice sounded rough, as if she had been shouting. Another sip of tea helped sooth her throat. "I'm Namid. It was brigands." She waved her free hand in the general direction they had come from. "Earlier today. A ways away."

He released her hand and brushed her forehead with his fingertips. "You should rest, too. I'll return to check on you both in the morning."

Namid nodded and gave him a slight smile. "Thank you. For us both."

He smiled and gave her a slight bow.

She waited until he had left, then struggled out of her chair and over to Aahmes. His color looked better and he breathed easily. Mehratar had bandaged him again, but Namid saw no blood seeping through. Aahmes looked only deeply asleep now.

"Shall we place the chair by the bed?"

Namid jumped and spun around, a dagger held ready.

Garai's eyes widened and he backed up a pace, hands raised in front of him. "Sorry, lass. Didna mean to startle you."

Namid straightened and sheathed her dagger. "I'm the one who's sorry," she said. "I'm a little on edge."

Garai moved the chair around the bed. "Understandable. Mehratar said it was brigands?"

Namid nodded and backed out of Garai's way, then watched him position the bulky chair close to the bed. Aahmes moved a little and muttered something but did not wake.

"We'll keep a watch this night."

"I don't think that's needed," Namid said. "We weren't close to the village when they attacked."

Garai studied her face, then motioned her to take her seat. "Safer with a watch, anyway," he said. "Now rest and don't you worry about a thing."

He gave her shoulder a pat, then left.

Namid settled back in her chair. She wrapped herself in her blankets and watched Aahmes until she fell asleep.

CHAPTER 9

During the night, Namid woke several times from disturbing dreams of people falling into dust, including Aahmes and her family, of Wesh having actually become her, of her having become Wesh. The dreams left her apprehensive, a feeling she had difficulty shaking. Each time she woke, she checked on Aahmes. He had shifted position a couple of times but still slept every time she looked.

The next morning, soon after dawn, Mehratar returned. Namid was already awake and had checked on Aahmes yet again. Mehratar greeted her in a soft voice and touched the back of her hand with his fingertips. She felt a brief touch of his Power and he smiled at her.

"Better," he said, and turned to Aahmes.

Namid watched as he placed a hand atop the bandages that covered the wound, and she felt a surge of Healing Power. Aahmes opened his eyes and looked around, stopping when he spotted her. Then he studied the Healer standing over him.

Mehratar nodded at Aahmes and introduced himself.

"Aahmes," he managed to croak out. His voice

sounded as rough as Namid's had the previous night. "What…?"

"You were gravely wounded," Mehratar said. "Fortunately, I was here. The rest I'll leave to your companion to tell you. You'll need to rest here a couple of days, or so." He held up a hand, with a smile, as Aahmes looked ready to argue. "As your Healer, I say this."

Namid nodded when Aahmes looked at her.

"And now I'll have some food and drink sent in to you two," Mehratar said and turned toward the door. But he leaned back to Namid before he left. "You rest, too. And when you're up for it, we need to talk," he said in a quiet voice.

Namid gave him a perplexed look, but he was already headed out the door.

Namid stretched in her chair and told Aahmes all the events of the previous day.

"The sword?" Aahmes said. "You still have it?"

Namid nodded. "It should still be with the horses' gear. Probably in a stable here."

"I need to see it again. There was something—" He broke off as the door opened again. Garai entered, followed by three others. They all exchanged introductions while the villagers set out food and hot tea. Namid learned then that Chall was Garai's eldest, and he was the one with the wavier hair of Garai's sons. The young woman who had assisted Mehratar was next eldest and named Thalace. Nolan was the youngest of these three, with the absent Tarn youngest of them all.

After Garai arranged everything to his satisfaction, he shooed his children out. He encouraged Aahmes and Namid to eat.

"No sign of brigands this past night," he told them as he leaned against the wall next to the door. "But now we're warned, I'm not worried."

"The sword?" Aahmes said around a bite of food.

Garai gave them both a questioning look.

"I grabbed one of their swords," Namid explained, "and tucked it with our gear. Could we have it, please?"

Garai looked around the room. "Such a fuss last night, we didna bring in any of your stuff. How about I have everything that's not tack brought to you?"

"Thank you."

"The horses are well cared for?" Aahmes said.

"Don't you worry about them, lad. They're happy and warm in Fabor's stable. We know how to care for the animals. You just follow Mehratar's directions and get yourself healed."

He left them to their meal.

Less than a quarter candle-mark later, Chall returned with their packs. He plopped them in a corner and left again, with a smile and a wave.

Namid chewed the last of her slice of bread as she dug through the packs.

"What's the deal about the sword?"

"Thought I recognized something on it," Aahmes said. "Distracted me and I ended up getting skewered."

Namid tsked at him. "Here it is." She pulled out the brigand's short sword and handed it to Aahmes.

He studied the sword and swiped a thumb across the chappe to clear it of ash. That revealed an intricate symbol stamped into the leather.

"What I thought," he said.

"And that is…" Namid prompted.

Aahmes looked up with a grim expression. "It's Belaraketh's symbol. They weren't common brigands."

"He sent people after us?" Namid's voice cracked with her surprise.

Aahmes nodded and returned the sword. "Looks like. Better hide that," he said. "I don't think we can linger here." He tried to rise but fell back with a gasp.

Namid frowned. "Not much choice. Just stay put. I'll talk to the Healer. See if he can get you moving sooner."

As she left, she heard Aahmes grumble something

behind her. She decided that she did not want to know what he had said.

She found no one else in the house, and outside, the village was quiet. She felt welcome warmth from the sun, but the air still held a chill.

She walked through the village, looking around to spot anyone. All the buildings were built of wood, mostly small houses, well cared for, many with stone chimneys. At the other end of the village, she finally heard something and poked her head inside what looked to be a smithy. Sounds came from the back somewhere.

"Hello?"

"Back room," a deep voice called.

Namid eased through the crowded smithy and paused in the doorway to the next room.

Inside two men worked at shoeing a horse. One of the men was Garai. Namid had not seen the other before.

When they finished, both men looked up. Garai smiled and the other man gave her a friendly nod.

"Ah, lass, good to see you up and about," Garai said.

"Thanks. Where can I find Mehratar?"

Garai looked alarmed. "Is aught wrong?"

"No, no," Namid tried to reassure him. "I just have some questions."

"Ah, good to hear all's well with you and the lad. Mehratar might be at the house he uses when he's in the village, second house from the end on the other side of the street. If not, then he's out at the fields with the others." Garai waved a hand in the general direction of the back of the shop. "Planting time, you know."

Namid nodded. Not that she did know, except by hearsay, city-bred as she was. She thanked Garai and headed to the Healer's house.

She found Mehratar's door ajar, so she peered inside. She saw a simply furnished front room, everything well made. She spotted Mehratar in a chair toward the back of the room. He sat tailor-style, his hands resting on his knees and his eyes closed. Namid looked back out in the street. No one there. She looked back at the Healer, uncertain what to do.

She said his name, loud enough that he should hear her if he was awake, but not so loud as to disturb him if he was asleep. He took a deep breath after she spoke but did not open his eyes. She leaned against the doorframe, planning to wait a while to see if he noticed her.

Before too long, he opened his eyes and stood.

"Welcome. You and Aahmes are both doing well?" He motioned her inside.

"Yes. Thank you. Is there any way Aahmes can be ready to move on today? We need to keep moving."

His intent gaze made her wonder what he was seeing.

"It wouldn't be wise, even with my Healing. Please, sit." He snagged one of his chairs and pulled it close to her.

"His wound was deep and dangerous. Another day of rest, at least, with more Healing would serve him best. Also, I wouldn't see you leave in your state."

Namid gave him a puzzled look. "My state? I'm still just a little tired, but otherwise I'm fine."

He studied her in a silence that stretched, and she shifted on her chair.

"What?"

"Your Power is off-balance. And getting worse. Certainly, you've noticed something wrong."

Namid thought back to what she had done to the brigands, and the times before when her Power had gone inexplicably awry. She nodded. "I suppose I have."

"I can help. I can't see you leave the village as you are."

Namid considered that. "How long will this need? And what's involved?"

"I'll need to take a close look to be able to answer with any confidence. Right now, I suspect something is interfering with your Power, or your control, something like that." He leaned closer. "May I?"

Namid nodded. He placed one hand over hers on her lap and touched her forehead with the fingertips of his other hand. She felt his Power wrap around her but could not tell what he was doing with it. After a few breaths-of-time, he sat back and again studied her, this time with a worried expression.

"Old injuries, now scars," he said. "Someone has deliberately blighted you."

Namid shuddered. She knew what he referred to. She flashed back to memories from more than twelve years earlier of the Dark Priests' chastisement that she had endured. The pain, the resulting scars on her back… and Randoq, the High Dark Priest. He had to be behind this new torment.

"I know a form of Healing that will help you," Mehratar said. "We'll need a couple of days, at least. Maybe more. It'll be draining. For us both."

"A Healer friend told me that it's been so long, the scars can't be Healed."

Mehratar smiled. "Your Healer friend had perhaps not yet reached the highest levels?" At Namid's nod, he continued. "And even then, few Master Healers would be able to do this. I am one who can. Although, your Healer friend was partly right. It's likely even I won't be able to remove the scars, not completely anyway."

Namid met his intense gaze, and she believed him. She took a deep breath to try to order her thoughts. For some reason, this frightened her.

"What do I do?" she said.

Mehratar gave her shoulder a quick squeeze as he rose. "First, we return to your friend," he said. "I'll see if he can take faster Healing. And you'll likely want his company for this."

Namid frowned. That did not sound good.

She followed the Healer back to Garai's house and watched as he spoke with Aahmes, then applied more Healing Power to his wound. She flinched when Mehratar turned to her.

"What is it?" Aahmes demanded.

Namid explained what the Healer had told her.

"Will this hurt her?" Aahmes asked Mehratar.

"Probably," Namid answered for the Healer. "Considering the source. But if that means fixing the problem, maybe even fixing some of the scarring…."

Aahmes nodded his understanding.

"Good. We'll begin with some caution," Mehratar said. He moved the cushioned chair back to its original spot and brought a wooden stool from another room. This he placed right next to Aahmes and told Namid to sit. She did and squirmed around trying to find a comfortable position. Aahmes gave one of her hands a quick squeeze of support. Mehratar crouched next to her, opposite Aahmes, and captured her attention.

"I'll start with just a small test, if you want to call it that. That'll give us a both a better idea of what we're dealing with. Ready?"

Namid nodded, with a deep sigh.

Mehratar rose and stood at Namid's right, in a spot where she could just see him without turning her head. He placed a gentle hand high on her back, in the center. She jumped when he touched her.

"Ready?" he repeated.

"Yeah. Go ahead."

A little bit at a time, Namid felt Power wrapped in warmth spread out across her back from Mehratar's hand. Then, for a time, nothing seemed to happen. She sensed that he worked with the Power but had no clue what he was doing.

Just as she had begun to relax, sharp pains sliced across her back. It felt much like the original whipping that had caused the scars. She gasped. Warm blood trickled down her back.

Mehratar murmured, "My apologies." And she felt an increase in his Power.

Without warning, she found herself back in Corentris, a girl as she had been then, standing chained between those pillars. The whip cracked and sliced into her. She cried out.

"Namid…."

She tried to pull away, tried to escape.

"Namid!"

Power touched her, and she gathered her own to strike out, then recognized the touch. Tamping down the Power, she fought her way out of the memories to see two concerned faces peering at her. She shuddered and drooped. Mehratar caught her shoulders to keep her from falling off the stool.

"What did you do?" Aahmes demanded of the Healer.

"I'm all right," Namid said, hoping to calm him. The pain had vanished, so she was even telling him the truth. "It wasn't his fault."

Aahmes gave her a look of disbelief but sank back on his pillow again. Namid looked to Mehratar for an explanation.

"It's complex," he said. "I *can* help, but we'll need to go slowly. Someone has tied Power into your wounds, now scars, that reopens them if Healing is attempted."

"And throws me back to the time they were made," Namid added.

"So, every time you try to Heal her, she relives that time? And is injured anew?" Aahmes said.

Mehratar nodded. "On the good side, though, I'll be able to mostly Heal your scars, at least. And, from what I felt, the more we can Heal, the less trouble your Power will give you."

Aahmes and Namid exchanged glances.

"I don't know that we should stay in one place that long," Namid murmured.

A commotion outside drew their attention. Aahmes tried to rise, but Mehratar stopped him with a firm hand on his shoulder.

"Not yet," the Healer told him. And when Namid tried

to stand, he shook his head at her. "Nor you, either. I'll see what it is and come tell you."

On his way out the door, he pointed at the remnants of their breakfast that still sat on a small table by the bed. "Eat," he ordered. "It'll help."

Aahmes and Namid exchanged glances but followed his directions. And they did feel better after they had finished. Mehratar returned before too long.

"You came from the west, right?" he said.

At their nods, he looked thoughtful. And troubled.

"What is it?" Namid said.

"There's smoke to the northeast. Hard to tell how far away, but we see no flames from here. At least the wind's not blowing it toward us."

"Another village?" Aahmes said.

Mehratar shook his head. "There's wilderness that direction, for the most part. A few isolated family settlements." Then he added, "And Jelth's temple complex, with all its instructors and students, buildings and fields."

Namid looked at Aahmes and saw the horror in his expression that she felt, too. "They wouldn't, would they? Is it starting all over?"

Aahmes shrugged. "Could be. From what we know, they've shown themselves quick to attack each other before."

"But the Healers?"

Aahmes shrugged. "Makes sense to take out anyone who can help your enemy."

"You mean the so-called gods and their penchant for mutual destruction?" Mehratar said.

Namid tried to keep her expression blank. "So-called?"

The Healer nodded. "I read an ancient journal, written by Jelth…. They're all just a bunch of old mages with too much knowledge and Power, and too little wisdom and self-control." Anger crossed his expression, then was gone so quickly Namid wondered if she had imagined it.

Mehratar looked from Namid to Aahmes and back. "And you two are completely unsurprised to hear that."

Namid shrugged. "Last autumn, we learned something to that effect."

Mehratar's expression invited her to explain, but she did not want to go into the whole thing right then, so she returned to the original topic.

"Is someone going to see if it's Jelth's temple?" she said.

Mehratar nodded. "A couple of the villagers are heading out...."

He stared in the direction of the temple complex, as if he could see it through the wall, his expression troubled. "There'll be injured, probably more than they can help," he muttered. "I need to go, too."

He returned his attention to Aahmes and Namid. "It'll likely be several candle-marks before we're back."

He glanced at the small table, now empty of any food. "Both of you rest. While you can," he told them and headed back outside.

"Yeah. My favorite thing," Aahmes said. "Lying around... healing." He yawned.

"Better than lying back there bleeding," Namid said as she moved back to the padded chair and curled up on it, pulling a blanket over herself. Then she sat up with a curse.

"What?"

"The reopened wounds mean another bloodied shirt," Namid said with a frown. She shook out the blanket and examined it. "Well, at least I didn't bleed all over Garai's blanket."

Aahmes chuckled, then winced. "Don't make me laugh yet."

CHAPTER 10

Namid woke in the afternoon, to the sounds of another commotion from outside. She saw that Aahmes was awake, too. This time they both went to the door of Garai's house to see. Aahmes braced himself against the doorframe. To help him remain upright, Namid thought, looking at the determination in his expression.

Two soot-covered villagers stumbled down the street supporting a third man between them. Mehratar followed behind, also soot-covered. Garai met the group, almost right in front of the door where Aahmes and Namid stood. Other villagers had gathered, too.

The three soot-blackened men in front of the Healer all spoke at once.

"It's bad, Garai. Whole temple complex burnt."

"Didn't see any survivors 'cept this fellow."

"I bring dire warning," the temple complex survivor said. "One of the temple guards saw who did this. He told me before he died." The man paused to cough, then resumed in a raspy voice. "Two of them, it was. A man and a woman. Looked like sibs, he said. Straight black hair, red-brown skin. Thin...."

109

He caught sight of Namid and Aahmes. "It's them!" he shrieked. "Run! They'll kill us all." Before anyone could stop him, he ran back down the street, screaming.

Everyone looked at Namid and Aahmes, who returned the looks with blank ones of their own.

"Want we should catch him?" one of the villagers asked Garai, with a wave of one hand toward the fleeing man.

"I doubt you'd be able to," Mehratar observed. He turned to Garai and gestured at Namid and Aahmes. "They've been here," he said. "Neither could have gotten to the temple and back at the time they were supposed to have destroyed it."

Garai nodded. "I hear you." He looked at Namid and Aahmes. "But it's a curious thing, ain't it? How could someone describe you so well? Why be after you two with such a wild tale? You two couldna do—" He broke off at the sight of their expressions.

Mehratar stepped up and patted the older man on the shoulder. "I've got this," he said.

Garai nodded and gave his two guests a pained look as he walked away. Mehratar urged Aahmes and Namid back into the house and closed the door. He motioned them to seats in the front room then grabbed a cloth, which he wet from a small pitcher of water that sat near the cook-stove. He used the damp cloth to clean the soot from his hands and face.

"How about you tell me about it," he said, his voice muffled in the cloth.

Aahmes and Namid exchanged glances, then—with Aahmes' help—Namid told the Healer about the quest to find the sword the previous autumn, as succinctly as she could. She skipped over many of the details, and deliberately left out her parentage and Aahmes', as well as the heritance that came to them both at Sesaisyd's death.

After they finished the tale, Mehratar stared at them in astonishment. "You were two of the heroes…."

Namid shrugged. "Yeah, we sort of got caught up in the whole thing."

Aahmes chuckled.

"From what you've said, Sesaisyd doesn't sound much like one would expect the 'evil god' to be. Although those Dark Priests are certainly heinous," Mehratar said.

"The winners get to tell the tale," Aahmes muttered. "It must have served the other 'gods' somehow to have Sesaisyd labeled as the evil one."

No one argued.

Mehratar studied them with that intense look of his. "The two of you together *could* have destroyed the temple complex, as I saw. You've got the Power…." He held up a hand to forestall their protests. "But I know you didn't. Why is someone trying to make you the culprits. And who?"

Namid looked at Aahmes.

Should we? she asked, using hand-talk, that secret language they had both learned as Shadowers.

Aahmes looked back at the Healer, who met his gaze. Namid felt him brush Mehratar with a tendril of Power. Mehratar frowned, but otherwise did not react.

I think yes, Aahmes answered Namid, also using hand-talk. *He already knows some. He's taken our side here. He might have helpful thoughts.*

So Namid told Mehratar more details. She told him about how she and Aahmes had both been able to use the Wild Power the previous autumn, when others could not, and how Power had come to both of them when Sesaisyd died. And she mentioned the gods' recent attack on them. Aahmes told of the brigand attack and the blades marked with Belaraketh's sign.

Mehratar studied them in silence for a long time after they finished.

Namid broke the silence. "I think we need to leave as soon as we can," she said.

Mehratar nodded. "For the health of the village, I have

to agree. But first…."

He Healed them both again. This time he took longer with Namid, and it was just as bad as the first time. Afterward, when she stopped shaking, she slipped into the next room to dig out a shirt and tunic and change out of her bloody ones. She bundled the bloody clothes together and stuffed them in the bottom of her pack to deal with later. She brought the pack into the front room with her, and Aahmes' pack, too.

Mehratar stopped them at the door. "Bide a breath-of-time. I won't keep you from leaving but think on this. You seem to be under two types of attacks, possibly from diverse sources. One to try to discredit you. Maybe to isolate you…"—then at their looks—"isolate you even further, anyway. And the other to try to kill you."

"But, consider," he continued. "The attacks on you might only be events at the edge of something else, something bigger. If the 'gods' have decided to wage war on each other again, they might see you as allies of their opponents or even favored of their opponents and so worth destroying just as Aahmes said of the elimination of the Healers' temple."

He stepped out of their way. "I don't like sending you both off incompletely Healed." He shook his head. "Be careful." Then he gave them a slight smile. "If you can."

He clapped Aahmes on the shoulder and gave Namid a long look as they stepped out the door. Outside, they found their horses waiting for them, tacked up and ready to go, each carrying an extra bag of provisions. Namid loaded their packs on the horses, to spare Aahmes the risk of pulling at his mostly healed wound, and they mounted and headed out at a brisk walk.

Namid glanced back to see only Mehratar standing in the street. He raised a hand and she returned the gesture. Then she lost sight of the village around a curve and beyond the thickening forest.

They had traveled only a little further when they both

felt it. Power, in quantity. Surging in their direction from the west. They pulled up and turned.

"Us?" Aahmes said.

"No. The village!" And Namid raced back. She recklessly pulled on her reserve of Power and tried to throw it ahead of her, over the village, to protect it. Aahmes followed hard on her horse's heels and added what he could of his Power and control to hers.

They heard a crack, followed by a roar, and a hot wind swept over them.

"No!" Namid urged her horse faster, then pulled up sharp as the village came in sight. Or rather the towering black cloud of smoke where the village had been.

They raced forward again and threw out Power to try to clear smoke and smother fires, with limited success. At the edge of the village, they both slid off their horses before they stopped completely. Aahmes gasped and clutched his side at the movement. And they stared.

The buildings were little more than piles of blackened rubbish, burnt wood, and stones that looked like they had also burned somehow. Smoke boiled into the sky from the direction of the fields, too.

Nothing moved.

Aahmes held Power around them, in case another attack came, but Namid's Power drained away from her control as she fought sudden despair.

"No!" she shouted. "They weren't part of this!" She stood in the middle of the street and stared at the destruction. Aahmes gave her shoulder a quick squeeze and sent a stream of Power to the fields to try to dampen the fires there.

A scraping sound ahead and to their left caught their attention. They ran to the wreck that had been Garai's house.

"There's Power there," Aahmes said.

Namid nodded and used her Power to drag the heat from the destroyed building. Then she hauled at the debris.

Aahmes helped as he could, being careful of his healing wound, and still maintained a watch with Power.

Eventually, Namid uncovered an arm, then the rest of the man. Mehratar had surrounded himself with a thin layer of Power, just enough to keep him from harm. He was barely recognizable under the filth from the smoke and ashes from the destroyed house. When Namid touched his arm, his Power defense vanished. He groaned and rolled over slightly. The Healer looked at her with little recognition but was able to help clear enough of the debris to fight free of it.

He staggered to his feet and out into the street, refusing any help. He spun around to see the destruction of the village and the lingering smoke from the direction of the fields.

Namid felt him send out a wave of Power that swept through the village and out to the fields. Then he sank to the ground, head hanging, and shoulders slumped.

"All of them," he murmured. Namid knelt next to him and reached a tentative hand toward him but did not touch him.

Namid sent out her own Power and touched nothing alive except the three of them and the two horses. Although she had found it difficult before to find people who did not have Power themselves.

"I'm sorry. I'm so sorry. We shouldn't have stayed so long. We should've left—"

Mehratar gave her a fierce look. "This is not your doing. *They* are responsible. Don't take on the blame that rests squarely with them." He waved a hand vaguely toward the west.

"He's right," Aahmes said, then added, "Belaraketh's temple complex is that way. Wager who sent that blast?"

Namid shook her head. "No wager." She looked back at Mehratar. "You're sure no one else survived?"

He nodded, his expression one of misery. "I'd be able to sense them in the Power if they had. It goes along with the Healing Power." He slumped down and stared at the ground between his slack hands. But he stayed like that only a short time. Then he levered himself to his feet.

"I can't help them now," Mehratar said. "But you would still benefit from more Healing. I'm coming with you."

Namid and Aahmes exchanged glances.

"Traveling with us might not be your best choice," Namid said.

"Not as bad as this. And I'll be able to help better with you. If you'd been stronger, perhaps you might've turned aside the attack. Yes, I felt you trying."

Mehratar stumbled to the ruin that had been his house and dug through it, muttering about seeing if he could salvage anything.

Aahmes leaned close to Namid. "I don't know about this. We don't really know him."

"We know he's a Healer, a cursed good one. And he knows the reality about the gods, as we do. He seems an ally."

Aahmes did not look convinced. "Where's the annoying oh-so-noble Healer lady when you want her?" he muttered.

Namid grinned at him. "Could it be? Do you actually miss Cameni? Perhaps have a soft spot in your heart for her?" she teased.

He looked at her with a startled expression, and Namid realized that they had not really bantered like this since he returned. She had missed it.

"Don't say such things. You know what a hard-hearted guy I am," he said with an overly solemn expression.

"Hah! Liar." She leaned closer and looked up at him. "I happen to have seen proof last autumn to the contrary."

Aahmes gave her a mock frown but the corners of his lips twitched upward. "I can't imagine *what* you might be talking about."

Clattering from behind them drew their attention.

Mehratar kicked at a half-burned board and turned toward them.

"Nothing," he said. As he approached them, he tried to brush off the soot and grime that covered him. "First stream we come to, I'm jumping in," he said with a faint smile.

He took a last look around, and Namid watched his expression fall into heavy sorrow. Then he seemed to push that aside as he turned to them and gestured down the road.

"We should put some distance between us and this devastation."

"We should at least give them a proper burial before leaving," Namid said.

The sorrow crossed Mehratar's face again. "Nothing left to bury," he said in a soft voice. "Look there. I know that Garai was there." He pointed to the smithy.

Namid walked over and poked around in the debris. Mehratar was right, nothing but ashes there, with the remnants of a few charred boards and stones. All the metal in the shop had melted into dull puddles. She shuddered. This looked too much like what she had done to the brigands.

Was she going to become as self-centered and callous as the mages-turned-gods? Could the Power she and Aahmes had inherited from Sesaisyd do that to them?

A hand on her shoulder made her jump.

Mehratar gave her arm a gentle squeeze of reassurance. "We need to go. There's nothing we can do now."

"One thing we can do," Aahmes said from behind them.

Turning, Namid caught him glaring at Mehratar, but the expression vanished so fast that she wondered if she had imagined it. Mehratar dropped his hand.

"What's that?" Namid asked Aahmes.

Aahmes led the way to a knee-high rock that was about half a pace long. It sat near the edge of the town, and near the road.

"Have you ever carved with Power?" Aahmes said.

Both Namid and Mehratar shook their heads.

"My people create memory stones for our dead," Aahmes said, staring at the rock. "They don't use Power for it, but I figured out a way to do so. I think this village deserves that."

Mehratar gave him a grateful look, and Namid saw tears in his eyes. "Thank you," he said.

Aahmes gave a quick nod. "Just tell me their names."

Namid sat on the ground and watched as Aahmes used the thinnest tendril of Power to carve the names that Mehratar told him.

"I wish we could do more," Namid said, after Aahmes finished the last carving: Arndu—the name of the village—and the date.

Mehratar helped her to her feet. "We can stop these butchers from doing this again," he growled.

Namid and Aahmes exchanged glances.

"Yeah," Namid said.

They collected the horses and left the destroyed village behind them.

CHAPTER 11

True to his word, Mehratar plunged, completely clothed, into the first stream they came to. It was near nightfall and they had left the road, deciding it safer to take the harder path and make their own way through the forest. Mehratar gasped at the icy water but stayed in long enough to get rid of the worst of the grime. Aahmes tossed him some dry clothes to change into when he was done. The Healer frowned at the clothes but took them.

Namid and Aahmes both hauled out their bloodstained clothes and rinsed them in the stream as well. At one point, Namid saw Aahmes finger the long slit from where he had been stabbed and Mehratar had sliced his shirt away from the wound, a worried look on his face. She turned away, not wanting him to see her own worry.

They decided against a fire, so Aahmes dug out some of their dried meat, and some hard bread, while Namid and Mehratar tended to the two horses. Aahmes also hauled out blankets while he was digging around in the packs.

"Is there someone nearby who might be willing to sell us a horse?" Namid asked the Healer as they worked. "I'd rather not continue having one horse carry double, if possible."

"Maybe," Mehratar said. "There are scattered settlements in the area. And further down the road, the way we've been going, is the next village. About half a day away, right now."

"I don't know that we should risk villages," Aahmes said.

Namid sighed. "And just when I thought we might be done with the camps in the wilds…."

Aahmes chuckled. "But we've gotten so good at them."

Mehratar looked from one of them to the other and shook his head slightly. "After we eat, I'll Heal you both again. This will be the last you'll need," he told Aahmes.

"How many more for me?" Namid said.

"I can't say exactly. Several, at least. I don't want to overwhelm you."

"I want to push this along," Namid said. "I can't have the Power getting away from me. Especially now."

"I wouldn't cause you increased pain. That's not—"

"Why not see how bad it gets before saying we can't do it," Namid said.

"You might be surprised," Aahmes told Mehratar.

Mehratar studied each of them in turn, then shrugged while shaking his head. "Be prepared for both of us to fall on our faces," he told Aahmes.

They made sure the horses were settled and their camp as set up as it was going to be, without the fire. After they ate, Mehratar Healed Aahmes, who then stretched elaborately, with a pleased smile, and thanked him.

"Your turn," Mehratar told Namid.

"Do you want to change into the stained shirt, so you don't bleed all over another one?" Aahmes asked her.

"Hmm, good point," Namid said. "But it's still wet."

"Easy enough to take care of," Mehratar said. He held out a hand for the shirt, then held it up, thumb and first finger of each hand clasping a shoulder of the shirt. He sent a thin tendril of Power through his fingers, spreading warmth through the shirt, until it dried.

"Nice," Aahmes commented.

Namid slipped off into the darkness to change.

When she returned, Mehratar had her lie atop her blankets, on her stomach. He sat tailor-fashion on another blanket next to her. Aahmes settled on her other side, keeping watch.

When Namid looked at him, she saw a strange expression on his face, but then he smiled at her.

Namid took a deep breath, trying for calm. She still jumped when Mehratar placed his hands on the middle of her back.

"Tell me if it gets to be too much," Mehratar said, and began.

At first, it was no worse than the previous times. The familiar pain, the dreaded memories, then something shifted. Other memories of her time in Corentris surfaced, then imaginings and nightmares, things she did not remember happening, did not remember even imagining could happen. She screamed, but no sound came.

She tried to drag herself out of the memories. Something held her there. She called up her Power. Nothing. She reached for Power around her. Nothing. Frantic, she reached for Wild Power. Nothing... something?

The Wild Power raged into her, feeling much like when Sesaisyd's heritance came to her. Then it exploded out from her, to free her from what held her.

Only in the last breath-of-time did she recognize the danger and manage to blunt its effect on her two companions.

She opened her eyes, surprised to find herself soaked with sweat and panting as if she had run a great distance, surprised also at how quiet the night was. Then remembered Aahmes and Mehratar. She sat bolt upright, ignoring the pain that shot across her back.

Both men lay some distance away from her, looking

like they had been flung back. Before she could rise, they both struggled upright.

Namid gave Aahmes a stricken look and turned toward Mehratar. She began to speak but the Healer overrode her.

"I didn't expect anything like that," he said. "Someone set a sort of trap for anyone who tried to Heal you, and we both got caught up in it. I'd nearly worked through it when you broke it." He winced then as he tried to stand. "Although can I say 'ouch'? Good thing you blunted the Power at the end there."

He limped to Namid's side and dropped back to the ground, then seemed to notice the other two staring at him. He grinned at them. "Felt a lot like getting kicked by a horse. An exceptionally large, incredibly angry horse. No… maybe an angry bull."

He stretched with a grimace, then turned his intent gaze on Namid.

"Now turn around and let me see your back," he instructed. "Since we couldn't finish…."

Namid looked back at Aahmes and wriggled around so she faced him, her back to the Healer. Aahmes had that strange look in his eyes as he watched Mehratar gently lift the back of Namid's shirt to examine the scars. The look vanished when he saw Namid looking at him.

"You all right?" he said.

She nodded, then sucked in her breath as Mehratar touched a particularly tender spot. "How bad is it?" she asked the Healer.

"Not as bad as I expected. Nothing is bleeding, although the scars look angrier than they did before. I think you managed to completely break whatever the trap was. I can give you some relief from the pain."

"I wouldn't say no to that."

"And then I *will* need to fall on my face for more than a few candle-marks."

Namid nodded. "I feel the same."

She gave Aahmes a smile while Mehratar eased the

pain. "It does feel better," she murmured. "Much better than it has in a long time. But that was rough. I hope that's the worst of it."

"Me too," Aahmes said and handed her another blanket when the Healer had finished.

~ ~ ~

Namid woke stiff the next morning. When she rolled over, she found Aahmes seated half-dozing a short distance away. He started when she moved and grinned at her questioning look.

"You two were out of it. Just wanted to make sure nothing came sneaking up on us."

Namid nodded and tried to rise, then dropped back down. "Ugh. I have no strength this morning."

"He said that was likely," Aahmes said and nodded toward a point behind her. She glanced back and saw Mehratar sitting as she had seen him before, eyes closed, hands resting on his knees, apparently oblivious to the world.

"At least it's not unexpected," Namid said. "So, let's have a fire—it'll be less visible during the day—and just rest here today."

With only a little help from Namid, Aahmes set up their camp a bit better. When Mehratar joined them, they enjoyed a hot, if bland, breakfast. Mehratar took a last look at Aahmes' wound, now an almost invisible line on his side and pronounced him healed.

They spent the day mostly at leisure, glad for time to make some minor repairs and better sort out a few more items of clothing for Mehratar. And Mehratar Healed Namid again, this time a longer session that left them both weary and napping the afternoon away, but with no memories to fight nor any added pain.

That evening, Namid fiercely kept from thinking about the attacks and what they might be traveling to. But the next morning, the subject of their journey came up as they packed to move on.

"If you don't plan to go to the next village," Mehratar said, "where *are* you two heading? Or are you just fleeing right now?"

Aahmes grunted a non-answer as he mounted his horse and reached down to help Namid up behind him.

She waited to answer until Mehratar mounted the other horse and they headed out.

"Certainly, we're fleeing right now. Staying in one place seems unwise. But we're also traveling to Kilaadi. I... my brother is missing, and that's the last place I saw him."

"You didn't mention him before," Mehratar said.

"No," Namid agreed. "Of my siblings, only he is left alive. Probably, anyway. I hope. The others were all killed by the Dark Priests. I need to find him."

Mehratar gave her a questioning look. Perhaps he could sense that she had left out some important parts of the story. Aahmes twisted around to look at her from the corner of one eye.

"Might as well tell the rest," he said. "Remember how well being secretive turned out last autumn."

Namid sighed.

"Better sooner than later," Aahmes said.

"I suppose." She glanced back at Mehratar. "My parents are Levil Eisunal Shartov and Yokana Zianya Shartov, Monarch and Lady Royal of the Six Realms." She frowned. "And if I can't find my older brother, I'm afraid they—and everyone else in Kilaadi—will try to stuff me into the position of heir."

Silence met her statement. She twisted around to look back at Mehratar.

"Oh," he said.

Aahmes chuckled. "Not quite what you expected?"

"Well, no," Mehratar admitted. "Although I'm not sure what I expected. And what of you, Aahmes?"

"Oh, he's the exiled not-heir to the High Chieftainship

of the northern clans," Namid said with a grin.

"Ah. Well…. Not-heir?"

"No living clansmates, so no clan, so no claim," Aahmes said shortly.

"So, you both aren't of the same clan?"

Namid shook her head. "As far back as I know my ancestors—and it's way too far—there are no clansfolk at all."

"And you can still wield the Wild Power," Mehratar said. "That *was* what you used to break that trap earlier, right?"

Namid nodded.

"It's unlikely that anyone else can still even sense the Wild Power, not since last autumn," Mehratar muttered. Then he spoke louder. "I can see why you said being with you two might not be my best choice."

"You don't have to stay with us," Aahmes said, sounding cheerful at the prospect. "We can give you some provisions, too, if you want to go your own way."

Namid glanced at Mehratar to see his reaction. He looked thoughtful, then gave her a brilliant smile.

"I'll see if the next village needs a Healer," he said. "But if not, I'll travel with you yet a while."

~ ~ ~

They came within sight of the next village soon after midday. Mehratar walked into town while Aahmes and Namid waited hidden in the forest. They both still tired easily, so they took the opportunity to rest while they waited. They stretched out on the ground and gazed at the sky through the trees. Namid noticed Aahmes studying one clump of trees, but then he settled back on the ground.

"What is it?" she asked.

"Hmm? What?"

She tilted her head in the direction he had been

looking. "What's that about?"

"Oh. I just have a feeling of being watched. It started last night, but I've not seen anyone. Nor sensed them."

Namid sent out a tendril of Power.

"I don't sense anyone…." Still, now that Aahmes had mentioned it, she too felt like she was the object of someone's attention.

"Hope it's not the 'gods' again," she murmured.

"We'd recognize two of them, anyway," Aahmes said.

"True. And shouldn't have any trouble sensing the others, I'd think." Namid contemplated the sky then.

"Aren't you worried that Kilaadi will be destroyed, as that village was, if we go there?" Aahmes said.

"Yes. But I have to wonder. Nothing happened to the village until after that man saw us, and seemingly identified us, at least in a general sense. The attack on Jelth's temple complex might have been exactly what you said – taking out the Healers. But then that man saw us… maybe Jelth found out we were there through him."

"But the attack came from Belaraketh's temple complex. At least, we think it did," Aahmes said.

"We know he's after us. But we don't actually know who destroyed Jelth's temple. Think about it." Namid sat up to look at Aahmes as she tried to explain her thoughts.

"Before last autumn, there were a certain number of 'gods' and they seemed basically at peace with each other. Or at least not actively attacking each other. Sesaisyd was no threat and the others went about doing whatever they were doing. But then Sesaisyd died, and we both got a share of his Power. Added to our own, I suspect that makes us among the most Powerful non-gods around. So now we are two Powers, where there was previously just the one."

"Sesaisyd," Aahmes said.

"Yes. And on top of that, we work together. We're not out to kill each other – not counting that one time, anyway…."

Aahmes winced at the reminder.

Namid continued, "We're not out to steal each other's Power, or any of those things. They, the 'gods', might now believe that the sort of peaceful balance they had achieved is broken. And they're again scrambling for Power, maybe over each other, and maybe fearing that we're going to join in the fight."

"Or maybe fearing that we're going to reveal what we know," Aahmes said. "About them not being gods at all. Can you picture the mess, the chaos that would cause? And everywhere in the Six Realms."

Namid nodded. "I suspect that they can't grasp that we're not interested in playing their Power game at all. In scrambling for more." She gave him a sidelong look. "You're *not* interested in that, are you? In becoming a self-declared god?"

Aahmes chuckled and shook his head. "Not at all. Too much work. Too much trouble. My interests lie elsewhere." He glanced around, then gave her a long look. A slight smile touched his lips.

Namid gave him another sidelong look. "Oh, really?"

"Mhm—"

At that moment, something came crashing through the underbrush toward them. They both jumped up, daggers ready. And Mehratar almost rode them over, atop what looked like a workhorse rather than a riding horse. He led a packhorse, too. He pulled up his mount before it plowed into them.

"Not the best option, nor my preference," he said as he slid off his horse. "But at least we won't have to double up. And we can switch the packs to the packhorse."

"So, you still plan to continue on with us," Aahmes said.

Mehratar nodded. "This village has an… adequate Healer and a barely adequate apprentice. They'll take over my circuit of villages. Namid still needs Healing, so I'll see her as Healed as I can manage. That will serve you both best in whatever you're getting yourselves into."

He smiled at the expressions on their faces. "I might not know all of what's going on, but I certainly get a feel for the danger and potential for violence." He started transferring their things to the packhorse.

"Everything I had is gone," he said over his shoulder. "I'll travel with you to Kilaadi. See what might be there for me after Namid's Healed."

~ ~ ~

They traveled slowly, heading east and picking their way through increasingly dense trees. The pace allowed Aahmes to finish recovering and kept from taxing Mehratar and Namid as they continued to work at Healing Namid's scars.

From time to time, Namid still felt like someone watched them, but never spotted anyone or sensed anything through the Power. She saw Aahmes keeping an eye on their surroundings, too, but when she caught his attention, he always just shook his head.

Three days out from the village where Mehratar had gotten the horses a sudden afternoon rainstorm drenched them. They scrambled through the dripping forest looking for shelter from the chilly rain. It had changed to a drizzle when a voice came to them from somewhere in the trees. "Well, that is one creature that's certainly not unheard."

"I know that voice," Aahmes said peering through the dripping trees.

Namid looked around, surprised. "Inezha? How…."

The dark-skinned, dark-haired Prazny stepped out from the trees with a delighted laugh and waved a hand at Mehratar's horse. Her own horse followed her, almost as silent as she. Inezha wore trousers and a simple tunic of a mottled brown, rather than the colorful Prazny clothes she had worn when they first met. Her tooled leather boots were a darker brown.

"I'm happy to greet you two again. I've found a drier spot if you wish to join me," Inezha said with a smile for Namid and a wider one for Aahmes. She gave him a good long look, from head to toes, Namid noticed. Aahmes returned her perusal with a languid smirk.

Inezha then nodded to Mehratar. "I give you greetings, too. I'm Inezha, formerly of Staehw's van, now traveling on my own. I'm known to Namid and Aahmes from some excitement we shared many weeks past."

Mehratar introduced himself, then looked to Aahmes and Namid.

"Or you can just stay here dripping," Inezha said with a laugh as they hesitated to take her up on her offer.

With a shrug for Namid, Aahmes turned back to Inezha. "Lead on."

"You're traveling without a van, now?" Namid said as they followed the Prazny through the trees.

Inezha nodded. "With the demise of the Dark Priests, leaving their promises to the Praznies unfulfilled, the van splintered. Not that I would've followed Staehw again."

"Promises?" Aahmes said. "What promises?" His tone held a hint of suspicion.

Inezha gave Aahmes a woeful look over her shoulder. "For a time now, the Praznies have been less than what we once were. Sesaisyd's people promised a return to greatness. If the Praznies followed them."

"Ah."

"But they could not honor their side of the bargain and now the Praznies are even more scattered. It's a sad time for my people." She looked at the ground and scuffed one booted foot in the mud, then glanced up at them. "But it's good fortune to meet friends on the road. Perhaps we can feast this evening, diminished as it will necessarily be from times before, and exchange tales."

"I don't know that it'll be worthy of being called a feast," Namid said. "But certainly a dry spot to spend the night will be welcome." Some skeptical part of her wondered at this chance encounter with Inezha. It seemed rather unlikely.

"I'll add what I can to help with the evening meal." Inezha said. "Just through here."

She led them to a wide, shallow cave beneath an overhang on the bank of a small stream. The cave was large enough for all of them to fit in its shelter, and dense trees nearby would provide some shelter for the horses. They set up camp there. Inezha shared her provisions, dried fruits and some of the sticky pastry Praznies loved, which helped make the evening meal more like a feast than it would have been otherwise.

Afterward, they sat close to the small fire, relishing its warmth, and shared tales. Aahmes and Namid told an abbreviated version of what had happened after they last saw Inezha, leaving out their heritage and the truth about the 'gods', but including their parentage. Inezha seemed little surprised to hear about their respective families.

Inezha, in turn, regaled them all with fantastic tales of traveling about during the winter and managed to avoid telling them anything of import about the Praznies. Mehratar shared a couple of tales of silly mishaps from his days learning to Heal.

"And how do you come to be traveling in this region?" Aahmes asked Inezha, when the tale-telling had petered out.

She leaned close to him with a bright smile and said in an exaggerated whisper, "The trees. Staehw had always favored traveling the southern roads, the plains. And I wanted to see forests."

"Good place for it," Aahmes said. "Now that you've gotten to see the forests, where next?"

"And what about the other Praznies?" Namid added. "Are all of you now wandering on your own?"

Inezha shrugged. "Some are. Some still try to hold their vans together. At this latest betrayal, every Prazny I've encountered seems lost. But at least I haven't seen Staehw again."

"As for where next...." She looked at Aahmes and laid a hand on his arm. "Now that I've had the fortune to meet up with you again, I'm of a mind to journey with you, my friends."

CHAPTER 12

In the morning, Namid snatched a moment to speak with Aahmes as they cleaned the dishes in the stream.

"So, Inezha…" she said, keeping her voice barely louder than the stream's burbling.

"Yes," he murmured back. "Think she's the one who's been watching us?"

Namid splashed some frigid water into a pan. "Wouldn't surprise me. Unlikely coincidence meeting her out here."

"Yeah. And yet, Praznies *do* wander. A lot. So, it's not completely unreasonable. But, could she be allied with one of the 'gods'? Keeping track of us, maybe?"

Namid glanced over a shoulder at Inezha and waved back when the Prazny smiled and waved at her. "I don't see that. But, still, this chance meeting makes me wonder."

Aahmes nodded. "Back to suspicions, again."

"Yeah, but suspicions of what?"

A final rinse of the dishes and they rejoined the others to finish packing to head out.

~ ~ ~

As the four traveled slowly toward Kilaadi, Mehratar continued the Healing sessions with Namid most evenings when they stopped to camp. Inezha asked about them at first, but soon lost interest and just sat talking with Aahmes during them.

After another five days, Mehratar announced that he could do no more. Namid's skin still showed the marks from the whip, but they were fainter and not nearly as raised as they had been. They no longer caused her any discomfort.

As the small group traveled, they stayed near roads, to help guide them. Periodically Mehratar or Inezha ventured into villages to supplement their provisions. Mehratar also bought a well-made cloak for himself, along with a couple of shirts of better quality than those he had been forced to borrow from Aahmes.

They moved further from lingering end-of-winter into the warmth that marked spring. The pine forests began to give way to trees just sprouting their new leaves, interspersed with large grassy areas, which forced them to ride further from the road to keep from being seen.

Mostly the weather had been kind to them, with minimal snow and less rain. As the days passed and the land began to look more like that near Kilaadi, Namid became increasingly twitchy. She slept poorly and fought to keep her thoughts from drifting to what-ifs. She began to practice with the Power again, each night after they had eaten. Aahmes usually worked with her, while Mehratar and Inezha stayed out of the way and watched. Sometimes it seemed Inezha watched with particular interest, her gaze focused on Aahmes. And Mehratar Healed the occasional injury when Aahmes and Namid got too ambitious or careless. Namid's Power still often felt slippery, but she seemed better able to work with it.

After a point, the underbrush beneath the trees became too thick to be worth fighting through, and they returned to the road at the next one they encountered that ran south. Although she had not traveled this particular portion of the road, Namid felt certain it was the one that led to the northern gate of Kilaadi. And she thought that another couple of days or so would see them at the capital.

"Nervous?" Aahmes said, the corners of his gray-brown eyes crinkled in amusement like he already knew the answer. He somehow managed to guide his horse around a large washed-out area of the road while looking over his shoulder at her.

"Is it showing that badly?" she responded as she guided her horse around the same area.

"Honestly.... Yes."

"Aren't you? After all, you're soon to meet the Monarch—"

"After returning with his only remaining daughter who's been missing for years. The daughter who's just possibly the heir to the throne?" Aahmes broke in.

"Well... yes. And I wish you wouldn't bring up the heir part."

He chuckled and brushed back his hair with one hand.

"Namid, it'll be all right," he said, as he guided his horse around yet another wash-out.

"You've been missing for years?" Mehratar said to Namid and urged his horse closer.

"Well, sort of..." Namid said. She brought her horse even with Aahmes'.

Aahmes snorted at her understatement and she glared at him.

"I was about thirteen when I last saw my parents."

Inezha whistled softly.

Aahmes nodded. "Yeah. I just know this is going to be so pleasant...."

Namid leaned over and punched him in the arm. "You're no help."

He just grinned at her.

Namid's thoughts turned to their companions from the

previous autumn and she wondered where they were now and what they were doing.

"What do you suppose the others are up to?" Aahmes said, somehow voicing her thoughts.

Namid shrugged. "I'd guess Enric and Cameni are working to convince their families that they should be wed soon. And Haeith's probably still guarding Cameni."

Aahmes nodded and chuckled.

"Odasoro had said he planned to travel to Kilaadi in the spring," Namid continued. "If so, we'll probably see him."

"These are the others who helped you overthrow Sesaisyd last autumn?" Mehratar said.

"Ah, well, 'overthrow' is one way to put it," Namid said.

Then she and Aahmes told tales of Enric's quest and what really happened, giving more details than they had before. It passed the time as they traveled.

Later they fell silent again and returned to riding one behind the other, Aahmes in the lead.

Namid brushed a strand of her hair out of her eyes and tried to tuck it back into her braid. But when she let go of it, the wind caught it again and whipped it right back into her face. She sighed and tried to ignore it.

Namid studied Aahmes' back as she followed him. He rode muffled in a heavy midnight blue cloak, over sturdy dusty-blue clothes—trousers, shirt and layered tunics—that he had found in Chendrukhar's things. She wore similar attire, from the same source, although in shades of dusty green. The hood on his cloak had fallen back in the wind, as had hers.

Just a couple of seasons ago, she would never have imagined that she would work with him, that they would be friendly. Or more than friendly. Perhaps.

And now they traveled together to her father's citadel to learn what aftermath might lurk there from the Dark Priests' demise. And she hoped to learn more about her brothers' visit to Navele, something to lead her to Tal.

So many years had passed since Namid had last called Kilaadi home. So much had changed in that time. For one thing, she had grown from a sheltered child, youngest of the Monarch's children, into an accomplished thief and mage. She suspected that she might no longer know how to fit into life at court. She doubted that she wanted to.

But she worried what condition her parents would be in after having been under the Dark Priests' control for these many years.

Namid realized that she had let her mind wander when her horse meandered to a stop in the road.

"Namid?" Aahmes said, giving her a concerned look.

"What? Oh, sorry… lost in thought."

Aahmes smiled. "I said, do we want to risk stopping in that town ahead, so we can be well rested for the end of this journey? Maybe clean up, too? Or we don't have to, if it's not worth the risk…."

Namid glanced at the westering sun, then looked at Mehratar and Inezha.

"What is this risk?" Inezha said.

Namid exchanged a look with Aahmes. How to tell her without revealing the truth about the 'gods'? Namid settled on a part of the truth.

"We think there might still be some Dark Priests out there," she said. "They'd probably love to get their hands on us and wouldn't have a care for anyone who got between them and us."

Inezha frowned at the mention of Dark Priests.

Namid gave that some thought, then turned to Aahmes. "Can you do that minimal glamour again? Like the one you put on all of us when we rescued Inezha from Staehw?"

Aahmes nodded.

Mehratar looked from one of them to the other. "Minimal glamour? What's this?"

"A very light veneer of Power that makes us look

unlike ourselves. You'll both still see us as you know us, but to others we'll look different enough that, hopefully, they won't pick us out like the man from Jelth's temple did."

"Interesting. I'd say do it."

Inezha agreed, so Aahmes stopped his horse to concentrate.

"It's done. And it'll hold for a while before needing to be renewed."

He grinned suddenly. *~I like having this much Power to work with,~* he said to Namid using thought-speech.

Namid grinned back at him.

~ ~ ~

"So, once we get to the Monarch's citadel, must we start addressing you as 'Your Highness' and 'Princess Tanyala'?" Aahmes asked Namid with a wicked grin, shortly before they reached the town gate.

Namid shrugged. "I hadn't thought about that. You know I'd rather avoid all that. And anyway, it's been so long since I used my first name, I'm not sure I'll recognize that people are talking to me when they say 'Tanyala'. They'll probably think I'm ignoring them."

"Probably. Are you up to this? I imagine being at court will be very different from Rhadanthus."

"I need to find out if my brother ever returned home," Namid said. "And I should see my parents."

"Certainly."

They passed through the gate and Mehratar pointed to an inn further down the street. "That one looks suitable."

"Sure," Namid said.

After they saw the horses well cared for and secured rooms for the night, they settled at a table in one corner of the inn's common room to enjoy a hot meal. Namid watched the other patrons while they ate. Most of them seemed to be locals, or at least well known to the innkeeper, who greeted many of them by name. By their attire, most seemed to be doing well enough at their livelihoods. And for the most part they acted cheerful.

Quite a change from just the past autumn when the Dark Priests held sway over much of the realm of Paronia. She mentioned this to the others as they relaxed after the meal with a bottle of wine.

"Just remember, their influence might still be affecting people, " Aahmes pointed out. "Even under this cheerful exterior. After all, we don't know how many of the Dark Priests weren't in Corentris when it fell."

Namid nodded. "True. And I do worry about running into some again, in whatever capacity they're now working their evil."

"That's not the only concern, you know…" Mehratar said, focusing on Namid.

"You mean the gods who aren't?" Inezha said in a quiet voice.

The others gave her blank looks and she laughed. "Yes, I've heard about them."

Mehratar leaned forward and spoke in a quiet voice. "So, then, what about what we all know regarding those who have called themselves gods these several millennia?" He looked at the table and absently traced a mark in the wood with a finger. "Is that knowledge we should keep to ourselves… that they are very Powerful, but aren't gods?"

"Namid and I have struggled with that question," Aahmes said.

"I do wonder if I should've at least told our companions last autumn," Namid said.

"Perhaps," Aahmes said.

"It would be a difficult thing to tell people the gods they've believed in all their lives aren't really gods at all," Inezha said.

Aahmes looked up at Namid through a few strands of hair that had fallen across his face. "I think we both took the news fairly well."

Namid thought back to how the information had come to her from Sesaisyd, and she had passed it on to Aahmes. At the time, they had been quite occupied trying to stay alive and out from under the control of two rival factions of Dark Priests.

"We had more immediate concerns on our minds at that moment," she said. "And when I, at least, had the time and inclination to even think about it, several weeks had passed. By then, it didn't seem nearly as shocking as it might have."

Aahmes nodded.

"So, we keep that information quiet," Mehratar said. "I can see both sides of the question, but I think we shouldn't be the ones to spread the word. At least right now." He gave Aahmes and Namid a slight smile. "No need to give them more reasons to hunt you two."

Inezha looked from Namid to Aahmes. "Give who more reasons to hunt you? Those who claim to be gods?"

Aahmes brushed his hair back with one hand. "Yeah. So, maybe you'd want to find other friends to travel with…."

Inezha gave him a bright smile. "Oh, no. You are by far the most interesting." She shared her smile with Mehratar and Namid.

Mehratar gulped the rest of his wine and rose. "I must find some better clothes for our time in the capital. Anyone else care to join me?"

Inezha jumped up. "I will. I'd like to explore the town, anyway."

Aahmes and Namid watched them leave, then finished the last of the wine, split between their two glasses, before they headed to their rooms to sleep.

~ ~ ~

The group started out later the next morning than they had planned, after sleeping until well past dawn, then taking the time to leisurely enjoy the excellent breakfast served them. So, midmorning found them finally riding out of town. Mehratar had found some new clothes the previous night and wore them that morning with a pleased expression. Looking at him, Namid wondered whether she should have gotten something, too.

Oh well, time enough in Kilaadi….

"What would you think of stopping in an inn in Kilaadi and spending some time seeing how things are in the capital?" Namid said, voicing the thought that had come to her.

Aahmes gave her a sidelong look. "More second thoughts about going home?"

"Well, partly," she admitted. "But it also occurred to me that it might be good to see if we can discover how things are before just walking right in."

"Seems reasonable," Mehratar said. "I plan to explore the city, when we get there. If I can be of help in discovering things, let me know."

"And me, as well," Inezha said.

Namid nodded.

Their ride to Kilaadi took the rest of the day. The road was well traveled, but they drew no unusual regard. At the city gate, two guards watched the influx of people, but made no move to detain anyone.

"No Dark Priests, so far," Aahmes said in a quiet voice after they had passed through the gate.

Namid nodded. "Promising," she said.

She led them to a modest, well-kept inn not too far from the gate.

"Let's stay here for now," she said.

They arranged for rooms and stabling for the horses, then met in the common room for a late evening meal. A minstrel played soft music from his place near the room's large fireplace, a cap by his knee to collect any coins that patrons might care to give him

"Do you have a plan?" Mehratar said as they finished

their meal. "How can I help?"

"We," Inezha said, with a smile for Mehratar.

Aahmes gave the Healer a sharp look. "What kind of help were you thinking of?"

Mehratar shrugged. "People chat with Healers. Along with details of their ailments, I might hear something useful. But what would be useful?"

"Certainly any mention of the Dark Priests," Namid said. "And any talk about the court, any gossip about the Monarch and Lady Royal, or anything related."

"Any mention of people out to destroy the gods, or anyone the gods say must be destroyed," Aahmes added.

Namid nodded. "Also, perhaps any talk of Powerful twins or brother and sister, and anything about the 'heroes' who killed Sesaisyd this past autumn."

"Is that all?" Inezha said with a grin.

"I think it's enough," Namid said with a matching grin.

Mehratar nodded. "Tomorrow I'll seek out Jelth's temple here and see what might be discovered."

"Is that wise?" Namid said.

Mehratar shrugged. "No one alive has seen me with the real you, the non-glamoured two of you. There's nothing to connect us."

"And I shall explore the city, see what people are speaking of," Inezha declared.

"And we'll go elsewhere in the city. See if we hear anything," Namid said, gesturing to herself and Aahmes. "Let's all plan to meet back here in the evening."

"Our glamour should last at least another couple of days," Aahmes said. "But I'll check it tomorrow night when we all return here and make any adjustments, if needed."

After they finished their meal and a couple of glasses of wine, they all headed to their rooms, intending to make an early start in the morning. As she headed to the stairs, Namid happened to meet the minstrel's gaze. He smiled at her and gave her a seated bow.

For a breath-of-time, she wondered if he knew her. She did not recognize him. Could he have seen through the glamour somehow? She dismissed those concerns when she saw him next smile at another patron. He must just be trying to ensure he got some coins for the evening's entertainment. She made sure to drop a navn into his cap as she passed.

CHAPTER 13

Aahmes and Namid trudged back to the inn near dusk, tired and unenlightened. They plopped down at the table where Mehratar already sat and ordered drinks first, then their meals. Inezha arrived just as the meals did and asked the server to bring her the same thing.

"Seems almost as if the Dark Priests were never here," Namid muttered.

Aahmes nodded. Mehratar glanced at them both but stayed silent and nursed a drink of his own.

"Might that not be a good thing?" Inezha said. "Everyone able to return to their lives? I know I'd want that."

"Possibly. But it makes my skin crawl," Namid said. "It's too 'normal'. And yeah, I know it's been more than a season since Corentris, but did you notice how no one seemed to want to gossip about the 'heroes'? They just kind of slide away from the subject."

"No gossiping about anything happening at court, either," Aahmes said.

"I heard one thing about court," Mehratar said. "Only in passing, but several people at Jelth's temple mentioned that the heir is expected to return soon."

Namid groaned, then waited while the server placed Inezha's meal on the table.

"Somehow they know I'm around?" Namid said in a quiet voice.

"Not necessarily," Mehratar said. "It was just along the line of 'I hear they're readying for the heir to return' but no details about who that is or when."

Namid shook her head. "Something here is off."

The others did not disagree, and they finished their meal in silence.

Then Inezha pulled something out of a pouch, a folded piece of parchment. "I discovered this while I was out and about," she said. She handed it to Aahmes, who unfolded it and spread it out on the table.

Two faces had been drawn on the parchment, clearly Namid and Aahmes. Beneath the drawing was a terse, but accurate description of them. Aahmes refolded it after they had all seen it.

"Good thing for the glamour," Mehratar said in a quiet voice.

The others nodded. Namid felt a brief touch of Aahmes' Power.

"And it's holding just fine," he said. He looked around to see if anyone paid them particular attention, then froze. "The troubadour."

Namid looked up and spotted Odasoro making his way between the tables, headed roughly their direction. His lute case hung from its strap from one shoulder. When Inezha turned to look, he smiled and raised a hand to her. He did not seem surprised to see her.

"Inezha!"

The Prazny gave Aahmes and Namid a quick look then turned back to the troubadour with a smile of her own.

"Odasoro! It's glad I am to greet you again, but also surprised. I'd not looked to see you here."

Odasoro clasped her hand in greeting and glanced at the others at the table, his gaze passing over Aahmes and

Namid without recognition. While he looked much the same as when Namid last saw him, his dark hair and beard held more white streaks than she remembered. And he had a tension about him, a wariness, that she had not seen in him before.

"Might your companions excuse you for just a few breaths-of-time?" Odasoro said to Inezha, with another glance at the others at the table.

Mehratar rose immediately and gave the troubadour a slight bow. "Certainly. Old friends who haven't seen each other in a while must have much to catch up on," he said, then headed toward the stairs to the second floor.

Odasoro looked at Aahmes and Namid, who had not moved.

"We can speak in front of them," Inezha said. She managed to keep her expression bland, but the corners of her eyes crinkled with amusement.

"Perhaps if there's a private dining room we might borrow," Namid said in a quiet voice, then smiled at Odasoro's look of astonishment.

"Namid?" he whispered, leaning close.

At her nod, he straightened again. "There's a small room the innkeeper sometimes lets people use," he said. "I'll meet you there." He nodded toward a door under the staircase, then headed over to speak with the innkeeper.

Namid, Aahmes and Inezha gathered up their cups and the jug of wine, then made their way through the tables to the door Odasoro had indicated. As Aahmes opened the door, Namid glanced at the innkeeper and acknowledged his nod. Odasoro joined them as they filed into the small room. He carried a cup of his own and a lit candle.

A single table sat in the room's center, with five chairs around it. Odasoro placed the candle in the center of the table, then reached for the jug that Inezha had carried. Inezha and Aahmes took seats at the table as Odasoro turned back to Namid, who leaned against the closed door.

~*Please drop the glamour,*~ she told Aahmes using

thought-speech.

She could tell from Odasoro's expression when he could see her own features. He caught her in a quick embrace.

"You certainly took your time," he said, then turned toward the table.

Namid had to grin at the expression on the troubadour's face when he caught sight of Aahmes. And she quickly reached out to rescue Odasoro's lute when it slipped unheeded from his shoulder. A glance back at Aahmes showed him brushing his hair back with one hand and giving the troubadour a rakish grin.

"What? How…?" Odasoro stammered.

"Aha," Aahmes said. "I finally caught you wordless."

Odasoro laughed and seemed to recover himself somewhat. "But how…."

Aahmes poured himself more wine and gestured to the other chairs. Namid placed the lute on the table as she and Odasoro joined the other two. Aahmes placed the glamour again on himself and Namid.

"Well, in short, Das, Aahmes escaped Corentris much like we did. He found me again in Rhadanthus, where we both wintered," Namid said. "We're here now with a Healer we met on the way, Mehratar. You sort of met him." She waved a hand at the outer room. "And we met Inezha on the way, too."

Odasoro nodded. "Along the same line, I returned here before the snows in the plains got too heavy. Cameni, Enric and Haeith thought they might travel this direction once the weather improved, but I don't know if they were thinking of visiting the city."

"You didn't seem surprised to see Inezha," Namid said.

Odasoro smiled. "I've had some people watching for you, Namid, and letting me know about any strangers who have come to Kilaadi. When my man in the inn here described Inezha, I recognized her. So I came to see her and see if she might have any word of you."

"You've had people watching?" Namid said.

Odasoro smiled and nodded. "Troubadours and minstrels are in a unique position to observe many things," he said. "With things the way they are here, I've expanded my connections in the city."

Namid exchanged a look with Aahmes.

"So you've just become some sort of spymaster?" Aahmes said.

Odasoro gave him an enigmatic smile. "I don't know that I'd say 'spymaster'. Nor would I say 'just become'." He drained his mug and looked at the others.

"I certainly had not expected that I'd find you here, Namid. And my time is short this evening. I must return to the citadel soon. But you should know that the situation in the citadel is… strange. Your father has a new advisor, has had for about a season, now. But the Monarch's acting different. And your mother is guarded. I've been watching out for her…."

He stood. "Perhaps I can return tomorrow, with more time to talk…."

"Wait!" Namid clutched his arm then looked at Aahmes. "The book."

With a nod, Aahmes hurried out the door, closing it again behind him.

"Book?" Odasoro said.

"We found a book in Rhadanthus," Namid said. "Written in no language I recognize. It was with some of Wesh's things."

Inezha made a small sound of surprise, but when Namid looked at her, she waved it off and poured herself more wine.

"I'm hoping you might be able to decipher it," Namid said to Odasoro.

Odasoro gave her a quick nod. "I'll do what I can. But I really must go." He reached for his lute case as Aahmes opened the door again and slipped inside. Aahmes pulled the book from his tunic and handed it to Odasoro, who took a quick look at it, but did not open it.

"You should probably keep it hidden," Aahmes said.

With a nod, Odasoro retrieved his lute case and tucked the book into it next to his lute.

"I'll try to see you again tomorrow," he said and then was gone.

The three stared at the closed door, then Namid grabbed Odasoro's empty cup to take it back into the common room, along with her own.

"I guess same thing tomorrow, then, for us – see what we can learn, maybe different places. Good night." And she left Aahmes and Inezha staring after her.

With Odasoro's enigmatic information whirling in her thoughts, sleep was a long time coming to her.

~ ~ ~

The next morning, Namid woke shortly after dawn, still feeling tired. She dug through her pack and found some relatively clean clothes, though very plain and a little ragged.

Have to do something about that soon, she thought.

She had just begun to comb out her hair when she caught a whiff of Power. She dropped the comb and threw a defensive shell around herself. She grabbed a dagger, too, just in case.

A small whirlwind of black sparkles appeared right in front of her. She backed up to her door, a matter of only a single step, and reached back to unlock it.

The whirlwind spun in the center of her room and slowly grew smaller and lighter in color, then coalesced into what looked like a letter. It dropped to the floor. And Namid jumped as someone pounded on her door.

"Namid?"

She opened the door, keeping her distance from the letter on the floor. "I'm all right," she reassured Aahmes. She spotted Mehratar just behind him in the hall. "Come

147

in and see."

She closed the door behind the two men after they crowded in with her and they all stared at the letter. Namid brushed it with Power and felt nothing unusual about it, in spite of its dramatic arrival. She eased her defenses and sheathed her dagger.

Namid picked up the letter and turned it over but saw no markings on the outside. It was folded in thirds and sealed with wax that bore an imprint she knew, not the seal of the Monarch, but rather her family's personal seal. Namid turned it over again but found no clues about it on the outside.

"Are you going to open it or just continue to admire the paper?" Aahmes said.

Namid glared at him but did open the letter. It contained only one line, in handwriting she did not recognize.

Your presence is required at the citadel immediately, it stated. There was no signature.

Namid passed it to Aahmes and watched his face as he read it. When he finished, he gave her a perplexed look, and passed it to Mehratar.

"Seems we are found out," the Healer said.

"Me, anyway," Namid said.

"Any idea who wrote this?" Aahmes said.

Namid shook her head. "No. The seal is my family's, but I don't recognize the handwriting. And I don't see how anyone could have found me out."

"Well someone has. Maybe the Power?" Aahmes said.

Namid shook her head again and gathered her messy hair in one hand after it flopped in her face. "I was the only one at court with Power. Well, except for the Dark Priests who were there when I left."

"I don't like this. We're pretty certain some Priests survived their god's demise. They could still be lurking in the citadel," Aahmes said.

He and Namid locked gazes, not sharing thoughts but

simply reading what they saw in the other's expression. Then Namid shrugged. "I suppose I'd better just go find out," she said.

"*We'll* go," Aahmes said. "You might need someone watching your back."

Namid studied his expression, then nodded.

She turned to Mehratar. "Aahmes and I will go there soon. If it's any of the people we suspect, they already know about us both. Will you stay here, outside the court?"

"Give you someone on the outside?" Mehratar said with a nod.

Namid nodded too.

"Where's Inezha?" she said as she just then noticed the Prazny's absence.

"She went out early," Aahmes said. "Said she wanted to get through as much of the city today as she could manage." He shrugged.

"If I see her before you return, I'll let her know what's going on," Mehratar said and left them to any preparations they might need to make.

Namid retrieved her comb and resumed pulling it through the tangles. Aahmes leaned against the wall next to the door and watched her, then grinned.

"What?" she demanded.

"I knew things had been too quiet…. We'd been due for something to stir things up."

Namid groaned dramatically. "Don't say such things. You know what that'll mean…."

He nodded. "Be honest, Namid. You'd gotten bored this past season with the rebuilding, with long, idyllic days of little to do while it snowed."

Namid frowned at him. "I don't know that I'd call it idyllic… flinging Power around every day, with heavy snowstorms every week or so. Attacked by 'gods'. And then the muddy and washed-out roads we've traveled. And I'll never admit to anything anyway, you know."

"Don't I know it."

He headed out the door. "I'll meet you downstairs. Going to grab a couple things then see about getting something to eat."

Namid finished getting ready. She braided her hair and gathered and stashed her small arsenal about her person. She hesitated to bring Tal's ring and brooch and the letter, but decided they were better with her than left in her room. She also buckled on the belt that held her sheathed sword—probably time to get it back to the family armory—then grabbed her cloak and ran downstairs.

From the bottom of the stairs, she spotted Aahmes at the inn's front door, flanked by two men in the uniforms of citadel guards. The guards straightened when Namid appeared then bowed to her.

"We're here ensure you arrive safely at the citadel," one of them said.

"Apparently we have escorts," Aahmes said with a grimace and shrugged on his cloak. He handed her a slice of warm bread. "And not even time for a real breakfast."

~The glamour's gone,~ he told her using thought-speech. *~These two knew me when I entered the room.~*

She almost choked on her mouthful of bread but waved away the guard who would have helped her. *~What? How?~*

Aahmes shook his head and looked around as they all stepped into the street, although Namid could tell he was not actually seeing the street and buildings around them. She felt a brush of his Power. Their guards took up positions with one in front of them to lead the way, and one behind.

To keep them from running, Namid thought nastily.

~There's a very subtle Power lurking,~ Aahmes told her using thought-speech. *~It wasn't here when we arrived. It's got a hint of that nasty Dark Priest tang to it. It must have taken down the glamour.~*

Namid sent her own Power out, just a small amount,

and hoped it would be unnoticed. She agreed with Aahmes' assessment.

She leaned close to him. "This isn't likely to be an enjoyable meeting," she said in a quiet voice.

He nodded. "But maybe we'll start getting some answers."

"I hope."

Namid looked around. They were not alone on the street, but no one paid them any particular attention. She happened to catch one man's eye and he just gave her a slight nod of greeting and continued on his way.

"I have to assume if our friend found that one drawing of us, there are more out there," Namid said, still in a quiet voice.

"But no one seems inclined to run screaming from us," Aahmes said.

"Yeah…."

With simultaneous shrugs, they continued to the Monarch's citadel. At the entrance to the citadel grounds—an ornate silvery metal gate set into tall, stone walls—their guards nodded to the two who stood there and escorted them inside. When the gate clanged shut behind them, they found themselves in one of the citadel's several gardens, plainer and less well tended than Namid remembered.

Four more guards joined them, two men and two women. Namid noticed one of the female guards in particular. The woman's hair was the most unique shade of red-orange, curly, and worn secured at the back of her head. The guard with the captain's insignia stepped forward and bowed to Namid.

"My apologies, Your Highness," he said. "We must hold your weapons for now."

Namid and Aahmes exchanged a look.

~*We still have the Power,*~ Aahmes commented.

Namid shrugged and divested herself of all carefully placed blades. She grinned at the guards' expressions as she and Aahmes loaded them down with a small arsenal of blades, as well as her two blade-concealing armguards. Last, she unbuckled the belt that held her sword.

"Take careful note of this blade," she told the guards. "The family will not be pleased if any mischance comes to it." With a few tugs, she pulled away the rough leather that wrapped the ornate, golden hilt to reveal the crest there. The guards' eyes widened. They all bowed.

"Of course, Your Highness," said the one who held the sword.

Aahmes leaned over and whispered in Namid's ear. "Yes, Your Highness. Of course, Your Highness."

Namid almost managed to stifle her laughter.

The guards holding all the weaponry stepped aside, and two of the others, one of them the captain, formed up in front of Namid and Aahmes.

"This way, Your Highness," said the captain and led them toward the citadel.

~ ~ ~

Uneasiness dogged Namid as she and Aahmes followed the guards into the citadel proper. She knew none of the people they passed, not a servant, retainer, or noble. Of the few who met her gaze, some gave her indifferent looks, but most seemed outright hostile. She felt twitchy with her back exposed to them after they passed. Aahmes gave her a concerned look.

This is very wrong, she told him by hand-talk.

Specifics? he asked the same way.

Namid switched to thought-speech and described her observations for him. When she finished, he gave her a grim look and dropped back to walk behind her.

~*What are you doing?*~ Namid demanded.

~*Trust me. I have some experience with back-stabbing sorts.*~

~*Well, yeah. You think there's really something to my concerns,*

152

then?~

~Since Sesaisyd's Power descended on us, I've been more sensitive to the nuances around…. Haven't you, too?~

~Maybe… I think….~ Namid shrugged.

~The Dark Priests were in control here for a long time. We don't yet know what they've wrought,~ Aahmes continued.

~I don't want you falling to an attack.~

His chuckle rang in her thoughts and helped lighten her mood. *~I have a few tricks.~*

In the time it took them to exchange those few unspoken comments, the guards brought them to the double doors that led to the great hall where the Monarch usually held court. The captain asked them to wait and slipped through the left door without opening it far enough for them to see inside. Their other guard took up a position next to the door, next to the guard already standing there.

Namid heard a number of people speaking loudly, before the door swung shut behind the captain. The guards who stood at either side of the doors seemed to be ignoring them, but Namid felt their gazes on her. However, every time she looked, their attention was studiously elsewhere.

She tried not to fidget while waiting. But eventually, she began to pace and worry about whether they should have insisted on time to clean up better, maybe get clothes of better quality.

And Aahmes was not helping at all. He leaned against the wall opposite one of the motionless guards apparently trying to match him stare for stare.

Namid's wager was on Aahmes.

Finally, the door opened again, and the captain beckoned them in. They stepped inside to total silence and what felt like hundreds of hostile gazes. Namid felt a light touch of reassurance from Aahmes brush her thoughts as she walked in the open aisle between the two groups of staring courtiers who stood to either side of the hall.

The hall looked the same as she remembered it. The dark wood floor gleamed as if freshly polished and the pale stone pillars that formed two columns from the door to the dais marked the edges of the open aisle. Again, as out in the hallways, Namid recognized no one among the courtiers, but she only noticed them in passing as the man on the throne at the other end of the room held most of her attention. Monarch Levil Eisunal Shartov.

At first, Namid thought he looked mostly unchanged, except his short-cropped hair hung longer than she remembered and had gone completely white. But as she approached him, she saw that his rich blue robes hung on him, like he had lost a great deal of weight. And the lines in his face were etched much deeper than they had been, with many new ones showing. His eyes were a faded brown, much lighter than she remembered them, and his red-brown skin also looked faded.

Namid stopped one pace from the bottom step of the dais, mildly surprised that she remembered the proper distance. She heard Aahmes move up on her left. Since a curtsey without a skirt would have looked rather odd, she bowed instead, noting out of the corner of her eye that Aahmes bowed at the same moment, almost as if they had rehearsed it.

As she straightened, her father rose from his throne, slowly like his joints pained him, and descended the two steps to stand before her. She realized with surprise that she now stood as tall as he. When she had last seen him, he had still seemed to tower over her.

Without warning, he slapped her across the face, hard enough to knock her back a step. She almost struck back but stopped herself. This was her *father*.... But his action so shocked her that she could only stare back at him, fingers pressed to her split lip.

"How dare you return like this?" he hissed, loud enough that she was certain the entire room heard his words. "Waltzing in here as if you already ruled here. You could not have remembered your duty to your family years ago, when it would have mattered? It's about time you returned home. I would never have thought it of you to run off so irresponsibly. And not a word from you in all this time. And now here you stand, looking like some low-born ruffian, expecting to be welcomed back with open arms as if you had not deserted your family and duties at a critical time, acting as if you had done nothing wrong!"

He took a deliberate step toward her, ready to strike her again. Without thinking, Namid blocked his blow, catching his wrist in a firm grip. "No."

They stood like that for several long breaths-of-time and stared into each other's eyes. For just an instant, Namid thought she saw the father she knew looking back at her. Then he was gone again as he wretched free of her grasp and rubbed his wrist.

"You sicken me." He turned his back on her and stalked back to the throne while she remained standing there, frozen and shocked.

Namid could think of nothing intelligent to say. He had never before spoken to her that way. She had no idea how to respond, how she *could* respond.

Might she have come to the wrong citadel and ruler?

She dismissed that fanciful thought.

Outwardly, this was her father and Monarch of the Six Realms, but the man she remembered seemed to have been replaced by this unfeeling martinet. She went from surprise and dismay to chagrin, then confusion. How could she respond that wouldn't make it worse?

Namid glanced helplessly at Aahmes. Unfortunately, this brought him to the Monarch's attention as the latter settled into his throne.

"And you, vagabond!" he shouted at Aahmes, who only bowed again. Namid did not think she had ever seen Aahmes so expressionless.

The Monarch looked him up and down, disapproval clear in his expression. "Nothing to look at, are you? And

S. Lynn Helton

worth as much, no doubt. I can see her taste in companions has gone the way of her devotion to her duty. Well, I supposed I'll allow you to partake of my hospitality, but I do not wish to see your face again. Do I make myself clear?"

Aahmes nodded, bowed yet again, and backed up a couple of steps.

Suddenly Namid's surprise and confusion at her father's unjust words turned to anger and she shook with the effort of containing it. The Monarch noticed her distress. A fierce expression spread across his face.

"So, you fear me," he said, misreading her expression. "That's as it should be. See that you remember this. Now, get out of my sight."

Namid just managed an appropriate bow. Then she escaped back down the long hall and out the doors before her anger got away from her and she did something extreme, something she would regret.

CHAPTER 14

Namid found a clearing in one of the gardens where no one could approach unseen. Aahmes followed on her heels without a word and sat next to her on one of the stone benches.

Namid stared at her clenched hands. What was going on here?

She had felt no touch of Power around her father, and yet had sensed something in that eye contact. She glanced sidelong at Aahmes and could tell by his clenched jaw that he was seething. But when he spoke, his voice showed no sign of it.

"So, where did that reaction come from?" he said.

Namid shrugged. "I have no idea. I've never seen him like this, not even at his angriest. Not even when he exiled me all those years ago." She gingerly touched her split lip.

"Is it possible that it's not him at all?"

Namid gave him a horrified look. "You mean like Wesh? I don't know. I suppose it's possible. We'll have to check, I guess."

"I don't know that it's wise to stay here for too long. I noticed many of the courtiers watching the exchange perhaps a little too avidly. If they all thought you dead, or at least never coming back, your return might not please them at all. Someone might decide that you should never have returned and take steps to remedy that."

Namid sighed. "This is certainly not what I expected. Or hoped for. I feel somewhat at a loss here."

He nodded. "When you left here, it was as a child. And so you hadn't gotten involved in any of the intrigues that seem to naturally flourish in the courts of the powerful. But now you're at the center of it. I think your status in everyone's eyes has changed, and I'm uncertain that it's a good thing. I think you've become a player in whatever games are going on here."

Namid nodded. "I didn't see Tal there. But he could've been elsewhere. I didn't see mother there, either."

She looked up as one of the guards stepped into the garden: the woman with the red-orange hair. Namid studied her as she approached. The woman looked to be about her own age, well-muscled, with pale skin and blue eyes. No doubt she could handle the sword she wore at her hip. Namid rose as the guard drew close. The woman stood a little taller than her.

"Your Highness," the guard said and gave Namid a deep bow. "I'm here to escort you to your rooms. And your friend to his, as well." She inclined her head to Aahmes.

"Please," Namid said. "Don't keep Your Highness-ing me."

The guard looked confused and troubled at the same time.

"Uh," she said. "My lady, then?"

Aahmes snorted and Namid backhanded his shoulder, not too hard. He laughed.

Namid sighed. "I suppose that'll do, for now. Where are they putting us?" She walked back toward the door she had used to enter the garden. She heard the others follow.

"Well, Your— my lady, you have rooms in the royal wing, of course. And your friend is in the guest wing."

~Are you worried about being separated?~ Namid asked Aahmes in thought-speech.

~Not unless you are,~ he replied.

"Fine," Namid said aloud. "Let's see which rooms they gave Aahmes, then we'll see where I am."

~ ~ ~

Aahmes had been given the use of the first suite upon entering the guest wing. Spacious and elegant, it opened onto another of the gardens on the grounds.

Namid gave the guards at the entrance to the royal wing some anxious moments when she insisted that Aahmes was allowed there and was also allowed to know which rooms were hers. They relented in the face of no actual orders to the contrary but looked unhappy. Namid smiled as she made them even more unhappy when she demanded the return of her blades, and Aahmes', and informed them that Aahmes was allowed to walk about the citadel armed.

When their guard—they learned her name was Ordra—stopped outside the double doors that she said opened to Namid's rooms, Namid balked.

"These are the heir's rooms," Namid said, backing up. "That's not me. What's wrong with my old rooms?"

Ordra looked pained. "His Majesty, the Monarch, specified that you are to be given these rooms.

Namid glanced at Aahmes, who gave her a blank look in return.

"Please, Your— my lady. He was most insistent."

Namid relented at the misery in Ordra's expression. "All right. For now."

She stepped through the door Ordra opened for her and looked around. The suite was as ostentatious as she had expected, with a large fireplace, rich rugs and colorful tapestries, a plush couch, and several tables and cushioned chairs scattered about. Two servant girls scurried about arranging early spring flowers in vases on the tables. When they noticed Namid, the girls curtseyed, then hurried out the door. Ordra gave Aahmes a dubious look as he prowled around the sitting room.

Ordra took Namid on a brief tour of the other two rooms, a more private sitting room with a desk and some empty bookcases, and the bedroom with its wide, lush bed and large wardrobe. Namid noted the wardrobe's door was not quite closed. She spotted what looked like several rich gowns hanging within. She suppressed a sigh and returned to the main sitting room.

Aahmes had made himself comfortable there in one of the cushioned chairs, leaning back with his legs outstretched. Ordra glanced at him and turned away with a slight shake of her head. He grinned at Namid.

"Any chance of getting something to eat?" Aahmes asked Ordra. "The early-morning summons made us miss breakfast."

"Of course," Ordra pulled a thick cord that hung near the fireplace then spoke softly with the page who answered the summons. She turned to Aahmes as the page ran off.

"Sir, your meal will be delivered to your roo—"

"No," Namid broke in. "He… we… will eat right here, thank you."

Ordra glanced between the two of them. "I don't think His Majesty approves…."

"I don't care," Namid said. "If everyone is going to be Your Highness-ing me, you're going to have to put up with following my directives, too."

The guard stared at her, then bowed. "Your meal should be here shortly."

She left, closing the door behind her.

Namid and Aahmes stared at each other a breath-of-time and Aahmes' lips quirked up at the edges.

"What?" Namid demanded.

He grinned. "You seem to be doing just fine at the princess-ing thing."

Namid made a rude noise and plopped into a chair. "So far, not much different from dealing with all the annoyances I had to as a leader in the Shadowers," she commented.

Aahmes nodded.

Someone knocked at the door.

Namid levered herself to her feet. "That was fast."

But when she opened the door, it was not their food that met her. A guard bowed to her.

"Your Highness, you—" He broke off as he was gently pushed aside.

"Now you just be about your duties, Padrag. No need at all to announce me to my own baby girl." A woman a few finger-widths shorter than Namid swept into the room and shut the door behind her. Namid heard Aahmes' chortle and swore to herself she would do him some serious harm when he mentioned the 'baby girl' thing.

Before she had a chance to speak, Namid was caught up in the woman's embrace. She tentatively hugged her back. From what she remembered, her mother had not previously been inclined to exchange hugs with anyone.

"Mother?"

"Oh, how I've missed you," the woman said. She held Namid at armlength, then. "Oh, baby girl, you're so thin. Haven't you been eating well? And what are these clothes? I wouldn't let a disgraced stablehand be seen in such things. Fortunately, I had them move some of my gowns in here for you. I see we're much of a size, so you should do well in them until we can get a dressmaker to make you new ones."

All this she said without seeming to pause for breath. She also spoke rather loudly, as if perhaps she could not hear well.

"Mother—" Namid said, and only got that far.

"And look how you've grown," her mother went on without pause. "And so pretty, now, too. And your hair. My hair used to be so beautiful, too." She ran her hands over her long, iron-gray braids. Keeping hold of Namid's hand, she turned toward Aahmes—who had risen to his feet—and pulled up short.

"Oh, my! They spoke truth. You two *do* look alike." She turned from one of them to the other. "Remarkable. Who would have thought?" She approached Aahmes and reached up to gently touch his face. Over her head, his eyes met Namid's. He looked bemused.

Namid touched her mother's arm. "Mother, this is Aahmes. Aahmes, my mother, the Lady Royal, Yokana Zianya Shartov."

Aahmes clasped her mother's hand in a gentle grip and bowed. "Aahmestharq Fathir Harunsson, of the clan Naalin, Lady Royal," he said. "I'm honored to meet you."

"Delightful," Namid's mother murmured. "But we don't need titles and formality when it's just us three. Call me Yokana."

Namid gave Aahmes a questioning look. With his free hand he told her by hand-talk, *I've been practicing.*

A laugh slipped out before Namid could stop it, but she was serious again when her mother turned back to her.

"Ah, baby girl, I see your sister in you." Yokana grabbed Namid's hands and squeezed them. "You still hold yourself as Chimirya did. Do you still tilt your head so endearingly, too, just as she did, when you ponder some puzzle?"

Namid felt her face grow warm. She gently pulled her hands back. "Mother…."

"I've seen her do so," Aahmes told Yokana. Namid could hear the suppressed laugher in his voice. She glared at him and he only grinned at her.

Yokana nodded and clasped Aahmes' hand next. "Tanyala used to follow Chimirya everywhere. Imitating her older sister's mannerisms and trying so hard to be like her." Yokana leaned close, but still spoke loudly. "Did you know that some of our guards nicknamed her 'Little Mira'?"

Namid sighed and glared harder at Aahmes as he struggled to contain his mirth. Yokana released his hand and turned to look around the room.

"But enough of memories. Let me make sure they've set you up perfectly in here, dear girl." And the Lady Royal began to examine the details in the room, all the while maintaining a running narrative, rather loudly. Aahmes and Namid watched.

"So that's your mother…" Aahmes said. He kept his voice low.

Namid nodded and shrugged at the same time. "Not the way I remember her." She sent out a tendril of Power. "But, yes, it's really her. No Power taint about her."

Aahmes gave Namid a sidelong look, with a familiar glint in his eyes. "So, ba—"

Namid cut him off. "Don't even," she warned.

He grinned.

"Dears," Yokana called out to them. "You simply must take a close look at this tapestry. Come."

Exchanging puzzled looks, Namid and Aahmes joined her at the wall near the fireplace. Prepared to endure admiring some minute detail of fine stitchery, Namid was surprised when her mother flipped up a corner of the long tapestry, all the while extolling the virtues of the stitches. Gesturing them close with her other hand, Yokana twisted one of the pieces of wood trim, rotating it, and they all heard a faint click. A panel about half Namid's height popped open.

Continuing her chatter, Yokana pulled it all the way open and peered inside. Then she closed it, gesturing again for them to watch as she secured it again. She dropped the tapestry and leaned close, taking a deep breath.

"Thank goodness," she said barely above a whisper. "The prattling gets wearying after a time, but I couldn't remember at first where that panel was."

At a knock on the door, she smiled brightly, and her expression returned to the nearly vacant look she had worn when she arrived. She hurried to open the door.

"Ah, lovely!" She gestured the servants inside. They carried several serving dishes. The Lady Royal pointed them to a low table along one wall. "There. That will do." She supervised the placement of each dish just so and shooed the servants back out. At the door she leaned out and spoke to someone, then closed the door firmly.

"I've told them to send along my troubadour. We simply must have some music with our repast. But don't wait, dears. I'm sure you're hungry." She placed a finger across her lips and pointed to the door. Then she turned away and paced while Aahmes and Namid filled their plates.

"Mother, aren't you going to eat anything?" Namid said, following her mother's example and speaking a little louder than normal.

"Oh, so sweet to think of me, dear girl. I'm fine. You two enjoy." She looked up at a sound from the door. "Come in."

Odasoro entered, carrying his lute case. He closed the door firmly behind him and bowed.

"You remember our troubadour, Odasoro, don't you, dear?" Yokana said to Namid.

At Namid's nod, Yokana turned to Odasoro. "I must have some music," she said and gestured toward the door. "If you please."

Odasoro bowed to her and settled right by the door and began to play loudly. Between notes, he beckoned Namid over.

"I didn't say so last night, but I had begun to worry when you hadn't returned before now," he said in a quiet voice, leaning close to Namid's ear.

"A few things have happened," Namid said.

"Somehow I'm not surprised," Odasoro said. "We'll talk more later." He inclined his head toward Yokana who was beckoning Namid and Aahmes across the room.

Namid added a little more food to her plate and joined

her mother and Aahmes on the other side of the room.

"I understand the joy of catching up, Tanyala," Yokana said to Namid when she and Aahmes came close. Her mother's manner was completely different from before and her voice low. "But it will have to wait. Das has told me what happened last autumn. Are you truly all right?"

Namid nodded. "I go by Namid now, mother. And yes, I'm all right. But things are happening again—"

"We'll get to that soon," Yokana broke in. "There are things you need to know here."

She turned to Aahmes. "First, you have all my gratitude for staying by my daughter's side and watching out for her."

Aahmes looked a little flustered and hid it with a bow. "Of course," he said.

Yokana gave him a shrewd look, then looked at Namid and nodded slightly.

"We won't have much time, so first things first," she said. "Can you both use the magic that came to you to defend yourselves, if you must? And attack, if you must."

Namid and Aahmes exchanged glances. "Yes," Namid said.

"Good. I hope you won't have to, but it's best to be prepared. When Sesaisyd died, all the Dark Priests here dropped senseless and those of us who regained their wits fast enough eliminated them. I'd thought your father had begun to recover from their tight control, but then a new advisor came to him. I don't know for certain that he used to be a Dark Priest, but he easily controls your father, as the Priests did, and I have no way to counter him. I've seen him use magic, and he is both powerful and dangerous. And much as I wish you could stay, I think you should leave as soon as you can. Probably secretly, as I don't see your father's advisor allowing him to let you go freely."

She leaned close. "And you need to find your brother. I don't like the look in this advisor's eyes when he speaks of getting the family together again. I think he searches for Talorisin. You need to find him first."

"Who is this advisor?" Namid said.

"His name is Andrin. I don't know anything about him, not his background, nor where he came from—"

Aahmes held up a hand, stopping her. "We have company," he said in a quiet voice.

Someone knocked on the door and opened it without waiting for an answer. Two men entered, Namid's father and another man she had not seen before.

Odasoro looked up and stopped playing. He rose and bowed. Yokana dropped into a low curtsey. Aahmes and Namid gave belated bows.

"My lord husband," Yokana said. "I'm so pleased you came to join us. The cooks have managed some truly marvelous dainties for our repast." She headed to the food and filled a plate.

Namid resumed eating and studied the man who stood slightly behind her father and to his left. The man was much younger than her father, although she guessed probably several years older than herself. He wore a rich green doublet and matching trousers, both of fine material, appropriate for the court. His skin was light brown, his hair a few shades darker, and his eyes a striking blue. Something about him seemed familiar, yet she did not know him.

"I've eaten, Yokana," Monarch Levil said. He glared at Aahmes but said nothing. Then he turned to Namid.

"Tanyala, it is time you met Andrin, my advisor. You will work closely with him from this day forward." He ran his gaze over her from head to feet. "And I expect you to divest yourself of those rags immediately and dress and comport yourself properly for one in your position. That includes sending your 'friend' on his way. He has rooms, he should make use of them while he has the chance."

Namid set her plate down so she wouldn't throw it and caught sight of the smile on Andrin's face. And, although his face was different, she knew that smile.

Randoq.

She pulled Power to herself, and felt Aahmes do the same, although she could sense his confusion, too.

~*It's Randoq,*~ she told him with thought-speech.

A twist of Power swept through the room and Odasoro, the Monarch and the Lady Royal all stopped moving, seemingly frozen in place. The Monarch blinked, once. Nothing further.

Namid drew more Power. "What have you done to them, Randoq?"

"Calm yourself," Andrin said as he smiled Randoq's smile again. "No need to get destructive. I'd hate to see the others in this room come to any harm, helpless as they are before our Power. And it's Andrin, now."

Namid glared at him and did not release the Power. "Free them. Get away from them," she said.

"This is just a little trick I've been working on. They'll be back to themselves soon. And will be unaware that they were even held," Andrin said. "I'd get away from them, as you so sweetly asked, but I'd so hate to see your father suffer. And even die. See for yourself."

Namid felt Aahmes step up behind her as she looked through the Power and discovered a well-hidden link between Andrin and her father, a link Andrin was using to keep the Monarch alive.

"Why?" she said.

At that moment, whatever Andrin had done to the others dissipated. Yokana gave Aahmes a puzzled look but said nothing.

With a sudden change of manner, Andrin stepped close to Namid and captured one of her hands. She stiffened. He raised her hand to brush the back with his lips as he bowed to her. She stared at him when he released her hand and he just gave her a slight smile.

"Words cannot adequately express how pleased I am that you've finally returned, my lady. I only wish you hadn't been gone so long," he said, then returned to the Monarch's side.

"Shall we set that formal celebration you wanted, Your Majesty, for tomorrow evening?" Andrin said as he touched the Monarch lightly on one arm.

"Wha— Oh… certainly…."

"Formal celebration?" Namid said and looked from her father to her mother and back.

Yokana clapped her hands like an excited child. "What a marvelous notion, Levil," she said. "A grand celebration to welcome back our baby girl!"

Namid winced and caught the look of amusement on Andrin's face.

The adviser bowed. "We should let the ladies begin their preparations then, Your Majesty," he said. "Tomorrow evening will be here all too soon."

He looked to Yokana. "I'll send your handmaidens to help, Lady Royal?"

"Yes, yes," Yokana said with a casual wave of one hand. She turned to Namid. "And we must see about getting you your own handmaidens. Now to decide what to wear…." Yokana steered Namid toward the bedroom and the gowns that waited there.

Namid glanced back to see Andrin guiding all the men out the door.

Later, Aahmes told her with hand-talk as he left.

"Your Highness," Andrin said to Namid with a smile and bow as he closed the outer door.

After a breath-of-time, Namid sent a tendril of Power to secure the secret panel behind the tapestry. Then she slowly released the Power she held.

Yokana closed the bedroom door behind them and drew Namid to the wardrobe.

"What was that out there?" she whispered to Namid while she looked through gowns. "Did you do something with your magic?"

"Not really" Namid answered the second question first.

"I can tell you that father's advisor used to be one of the Dark Priests. His real name is Randoq. And yes, he's dangerous."

"I knew I didn't trust him. I'll continue to stay clear of him as much as possible then." Yokana began to pull elaborate gowns from the wardrobe and lay them on the bed. By the time a knock came at the door, she had seven laid out.

Each worse than the last, Namid thought.

"Oh, good, here are the handmaidens," Yokana said. "Now which color is best for today and what shall you wear for the celebration? We might even just have time to have a gown altered for you."

Namid sighed as her mother's handmaidens gathered around to help Yokana change her into the royal daughter.

Chapter 15

Namid slouched in a plush chair in her plush sitting room and fumed. She had managed to persuade her bevy of helpers earlier that she would be just fine, at least for the day, in a dark-red gown that had few embellishments. But they had insisted on arranging her hair in an elaborate tangle of braids and shiny threads. At least she had been able to convince them that she was perfectly capable, on her own, of changing into the chemise that went under the fine gown. She had not wanted them, and particularly her mother, to see the scars she carried.

Namid twisted one loose strand of her hair around a finger and glowered. She had also delayed choosing tomorrow evening's attire, for a while anyway. She dreaded the thought of it and the hair arrangement.

Have to get away as soon as possible.

But now she was stuck in her sitting room. Yokana had urged her to remain there, in safety, for the time being. Then she had left, taking all her chattering helpers with her.

Namid glared around the room. Nothing of interest, no books, no weapons…. Right, her blades.

She jumped up and opened the door. The two citadel

guards who flanked her doorway straightened in haste and bowed to her. One of them was Ordra.

"Your Highness," the man to Namid's left said.

Namid resisted sighing. "When my friend and I arrived, some of the guards confiscated our weapons before we were allowed into the great hall. I require their return. As quickly as someone can run them to each of us."

The two guards exchanged looks.

"What is it?" Namid said.

"Lord Andrin had them all taken to the armory," Ordra said. "He said you and your guest would not need them."

"I see." Namid studied the two guards long enough that they shifted around uneasily. "I suppose he also instructed that you two ensure I remain in my rooms until called for?"

The man's light skin flushed, and he avoided meeting her gaze. "Yes, Your Highness."

So Randoq thought to control her. Or rather Andrin, or whatever he wanted to call himself. Namid frowned and made her decision. She might scandalize many, turn them against her – although with Randoq in a position of power, she had to assume many already would be against her. So, she was not inclined to behave cautiously here anyway, why even start? This was Namid, here, not the princess or heir.

"I know Ordra… what's your name?" she said to the other guard.

"I'm Krendl, Your Highness," he said. "Ordra and I are partners in the guards. We've been assigned as your personal guards."

"And I'm Namid. Unless we're around some high-muck-a-muck who'll get his trousers in a twist, I'm not 'Your Highness' or 'Princess' or even 'my lady'." She smiled at his shocked expression. "But speaking of high muck-a-mucks… who exactly has the higher rank? Me or Lord Andrin?"

The guards exchanged glances again and Ordra shook

her head slightly with a grin. "You, of course, your... uh, Namid."

"Exactly," Namid clapped them on the shoulders and closed the door to her room.

"My rooms are very dull," she told them with a mischievous grin. "I think I should inspect the armory. And my guest would also be interested. So, we'll liberate him from his rooms, assuming he hasn't done so himself already, and then you two will help me remember the way to the armory."

Ordra and Krendl both gave her slight bows, grinning the while, and fell in on either side as she headed for the guest wing. As Namid strode through the citadel, she tried not to wince every time someone dropped a curtsey or bowed to her.

She turned the corner into the guest wing and had to grin at the sight that greeted her. The door to Aahmes' room stood open and he leaned against the doorframe. He looked completely at ease, engaging his guards in some animated conversation. Both of his guards wore grins and seemed to be enjoying whatever he was telling them.

For a breath-of-time, Namid lost herself in just gazing at him. He, too, wore fine clothes, of dark blue, and they helped emphasize his broad shoulders and lean legs. She pulled herself out of her contemplation as they got closer.

When Namid and her guards approached, Aahmes' guards suddenly straightened and bowed.

This time Namid did sigh, and Aahmes chuckled.

"You're not telling tales about me, are you?" Namid asked him.

He gave her an innocent look. "How could you think such a thing?"

"Right." Namid looked at his guards. "I see you're getting along."

"You know what a friendly guy I am..." Aahmes said, the corner of his mouth quirking.

She gave Aahmes an impudent grin. "Aren't you going

to introduce us?"

"Of course, Your Highness," Aahmes said.

"Don't. Just… don't," Namid said. She heard Ordra stifle a laugh.

Aahmes grinned and introduced the two guards, Finor and Lazarn. Brothers, it turned out. And Namid made it clear to them how she wanted to be addressed, as she had to her guards.

"And now that we have that all settled," she said. "Let's visit the armory."

Finor looked about to object, but Krendl pulled him aside and explained things. And soon Aahmes and Namid stalked through the citadel with their entourage of not-quite-smiling guards.

Aahmes leaned close and spoke for Namid's ears only. "You seem to be doing just fine at the noble games here."

"No," she countered. "I'm doing my best at ignoring them and doing what we need to."

Aahmes smiled. "Good. That's the Shadower I know."

Namid laughed.

"And I'd like to add," Aahmes said. "That she looks rather splendid in that gown and with her hair styled so elaborately."

Namid shot him a sidelong look. "I know a certain Shadower who's looking rather splendid himself." And she felt her face heat up.

"Ah, you noticed."

Namid shook her head and gave him an exasperated look. He chuckled softly.

At the armory, the guards seemed inclined to cause trouble, but subsided when Namid sailed past, ignoring their protests, and looked for her blades. Aahmes followed her example and, before long, they had retrieved all their weapons. Aahmes buckled his worn belt around his waist so at least two of his daggers would be at hand. Namid strapped on her armguards beneath her long loose sleeves. She debated about the rest of her blades, then just bundled them up for the time being, but carried them so she could unsheathe one easily, if needed.

On the return trip to the hallway, she paused by one of the armory guards.

"Where will I find my mother, do you know?"

"I'm sorry, Your Highness, I don't."

Krendl leaned toward Namid. "The Lady Royal mentioned something about cakes for the upcoming celebration. I suspect she is in the kitchen ensuring they are made to her specifications."

"Well, then, let's go."

~ ~ ~

With some reminders of the path from her guards, Namid led them to the citadel's large kitchen. They paused inside the door to avoid being bowled over by the bustle of busy cooks and helpers. Namid peered through the confusion and spotted Yokana at the far side. She led her little entourage through the tumult.

Yokana smiled as she approached. "Oh, baby girl. You look stunning."

Namid winced. "Mother, please."

Yokana just giggled. "Come, all of you. You must see the lovely little cakes the bakers have created."

Yokana led them off to a quieter spot to one side where a variety of fancifully decorated hand-sized cakes sat. And while the guards admired them, Yokana pulled Namid aside just far enough to be beyond their hearing.

"Do be careful wandering around," she urged Namid. "Don't trust to the dubious safety of having people about."

"That's part of why I retrieved these," Namid said of her daggers. "But mother, we need to get out of here. And what can you tell me about my brothers' visit to Navele? Anything might help me figure out where Tal might be."

"Yes, of course. But later. You'll have a better chance

of getting away unnoticed sometime after tomorrow's celebration, I'd say. Until then, can you act like you are joining in with the spirit of the thing? I think it'll help." Yokana glanced around and dropped her voice even more. "Also, you can trust Ordra, or Odasoro, of course, if you need anything. And a few of the servants, too – I'll have to make them known to you. Later. I can't speak for the rest of your guards. Or Aahmes'."

Namid nodded, then jumped as someone touched her shoulder. It was just Aahmes. "Randoq," he whispered and glided back to the cakes.

"Andrin," Namid told her mother, who immediately resumed her flighty persona. She grasped Namid's shoulders and spun her around.

"Now let me just look you over, baby girl. Yes, perfect. But I do wish you had worn one of the fancier gowns. Still, for the celebration tomorrow, you certainly will."

As she turned, Namid caught sight of Andrin making his way toward them through the confusion. Then she faced Yokana again, who whispered, "Remember... act like you're joining in the spirit of all this. Fewer complications." Then she said aloud, "So, what do you think, dear? Shall we have more of the oval cakes? Or the round ones?"

Andrin joined them and bowed. "Ladies." He leaned toward Namid. "I'd not looked to find you here in the kitchens." He glared at her guards, who looked nervous and chagrined at the same time.

Namid flicked a glance at Aahmes, then deliberately giggled at Andrin and played with some strands of her hair. "I was so *very* bored in my rooms. Not even a book to look at. And when I heard that mother had some lovely cake ideas...."

"You felt you had to bring your weapons to the kitchen?" Andrin said with raised eyebrows.

Namid giggled again, making Andrin's eyebrows climb higher.

"Of course not. Since I was out and about, I took the opportunity to retrieve these poor blades from the armory. They really don't belong there with all the fine blades father keeps."

Andrin gave her a dubious look, then moved closer. He reached for her free hand, but she tucked it behind her.

With a resigned look, he bowed again. "I am sorry for whatever I've done to upset you so. I hope that you'll allow me to make amends now that you are back home."

Namid struggled not to openly gape at him. How could he possibly think he could make amends for what he had done to her, to her sister, when he had been one of the Dark Priests holding them years ago?

He leaned close to whisper in her ear. "It's my pleasure to keep your family perfectly safe, just as I've been doing already this past season," he said then stepped back.

Working to hide her consternation, Namid turned to Yokana. "I adore the decorations on the round cakes, so maybe more of those?" she said. Then she turned to the guards. "I find all this noise is making my head ache." She shot a look at Andrin and turned away again. "Come on."

As they left the room, Andrin called after her. "No doubt Your Highness would benefit from an extended rest in your rooms, with no distractions."

Namid just waved a hand back at him and led Aahmes and their guards from the kitchen to the quieter hallway. There she announced she wanted a book from the library and then would return to her rooms.

But after she wandered through the family's private library, she changed her mind and took Aahmes, with the help of their guards, on a tour of the citadel. She had several reasons for this. First to give Aahmes an idea of the layout. With his uncanny ability to find his way around with only a casual knowledge of a place, she felt this was critical. Second, she needed to refresh her own memory of the building.

On top of these reasons, she wanted to see how many

guards Andrin had around the citadel and whether they might just be able to leave as they willed.

They could not, of course.

And finally, she did it to irritate Andrin, if he should happen to think he could just find her where he thought she should be.

After the jaunt through the citadel, the small group did return to Namid's sitting room, where she called for some food for a late midday meal. She and Aahmes relaxed and ate. Ordra and Krendl stood guard at opposite edges of the room, while Aahmes' guards flanked the door outside.

Both Ordra and Krendl refused food when Namid offered it. With a glance at them, she scooted her chair close to Aahmes' so they could talk.

"I don't see us walking out the gate," Namid said.

"No. Perhaps the way your mother showed us."

"Agreed. How much of that with Andrin earlier did you sense?"

"You mean the link to the Monarch?"

"Yes. It seems he's keeping my father alive. Not sure why. I'd like to get Mehratar to take a look at father, if we can, but I don't think it's likely. I'd like to get word to him anyway. I think I can't avoid attending this celebration tomorrow. So we'll make our escape afterward, while everyone's wearied and sated from the party. Hopefully before then, I can find out from mother about my brothers' trip to Navele."

Aahmes nodded. "I can prowl around. See how much freedom I've got when alone. See what I can get away with."

Namid grinned. "Sounds good."

"And what was that with Andrin?" Aahmes said. "In the kitchen, and before when he and your father came here?"

Namid shook her head. "I don't know. I suspect an act of some kind to help keep anyone else from figuring out what he's up to…."

They both looked up at a knock on the door. Ordra opened it to admit Yokana and a handmaiden who hovered so close behind Yokana that she was nearly hidden.

"Good, you've eaten," Yokana said. "We need to devote some time to planning your attire for tomorrow."

Namid groaned. Aahmes patted her arm as he rose. "I will take my leave, then." He bowed over Yokana's hand then left, his guards following him.

Yokana smiled after him, then shooed Namid's guards outside, telling them to resume their places at the door. After she closed the door behind them, she turned to Namid with a smile. "I've brought your new handmaiden. Your friend Ina?"

She gestured the handmaiden forward. And as the woman lifted her head, Namid realized that it was Inezha, wearing a plain dress much like a citadel servant's attire.

"Ina!" Namid repeated the name. "How?"

The Prazny grinned.

"I saw the guards escorting you to the citadel this morning," Inezha said. "And so I took it upon myself to pester the servants about getting a position now that the princess has returned."

"And fortunately, she approached one of the few people here I can trust and let us know that she was known to you," Yokana said and gave Namid a questioning look.

Namid nodded.

Inezha dropped into a deep curtsey. "I'm pleased to be able to help Your Highness," she said, with a mischievous glint in her eye.

"Yes, yes," Yokana said. "We don't need formalities when we're here alone." She turned to Namid. "While we pick out tomorrow's attire and decide how to do your hair, we'll talk about Tal."

So again, out came dresses to be laid across the bed and discussed and tried on over Namid's chemise. Inezha proved adept with all the laces and buttons, and blunt in her assessment of the dresses, and so was more help than Namid had anticipated. And during this activity Yokana told Namid about the journey her brothers had taken all those years ago.

"Your father received a letter from Lady Estaevi of Navele, one of the lesser nobles in that land, who nevertheless counted more than one town among her holdings. Mezeft, Breln and Urel, that I know of," Yokana told Namid. "Lady Estaevi wrote that she had a number of sons and daughters, and even nieces and nephews—apparently the family's quite large—who were all of marriageable age, and her family desired closer ties to ours. So, would we consider, she inquired, letting some of the young people of both families meet and spend some time together? Well, I don't know if you remember, but your brothers had become quite… rambunctious…."

"And bored, and destructive," Namid added.

"Indeed. I think at times your father was about ready to toss them out on their ears. But this was a better solution. A long journey, some responsibility, and perhaps some nice young ladies to meet, as well. So we, your father and I, decided they would journey to Navele and spend some time there. After that, the plan was to return the courtesy and have some of Lady Estaevi's young people visit here."

"But that didn't ever happen, did it?" Namid said. "I'm sure I'd remember…."

"That's right," Yokana said. "For a couple of seasons, messengers carried letters back and forth. Your brothers were enjoying their visit and eventually asked, with Lady Estaevi's permission, whether they might extend it and accompany the other young people in a journey around Navele, to visit various other lords and ladies, and get to know other nobles in the land. Lady Estaevi assured us of their safety. She planned to have Flame Warriors accompany them. We agreed and the boys traveled with their friends for about a year. Letters still came periodically, but then they stopped. Silence met our inquiries for a time, then finally we received word from Lady Estaevi's eldest daughter."

Namid shuddered, certain she knew at least some of what came next, but still dreading to hear it. And she feared the connection to the Flame Warriors. Haeith had been a Flame Warrior....

Yokana dabbed at her eyes with a cloth she pulled from a pocket. "It's still hard to speak of...."

Namid put a hand on her mother's. "Then don't. I can figure out the rest, I think."

Yokana shook her head. "You need to know to be able to find Tal, because all was not as it seemed. That last letter said that bandits had ambushed the young people, and captured some for ransom, but killed most of them, our sons among the latter. But right after that letter, came another, this from Lady Estaevi supposedly. It said that the attack was by unknown assailants and the young people had all been taken, none killed. Then a third letter came...."

"Such a mess," Inezha murmured.

Yokana nodded. "It was. The third letter came from someone called Wesh. It assured us of our sons' safety and said that they had chosen to join the Dark Priests."

Namid and Inezha exchanged glances at hearing of Wesh.

"But that's not true!" Namid said.

Yokana laid a calming hand on her arm. "I know that now. But at the time, it was the best of the news we'd heard. Naturally we sent some of our people to determine the truth, and when they returned, they said the last letter held the truth. Of course, this was around the time the Dark Priests extended their influence over us, over your father. And you and your sister were gone from us, then only you returned—"

"Yes," Namid interrupted, not wanting at all to revisit that time. "But I saw both Kalon and Jiro this past autumn and they had been prisoners of the Dark Priests. They didn't join them—"

"I know," Yokana said. "Odasoro told me of their deaths and that you learned Tal had escaped. And Andrin's desire to bring our family together seems to support the thought that the Dark Priests did not have Tal."

Namid nodded and tried on the next dress.

"So, look for the truth in Navele," Yokana said. "Maybe see if you can find out something from the Flame Warriors who accompanied the young people on their tour, if any still live. Find Tal before Andrin does. You should leave soon, before you become too entangled in the goings-on here."

"We plan to—"

"No," Yokana cut her off. "Don't share your plans with me. Just in case. But get away from here soon."

Namid nodded. "Do you still have any of the letters?"

Yokana shook her head. "I burned them all when Andrin began to speak of bringing the family together. I just felt I had to keep them from him. I'm sorry. You could perhaps have used them…."

Namid shrugged. "I'll manage," she said. "But one thing that would be of immense help, if you have it, is a drawing or portrait miniature of Tal. Even though he'll be older, that might help."

Yokana nodded. "I think I can get you one." She looked at Inezha, then. "And what of this dress?"

Inezha grinned. "It will take a little work to make it fit perfectly. But I think it's the best of the lot for her."

Namid looked at the rich red dress—a brighter red than what she had been wearing earlier—with its abundance of silvery embroidery. Inezha was right. It would be the best. And at least she liked the color, so she nodded.

Yokana smiled. "Wonderful! I think we have just enough time before the evening meal to try a few different stylings for your hair," she told Namid.

Chapter 16

Struggling to look more interested in the whole affair than she felt, Namid endured the fancy evening meal. She could not even exchange quips with Aahmes, as he was trapped at one of the lower tables while she ate with the family, and Andrin, at the high table. It seemed like every one of the many courtiers and nobles made a point of speaking with her, complimenting her dress and hair, trying to engage her in talk of some scandal or other. She felt they were all just trying to find some fault with her. She modeled her behavior after her mother's, but more subdued, and just endured until she could escape back to her rooms for the night.

On her way back, she took note of the considerable number of guards about. Clearly, just walking out the front gate was not going to be an option when they left. Perhaps that hidden door in her sitting room, as they had thought....

Back in her rooms, she secured her outer door with a bit of Power, like she had secured the secret panel earlier, so no one would be able to just open it. Someone had lit several candles in all three rooms, so she next checked around for any unwelcome surprises. She found none.

Inezha had not yet returned from her planned trip to meet with Mehratar to let him know what was going on.

Namid changed out of her finery as fast as she could, back into the simple tunic and trousers she had worn earlier, and combed out her fancy hairstyle. She tied her hair at the nape of her neck, not bothering to braid it for this.

She had just finished arming herself when she heard a light tapping sound. She traced it to the panel next to the fireplace and opened it, a dagger held ready.

Aahmes looked up at her from the opening with a slight smile.

"I'd planned to do that," Namid said as she clasped his hand to help him through the awkward opening. She closed the panel behind him and secured it again with a touch of Power.

He chuckled. "I'm sure I had fewer frills to shed," he said. Namid saw that he also wore his own clothes. He reached out and playfully flipped her tail of hair up over her head. It slid right back down. "I like this style... baby girl."

"Don't call me that." Namid swung her fist at him, but he caught her hand before she could connect with his shoulder. He held her gaze, then gave her a rakish grin and released her hand.

Namid glared at him. "You're in a mood."

"I haven't felt much like myself with all this m'lord-ing, and rebuilding a city before that. I'm much happier when I can skulk about," Aahmes said.

Namid nodded, with a small smile. "So, what did you learn while skulking about?"

He plopped down in a chair and stretched his legs out in front of him. "I could get used to this, though. Nice furniture, food whenever I want, servants...."

"Guards at every turn, plots and intrigue...."

"True, not so many guards, so much. But the plots and intrigue aren't so different from Rhadanthus. Maybe rather less honest."

"Aahmes…."

He gave her an innocent look, but the corners of his mouth quirked just a bit. "My companions were quite entertaining…."

"I noticed the two ladies practically hanging on you."

He laughed and waved a hand in the air. "Nice enough, but not truly appealing. But what they had to say is something else entirely. Do you know that you are the object of no fewer than six noblemen's marital ambitions?"

Namid groaned and plopped into a chair opposite him.

"Word is they each plan to speak with your father, maybe even this night. What a sight it must be, them all running into each other as they try to see him first."

Namid glared at him, but then chuckled. "Lovely. Even more reason to get away from here."

Aahmes nodded. "I haven't had time to check all the passages," he said with a wave of one hand at the panel behind him. "But I did find one that led to the kitchens. From there, it's likely an easy walk out one of the servants' doors. Another passage led to an overgrown garden along the outer wall, thick with bushes and trees. So, two possibilities already."

"Good." Namid told him about Inezha's presence in the citadel and how the Prazny had come to be her handmaiden. "Inezha will probably also know a way out. She said she was leaving, after the servants ate, to return to the inn to tell Mehratar all that's happened. Then I think she'll return here."

Aahmes nodded. "Is she going to stay the night in here, too?"

Namid nodded. "We'll take turns keeping watch. But what about you?"

"I've got my door secured much like yours," Aahmes said. "I don't think anyone will be getting in there tonight. But I'd planned to take over that couch of yours, especially after learning that Dark Priest's here and in a position of authority. That was before I knew Inezha would be here."

"You still can," Namid said. "I'd be happier with none of us off alone. I don't trust Andrin's apparently civilized behavior at all."

"Agreed."

"And I'm worried about Odasoro. He said we'd speak again, but I haven't even seen him."

"I caught sight of him at the feast," Aahmes said. "But he kept himself behind the other musicians and shook his head the one time I managed to catch his gaze."

Namid then shared with Aahmes all she had learned about her brothers' journey to Navele.

When she paused, he shook his head slightly.

"What?"

He grinned at her. "Running off across a realm or two to meet some lovely ladies…."

"Really?"

His grin widened, but then he sobered. "Do we bring Odasoro into this?"

Namid gave that some thought, her head tilted slightly. "I don't think so. He's been here watching out for mother and should probably continue to do so. Otherwise, it sounds like she's only got Ordra and a few servants that she trusts. And he seems to have some other things going on, as well. I think the fewer people who know what we're doing, the better."

Aahmes nodded.

Namid leaned back and stared at the ceiling as she tried to gather her thoughts.

"What is it?" Aahmes said.

Namid sighed. "Something I learned last autumn. Something I don't think you knew…." She leaned forward and gave Aahmes an intent look. "I learned that Haeith used to be a Flame Warrior…."

Aahmes gave her a sharp look. "And your brothers supposedly traveled with Flame Warriors, for a time, anyway. Interesting coincidence. And considering what we both think of coincidences…."

"Yeah. I know something bad happened, which is why Haeith is no longer one of those elite warriors. I have to wonder if he was one of the ones supposed to guard my brothers."

"Did he speak of them at all?"

"Why would he? Anyone who had seen them wouldn't automatically think we were related. And you remember how Cameni acted when we first met her. From what I remember, most of those of higher rank in Navele have as little as possible to do with those below them. It's entirely possible that Haeith might not even have known who his charges were, if he even *was* one of those Flame Warriors."

Aahmes nodded, lost in thought. Namid watched him, trying to guess the path of his thoughts from slight changes in his expression. And just enjoying looking at him.

After a time, she yawned, just as he looked at her. He chuckled.

"Why not get some sleep?" He waved a hand toward the bedroom door. "I'll stay awake until Inezha returns."

Namid nodded. "Or wake me after a reasonable amount of time if she's not back yet and I'll watch while you sleep."

Aahmes nodded and slouched further in his chair. Namid doused all but one candle in the sitting room, and all of them in the private sitting room, before she went into the bedroom and closed the door most of the way.

A muffled thump came from the outer door as Namid had just doused the last candle in the bedroom, after having changed into one of the sleeping shifts she found in the wardrobe. With a groan of complaint, she padded barefoot into the sitting room, carrying a dagger. Aahmes stood at the outer door, but off to the side so he would not be visible when it opened. He looked at Namid with a grin when she appeared and waved a hand at the door.

~*You didn't set the Power so I could open it,*~ he said using thought-speech. ~*And while I could probably break through it, I'd not like the display it would make.*~

Namid sighed. ~*Yeah, I forgot,*~ she replied the same way.

Aloud she shouted in the direction of the outer door, "I'm coming." She hurried to open it, but just a little. Next to her, well hidden, Aahmes held a dagger ready. She held her own dagger to the side, out of sight from the door.

Inezha stood outside in the hall, a bundle of some fabric, blankets maybe, in her arms. She dropped a curtsey as Namid opened the door wider.

"Sorry for the noise, Your Highness," Inezha said. "But these lumps of guards insisted no one was allowed to disturb you." She tilted her head to one side then the other.

Namid peeked out at the two guards who stood to either side of her door. She recognized neither of them. They bowed to her, but otherwise held themselves stiffly at their spots.

"Ridiculous," Namid said, directing her words to the guards. "What utter nonsense! Of course my handmaiden is allowed to disturb me, especially when she's brought what I asked for."

Namid opened the door just wide enough to let Inezha inside. She then glared at the two guards long enough that they shifted in discomfort.

"See that you don't keep my handmaiden from her duties again," she said and slammed the door. She secured it again with a touch of Power, this time setting it so it would only keep anyone other than the three of them from opening the door. She changed the Power that secured the hidden panel to allow the same, then looked at her companions, both of whom were grinning at her.

"What a proper royal scolding you gave them," Inezha said in a quiet voice as she dropped her bundle on a chair. It *was* blankets.

Aahmes tugged gently on a bit of the lace that decorated the cuff of Namid's sleeping shift. "Fancy," he said.

Namid glared at him. "It's nice to not have to sleep in my clothes for once," she said. "And this was the plainest of the ones mother left for me."

He gave her a long look. "Pretty," he said and returned to slouch in his chair.

Inezha shook her head in his direction and tossed him a blanket. She grabbed the other blanket and settled herself on the couch.

"I'd ask for one of the fancier shifts for myself," she said to Namid. "But it would raise questions if I have to answer the door before I can change back into this." She tugged at the servant's gown she wore.

Aahmes sighed and shifted his chair so he faced the outer door more than the two of them.

Namid and Inezha shared a smile.

"Did Mehratar have anything to say?" Namid asked Inezha, keeping her voice low.

"He expressed appropriate astonishment at the tale," Inezha said quietly. "And he'll make certain the horses and everyone's packs are ready when we are, like you asked. He also said he's coming with us."

"Us?" Aahmes said, also in a quiet voice.

"I cannot remain after you two have gone," Inezha said. "I know too much, and don't truly wish to be a citadel handmaiden, charming as your mother is, Namid. I would not stay in Kilaadi, either. Too close. So I'll come with you." She gave Aahmes a bright smile.

"As welcome as your company is, you don't have to," Namid said. "There's no telling how far we'll have to go or what we'll find."

"An adventure it is then," Inezha said, delight clear in her voice and expression. "Who knows, you might find my skills welcome." She gave Aahmes a long look. "And my daggers helpful, too. I've travelled too much of my life to be happy staying in one place for long."

Namid studied Aahmes to see his reaction. When he noticed her scrutiny, he just shrugged.

So Namid nodded to Inezha. "All right. And we'll speak with Mehratar, before we drag him along on this. I can't imagine why he'd want to come along...."

Aahmes murmured something that sounded like "I can." But when Namid gave him a quizzical look, he just turned his attention to the closed door.

"Wake me for my watch, then," Namid said to the two of them, and retreated to her bedroom.

~ ~ ~

Early the next morning, Aahmes returned to the hidden passage to return to his rooms. Yokana arrived shortly after he left and kept Namid busy the rest of the morning with preparations for the evening's celebration, tasting various foods, trying on her gown several times to get the adjustments exactly right, and trying even more hair styles until Yokana decided on the perfect one.

Inezha stayed with Namid nearly the whole time, perfectly acting her role as handmaiden. Namid only saw Aahmes once in the kitchen, when she and Yokana were there to taste some different soups.

Aahmes bowed to them from across the room but did not join them.

~Avoiding attention as much as possible,~ he told Namid using thought-speech and left the room.

After they had tasted too many dishes to count, and Namid no longer felt the need for any formal midday meal, she allowed her mother to take her back to her rooms to rest for the afternoon, in preparation for the evening. On the way, Namid spotted Inezha down a side corridor, talking with someone. She slowed to better see who and realized it was Andrin.

The advisor had Inezha backed to a wall, standing too

189

close to her and speaking intently, his whole focus on her. Inezha shook her head a couple of times. Namid slowed further, letting her mother pull ahead, to see if Inezha needed help. She saw Andrin lean in close and either whisper something in her ear or kiss her. Inezha pushed him away hard enough that he almost fell. Then she hurried away down the hall.

Andrin smoothed his doublet—green again, just like the previous day—and looked around, spotting Namid. He gave her a smooth bow and a leer of a smile, then sauntered down an adjoining corridor.

Yokana tugged on Namid's arm, having returned in time to see Inezha shove the advisor away. "The sooner you're away, and can take your friend with you…." she whispered.

Namid nodded. "We've made arrangements."

"Good." Then Yokana spoke louder. "You might not feel tired right now, baby girl, but you simply must rest before this evening. You won't want to wilt at a party in your honor."

"Of course, mother," Namid said.

~ ~ ~

When they reached Namid's rooms, both nodded to the guards at her door, another pair Namid did not know, and slipped inside. Yokana then insisted in a loud voice that she help Namid refresh her memory on court dances before she rested. They spent a long candle-mark reviewing steps of the dances Namid would need to know for the coming celebration, while Yokana quietly filled her in on recent happenings — mostly tales of alliances and fallings-out of various nobles whose names were only slightly familiar to Namid. She could tell Namid nothing more about Andrin, however.

When Yokana was satisfied that Namid would be able to manage well enough at the dances, she left her with an admonition to rest before they needed to prepare her for the evening. As had become her habit, Namid secured the door behind her mother with a bit of Power.

She stretched out on the couch in the sitting room, not feeling tired, but well aware that the night might be a long one, with the party followed by their planned departure from the citadel.

Namid managed to doze for a bit before her mother and a bevy of handmaidens descended on her. The rest of her time before the celebration was consumed with all the preparations. In the bathing room two doors down from her rooms, Namid bathed in warm, scented water—a part of the preparations she actually enjoyed—and managed to keep anyone from seeing her scars when she dried off afterward and pulled on a fancy chemise and robe over that. Back in her rooms, one of the handmaidens trimmed the ragged edges of her hair. Next came dressing in the layers of underskirts and gown needed for proper formal attire—each appropriately arranged before she put on the next—then sitting still for the handmaidens to apply cosmetics and artfully arrange her hair. They even put many small red cornelian gemstones in her hair, the largest barely the size of her smallest fingertip.

Yokana took over part of Namid's rooms for her own preparations and kept up a steady, light conversation the whole time the handmaidens fussed around them.

When the handmaidens finished, Yokana shooed them all away, except for Inezha, and retrieved a small wooden box from the depths of the wardrobe. She opened it and pulled out a delicate gold chain from which hung a ruby in a gold setting. The oval ruby itself was beautiful, about the size of the nail of Namid's smallest finger, with a highly polished, rounded top. But the setting was an ugly twisted snarl of gold clumps and wires that almost looked like it had been partially melted around the brilliant stone.

Namid gave her mother a questioning look as the latter handed her the pendant.

"Yes, I've also always thought the setting ugly," Yokana said. "But you can sell it for quite a lot, I'd imagine. Wear it tonight – the stone is a lovely match for your dress. And take it with you when you leave. Get as much for it as you can to help ease your travels."

Yokana turned back to the dress she had worn earlier, now tossed across Namid's bed, and pulled a small roll of parchment out of the pocket.

"And here's this." Yokana handed it to Namid.

Namid unrolled it to find a small sketch of her brother Tal, as she remembered him from just before her three brothers had left.

"The artist who always painted our portraits drew that before she moved on to the painting itself," Yokana told her.

Namid rerolled it and tucked it away in her own pocket.

"I'll take good care of it and return it to you," she said.

"Just return yourself and Tal safely," Yokana said, blinking at tears. "I'll say good-bye now, in case you plan to leave when I think you might." She hugged Namid and left the room.

Inezha leaned close after the outer door closed behind Yokana. "I'll get everything ready while you're at this celebration," she said. "So we can get out of here as soon as possible after it's over."

Namid nodded and headed out of her rooms as Inezha began to straighten the mess left from the preparations.

CHAPTER 17

As she had expected, Namid found the celebration tedious. The food was delicious, but the conversation did not interest her. She was seated between her father and Andrin, which added another level of unpleasantness. She saw Aahmes seated again at one of the lower tables, surrounded by young ladies. Aahmes wore dark red this time. When Andrin saw the direction of her gaze, he leaned close.

"Your friend seems quite enamored of the beauties to be found in court. He would do well to choose one. Which do you think it'll be? I think he favors the lady with the dark hair. The one to his right. What do you think of her? I'm sure I could convince your father to encourage a match with whichever one he prefers."

Namid glared at him but did not respond. Aahmes did seem to be enjoying himself.

The meal ended not too soon for Namid. After the servants cleared away the remnants of the meal, but before they brought in the sweet treats, a fanfare of horns from behind the high table heralded an announcement by the Monarch.

Monarch Levil stood slowly. Namid thought she saw a

flash of pain cross his face. She felt a surge of Power come from Andrin and glanced at him. He nodded and returned his attention to the Monarch, who smiled at the assemblage.

First the Monarch spoke about how wonderful it was that Princess Tanyala had returned to them. He went on at some length about how pleased they were to welcome her back into the family after the misunderstandings of years ago.

Namid only half listened and firmly reminded herself not to argue with this interpretation of events. She did not plan to stay, anyway.

But his next words caught her whole attention.

"Midday on the morrow, we will hold the ceremony to officially seal the Princess Tanyala as our heir," Monarch Levil said. "And we accept Lord Andrin's suit to be consort to the princess, to be made official as part of that same ceremony."

Namid glimpsed her mother's expression over the Monarch's shoulder. The Lady Royal looked grim, but unsurprised.

Although she had not suspected that events would head this direction, Namid realized she was also unsurprised. After all, she had learned the past autumn that Randoq, now Andrin, planned to gain power over the Six Lands, originally through her sister but now he had apparently decided Namid would suit his plans. Yet another reason to get away from here. Namid stared down at the table, working to hide her grimace.

Then Andrin clasped her arm and lifted her to her feet to accept the accolades of the party guests.

He leaned close to her, while smiling and waving to the crowd, and whispered, "I promised we would wed, my dear. Now we'll be together as we're supposed to be. And they'll naturally accept my rule, when your father's health fails. I'll keep him alive for you, as I have been. My dear Mira, I can't properly express how delighted I am that you've come back to me."

Namid froze, only barely managing to keep her shock from her expression. What was this? Did he genuinely think she was her sister Chimirya, dead now these many years?

Over the clapping and cheers, one voice came from the back of the room.

"What?" Aahmes yelled, echoing Namid's own thoughts.

Andrin lifted a hand and several guards moved toward Aahmes from the sides of the room. The advisor draped an arm around Namid's shoulders and leaned close.

"It'd be such a shame for your friend to rot in some dungeon cell," he murmured, his manner much different from before. "Such a pity."

Namid glared at him and slid out from beneath his arm, then turned back to Aahmes' plight. The guards now surrounded him and were easing him toward one of the doors out of the hall. He was not looking in her direction, so she tried to use thought-speech, uncertain if it would reach him as far away as he was.

~Don't get yourself imprisoned,~ she told him.

Aahmes glanced back over a shoulder at her and nodded once. He spoke emphatically with the guards, and they soon let him return to his place.

The servants brought the after-meal sweets and also moved the lower tables aside to clear an area for dancing.

Namid resumed her seat and tried to act like she was enjoying the delicious sweets, but she tasted nothing. Beside her, Andrin spoke and laughed with the courtiers who came to the table to offer congratulations. Namid went through the motions of acting pleased with the news, but her thoughts were on the escape plan for later.

Andrin played his part well, acting the attentive swain, picking out sweets to tempt her, leaning close to whisper to her. Namid kept her head tilted down as she found it increasingly difficult to school her expression into something pleasant.

"This is as it's meant to be," Andrin told her when the rush of congratulatory courtiers eased. "Your father is failing, but I've helped him. He'll live long enough for us to be wed and make everyone see that I'm the best next Monarch. Much better than that last remaining brother of yours, who hasn't even been around for years. Of course, we can't have Talorisin coming back and ruining everything."

Namid gave him a quick, sharp look. Maybe he knew something that could help her find Tal. "Well then, where did he go after he escaped Corentris?"

Andrin laughed lightly. "My dear, he was never in Corentris. Only your two eldest brothers were captured that day." He sliced a bite off the small, elaborately decorated cake on Namid's plate and held it out to her as his manner shifted again.

"But you haven't touched this delicacy yet. Here…. Oh, my Mira, how I've looked forward to this, to being together again with you. I know it hurts your father sometimes, but this is the best way. If he dies too soon, these privileged, self-important twits will claim they should rule instead of me. Instead of us. We can't have that."

Namid glanced up, looking him in the eyes and realized that something had broken deep within him. One of the most Powerful Dark Priests… was stark, staring mad! She shuddered and returned her gaze to the tabletop. Andrin continued sampling the sweet delicacies and turned his attention to banal chatter with another courtier who approached with congratulations. At least the advisor did not seem to have seen her realization in her expression.

Namid felt the Wild Power seep into the room, coming to her, pooling about her feet, and marveled that Andrin seemed oblivious to its presence. Much as she wanted to grab the Wild Power and fling it in Andrin's face, she willed herself to indifferent calm and soon the Wild Power drifted away.

Then came the dancing.

Namid endured several dances with Andrin, deaf to his inane conversation and numb to the motions of the various court dances. Her missteps were minimal, thanks to her mother's help earlier. She tried to smile but felt more like snarling. She suspected her smile looked more like a snarl, too. This was not at all what she would have hoped for her homecoming.

After several dances, Andrin returned to his seat next to the Monarch, leaving Namid with the message to enjoy a last dance with her friend—here he nodded in Aahmes' direction—as on the morrow, things would be vastly different.

Namid chose to rest and have some wine to drink, tired of dancing, of the whole gathering really. She was halfway through the wine in her goblet, when Aahmes took the seat next to her.

"I told them I was just so astonished that Lord Desmon hadn't won your hand," he told her with a grin. "I'd been certain his was the strongest suit."

Namid tried to smile. This time she knew for certain it looked more like a snarl.

"Not much longer," Aahmes assured her with a glance toward the high table. The Monarch and the Lady Royal had remained seated there the whole time and had not taken part in any of the dancing.

Namid followed his gaze. Yokana leaned toward the Monarch, speaking to him and giving a good appearance of extreme fatigue. Namid nodded. Once they left, the rest of the guests would probably follow their example in less than a candle-mark.

Namid leaned back in her chair.

"I hate this, the playing with people's lives."

Aahmes nodded and grasped her hand. "Let's dance."

She looked up, surprised, then spotted a noble headed her way.

"Certainly."

In spite of her awareness of the glares directed at them from all sides, Namid began to enjoy the dance. Aahmes moved as smoothly through the dance steps—even his missteps—as he did when sneaking through dark alleys. The dance was one of the slower court dances, and Namid was very aware of the warmth of Aahmes' hand at her waist and how close they moved together in the steps of the dance.

She felt her face grow warm and looked away to distract herself, right into Andrin's smug smile. She stared at him with no expression until the smile slipped, then returned her attention to Aahmes.

"You can loosen your grip, now," Aahmes said. "My hand isn't the blackguard's neck."

"Sorry."

"Although I appreciate the sentiment," Aahmes added and threw Andrin a glare.

"I didn't know you knew court dances," Namid said.

"I learn quickly," Aahmes said. "They did this dance earlier and I watched carefully."

Namid looked up at him. "You've never danced this before?"

Aahmes shook his head. "The dances I remember from my home are much more spirited. I'll show you, sometime."

"I'd like that." Namid watched the other dancers for a breath-of-time.

"I can't wait to get out of here. I hope everything's ready as soon as this ends."

"Inezha knows what she's about," Aahmes said. "And I find I'm actually enjoying this one particular part of our visit to the citadel."

Namid studied him to see if he meant it. When she saw that he did, she gave him a slow smile and a nod. "Me too."

He leaned closer. "Mm, you smell good."

Namid gave him a startled look, then smiled. "Thank

you. It's from sweetberry blossoms, according to one of the handmaidens. They put it in my bath water."

"It suits you. Spicy and surprising."

The music ended. Aahmes stepped back and gave her a perfect bow.

"Thank you for the honor of the dance, Your Highness," he said, the corners of his mouth quirking up.

Namid curtseyed to him. "The honor, of course, is all yours," she said with a too-sweet smile.

He almost laughed.

The horns again sounded, announcing the Monarch's departure, the Lady Royal at his side. Andrin held out his hand toward Namid.

She flashed Aahmes a frustrated look. He bowed again and backed away from her.

~*Only a little longer,*~ came his voice in her thoughts.

She inclined her head to him, and briefly debated open opposition to Andrin's wishes. But that would probably be far from beneficial just then, so she joined Andrin and allowed him to take her arm to escort her from the celebration.

Just a little longer, she reminded herself.

CHAPTER 18

Back at her rooms, Namid found her door flanked by two guards she had not seen before. Andrin opened her door for her and bowed, gesturing her inward.

"I have taken the liberty, my princess, of replacing your normal guards with these two gentlemen from my elite corps. Now that you have been declared the heir, we cannot be too careful with guarding you."

Namid gave him a long look and tried to figure out what new twists he might be plotting to whatever game he was playing. "Of course," she murmured.

"I'll see you in the morning, then," Andrin said. "Sleep well."

Namid inclined her head to him and stepped inside, closing the door behind her. Inezha peeked out of the door to the unlit private sitting room, with a quizzical look.

Namid held a finger to her lips and leaned back against the closed outer door. She did not hear any voices, but she felt the tingle of Power. Being careful not to draw any Power herself, Namid opened herself to sense it and discovered Andrin putting some kind of seal on the outside of the door. Locking her in, no doubt. Not that it mattered.

Namid beckoned Inezha into the bedroom and joined her, closing the door behind them.

"Andrin's sealed the door with Power," she whispered. And has his people guarding it. Help me out of this dress, please."

Inezha made a face at Andrin's name and began loosening the laces that Namid could not reach on the dress.

"Your mother suggested we each take one nice dress with us, in case we need them in Navele," Inezha said in a quiet voice.

Namid nodded and struggled out of the dress. She dug her fingers into her elaborate hairstyle and grimaced at the feel of the sticky stuff the handmaidens had put in her hair to help hold the style and gems. She began undoing the hairstyle while she looked into the wardrobe. "Have you seen that gown I was wearing when you got here? And have you picked out something?"

Inezha joined her and pushed aside the bunch of gowns to find the red gown at the back. "Here it is," she said. "And I found a bright blue one that I like."

Namid grabbed the red gown and bundled it up. "Sure. Grab it."

"I already have," Inezha said with a grin, and held out a set of dull-colored clothes. "Your own clothes were gone, so I grabbed these."

Namid frowned. Some overzealous servant must have taken her tunic and trousers one of the times she had been elsewhere. She looked around and spotted two bags tucked behind the door. "This our stuff?"

At Inezha's nod, she tucked the red dress in the top of one bag and took the clothes Inezha offered. She shook them out and sighed to herself. A servant's shift and gown, much like what Inezha still wore. Namid would have preferred tunic and trousers, maybe a stablehand's attire, but this would do. At least it had no train. Unlike all the fancy gowns, this dress only hung to her ankles. She slipped it on then finished pulling her hair out of the fancy style and braided it into its customary single braid.

As she worked at the preparations to leave, misgivings plagued Namid. Should she go? What might Andrin do in her absence? He claimed he needed her father…. And she believed that he would take the easiest route to get what he wanted. That should mean she could believe that he would keep the Monarch alive, keep things much as he had for the past season. And she trusted her mother when she said they needed to find Tal, especially before Andrin did. There really was no one else to do that. With a mental sigh, Namid pushed aside her qualms and resolved to focus on the task at hand.

After she tied off her braid, Namid knelt next to her bed, sent a small tendril of Power sliding under to release the illusion she had set earlier and pulled out the small bundle of her cloak, boots, belt and blades. "Good thing I hid these," she muttered as she put everything on, including her dagger necklace that she pulled from a pocket of her belt.

"Oh, I encountered Odasoro earlier," Inezha said. "He gave me a message for you. He said to tell you that the book is going to take him a while. And he'll be sure to keep it safe while he's working on it."

Namid nodded again and looked over to see how Inezha was doing. The Prazny stood by the bedroom door, wearing a dark cloak and holding the two bags. Namid scooped up a double-handful of the gems that had fallen from her hair, added the ruby necklace from her mother, and stuffed the valuables into one bag, which she then grabbed from Inezha. Then Namid doused all the candles in the room.

"Let's go," she said.

In the sitting room, she paused and set her bag on the floor.

"Bide," she whispered to Inezha and pulled Power to herself, not trying to hide it. She let her anger color it for

Andrin to sense later, or even right then, if he was paying attention. She flung the Power deliberately at the outer door and smiled to herself when Andrin's Power flashed momentarily into sight.

"What are you doing?" Inezha hissed. "Won't that bring him running?"

"I don't think so," Namid said. "He'll be able to tell I haven't broken through, so he should be confident he'll find me where he wants me in the morning. But I'm not going to make it easy."

This time, she drew upon her Power reserve, reaching for it several times as it slid from her, still as slippery as ever. Finally grasping enough Power, she spread a small bit along the walls of her rooms and pushed it into the structure to form a shell designed to keep anyone from hearing or sensing anything within the rooms. She was intentionally sloppy, leaving the Power shell slightly visible, and deliberately infused the Power with her anger and hatred of Andrin. Let him think she had done this out of spite and frustration, and that she had only tenuous control of the Power.

When it was sealed to her satisfaction, she nodded to Inezha and grabbed her bag again.

"And how are we to get out now?" Inezha said, her eyes wide in the slight glow from the Power.

Namid smiled and headed to the concealed panel her mother had shown her. She dissolved the seal she had previously put there and opened the panel. A faint shimmer of her Power shell glowed in the dark opening.

"Just go right through," Namid whispered.

Inezha did, with a look of surprise as the shimmer did nothing to stop her. Namid followed and closed the panel behind them. She created a small orb of reddish light and looked down the passage, pleased to see that it was tall enough to stand upright. No side passages were visible, so at least this first part would be easy. She hoped Aahmes was already in the passages and would meet them before they got lost. She wanted out of the citadel as soon as they could manage.

She and Inezha crept down the passage a few paces, then Namid called a halt.

"One more thing," she whispered.

She turned back to the panel and studied it through Power.

Should be possible. Not too different from fusing the rocks back at Shadow Keep, she decided.

Hoping that Andrin could not sense Wild Power, she pulled a small amount of it to her, only having to fight a little to call it. She then sent it sliding through the wood panel and into the surrounding wall, willing the separation between the two to vanish and leave a single, solid wall.

At first, nothing happened, then the Wild Power surged and seemed almost to take on a life of its own, seamlessly connecting the panel to its surrounding wall.

Namid let the excess Power slip away and turned back down the narrow, dirty passage. She saw that the dust on the floor had been disturbed. She hoped it only marked the times that Aahmes had walked there.

When they came to the first side passage, Namid studied the dusty floor to see if perhaps this one was the one Aahmes had come from. She had only a vague idea where they might be in relation to the citadel proper, but she did not think the new passage headed in the direction of his rooms. The dust looked disturbed only by something small, maybe rats or mice, so the two women stayed with the main passage. But Namid sent a tiny puff of Wild Power down the other passage to disturb the dust for a long way, to help confuse anyone who might come searching for them.

More than a quarter candle-mark later, after they had passed several more side passages, which Namid also disturbed to look like someone had gone there, Inezha pulled up short and glanced back at her.

Namid nodded. "I heard it. Aahmes, I hope," she

whispered.

Namid released the light orb and twisted one wrist to drop that armguard's stiletto into her hand. She used a small bit of Power to enhance her sight in the darkness and crouched, waiting, one hand on Inezha's arm to let her know where she was.

The slightest hint of a whisper came from somewhere ahead.

"Namid?"

Namid reached out with a sliver of Power. It was Aahmes.

"Here," she said, and brought back the light orb.

Aahmes stepped out of the gloom in front of them. He carried a small bundle and wore his cloak. He had a nod for Inezha and a smile for Namid.

"This way. Glad I caught you here. We need to follow side corridors starting just ahead," he said.

They now hurried through the passages to a panel Aahmes said led to the kitchens. Inezha went through first, claiming she would be the least recognizable, if seen. Before long, she returned to tell them the room was empty.

"Shouldn't we put up another glamour?" Namid said.

Aahmes shook his head. "Once it's up, it's hard to sense. But putting one on us here…. Andrin's got his Power blanketing the citadel. Lightly, but he'd still probably feel that much use of Power."

They stepped out from the hidden passage and closed the panel behind them. Namid doused her light orb. One low fire lit the huge room. Inezha pointed across the room to a low archway in one wall.

"The door the servants seem to use most," she told them, keeping her voice low.

Namid nodded, then took a second look at Aahmes. He still wore his finery from the evening, although mostly covered by his cloak.

"One of us doesn't match…" Namid whispered.

Inezha turned back to look. Aahmes just grinned.

"Unlike some," he whispered back, "I knew I wouldn't have to worry about trailing skirts, so I didn't bother to change. But let's get out of here."

They made for the archway Inezha had pointed out. When they got there, they found stairs going down to a landing, then extending down further to the right from there.

Aahmes stopped them at the top and drew them close.

"There's someone down there," he said, almost too softly to hear. "Probably a guard."

Inezha glanced that direction, although they could see nothing more from their vantage, and turned back to them with a grin.

She reached into her bag and pulled out a jug of wine. "I'd hoped to save this," she said, "but I think we who are about to have our own party would appreciate it." She winked at Aahmes and Namid, then held the jug out to Namid. "Can you get the cork out without extra noise?"

"I've got this," Aahmes said and grasped the cork with just his thumb and forefinger. A light touch of Power and he slid it out without a sound.

"Now a drink for each of us," Inezha said, "but we should act like we've had much more."

They passed the wine around once, then Inezha wobbled down the stairs, clasping the jug in one hand while sloshing some wine onto her dress. She held her bag in her other hand, concealed beneath her cloak. She stepped heavily on one step, exclaimed softly and giggled.

"Who's there," a man's voice came from below. "Show yourself."

Aahmes and Namid exchanged glances. Namid pulled up her hood to help conceal her face and they followed Inezha, also acting like they had already enjoyed more jugs of wine than the one Inezha carried.

"Confounded steps," Inezha said. "Be there in a breath-of-time, han'some."

The three bumbled their way down the stairs, stumbling into each other and trying to brace themselves together, with much merriment. When they reached the bottom landing, where the guard stood beneath a single lit torch, they saw he was clearly amused, but trying to look stern.

"The door is closed tonight," he said. "No one is to leave."

"Aww," Inezha said. "I wan' t' go have some fun...."

She grinned at the guard, then turned to Aahmes. She sidled up to him and pulled his arm around her shoulders. "You promised," she said with a pout and looked up at him.

Namid imitated the Prazny's actions at Aahmes' other side, drawing his other arm around her shoulders. She peered out at the guard from beneath her hood. Inezha ran her fingers across Aahmes' cheek while wobbling a little.

Aahmes hugged Namid close, then held his arms out in appeal to the guard. "Help a fellow out," he said in a whiny tone. "We've more fun planned than that stuffy party upstairs."

The guard almost smiled, but then gave the three a stern look. "I'm sorry, my lord. I can't. No one is to leave the citadel this night."

Inezha slipped away from Aahmes and sidled up to the guard. "A'right, a'right. But you're a nice fella. Why not have a drink to help you through your watch an' maybe we can meet up later." She gave him an exaggerated wink.

He started to reach for the wine, smiling all the while at Inezha, then stopped himself.

Inezha flicked a worried glance at Namid, who sighed to herself and stepped close to the guard's other side, slipping her finger-long dagger from its necklace sheath under cover of her cloak. She leaned in close and deliberately fell against him as if she had lost her balance, then stabbed the needle-like dagger into his arm in the gap between his glove and sleeve.

He kept her from falling, but then a look of alarm crossed his face. And he slumped to a seated position, leaning against the wall, eyes staring straight ahead. He breathed evenly, as if asleep. Namid wiped her tiny dagger on a corner of the guard's cloak and returned it to its sheath, then closed the man's eyes.

"Nice," Inezha said. "How long will it last?"

"Maybe a candle-mark," Aahmes said, already unlocking the door with a key he grabbed from the guard's belt. "Let's go."

Inezha took a last drink of the wine and placed the jug on the floor at the guard's left hand, splashing some on him in the process. "Such a shame to leave it behind."

Aahmes replaced the guard's key and followed Inezha and Namid through the door.

Outside they huddled in the shadows.

"I don't remember this door," Namid whispered. "Where are we?"

"The kitchen gardens are to our left," Inezha said. "There's a path that goes to the right toward the stables. Straight ahead somewhere is the outer wall."

"Which way then?" Aahmes said.

"Let's try the gardens," Namid said. "I remember paths there and, I think, a small gate in the outer wall."

"Wager it's guarded, too," Aahmes said as they headed into the gardens.

"Wouldn't be surprised," Namid said.

She led the way. As they got further away from the shadow of the citadel, moonlight fell on them and lit the way, letting them walk faster.

They traversed the gardens, working to avoid stepping on dried plants left over from the winter. Then Namid stopped them.

"The gate is just ahead," she said in a quiet voice. "And I don't see anyone there. It seems unlikely it's not guarded…."

She glanced back toward the citadel. The best she could

tell, everything looked still that way.

"I'll get a closer look," Inezha said. "I've the most silent steps of us three."

She slipped off ahead, while Aahmes and Namid crouched low by some bushy plants.

Namid began to fidget after a while. "She's been gone too—"

A single horn interrupted her. And Inezha's voice came out of the darkness ahead of them.

"Come on!"

Namid grabbed Aahmes' arm and together they sprinted toward the gate, plunging through plants on the way. At the gate, they found Inezha easing an unconscious guard to the ground. The horn he had sounded rolled almost under their feet.

Aahmes tried the gate.

"Locked," he said. He looked back into the garden. The sound of running footsteps came from that direction.

"I can't find a key," Inezha said as she pawed through the guard's clothes.

"No time," Namid said and sent a tiny tendril of Power into the lock to pop it open.

They dashed through the gate and Namid swung it shut behind them. Another bit of Power fused the gate to the gateposts and hinges. And they ran.

CHAPTER 19

Several streets away from the citadel, they paused in a narrow alley to catch their breath and listen for pursuit, which they heard all too close.

"Have they roused the city?" Inezha said.

"Sounds like," Aahmes said.

"Where are we meeting Mehratar?" Namid said.

"A stable down the street from our inn," Inezha said. "This way."

Inezha led them through many twists and turns, avoiding lighted areas as much as possible and the now-alert guards prowling the city.

Nearly a quarter candle-mark after leaving the citadel grounds, Inezha stopped them in some deep shadows behind a stable, easily identified from the smells.

"This one," she whispered.

A cloaked figure stepped out of the deeper darkness cast by the next building. All three of them drew daggers.

"Aahmes? Namid?"

"Oh good," Namid said as she recognized Mehratar's voice. She sheathed her dagger and stepped forward to greet the Healer.

Mehratar took them inside the stable where their

horses stood tacked up and ready. A new horse stood with the others, also tacked up and ready.

"You don't need to come with us," Namid said to the Healer.

"No need to stay in Kilaadi," Mehratar said. "The Healers here suffice."

"So find another town," Aahmes said as he checked over the gear and the packhorses. "Go instruct some apprentices or something. Why even come with us, anyway?"

"Traveling with us has just become more hazardous," Namid added. "And that's likely to just get worse."

Sudden lanternlight momentarily blinded them.

"Here, what're you doing…" said a man standing in the doorway. His voice trailed off as he took in all their faces.

Namid groaned at the sight of the man's uniform. She darted toward him but was too slow. The guard dropped the lantern and let out a piercing whistle as he drew his sword.

Namid hit the guard before he could bring his sword properly to bear. She stabbed him with her tiny dagger at the base of his neck, right at the edge of his armor. They both fell to the ground, the poison affecting him almost immediately. Namid struggled free and back to her feet.

Other whistles pierced the darkness as they all scrambled to gather the horses. Without mounting his, Aahmes led the way out the door.

"Guess you're coming along after all, Healer," he said over his shoulder. "He saw you with us. You can't stay here."

With a nod, Mehratar grabbed his horse's reins and the lead rope of the workhorse he ridden previously, which now carried packs.

Aahmes led the way through the city. They kept to back ways as much as possible, with frequent pauses to avoid running into the increasing numbers of citadel and city guards who searched for them.

"Can you get us from here to that secret door out that Odasoro showed us last autumn?" Namid whispered to Aahmes as they waited nearly a candle-mark later for two guards to move past where they hid in the darkness near a rundown tavern. The tavern was almost as far from the citadel as a person could get and still be within the city walls.

"Not sure," he said.

After the guards turned a corner further down the street, Aahmes, Namid and Inezha took the opportunity to secure the packs they had carried from the citadel. Then everyone mounted their horses. Mehratar retained the lead rope to his workhorse now packhorse. Aahmes handed Inezha the lead rope of the other packhorse.

"Which way out will be best?" Mehratar said.

Namid glanced at the stars to judge the time and the direction.

"I'd say whatever's closest," Aahmes said. "It's clear we're not getting away unnoticed, so getting away fast would be the next best choice."

Namid nodded, not thinking that they might not see her action. "We need to go east...."

With a glance at the stars, Aahmes set off down the alley to their right. "This way, then," he said.

"I hope we're close to the outer wall," Inezha said.

"We should be," Namid said. "Judging by how far we've come from the citadel."

Only a few twists and turns of the alley and Namid spotted the outer wall ahead. All of a sudden, the horses' hooves sounded too loud to her in the quiet of the night and she called a halt.

She slid off her horse. "I think there's a small gate near here. Going to find it," she said in a quiet voice and slipped into the darkness.

Away from the others, she indulged in a couple of deep breaths to calm herself. They only helped a little. She hated to think what would happen if the guards managed to catch them.

She hurried through the streets, using all the skills she had learned as a Shadower, and made it to a corner within sight of the small gate without being discovered.

Only two guards stood there, but they looked alert. And the area approaching the gate was open and lit by torches.

Out of habit, Namid studied the wall, but of course going out that way would mean leaving the horses behind. At least this part of the city *was* quiet. That might mean that few other guards were close.

She returned to the others and told them what she had seen.

They tossed some ideas back and forth, but nothing sounded like it would get them away without being spotted.

"Not even that glamour you put up before?" Mehratar asked Aahmes.

Namid felt Aahmes send out a faint wave of Power, she assumed testing what other Power lurked in the night.

"I can't make us invisible," Aahmes said. "So they'd still see people trying to leave. And at this time of night, I'm sure they'd be suspicious anyway, even if not alerted for us."

He looked at Namid. "Maybe that semblance that you and Haeith created last autumn, of a nothingness that clung to us and hid us…. Wait, same problem. Unless you can make a semblance of the gate staying closed while we actually open it and go through?"

"Maybe, but I haven't done one like that before," Namid said. "I don't think I want to try something new right now."

"Why not just use your Power and destroy the gate?" Inezha said. "Then we can ride right through and be away while they are still surprised."

"Messy and noisy," Aahmes said.

"And anyone in the entire city who's sensitive to the

Power would likely feel it," Namid said. "It'd draw Andrin faster than anything." She tilted her head, considering. "But maybe a diversion…."

"Draw our pursuers somewhere else?" Aahmes said.

Namid nodded.

"Or I can do something," Mehratar said. "One of the things a Healer sometimes has to do is get someone to sleep for a while."

That caught their attention.

"Can you make an unwilling person sleep?" Namid said.

Mehratar nodded. "I've had to compel many sick or injured people to sleep. It'll just be a little more difficult with someone who's healthy. And I can get both guards at the same time. Also, it requires little Power, so someone more than a pace or so away is unlikely to even feel it."

"I say let's do that, then," Namid said.

"But can you sneak up to the guards well enough to reach them without raising an alarm?" Inezha challenged.

"I'll manage it," Mehratar assured her.

So Namid described the path to get to the gate. When she finished, Aahmes pulled out a wide strip of dark cloth from his tunic and tied it around the lower half of Mehratar's face, telling him to keep his hood up and pulled far forward. Then Mehratar set out on foot.

The three left waiting eased the horses to one side of the alley, close to the wall, trying to be less conspicuous. Namid toyed with her dagger necklace while they waited. She still had the poison. Maybe she should have just used it on the guards at the gate. But she could only get one at a time, maybe leaving the other enough time to sound the alarm….

"He's returning," Aahmes said.

"We should hurry," Mehratar said as he rejoined them. "They won't stay asleep as long as someone sick or injured. They'll begin waking in about half a candle-mark."

Leading the horses, they hastened to the gate and

through. Namid paused to use a tendril of Power to lock it behind them. By the time Andrin made it to this gate, if he ever did, any hint of her Power would be long gone. Aahmes reached through the bars of the gate and snatched the guards' pouches. He grinned when his gaze met Namid's.

"Why take—" Mehratar began, but Inezha interrupted.

"Good thought," she said. Then to Mehratar, "Now it looks like they were knocked out to be robbed, not for someone to go through the gate.

The Healer nodded his understanding and they all mounted up again.

They held the horses to a walk, to minimize the sounds of their passage along the road until they moved into thicker trees and out of sight of the gate. Then they increased their pace.

"What about that travel spell you have?" Inezha called to Aahmes, who rode in front.

"I haven't prepared for it," Aahmes said. "But I'll be able to hold it for a short time at least."

"That'll help," Inezha said.

Aahmes nodded. "Let's get further away from the city before I use it."

Mehratar dropped back to ride beside Namid. "Travel spell?"

"A way to use Power to travel further in a shorter amount of time. For a while. I know how it's supposed to work but haven't yet been able to do it myself."

Mehratar nodded.

They increased their pace again. Namid tried to listen for signs of pursuit and often turned to look back but detected nothing. Dim moonlight filtered through the still mostly bare tree branches and gave her plenty of light to see.

Close to a candle-mark after they had left the city, Aahmes called for them to slow to a walk and gather close. He pulled the Power around them and the world blurred in that way that had become familiar to Namid the past autumn. Namid called up a light orb, getting a smile from Mehratar. They continued on, to put as much distance as they could between them and Andrin before stopping.

When Aahmes released the Power a few candle-marks later, near dawn, they still traveled in a forested area. Some of the trees here had their leaves, although they were still the small early-spring ones. Aahmes slumped in his saddle and Namid started toward him. But Inezha got there first.

She spoke quietly to Aahmes, who straightened up a breath-of-time later and waved her away. He looked back at Namid and Mehratar.

"We need to stop, make a camp, before I do the falling on my face thing." He gave them a quick smile.

Inezha looked around. "There should be a stream off that way. Not too far."

"You've traveled this road before?" Mehratar said as they picked their way through the trees and undergrowth in the direction Inezha had indicated.

"Not this one," Inezha said with a grin. "But I have traveled many roads, for a long time. I know what to look for to find a good spot to camp."

Mehratar nodded. "Of course."

Inezha found them a small clearing in the trees, a few paces from a small stream. They dismounted and tended to the horses. Inezha cleared out an old fire ring that sat near the center of the clearing and started a fire, while Mehratar grabbed a water bag and headed to the stream.

Namid yawned and plopped down on the ground. She blinked a couple of times in an attempt to keep her eyes open. Aahmes sprawled next to her and did not even seem to try.

"So it begins again," he murmured.

"What?"

He grinned. "The traveling at night, hiding from those hunting us, the racing to get there."

Namid sighed. "Perhaps. But I don't think we really

need to travel at night. I doubt those hunting us will be deterred by darkness. And it's not much of a race, either. It's already been well over ten years since Tal headed to Navele."

"Those hunting you were unable to find you in Kilaadi," Inezha said.

Aahmes opened his eyes and gave Namid an enigmatic look.

"True, but I'm uncertain why not," Namid said. "That drawing you showed us was good enough that we should have been recognized, especially with the glamour gone."

"Maybe you have someone on your side," Inezha said as she stirred some grains from one of the bags into the pot and added water from a water skin.

"Someone other than us," Mehratar said as he returned with a full water bag. He set it on the ground next to Inezha.

"Obviously other than us," she said, but gave him a smile to take any sting out of her words.

Namid dropped her head into her hands with a groan. "I don't know. Maybe…."

She felt a faint touch of Mehratar's Power and looked up to meet his intent look. Out of the corner of her eye, she saw Aahmes roll over to face her.

Mehratar crouched down in front of them. "I can do something for your fatigue," he said. "Both of you. If we need to keep moving for a while. It'll only last for a brief time, though, and the fatigue *will* catch up with you."

Namid and Aahmes exchanged glances.

"Would you see if there are any people out as far as you can reach with your Power?" Aahmes said.

A surprised expression crossed Inezha's face, with Mehratar showing an almost identical one. Then he nodded. "Good idea. I hadn't thought of that for here…."

"You probably haven't been hunted like we have," Aahmes said and closed his eyes again.

Mehratar's gaze unfocused and Namid felt his Power

sweep out, but only because she was looking for it. She did not think anyone else would even notice it.

Mehratar shook his head. "No people are anywhere near us. I can't sense as far as Kilaadi – we've come quite a distance...."

"More than a day's normal travel," Aahmes murmured.

Mehratar's eyes widened at the news. "Well, I can sense out several leagues, and there are no people."

Namid nodded. "Then let's rest here." She looked at Inezha. "And that's smelling good. Is it ready to eat?"

CHAPTER 20

The four decided to spend the morning in their camp, to rest and also repack the things they had brought from the citadel. Aahmes slept most of the morning. The others napped and took turns at watch.

Namid was pleased to discover that Mehratar had brought all of their things from the inn. In her pack she still had a couple of tunics and trousers that were in decent shape. And from the looks of them, Mehratar had gotten them cleaned. So as midday approached, she slipped off to the stream to try to rinse out the stickiness of whatever the handmaidens had put in her hair the day before.

Whatever it was, it resisted her efforts. But she finally got it out, while slopping a fair amount of icy water onto herself and soaking the dress she still wore. She squeezed out as much water as she could, then tried using the Power to dry her hair as Mehratar had dried that shirt many days earlier. She was partly successful. At least her hair no longer dripped on her clothes.

She shivered. That water was cold!

Namid changed into her accustomed layered tunics and trousers and tried to warm herself using Aahmes' technique. As with her hair, she was only partly successful.

At a soft sound back toward the camp, she turned away from the stream. Aahmes stood at the edge of the trees, his fancy doublet dangling from one hand like he had just taken it off. He held a bundle of plainer clothes in his other arm. The breeze plastered his thin shirt to his body.

Namid shivered again. "Aren't you cold?"

He grinned and sauntered close. After a slight hesitation and a quick look around, he brushed his fingertips across her cheek, sending a tendril of Power through her to ward off the cold. Although not all the warmth she felt came from that Power.

"Practice," he said and headed to the stream.

She glared at him, fingers resting lightly on her cheek where she still felt his touch. She turned back to the camp when she realized she had been admiring the way his clinging shirt revealed the wiry muscles of his arms and torso.

"We'll be heading out soon," she called over her shoulder.

He raised a hand in acknowledgement.

~ ~ ~

Everyone ate while they finished packing up the horses. Namid took the time to dig out the pendant her mother had given her and the small loose gems. She slipped the pendant over her head and tucked it into the top of her tunic next to her dagger necklace. The gems she divided among the four of them. Aahmes whistled when she dropped his gems into his hand.

"Won't have to pick any pockets on this journey," Namid said with a grin.

Aahmes and Inezha returned her grin, while Mehratar gave them all a startled look. After everyone tucked away their gems, they led their animals back to the road and mounted up.

"Will we use the travel spell again?" Inezha said with an

intent look for Aahmes.

Aahmes shrugged. "I'd rather call it a technique or method, not a spell. And we certainly could, although I don't know that we need to. I'd prefer to use the technique only when we really need it." He looked at Mehratar as they all mounted their horses. "Anyone getting close?"

Mehratar sent out his Power, then shook his head.

"Then let's just ride normally," Namid said. "The travel technique uses a lot of Power. It's exhausting."

"I have an idea to help with that," Mehratar said as he rode next to Namid, the two of them in the front of the little group. "But it'll have to wait until we stop again. How long of a journey do we have in front of us?"

Namid pictured a map of the Six Realms. "I think it's over a week to the border with Navele. After that, maybe a day to the first town on the other side of the border. It should be in Lady Estaevi's holdings. She's supposed to be a minor noble of Navele, but apparently her holdings include more than one town."

Mehratar nodded then turned the conversation to other things.

~ ~ ~

When they stopped for the evening, after they had eaten, Mehratar drew Namid and Aahmes a little away from the fire. Inezha stayed lounging on the ground in the circle of firelight, watching.

"Healers are taught a way to make the most of a very small amount of their Power," Mehratar told them. "The most-skilled Healers are few in number, so we must be able to do as much as we can with what we have, without exhausting ourselves to the point of falling over." Here he grinned.

"Unlike when you Healed Namid?" Aahmes said.

"Her wounds were a very unique circumstance. Not something a Healer normally encounters. I think this…

technique…"—he gave Aahmes a grin—"I think it will help you two. You don't have to save your Power that I can see. You've certainly got enough. Much more than most. But you both are sloppy. You throw more Power than you really need into things and so you exhaust yourselves when you don't have to, or much sooner than you should have to."

"Sloppy?" Aahmes said, with the vexed expression Namid knew only too well.

"He's trying to help," she told Aahmes.

Mehratar nodded and held Aahmes' gaze. Aahmes shrugged. "So how does this technique work?" he asked the Healer.

"I can't describe how it works, but I can show you." He held up one hand, inviting the contact needed to thoroughly show someone a use of Power.

Aahmes leaned back with a closed expression on his face. He tucked one arm behind his head and nodded to Namid. "You try it," he said.

~You're so eager to work with him,~ he added using thought-speech.

Namid frowned at him and placed her hand palm to palm with Mehratar's. She closed her eyes to concentrate and was startled when Mehratar gently drew her into his thoughts to follow how—before using Power to do anything—he formed it into a kind of woven strand that increased its effectiveness.

"Try it," he told Namid after he broke the contact.

She glanced at Aahmes, who just watched them with narrowed eyes.

Namid tried to form her Power as she had seen. It kept slipping away from her. After several tries, she growled in frustration.

"Something maybe only Healers can do?" Aahmes muttered.

Namid glared at him. "Why don't you try it?"

"He has been," Mehratar said. "My mentors said it's

something anyone who has Power can learn to do. But I'll tell you that I didn't get it to work for me for quite a while."

"Practice, practice," Namid said to Aahmes and grinned at the glare he gave her.

~ ~ ~

Namid and Aahmes continued to work on the technique as they traveled. The small group fell into a routine of rising with the sun and traveling most of the day, then stopping in the late afternoon to have time to work with Power and do anything else that might be needed, like washing clothes in a convenient stream. Mehratar sent out his Power morning and night to alert them to any people nearby. In this manner they discovered several small towns along their route in time to avoid them. Namid wanted to leave as little sign of their travel as possible, and they did not need anything from town anyway.

Before they left the first town behind them, Aahmes encouraged Mehratar to leave the small group and stay there, or even travel to another town. Mehratar countered with the argument that the small group might possibly find themselves in need of a Healer at some point, and so it made sense for him to continue on in their company. Inezha sided with Mehratar and so the Healer stayed with them.

While traveling, they tended to ride two and two, switching around partners every so often and chatting about inconsequential topics or just riding in silence. After a couple of days of travel, the road curved to the south to take them into northern Navele rather than southern Luag, just as Namid remembered from long-ago lessons about the Six Realms.

More than a week after they left Kilaadi, Mehratar told them he sensed a small group of people ahead of them.

Too few for a village and gathered near the road.

"The border with Navele?" Inezha said.

"Should be," Namid said. "How far?" she then asked Mehratar.

He sank back into the Power. "Certainly less than a full day's ride," he said. "I count only ten."

"Few enough if there's trouble," Aahmes muttered.

"So, we'll need to get all dressed up, then, in the morning," Inezha said.

Namid pictured her one fancy dress and shook her head. "Not yet. I'd rather save it for actually dealing with any nobles, which we shouldn't need to do at the border."

"Don't want to damage your pretty dress by riding in it," Aahmes said.

Namid gave him an irritated look. "Something like that. Can you work the glamour? I think for all of us this time, since both Inezha and Mehratar were seen with us in Kilaadi."

Aahmes concentrated for a breath-of-time, then nodded. "Whatever interfered in Kilaadi is gone," he said. "And I'll make us look less travel worn, too." He grinned and set the glamour on them.

CHAPTER 21

They traveled faster the next day than previously, but still took care to avoid tiring the horses. So late afternoon found them approaching the people Mehratar had sensed. Namid and her companions topped a low rise to see a small group of buildings clustered about the road ahead. When someone spotted them, two of the people moving among the buildings walked to the closest end of the cluster and stood waiting, hands resting on the hilts of their swords.

Aahmes dropped back to a spot behind Namid and to her left. "You take the lead on this," he told her with a grin.

"Thanks," she said and rode down the hill.

A glance behind her showed Mehratar taking a similar position to her right, and Inezha following them, in a line behind Namid's horse and leading both pack animals.

Namid smiled to herself. The precision of their placement might impress the border guards. She reached into her belt pouch and pulled out Tal's signet ring. She slipped it on her thumb. It fit, and not too loosely. Good thing Tal had it sized to wear on his smallest finger, otherwise she would not have been able to keep it on any of her own fingers.

As they approached the border post, Namid studied the two people who waited for them, a man and a woman. Both seemed tall and both looked very comfortable in their armor, which resembled what she remembered Haeith wearing. Their swords were not as massive as Haeith's. Their expressions were neutral, and showed no hint of hostility. Or recognition. Good so far.

She gave them a slight smile as she stopped her horse a half-pace from their position.

"You are about to enter Navele," the woman said. "Is that your intention?"

Namid studied the woman as she wondered at her phrasing. Did they often have people unintentionally enter Navele?

"Yes, it's our intent to enter Navele," Namid said.

The woman looked over each of them and sniffed. "There are certain expectations that you need to be aware of." She handed Namid a folded parchment. "You *can* read, right?" At Namid's nod, she continued. "Be certain you are familiar with everything written within. It's intended to keep out-land commoners such as yourselves out of trouble."

"We certainly don't want any trouble," Namid said.

The woman nodded to her companion, who stepped closer and held something out to Namid.

At Namid's slight hesitation, the woman gave her a nod. "Take them."

Namid held out her hand, then studied the four pendants the man gave her. She directed a questioning look at the woman.

"Wear them openly," the woman directed. "They mark you as free commoners from out-land, which will help avoid any misunderstandings."

~Not sure I like this emphasis on commoners,~ Aahmes' voice came into Namid's thoughts. *~Maybe I should have given us noble attire in the glamour.~*

Namid considered that, sharing Aahmes' concern about being labeled as commoners. Might make this whole thing harder. She had hoped to avoid revealing her status until they had traveled further into Navele, but it seemed sooner was going to be better.

To guide her bearing and attitude, Namid recalled her first meeting with Cameni, favored daughter of the Earl Navele. With a slight flourish, she held out the hand bearing the signet ring and adopted a haughty tone. "And what provisions are in place for out-land nobility, in order to avoid any misunderstandings?"

The woman studied the ring. Her eyes widened and she bowed deeply.

"Apologies, my lady," she said and waved at the man to bow, too. "Your appearance—"

"I could hardly be expected to be out traveling in my best clothes," Namid snapped. "It's anything but a short day-ride from Kilaadi."

"Of course, my lady. Of course not," the woman said. "My mistake."

"If I may?" the man murmured from Namid's other side as he reached to take back the pendants.

Namid pulled her hand back and tucked the pendants in her belt. "I still await the answer to my question," she said.

The woman bowed again. "We will get what you need right away. We ask that visiting nobles wear a pendant, also, one that is, of course, much better crafted and decorative. If you would consent to wait just a little while?"

Namid made a great show of studying the angle of the sun, then looked back at her companions. Both Inezha and Mehratar conveyed an air of confident detachment. Aahmes was trying not to grin.

"No rush," Namid said when she returned her attention to the woman. "I believe the first town along this road is too far away for us to arrive there until well after nightfall, isn't that correct?"

At the woman's nod, she continued. "Then we'll stay the night here. I assume you have adequate guest quarters. Don't you?"

The woman nodded again and sent her companion running.

"I will take you there myself, my lady," the woman said and led them further into the cluster of buildings. "You are our only guests, so you have the pick of the guest quarters."

"The best available, of course," Namid said. "And you have not yet informed me of your name and designation."

The woman bowed. "Of course, my lady. I am Cahodre, commander of this border post."

Namid nodded. "Thank you for your hospitality, Commander."

"Of course, my lady. Shall I have our cook prepare your evening meal. I assure you he is quite good."

Namid shook her head. "All we require of you are comfortable beds and a lack of disturbances for the night. And in the morning, those pendants, along with whatever else we need so we can continue our journey. And avoid any of these *misunderstandings.*"

Cahodre bowed again. "It shall be as you require, my lady." She opened the door to the largest building and stepped back. "I hope you'll find this satisfactory, my lady," she said. "If anything is not as you need, please tell me and I'll make sure it's corrected for you."

Namid slid off her horse and gave the interior a brief look. "I'm sure it'll be fine."

"I'll personally see that your mounts and packhorses are cared for," Cahodre said.

"I'll see to that," Aahmes said as he dismounted. "Just lead me to your stables."

Mehratar and Inezha also dismounted. The four pulled their packs from the packhorses and dropped them inside the door to the guest quarters.

"I'll join you, as well," Inezha said, laying a hand on Aahmes' arm as they followed Cahodre across the compound, leading the horses. Namid watched them. Inezha seemed to be talking the whole way, but Aahmes seemed to pay little attention. The commander acted as if she heard nothing of the one-sided conversation.

The man who had been with the commander ran up to Namid and bowed, trying to talk while catching his breath.

"My lady… here are the… pendants for you… and your companions. They'll ensure no… misunderstandings."

Namid examined the new pendants. They seemed to be made of gold and each bore a raised, elaborate design of whorls and swirls on the front. The backs bore no markings.

"Much better," Namid said. "So sweet of you to get these to us right away." The man's fair skin flushed, and he bowed again.

"Can I get you anything else, my lady?"

"Do you know where we are likely to find Lady Estaevi? I wish to meet with her."

"I don't know, my lady, but I'll see if any of the others can tell you."

"Good. But the morning will be soon enough," Namid said. "I'm weary from the ride and don't wish to be disturbed further this evening."

The man bowed. "Of course, my lady. I'll pass the word. May I be so bold as to wish you a good evening?"

Namid gave him a slight smile. "That's very nice of you."

She gave him a small wave, then she and Mehratar entered the guest quarters and closed the door.

Mehratar grabbed his pack and took it to one of the two beds nearest the door. He dropped it on the end of the bed and turned back to Namid.

Namid gave him a quizzical look at the odd look he gave her. She grabbed her pack and dropped it on another bed then prowled around the quarters. She found a smaller second room with a table and chairs, and an even smaller kitchen area at the back with another door that led outside.

"So that's what the nobility are like here," Mehratar said when she returned to the front room.

Namid grinned. "At least somewhat, based on the only Navelean noble I've actually met. Although I might've been a little heavy-handed about it."

"The guards seemed to accept it as appropriate." Mehratar dug around in his pack. "Good thing I bought this back in Kilaadi." He held up a dark-green doublet of fine cloth.

"Nice," Namid said. "So we each have one change of clothing that's suitably noble. I suppose we'll have to see about getting more." She frowned. "Maybe Aahmes can help with a glamour so we don't have to cart around a complete wardrobe."

Mehratar nodded and pulled out some of their food. "I'm getting hungry," he said and headed with the food toward the kitchen.

Namid followed. "I'll give you a hand. The others will be a while, I imagine, but should be ready to eat, too, when they return."

After Inezha and Aahmes returned, after they all ate and cleaned up, Namid and Aahmes created a Power shell that clung to the building's outer walls so no one outside could overhear them. Aahmes also secured the doors and windows against entry.

Don't trust anyone else, Aahmes told Namid using hand-talk.

Namid nodded at the reminder of Dar's last words to the two of them.

"What's all this?" Inezha said, waving a hand at the walls and door as they gathered around the table. "Why not use the Power instead to make them do what you need, tell us what you need to know?"

"That would be just like the Dark Priests," Aahmes

said.

"But it's effective," Inezha said. "Without worrying about *misunderstandings*. I wager with the Power you could even make people forget being made to do things, or make them think it was their idea the entire time."

"I suppose the Power can be used for that. But I don't want to *make* anyone do anything with Power," Namid said. "That's not how—"

"How is that different from acting the noble and commanding them?" Inezha said.

Namid shook her head. "I know. And I don't like that, either. But it's at least acting within the way things work. And they can always refuse, anyway."

Aahmes shook his head. "Not here, I think. I spoke with the commander. The hints we got from Cameni last autumn didn't really describe the gulf between commoners and the nobility here. Commoners are hardly better than serfs, not allowed to travel anywhere without permission from their local lord, not allowed to refuse a noble's demands, and certainly not allowed the freedom we'll need to find Tal."

Namid dropped her head to her hands. "So we do have to play nobility here…."

"But the glamour should help, right?" Mehratar said. "We'll just be some nobles from Paronia out traveling the land together, rather than the Monarch's daughter and friends."

Namid looked up. "True. So, we'd better settle on who we are, then, so we don't slip up."

"But you've already shown the commander that ring," Inezha objected. "She'll probably spread the word about it unless you make her forget about it."

Namid studied the ring. "It's not mine," she said after a while. "And while it's got the family crest on it, it doesn't imply a child of the Monarch. A relative would also be allowed to use it, especially if on business that concerned the family, as this venture surely does. So I'm a distant cousin, still with the right to wear the ring and use it, but not anything like heir." She gave them a brief glare and received grins in return.

"I can set a glamour to make us look better dressed than we are when we leave here, but we should at least pick up some better riding clothes to make things easier," Aahmes said. "I'll separately hold the glamour that changes our faces and keep that one up all the time. I'd rather not have to do that all the time with clothing, too. Especially in case we might need the Power otherwise."

Namid grinned at him. "I think you're just getting to like the fine fabrics," she teased.

He shrugged. "There *is* something to be said for silks and velvets, fine linen…."

"So what name shall we call you by, my good friend Lady…?" Inezha said with a glint in her eye. "I think I can just use my own name."

Namid nodded. "And Mehratar, you can too, I think. But Aahmes and I will need other names."

"I'll just use my second name, Fathir," Aahmes said. "Few others know it and none of those who do should be anywhere nearby. And I'll use my clan name, Naalin, for a second name."

"And you can be Namid's brother," Inezha said.

Aahmes winced and shook his head. "No," he said, with a glance at Namid. "Not a brother."

Aahmes' strange expression aroused Namid's curiosity, but she decided it would wait. "I already use my middle name," she said. "A shortened form anyway."

"From your first name, Tanyala, you could use Yala perhaps," Aahmes said, with a chuckle. "Or Anya. Or maybe Saina from your middle name Sainamid?"

"Definitely Saina," Mehratar said.

"Saina Shartov…" Namid said, trying it out with her family name. "It'll do."

"What second name for the two of us, though?" Inezha said, indicating herself and Mehratar.

"Something you'll remember easily," Aahmes said. "Maybe a relative's name or someplace you visited often?"

After she considered that, Inezha said, "I shall be Inezha Nazextas."

"That name sounds familiar," Mehratar muttered with a frown.

"Really?" Aahmes said to Inezha. "The Spirit-City?"

Inezha nodded. "As you might have noticed, the Praznies have a connection to that city," she said. "And it's unlikely anyone else has heard the name."

"What *is* the connection?" Namid said.

Inezha gave her an enigmatic smile. "It was our ancestral home. The Praznies weren't always scattered across the Six Realms," she said, then turned to Mehratar. "So what will you choose for your noble second name?"

"I'll use Arndu. Using the name of that village seems appropriate," Mehratar said with a sad smile.

"This should be fun," Inezha said with a broad smile. She jumped up to grab one of Aahmes' hands and curtsey to him. "If you please, Lord Fathir Naalin, would you be so kind as to show me the steps to the latest court dances?"

"I don't really know them…." Aahmes brushed his hair back with his free hand and glanced at Namid, who shrugged.

"I wouldn't think that we'd need to demonstrate our dancing abilities," Namid said.

"Wouldn't hurt to be prepared," Mehratar said as he stood and held a hand out to Namid. "Perhaps you would consent to help me learn the steps as well, Lady Saina Shartov? We certainly have the time this evening."

With a quick glance at Aahmes, catching a glower on his face before he saw her looking, Namid rose and took Mehratar's hand.

"It'd be easier if we had music…." And a wisp of Power flowed past her. A faint strain of music sounded in the room.

She glanced at Aahmes' smug smile. "Will that do?" he said.

She nodded and began showing Mehratar the easiest of the court dances.

And so they spent a pleasant evening trying dances, working to avoid stepping on each other's feet, laughing at all their missteps and enjoying themselves. They also settled on a bit of their story about how they knew each other and came to be traveling without all the retainers that nobles would usually take with them.

~ ~ ~

Sometime in the middle of the night, Namid woke. Holding herself still, she looked around, wondering what had disturbed her. She spotted Inezha standing by one of the windows. She rose and padded over to the other woman.

"What is it?" she said in a quiet voice.

Inezha started in surprise—although Namid had not thought she had been that quiet—and turned to her. "N-nothing. I had a strange feeling, thought maybe I heard something, but I haven't seen anything out there, out any of the windows."

Namid looked as well and saw nothing amiss.

Inezha brushed one hand along the wall. "This is like the Power shell you used in the citadel?"

"Yes, but not as sloppy as I made that one."

Inezha nodded. "Yeah, I can't see any of it. But I think I might feel something... maybe that's what disturbed me...."

Namid peered at Inezha. "Do you have Power? Have things happened around you that you couldn't explain any other way?"

Inezha shook her head. "I've seen people use Power, you know. I'd recognize if I was doing it myself. But sometimes I get strange feelings."

"Perhaps you sense it, then," Namid said. "That could be useful, especially if you can bring it under conscious control."

The two women looked at each other in silence. Then Inezha nodded. "Is that something that one of you can teach?"

Namid shrugged. "Let me think on it. But in the meantime…." She reached out to the Power in the walls and smoothed it and quieted it, hoping that would disturb Inezha less. "Can you still feel something from the Power?"

Inezha closed her eyes and stood still for a breath-of-time. Then she touched the wall. "Only if I touch the wall now. My thanks."

Namid nodded and watched Inezha return to her bed. What did it mean, if anything, that Inezha sensed Power but did not seem able to use it? Namid had been able to sense Power almost as soon as she discovered that she had it herself. She had never heard of someone who could sense it but not use it. She wondered if there were more out there with that ability.

As she returned to her own bed, Namid heard Aahmes' voice in her thoughts. *~Problem?~*

~I don't know,~ she replied the same way. *~Probably not. I just learned Inezha can sense the Power. She said our Power along the wall disturbed her sleep. So I tightened it, so she only senses it when in contact with it.~*

~Really? Interesting.~

~Yeah.~ Namid returned to her bed and tried to stifle a yawn. *~Something for later, though. I still need sleep.~*

She sensed more than heard his chuckle. *~Later, then.~*

~ ~ ~

The next morning, none of the border guards disturbed them so they were able to eat their breakfast and prepare for the day without the need to play their adopted roles.

They made sure they were dressed and all packed, then Aahmes built the glamour of better attire around them before he removed the Power shells both he and Namid had constructed.

"This is weird," Inezha said. "I think I can feel the glamour on me now."

Namid watched Aahmes make an adjustment to the Power and Inezha stopped twitching.

"Better?" he asked her.

She nodded, with a bright smile for him. "I can kind of see them, too. Is that normal?"

"I tried to set the glamours so we would know what we look like. Thought it might be a good idea."

Namid nodded to that and paused at the door to glance back at the others.

"Ready?"

At their nods, she opened the door. They stepped out and gave the guards who met them friendly, but aloof greetings. One guard ran off to one of the other buildings, Namid assumed to get the commander. Two came toward them from the stables, leading their horses and packhorses.

While they watched, the guards loaded all their packs for them and checked the horses' tack. They attached one packhorse's lead to Aahmes' saddle, at his direction, and the other's lead to Mehratar's saddle.

The man from the previous night approached Namid and bowed. "My lady?"

He flinched when she turned toward him and bowed again.

"I offer my most sincere apologies, my lady," he said. "No one here knows where Lady Estaevi might be found currently."

"Unfortunate, but not entirely unexpected," Namid said. "I suppose we'll just have to ask when we get to the next town. What's the town's name, anyway?"

"Breln, my lady. Likely they'll be able to help you. The town is one of Lady Estaevi's holdings."

"Thank you for trying to get the information for me."

He gave her an astonished look and managed to stammer, "You're welcome."

When she turned her attention to her companions, he hurried off.

Aahmes leaned close. "Poor fellow. Whatever did you say to him?"

"Uh, 'thank you'."

"Well there's the trouble." He grinned at her and mounted his horse.

The others mounted also, and they waited for the commander to join them.

Cahodre bowed when she arrived. "I have here a letter of passage for you," she said. She handed it to Aahmes when he held out a hand for it. "It just confirms that you have indeed passed through this post. However, if I might have your names to complete the letter?"

Aahmes read it over and passed it to Namid. It was exactly what the commander said, and sending out a brief tendril of Power only confirmed that for Namid. No hidden surprises. She handed it back to the commander.

"Of course," she said.

They followed the commander back to her office. There Namid introduced them all by the noble names they had chosen for themselves, and spelled them as needed, while the commander stood at her desk, with the door open, to write on the letter. Namid and her companions waited outside, still mounted. Cahodre blew lightly on the ink to help it dry and returned the letter to Namid.

"My thanks, my lady. What else can we do for you to make your journey more pleasant?"

Namid glanced at each of her companions, but no one seemed to think of anything they needed.

"We require nothing else. Thank you." She inclined her head to the woman and turned her horse toward the road into Navele as all the guards again bowed to them.

"Let's go," Namid said just loud enough for her

companions to hear and they trotted down the road until they were out of sight of the post.

"They do like to keep track of people, it seems," Mehratar said.

"Good thing we came up with our names last night," Inezha added.

CHAPTER 22

They reached Breln in the late afternoon and took rooms at an inn the gate-guard recommended to them: an inn exclusive to the nobility. After they changed into their finery, they visited a tailor that the innkeeper recommended to purchase two more sets of fine clothes each, one of them quality traveling clothes. The poor tailor was in a dither at receiving so many orders at once, but calmed some when they assured him that alterations to half-made garments he already had in his shop would be sufficient. Namid also handed over a couple of the small gems to allow him to hire help, which pleased him and calmed him even further.

While a strain for Aahmes to maintain the multiple glamours, he said that he would manage until they got their new clothes. But it would be easier if he did not have to hold them all the time. So they limited the times they ventured out of the inn, and all went together when they did.

After the tailor delivered some of their new clothes the third day they were in town, Aahmes dropped the glamour on their clothing. He refreshed the one on everyone's features, and announced he planned to rest the afternoon in his room.

The other three headed out to see what information they could find about Lady Estaevi.

Their attire and pendants won them visits with the minor nobles in town and they soon learned that Lady Estaevi was currently in her house in Urel, a town about a day and half away. She usually resided there for the spring, then moved on to Mezeft for the summer and autumn, wintering in Breln. So they had only missed her by a couple of weeks.

With this news, they waited impatiently the remaining days until the tailor completed their order, then took to the road again, this time with an additional packhorse to help carry their finery.

The innkeeper sent them off with enough food for the entire day and told them several times that he hoped they would visit again when they returned to Paronia.

They attracted more attention as they rode out of town in their new riding finery, each of them in a different color. Namid felt certain they made quite the sight and resigned herself to being on display – probably the whole time they were in Navele.

They arrived at Urel not long after midday the next day. Larger and busier than Breln, Urel also looked wealthier. The guards at the gate scrutinized their letter from the border post, their pendants and the signet ring Namid wore. They even pulled out a book and held Namid's ring close to one page within. Namid glanced over their shoulders and saw drawings of various insignias.

"That forger back in Rhadanthus would have given half his shop for that book," Aahmes murmured in her ear.

Namid nodded and smiled a little sadly at the thought of the man they both had once known.

Once the gate-guards were satisfied about their claim to nobility, they sent them into town with an escort to take them to Lady Estaevi.

During the short ride, the group attracted a lot of

attention. Namid endured it, but secretly wished herself back with the Shadowers. Aahmes kept his mount next to hers through the town and he reached over at one point and gave her hand a quick squeeze. When she looked at him, he nodded ahead to a low hill roughly in the center of town, atop which stood Lady Estaevi's grand house.

"Almost there."

Namid nodded. "None too soon."

Lady Estaevi's house in town was the largest structure they had seen there so far, but otherwise looked little different from many other buildings in town, down to the same white walls and chestnut brown roof, save for the stone wall that set it off from the rest of the town.

In the courtyard, servants took their horses and packs while the guards bowed and headed back to their duties at the gate. Other servants led them inside, where yet more servants waited with cloths in small bowls of water for them to clean the dust of travel from their hands and faces. A woman, clearly the head of the servants, approached them and curtseyed.

"Lords and Ladies, please follow me. Lady Estaevi is eager to meet with you."

She led them away from the front door and down a hall to the right to a set of closed double doors. One guard stood there. He bowed when they approached and opened one door for them.

The woman curtseyed and returned back the way she had brought them.

Namid and her companions filed through the door, which the guard then closed behind them. They found themselves in a room lined with filled bookcases. Several plush chairs formed small groupings throughout the room and lush rugs covered most of the shiny wood floor. At the far end of the room, an older woman—who looked to be of an age with Namid's father—rose from her chair in one of the larger groupings and came toward them.

"Welcome to my holdings and home. I am Lady

Estaevi Charov," she said. "Please call me Estaevi in this informal setting."

They introduced themselves, using the names they had chosen for their noble selves... Lord Fathir Naalin, Lady Saina Shartov, Lady Inezha Nazextas, and Lord Mehratar Arndu, all of them minor nobles from the realm of Paronia, and distantly related to each other. After completing the introductions all around, they followed their host to the chairs at the far end.

"Please forgive my eagerness..." Estaevi said as they seated themselves. "I'll have someone show you to your suite so you can properly refresh yourselves. But I had just had to hear right away.... Have you brought word from Kilaadi? It's been so many years since we've had word... since the tragedy.... I've feared that the Monarch and Lady Royal blamed us for what befell their sons."

"We don't exactly bring word, my lady," Namid said. "We hope to learn something more from you regarding Prince Talorisin. I can tell you that when I last spoke with the Lady Royal, my cousin, she was not contemplating condemnation. She just wishes to learn of his fate."

Estaevi nodded and seemed about to say something when a side door opened near them. A servant entered supporting a thin, pale young woman who resembled Lady Estaevi. The woman looked older than Namid. Her brown eyes held no expression, and her red-brown hair hung in dull strands. She clung to the servant's hand like a small child.

The servant's eyes widened when she saw Namid and her companions and she dropped into a quick curtsey. "Shall we return later, my lady?"

"No, no, let's not interrupt the pattern she's gotten used to. I'd like to think it brings her some comfort...."

The servant settled the woman in a chair next to Lady Estaevi and fussed over her before leaving again. The younger woman neither looked at anyone in the room nor said a word. Namid thought she seemed familiar somehow.

Estaevi shook her head slightly. "My daughter Stefe," she said. "If only she were as she used to be, she might be able to help determine what happened to your cousin."

Mehratar leaned forward with an intent expression and studied Stefe through narrowed eyes. Namid could not tell if he used Power, but she suspected it.

"How is that? What has done this to her?" Inezha said.

"I am a Healer," Mehratar said. "Perhaps I can help."

Estaevi sighed. "I would wish so, but she's seen innumerable Healers over the years. This is the best she's ever been. Before, she just lay in her bed and wouldn't even rise with help."

Namid studied the woman but could not think why she seemed familiar. She jumped when Aahmes tapped her arm.

"What is it, Saina?"

Namid shook her head. "There's something—"

They all jumped as Stefe let out a sudden shriek, her eyes wide and focused on Namid. While the others scrambled backward, shoving and overturning chairs, Stefe's scream grew louder and shriller. Both Aahmes and Namid jumped back with daggers drawn, searching the room for any threat.

Lady Estaevi's guards burst through the doors with weapons drawn, also looking for the threat. They focused on Aahmes and Namid and approached cautiously. Lady Stefe's handmaiden ran to her and attempted to calm her. Estaevi's voice cut through the clamor ordering everyone to hold.

Mehratar stepped forward and laid a hand on Stefe's forehead. Her gaze snapped to him and she stopped screaming. Then she slumped in her chair, her eyes closing.

"She'll sleep now," Mehratar told Estaevi before the latter assumed the worst.

Slowly, Aahmes and Namid sheathed their daggers and showed empty hands to the nervous guards, who only relaxed after Estaevi assured them that everything was fine. The guards did, however, position themselves inside the room by the doors.

Namid studied the sleeping woman and the memory came to her. She began to shake.

Aahmes reached a hand toward her but did not touch her. "Always wondered when you'd have that effect on someone...."

Namid choked out a sort of laugh, but still shivered. Mehratar saw her distress and hurried over. He and Aahmes guided her to a chair. There she pulled her knees up and wrapped her arms around them to try to stop the shivering. Estaevi ordered two guards to help Stefe's handmaiden return the lady to her rooms then joined the others near Namid.

"I remember..." Namid whispered. "She must have, too."

Estaevi crouched in front of Namid and gave her a stern look. "She hasn't acted this way before... not until you spoke. Explain."

Namid looked at her and fought to keep her voice steady. "She must have recognized my voice. The Dark Priests held us both... I never heard her name, nor she mine, I'm sure. But we saw each other enough... spoke sometimes...."

Mehratar lightly touched Estaevi's shoulder. "My lady let's all return to our seats... perhaps your servants could bring something to drink. As you've seen these years with your daughter, this past is very distressing to those who share it. Lady... Saina could use some time...."

Estaevi stood with a nod. "Yes, of course." She called for a servant to bring some light food and drink. She busied herself righting and rearranging the toppled chairs, then she sat and gazed at Namid.

After giving herself a severe, silent talking-to, Namid met Estaevi's gaze. Mehratar handed her a piece of warm bread and something cool in a cup.

She drank, eased her legs from their tight curl and drew a shuddering breath. She nodded at her companions and looked at Estaevi again.

"I'm sorry about Lady Stefe," Namid said. "We... those held by the Dark Priests those years ago saw and experienced horrors...."

Estaevi nodded. "You are so much better than my Stefe... perhaps what helped you might...."

A humorless laugh escaped Namid and she shook her head. "It's different for everyone, from what I've seen." She took a bite of the bread.

"I helped Saina," Mehratar said. "If you'd permit it, I'll see what I can do for your daughter."

The lady studied the Healer, then nodded. "At this point, I'm afraid to hope, but yes, please." Her gaze took in all of them. "And I've kept you too long from refreshing yourselves after your journey here. We can continue talking this evening."

She beckoned a guard over and told her to show them to their suite.

After an exchange of bows and curtseys, Namid and her companions followed the guard through the house and up a wide staircase to a suite of rooms near the top of the stairs. The guard opened the outer door for them and told them to let her know if they needed anything.

The first room they found themselves in was a lavish sitting room. Several doors led to bedrooms, one obviously for servants. All of their packs sat on the floor in the sitting room. A small table held more of the bread and cheese and drink that they had sampled downstairs.

Namid glanced at her packs, but then sank into one of the padded chairs and rested her head on the back.

Aahmes placed a thin shell of Power around the room to foil potential eavesdroppers, poured himself a drink and plopped down in another chair. He watched Namid but said nothing.

Aware of his scrutiny, Namid looked at him through

slit eyes. "Ugh," she said.

He grinned. "So you knew the Lady Stefe in Corentris?"

Namid shook her head. "Not knew her. Saw her, was all. Never knew that's who she was." She accepted a cup from Inezha.

"She is much more damaged from her time with the Dark Priests," Inezha said.

Aahmes gave her a sharp look, but Namid only shrugged, then looked around for something to change the subject. "We should probably unpack and wash up," she said, forcing some brightness into her voice. "I imagine we'll stay a couple of days, at least, if Lady Estaevi is willing."

Aahmes gave her a sidelong look. "You think Lady Stefe might be able to tell us something about Tal?"

Namid shrugged.

"It's unwise to push her currently," Mehratar said. "I'll need to take a closer look and see what help I can give her before we even consider any talk that might distress her." He gave Namid a pointed look.

She gazed back at him, then nodded.

After they finished their light repast, they separated to get cleaned up and changed for the evening meal. Before long, Namid poked her head out the door and requested a servant for each of them to help.

When the call to the evening meal came a couple of candle-marks later, they were ready. Namid and Aahmes had both chosen dark red attire, to their mutual amusement. Inezha wore the bright blue dress she had brought from Kilaadi and Mehratar wore a rich brown.

Estaevi received them in a small dining room, just the right size for the group, with one addition. Lady Stefe had joined them, seated at her mother's right hand. Her gaze still looked mostly blank, but Namid thought she detected a slight spark of life. At least Stefe ate well, if mechanically.

Estaevi kept the conversation light during the meal,

speaking of little of consequence. Namid kept her voice
low and spoke seldom, fearing to spark another screaming
fit. But the meal passed without incident.

Afterward, Estaevi led them to an even smaller room,
where the servants provided them with light wine and a
selection of sweets. Their host pulled several chairs
together and motioned for everyone to be seated. Stefe
again sat at her mother's side and now Namid was certain
she saw signs of life in her.

Estaevi first turned to Mehratar. "Lord Healer. I know
this is probably not the ideal arrangement, but would you
be able to see if Stefe is up to a short, although perhaps
trying discussion this evening?"

As she spoke, Namid watched Stefe's eyes travel slowly
over all of them. Her gaze settled on Mehratar when he
rose.

The Healer knelt in front of Stefe and lightly clasped
her hands between his own. He spoke softly to her, soft
enough that Namid did not catch what he said. At one
point Stefe gave him a slight nod. Mehratar placed a hand
on her forehead and was silent for a few breaths-of-time.
Then he turned to Estaevi.

"She is improved, mostly on her own, since we saw her
earlier," he said. "Perhaps the shock of encountering
someone from that time has helped bring her out of those
memories. I'll watch her for signs that our conversation is
too taxing."

"My thanks," Estaevi said. She leaned toward Stefe.
"Please let me know if this gets to be too much for you
and we won't continue." She covered her daughter's hand
with her own. Stefe looked at their hands and back at her
mother. Then her gaze returned to the others.

Estaevi nodded.

Keeping an eye on Stefe, Namid briefly told Estaevi
what they knew about what happened more than ten years
previously. She spoke of Estaevi's letter of invitation, what
the Lady Royal had said about the three princes' visit to

Navele and the letters exchanged, then about the three final letters that contained contradictory information about the tragedy, as Estaevi had labeled it. Estaevi listened without interruption until Namid spoke of two of the final letters that came supposedly from Estaevi and her eldest daughter.

"I have no knowledge of those letters," she said. "And some of what you've said doesn't match what I know. My eldest daughter was among those who were found dead after the attack, in the mountains to the southeast. We knew they were attacked. It was clear when we found the location. Only one person in the carnage still lived, barely, one of the Flame Warriors. All the rest of them were dead, as were most of the young people they were supposed to protect. A few were missing... Stefe here, and a couple of her cousins, and your three princes. We later learned that Stefe and her cousins had been taken by the Dark Priests. We never heard or saw anything further of the princes."

She turned to Stefe who had not moved while Namid and Estaevi spoke.

"Did you write letters to the Lady Royal?" Estaevi asked her daughter. "Perhaps the Dark Priests made you?"

Stefe looked back at her but did not answer. Estaevi glanced at Mehratar, who shook his head slightly.

"She *is* a little better," Mehratar said. "She can hear us, and I see nothing keeping her from speaking. She isn't distressed, but not entirely present here either."

"The Monarch and Lady Royal did receive one final letter that said that the princes had joined the Dark Priests," Namid said. "It came from someone called Wesh—"

"No!" Stefe stiffened in her chair at the name and began to shake. She jerked her head from side to side and moaned.

Mehratar sprang to her side and calmed her with a light touch of Power, but she still acted distressed. Then she froze, staring straight ahead.

"Hear my words and know them for truth," she said, but the voice was not hers. It was Wesh's. "I care not what has brought you down this path, but that you would hear this has been foretold."

Namid shivered and exchanged a horrified look with Aahmes. Not only was the voice Wesh's, but even the tone, the pattern of the words, sounded like him.

Stefe continued in Wesh's voice, "In order to foil Randoq's machinations, I have hidden Talorisin. You must find him. Seek the other survivor to find the path to your brother."

Then Stefe collapsed back in her chair, her eyes closed.

"Stefe!" Estaevi cried.

"She's all right," Mehratar hurried to offer reassurance. "She just sleeps again. Please call someone to return her to her room."

Estaevi nodded and accompanied the servants who took her daughter from the room. As she left, she asked the four to await her return.

"She... he... said 'your brother'," Inezha said.

Namid nodded. "Yeah. Seems I'll be letting Estaevi know who I really am," she said. Then to Aahmes, "Please remove my glamour when I say so. But only mine. I don't want to reveal any more than we have to."

Aahmes nodded.

Estaevi returned less than a quarter candle-mark later and grabbed a cup of wine before she took her seat again.

She gave them a stern look. "Perhaps there's more that you haven't yet told me?"

Namid nodded, then glanced at Aahmes, who dropped her glamour. Estaevi straightened in surprise.

"I'm Tal's younger sister," Namid told her. "My mother asked for my help to learn of Tal's fate. Because there are still some Dark Priests about, I'm traveling as only a cousin to protect myself and my task."

Estaevi nodded. "What about my daughter? What was that?"

"Apparently a message left for me." Namid studied Estaevi. "There are a number of intertwining and conflicting plots that we know of. This now seems yet another part of that. I can tell you more details… but I'd not like to embroil you any more than you already are."

Estaevi gulped the rest of her wine and poured herself more. She studied them all and nodded to Namid.

"I agree. While part of me wishes to hear what's going on, I have a duty to my holdings and people and this sounds too dangerous for us to handle. Stefe is my only remaining daughter. I want to improve her fate, not endanger her further."

She gave Mehratar a pleading look. "And please do all that you can for her. I'll be forever in your debt."

"Of course. She should sleep this night. Then I'll see her in the morning and see what more I can do."

Estaevi inclined her head to him. "My thanks."

She turned then to Namid. "What help I can give is yours. But please understand that I'm eager to see you on your way as soon as possible."

Namid glanced at her companions then turned back to their host. "Of course. I wouldn't see any further troubles fall on you or your house. So please, continue to treat us as just visiting minor nobles, as what you see."

~Please bring my glamour back,~ Namid told Aahmes with thought-speech. She grinned at Estaevi's start of surprise.

"I will leave you for the evening, then," Estaevi said. "If you need anything, my servants are ready to assist."

With a nod, she left them again.

"How soon will we be leaving, then?" Inezha said.

Namid turned to Mehratar. "Do you know yet how long you'll need with Stefe?"

The Healer shook his head. "But I'll know after I see her in the morning."

"Good enough," Namid said. "Tentatively, I'd say we'll stay only another day. Probably. I don't want to linger too long anywhere anyway."

"But then where?" Inezha said. "How are we to find this survivor? I assume it's that surviving Flame Warrior…."

Aahmes chuckled. "If it's who we think, Saina and I… we're going to be having a talk with Haeith."

CHAPTER 23

When Namid wandered into the shared sitting room late the next morning—barefoot and enjoying the feel of the lush rugs under her feet—she found Aahmes already there. She paused to admire the sight before her.

Aahmes lounged in one of the padded chairs with his feet propped on another. He wore just a loose white shirt and snug brown trousers. His feet were bare also. He ate with one hand, while in the other he held a slim book. A plate filled with food sat on a small table next to him. He seemed engrossed in his reading but after several long breaths-of-time he peered at Namid over the top of his book.

"Like what you see?" he said with a grin.

With an impish grin of her own, Namid deliberately took a long look at him from head to toe, admitting to herself that she did indeed like what she saw. Then she just padded to the table along the wall that held a variety of foods for breakfast. He chuckled.

"You seem to have settled in here," she said as she filled a plate for herself. "What're you reading?"

"Some warrior's writings from a couple hundred years ago or so about various aspects of warfare and how they apply to tactics and strategy," Aahmes said without looking up again from his book.

"Oh," Namid said as she took a chair nearby. "Light reading, then. Planning a war?"

"You never know."

"Where're the others?" Namid said.

"Mehratar's been with the Lady Stefe almost since we woke up. Inezha went with him."

"Any idea how Stefe's doing?" Namid said.

Aahmes set his book aside and pulled his plate into his lap. "Not yet. But the servant who came to escort Mehratar didn't seem upset."

Namid nodded.

"What more do we need from here?" Aahmes said.

Namid considered that while she ate.

"I feel bad about Stefe, but only Mehratar has a chance of doing anything for her, so we'll need to see how long he needs. Otherwise, we can see if Lady Estaevi knows where Haeith is, or at least Cameni. If not, we find out if the Flame Warriors maybe have a place they call their own and try—"

The outer door opened and Mehratar peered in.

"Good, you're awake," he said to Namid. "I think Stefe wants to see you. She keeps asking to speak to the 'Lady with the voice from the caves'. I assume that means you."

Namid and Aahmes exchanged looks, Aahmes smirking just a bit. Namid shook her head at him but knew he probably would pull out this new name for her at the most inopportune time.

"Do you know why?" Namid said, setting her plate aside.

"No, but she's still improved over when we first saw her. I think some spell was set in her, much like we've seen before, and somehow the sound of your voice set it off."

"Great," Namid muttered and headed for the door.

"You might want some shoes," Aahmes said.

Namid stopped. "Oh. Right."

Properly shod, she followed Mehratar and a servant through the halls to a large suite of rooms nearly at the other end of the house. The servant left them there, with Inezha, Stefe, and a couple of other servants.

Namid studied Stefe as she approached her. The older woman still looked pale, but her expression was more animated than before, and she looked back at Namid with clear eyes. Namid sat in the empty chair in front of her.

Stefe leaned forward to clasp her hand with her own cold ones. "I can't believe you've finally come," Stefe said. "Although you look different... no matter. I'm finally free. I thank you."

"Free? How do you mean, free?" Namid said. "Can you tell us anything more about the message?"

Stefe gave her head a violent shake and settled again. "He... that Wesh... set the spell, the message in me, but I don't know what it was. Although I do remember something odd. He seemed distraught and uncertain. He almost seemed frightened of me. And he kept muttering to himself, 'What does the Seer know that I don't?'" She shrugged. "Other than that, he made sure I knew that I would have to stay until I heard the voice of the intended recipient. You."

"Stay?" Namid repeated, feeling a sudden sense of unease. She darted a glance at Mehratar, who hurried to Stefe's side and placed a hand on her arm. Namid felt his Power flow out to surround the woman.

"Where would you go?" Inezha said.

Stefe glanced at Mehratar's hand and shook her head at him. "Won't make a difference now. I feel it unraveling...."

Alarmed, afraid she knew what was happening, Namid shouted to the servants to get Estaevi. Then she reached out with her own Power... and found a rapidly disintegrating mesh of Power around Stefe that reminded her of the link that Andrin held to keep the Monarch alive.

Inezha backed up to the far side of the room, her eyes

wide. Namid grasped Mehratar's arm and offered her Power ready for his use.

"Pull all you need," she told him. "Or tell me what I can do...."

He nodded and she felt him draw on her Power to bolster what he was doing. But she could not tell what that was.

Stefe slumped in the chair and her breathing slowed. "All I know is that his Seer is a woman...."

Estaevi burst into the room, wild eyed, and ran to her daughter's side. Namid linked to Mehratar so he could pull whatever Power he needed, then she backed away and joined Inezha across the room.

Namid could not hear what was said, but she saw Stefe say something to her mother. Estaevi said something to Mehratar, who shook his head.

"No," Namid whispered. Inezha clasped her arm tightly and watched with a sorrowful expression. Namid blinked against tears.

Estaevi said something more to Stefe then wrapped her daughter in her arms, her shoulders shaking. Mehratar backed away, his head hanging. He gave Namid and Inezha one glance of misery and left the room.

Namid and Inezha exchanged a look and followed. In the hall, Namid watched Mehratar speak briefly with Aahmes, who seemed to have been coming to join them. Aahmes clapped Mehratar on the shoulder and watched him walk away. He then turned to the two women as they joined him. At his questioning look, Namid shook her head.

"Let's get back to our rooms," she said in a quiet voice.

They found Mehratar slumped in a chair in the sitting room, sipping a glass of wine. After the others also poured themselves some wine and joined him, he looked up.

"She spoke truly," he said in a rough voice. "Nothing I did made any difference. The spell, the Power this Wesh set in her, was keeping her alive only for her to deliver the message." He frowned at his feet.

"To me," Namid said. She exchanged a glance with Aahmes, wondering if his thoughts were headed the same direction as hers.

"We'd better pack our things," Aahmes said, just as she had been thinking. "I'd not be surprised if Lady Estaevi won't want us to stay any longer."

Inezha looked from Aahmes to Namid. "Why wouldn't she...? Oh. She'd blame us because the message was for you?"

"It's possible she might feel that way," Namid said. "But even if she doesn't, I doubt she'll want the company of a group of—essentially—strangers in her house right now."

"But don't we need to find out from her where to find this survivor?" Inezha said.

Namid shrugged. "We can probably ask just about anyone where to find Cameni, or at least her father. If Haeith isn't still guarding Cameni, we can go from there."

They scattered to gather their belongings. As they piled their packs in the sitting room a knock came on the door. Namid answered it.

Estaevi stood there, looking haggard and much older than before. She briefly met Namid's gaze, then her eyes slid away.

Namid stepped back to allow her to enter the sitting room. "I'm so very sorry," she said as Estaevi walked past her. The lady nodded, glanced at their stacked packs, then gazed at each of them in turn.

She sat in the nearest chair and fixed her gaze on Mehratar. "I need to understand this." She glanced at Namid, then. "Not all the plots, but what they did to my Stefe. It was the Dark Priests, wasn't it?"

Namid nodded.

"We know that some of them can set Power, a spell, in a person, for a specific purpose," Mehratar said. "I have some experience eliminating such things. But I've never, before today, seen anything like what they did here."

"Two we know for sure have done this sort of thing," Namid said. "One is dead. Wesh. The one who set the spell in Stefe. He's probably responsible for her condition that required Power to keep her alive. The other still currently lives. He has set something similar on my father—"

"The Monarch?" Estaevi turned sharply to her. Mehratar and Inezha also gave her sharp looks.

Namid nodded.

Estaevi nodded too, her expression thoughtful. "I see you're preparing to leave. Probably for the best…."

"One bit of help you can give us… if you would, before we go?" Namid said.

Estaevi's expression told Namid she felt she had given too much already, but she nodded for Namid to continue.

"Do you know where we can find Lady Cameni Jiang?"

"What would you have from our Earl's daughter?" Estaevi said.

"Only information," Aahmes said. "She knows us, and she might be able to help us find this survivor that Wesh's message spoke of."

Estaevi studied them all and gave a slight nod. "I don't know where Lady Cameni is currently. I'd heard she was away somewhere. I don't know whether she's returned home yet. But I can direct you to her father's house. It's in the south, in the city of Kezenae. Like me, Earl Navele spends time in his various houses throughout his holdings, throughout the realm of Navele. But right now, he's there. And should still be there when you get there in about two weeks."

She rose and inclined her head slightly to them. "I don't think we'll speak again before you depart. I wish you a good journey and success in your endeavors. I'll instruct my staff to provide you with a map and any provisions you might need. I expect you'll make an expedient departure." Then she left, closing the door behind her.

They all exchanged looks.

"That could have gone much worse," Aahmes muttered.

"Yeah," Namid said and grabbed her packs. "Let's get going."

CHAPTER 24

With her chin on her knees, which she had tucked tight to her chest, her arms wrapped around them, Namid stared into the fire. She watched the flames form columns, break apart, and twist in the slight breeze. Two days out already from Urel and none of the small group could shake the gloom that hung over them. Namid's gloom had become increasingly tinted with an anger she could not shed.

She squeezed her eyes shut and still saw the flames. With a touch of Power, she sent them writhing across the logs, twisting into knots, breaking apart violently. They jumped when they overheated a pocket of sap. She sent them clashing against each other, but still her anger smoldered, much like the coals beneath the logs.

She opened her eyes again to meet the gazes of her companions. Unable to sit still any longer, she jumped to her feet and paced to try to shed her anger. Just as with the fire, her actions did not help.

"Do we have an axe?" Namid said, halting her pacing. "Think I'll chop some wood for the fire."

"Why not just use your Power?" Inezha said. "Wouldn't it be easier?"

"Probably," Namid said. "But I need to *do*

something…."

"There's nothing any of us could have done differently," Mehratar said, speaking to the source of their gloom. "She was truly dead long ago. Only the Power held her until she could deliver that message."

"And even *dead*, they're still controlling people, ruining their lives," Namid fumed. "What more will we run into? What of this Seer of Wesh's? Is she out there knowing everything we're going to do, plotting to thwart us? How can anything we do make *no* difference?"

"That's not how that Power works," Mehratar said.

"Oh?" Aahmes said.

From her seat next to Aahmes, Inezha looked at the Healer with interest.

Mehratar shook his head. "It's the rarest of the abilities of Power," he said. "Seers can perceive the best actions to take that lead toward achieving a very specific goal. They don't see any sort of fated future. I don't think there is such a thing."

"So Wesh's Seer would have known what he wanted to achieve, and she could see the exact actions he needed to take to get there," Namid said as she tried to wrap her thoughts around such a use of Power.

"Even actions to take in case he didn't achieve his main goal," Aahmes said. "Judging by that message he left."

"Not the *exact* actions, from what I've heard," Mehratar said. "More something like 'be in the corner tavern on the second day of spring', I believe. The person trying to follow the Seer's guidance still must decide exactly what they'll do to further their ambitions."

Namid paced again. "That's still very bad—"

"It's not completely certain," Mehratar said. "She sees the best actions to take to most likely lead to the goal. She would have known which possible actions were best, but not certain. A likelihood, not a guarantee."

"So maybe this Seer just gives someone better luck at their endeavors," Inezha said.

Mehratar nodded. "Something like that."

"But she's out there somewhere," Namid said. "What if she's a Dark Priest?" She whirled around to glare at her companions. "What if she's working with Andrin?"

Aahmes slid Inezha's hand from his arm and walked over to Namid. "Spar with me," he said.

"What?"

"Spar with me. Work off some of your anger. Before you set fire to something." He waved a hand at the thin forest around them.

Namid glared at him, then gave a sharp nod.

"No Power," Aahmes said as he shed his cloak. "And no daggers." He dropped his blades atop his cloak.

"Works for me," Namid said, likewise shedding her blades and cloak.

They stepped away from the fire into a small clearing a short distance away. Mehratar and Inezha followed but stayed at the edge of the clearing.

Aahmes sent a wave of Power out across the ground to sweep away loose rocks and sticks. As he and Namid faced off, he set a few dim Power orbs in the branches of the trees at the edges of the clearing to give them some light.

~*Talk to me,*~ he said then in thought-speech.

And he beckoned her with a taunting gesture the Shadowers often used on opponents.

Namid responded with a rush... fists, feet, knees.

Aahmes blocked and redirected her attacks but did not attack back.

Namid glared at him, already feeling somewhat better. Not that she would tell him that he had been right.

"Fight back," she growled as he continued to block her attacks but made no move to retaliate.

"See if you can hit me," Aahmes said. ~*And talk.*~

~*They used her, then killed her!*~ Namid shouted in thought-speech as she attacked again.

~*They've been doing that for years.*~ He blocked her and backed up, opening some space between them.

She charged him and attacked wildly, with little of her usual skill. *~They use everyone. Nothing seems to stop it! Wesh is dead and* still *he used that poor woman. He shouldn't have been able to. We can't fight that!~*

~I wager we can.~ Aahmes said as he twirled her around with a breath of Power.

"You said no Power," Namid said aloud

"Don't follow the rules. Gain an advantage…."

Namid had the feeling he was not talking just about this bout.

"Fine, then." Namid called Power to her hands and formed two daggers of flame. Aahmes grinned and copied her. And the fight continued in earnest.

~What else has you as tied up in knots as the ones you were making in the fire?~ Aahmes said, switching back to thought-speech after they exchanged several attacks and blocks.

Namid attacked again without answering, and almost got through his defense. This time, he returned the favor, sending her scuttling back to avoid his blows.

~Talk.~

~It's happened again!~ Namid shouted in thought-speech.

~What?~ Namid felt his annoyance behind the thought.

~Chased out again!~ Namid answered. *~Do you know how many times I've been cast out? For something that wasn't my fault? For something I would have stopped… would have fixed… if I could.~*

Aahmes nodded and blocked her next series of blows.

~So, we keep fighting. We're both getting better and stronger in the Power now. We can defeat this!~

~We? How can you say 'we'? You watched me for days and didn't let me know you lived. You even tried to stab me in the back. Literally!~

~I've explained that!~ Aahmes' thought-speech conveyed his frustration, shading into anger, even better than his

narrow-eyed expression.

Namid increased the pace of her attacks, and Aahmes matched her with blocks and counter-attacks just as fast.

~I trusted you! But Dar was right. And you can't even stand to be near me if there's a chance that anyone around might notice!~

Aahmes stopped cold, with a surprised expression. He dropped his guard. "What?"

Namid lunged at him and he barely avoided her attack. Then he let his flame daggers wink out and caught her wrists, stopping her. "Remember what I told you when you were a tyro about grappling with someone stronger than you," he said.

Namid glared. "I remember." She twisted suddenly and knocked them both off balance. They fell and rolled together across the clearing. One of her flame daggers came too close and scorched a line on his arm. She glimpsed Mehratar start toward them, then he stopped. Namid let the blades go and ignored Mehratar's attempt to get her attention.

They came to a stop almost at the edge of the clearing, lying face to face, mere finger-widths apart. Aahmes still gripped one of her wrists, a hold she easily broke. Namid looked into Aahmes' gray-brown eyes and for a breath-of-time lost track of what they had been yelling about. Then she remembered and frowned at him.

~I've seen it,~ Namid told him. *~How you're always looking to see if anyone's there to see us. Yet you and Inezha—~*

~No. She's noth—~

~You let her close….~

Aahmes shook his head and rolled away, avoiding her gaze. He ended up standing a short distance away, his back to her. Namid glimpsed Inezha and Mehratar giving them questioning looks, but they both stayed at the edge of the clearing.

~I'd thought we—~

~I… can't! I don't dare!~ Aahmes brushed his hair back with one hand but still did not turn back to her. *~You don't*

know—~

Namid scooted around him, rising to her feet, and planted herself right in front of him. ~*Then tell me. You said we fight back. But then you run from any 'we together'! So talk!*~

~*I can't let….*~

~*You can't let… what?!*~ She wanted to grab him and shake him but held back.

He turned away, but she did grab his arm then and pulled him back around. ~*Can't let me what? What is it?*~

He glared at her, shook his arm free of her grasp and backed away from her.

~*I can't let— can't have— If they know….*~ He gave her a desperate look, wild-eyed, as he shouted at her in thought-speech. ~*They'll kill you, too! I care for you… about you… too much! I can't let— I won't see that kill you!*~ A sense of his fear and horror at the last thought came to her behind his words, mixed with a wave of strong attraction and desire.

Namid glared back at him. ~*I care for you, too,*~ she shouted right back in thought-speech. ~*Probably too much! And I have no intention of letting anything or anyone kill me. Haven't you noticed that by now? You were the one who just said to keep fighting….*~

They stared at each other, then Aahmes dropped to the ground and rubbed at his temples with his fingers.

"What have I done?" he muttered.

Namid dropped down in front of him, within reach, but did not touch him. "You finally told me something important," she said.

"I shouldn't have—"

Namid punched him in the shoulder. Not too hard. "*Talk to me.*"

Aahmes rubbed at the spot she had punched and shook his head. His gaze met hers then slid away. She did not remember ever seeing him look so miserable before.

"Before I came to Rhadanthus, my entire clan was killed, as you know." He spoke looking at the ground. "What I didn't tell you was that it didn't happen all at once. I returned home one evening after spending the day with our herds to find my family brutally slaughtered in our home. My parents. My brothers and sisters. Even little Taakha still in her crib…."

He glanced at her and the deep anguish in his eyes cut right through her.

"I ran to my uncle's home. They took me in while the clan tried to find out what happened… determine whether it was bandits. Or what. They finally decided it was related to the leadership dispute that was going on. Although usually such things didn't turn so bloody."

Aahmes dropped his head to his hands. "A week later, again while I was away from the house, the same thing happened to my uncle and his family. And it happened again, just a few weeks later… one more time, to another relative who took me in. After that, I just ran and hid. But that didn't stop the slaughter. Before the next winter, my entire clan lay dead. Murdered. Everyone I had cared for. So, I ran further away. Much further."

He glanced at Namid again and switched back to thought-speech. *~Everyone I care for is killed. Look what happened to Dar. I can't— I can't see that happen to you.~*

Namid studied his bowed head. *~So the apparent animosity, the scorn….~*

He nodded. *~A way to show that you were nothing to me, to keep anyone from guessing otherwise. A way to keep that from happening to you. To try to keep from caring for you….~*

"The same thing happened in that village that sheltered me after Corentris," Aahmes whispered. "All of them…."

Namid sat back on her heels and shook her head. She tried to get her thoughts in order to absorb all this, but they kept tumbling around.

When Aahmes looked at her again, she tilted her head slightly and gave him an impish grin.

"We're stronger together, I think you said," she said. *~And I do like what I see. Even 'care for it', you might say,~* she added in thought-speech.

Aahmes chuckled. *~You did say. But then so did I….~*

~Even emphatically….~

Aahmes grinned. *~Well, yeah….~*

"So, where from here?" he added aloud.

"Fight, like you said. Even if this Seer is setting events against our goal, we fight through and fix what we can. And don't follow the rules."

"Break the pattern of exiling," Aahmes said.

Namid nodded. *~Now, about Inezha….~*

Aahmes groaned and ducked his head. She leaned closer to confirm what she thought she saw. His cheeks *had* darkened. *~Are you* blushing?*~*

Aahmes shook his head. *~She's made several rather… specific… suggestions.~*

~Oh? And….~

~Nothing! I'm not— not with——~ Aahmes turned away and brushed his hair back with one hand.

Namid felt his discomfort behind his thought-speech. *~She's had her eye on you almost since we first met her. Remember she sat with you every evening fest with Staehw's van.~*

~I remember.~ He shook his head again. *~She'll see from this point that I'm not——~*

Mehratar and Inezha joined them then, both wearing stern expressions.

Mehratar took in the burn on Aahmes' arm and the weary looks on both their faces and his expression eased to more of a questioning look. Inezha stood with hands on her hips and continued to glare at both of them.

"What was that?" she said.

Aahmes stood and claimed Namid's hand to help her to her feet. And he did not let go of her hand afterward.

"Just a few things to talk out," he said.

Mehratar looked from one of them to another. "About time," he muttered, softly enough that they could all pretend they had heard nothing. Louder, he told Aahmes that he would see to his burn over by the fire where the light was better.

"Talking by staring at each other?" Inezha said.

"Talking through the Power," Namid said.

Inezha glanced at their clasped hands, then studied both of their faces. Her stern expression softened into a thoughtful one. She turned away and returned to the dying fire, a few steps behind Mehratar. Aahmes and Namid followed at a slower pace. ·

"And what of Mehratar?" Aahmes whispered to Namid.

"What of...? No.... Mehratar? You think...?"

"I've seen the intent looks he gives you," Aahmes said.

Namid shook her head and gave Aahmes a sidelong look. "I've seen the glares you've been giving him."

He chuckled.

"If you'll notice, he does that with everyone," Namid said. "Gives them his full attention with the intent look. It's a little unnerving, actually."

Aahmes just grinned, then gave her a serious look. "So, did it work?"

"Did *what* work?"

"Do you feel a little better? Ready to take up the fight again? Maybe not so ready to burn down our campsite with twisted fire knots?" He held his serious expression, but his lips twitched just a bit.

She studied his face, waiting to see how long he could hold the expression. Finally, he grinned.

Then she nodded. And leaned her head against his shoulder.

"I've told you," he said. "I've got your back. Even when it means I have to fight you."

Namid grinned.

Chapter 25

A little less than two weeks after they left Urel, the four approached the city of Kezenae. Aahmes had used the travel technique a few times to hasten their journey without unduly tiring himself. The weather had settled firmly into spring and the roads had dried from the winter melt. They had ridden out of the thin forest a few days earlier and now crossed rolling green hills, similar to those near Rhadanthus, but much greener than that area ever got.

They paused atop one of the taller hills to look over what they could see of the city from their vantage point.

"I think it's larger even than Kilaadi," Namid said.

"The guards at the gate look very attentive," Inezha said. "Is the glamour still holding?"

Aahmes nodded. "And thanks to that technique from Mehratar, it takes hardly any Power and little attention. Now if Namid would only manage to hold her own...."

She scrunched her nose at him. "You know I've been trying."

He grinned.

"Expecting trouble here?" Mehratar said.

"I wouldn't think so," Namid said. "We should be able

to find out what we need without having to reveal the real reason behind our inquiries to anyone we don't already know."

Inezha studied the city. "That would be Earl Navele's home, would it not?" she said and pointed to the largest building that they could see from their hill. It sat atop a high point a good distance into the city, with some smaller buildings clustered with it. And while made of the same light-brown stones as much of the rest of the city, all of the clustered buildings, largest to smallest, seemed cleaner, brighter somehow. Near that group of buildings sat several other large buildings, but none quite as imposing.

"Could be," Namid said.

"No," Mehratar said. "Look at the symbol on the flag flying above the main structure."

"A scepter?" Inezha said.

"Roivah-neheb," Mehratar said, naming the head of the pantheon of so-called gods.

Namid shifted in her saddle. "He's got a temple complex here? I thought all the temple complexes were like their own towns almost, well away from any major settlement." She frowned. "I don't like this. His priests are supposed to be Powerful. If he's allied with Ilenii and Belaraketh…."

"We'll just do this as quickly as possible," Aahmes said.

"So, no plush rooms in the lord's grand house," Inezha said with a playful pout.

Namid shook her head. "A decent inn near one of the city gates will serve us better. Just in case."

Inezha shrugged. "We already use the glamour to make people believe they see someone other than the real us. I don't see why getting the knowledge we need and then using Power to make the person forget we were even here is so very different."

Namid shook her head. "I won't force Power on someone like that. Deceiving them is one thing. The glamour is just another form of disguise and it's used on us with our knowledge. It's not using Power to change something about someone else, which trying to make them forget would be."

Inezha shrugged and rode down the road toward the city gate. The others followed.

At the gate, the guards took their names and examined their pendants and the letter from the border post. They only glanced at Namid's signet ring then let them pass, with a few recommendations for lodging.

While busy, the streets that led from the gate were wide and clean. Namid spotted some narrower streets leading off to the sides, but those too looked clean.

The first inn that the guards had recommended had no rooms available, so they needed to ride further into the city to find lodging.

Finally, the third inn they tried had two rooms available, and stabling for their mounts and pack animals. The two rooms were the only rooms on the third floor, which was smaller than the two beneath. Their rooms included a third small room—holding a table and some chairs—between the two bedrooms. After they had settled their packs into their rooms—Inezha and Namid sharing the fancier bedroom and Mehratar and Aahmes taking the plainer one—they met back in the third room.

"We still have the afternoon," Inezha said. "Do we present ourselves to Earl Navele? Maybe get invited to the evening meal? I've never feasted with an Earl." She grinned.

"Maybe," Namid said. "Although we really need Haeith, which probably means getting to Cameni, and she won't know us by looking at us. Might not recognize our names, if we give the noble names we're using…."

Inezha grinned wider. "Except for mine. So, I'll speak for us to get us to Cameni." She jumped up and grabbed Mehratar's arm. "Be my escort. Let's go!"

Namid rose, too. "We'll all go." She looked everyone over and nodded. "The glamour's still holding—nothing like what happened in Kilaadi—and we look presentable enough."

~ ~ ~

The innkeeper directed them to the Earl's house and encouraged them to use the inn's carriage to travel there, for an extra fee, of course. After seeing his horrified reaction at even the thought that nobles would walk about the city, they paid for the carriage and a driver.

The ride took more than a half candle-mark but gave them a good view of that portion of the city. Few streets ran straight for long, so they saw several different areas of shops and houses on their way. When they reached their destination, they found themselves at the second-largest building in the city. And just across the street from Roivah-neheb's temple complex.

They stepped out of the carriage on the side away from the temple and Namid checked that the glamours still held. She sent the carriage back to the inn after everyone clambered out.

With one hand firmly clasping Mehratar's arm, Inezha led the way to the closed, wrought-iron gate of the Earl's dwelling. Aahmes took Namid's hand and they followed.

The guards within the courtyard on the other side of the gate approached to meet them but made no move to open the gate.

Inezha gave them one of her bright smiles.

"Ah, such prompt attention," she said. "Splendid. Inform the Lady Cameni that I, Lady Inezha Nazextas, have arrived for a surprise visit."

The guards bowed and the one with the most decoration on his uniform doublet stepped closer. "She left no word for us to watch for you, my lady," he said. "Is the Lady Cameni expecting you?"

Inezha waved her hand in the air and laughed. "Of course not, silly man! What would be the fun in surprising my good friend if she expected me?" She made a shooing motion at one of the other guards. "Now you just run on inside and let her know we're here."

The guard bowed but looked to his commander and hesitated. The commander bowed again to Inezha. "Of course, my lady. May we pass along your companions' names as well?"

Inezha glanced back at Namid and Aahmes. Namid nodded and stepped up.

"Of course, commander," she said and gave him their noble names. With a wave, the man sent two of the guards running inside.

"Please wait just a breath-of-time my lords and ladies. With the recent troubles, Earl Navele is cautious about anyone asking about any of his sons and daughters."

"Of course," Mehratar murmured.

Namid wondered what troubles the guard meant.

After less than a quarter candle-mark, there was a fuss across the courtyard and Cameni rushed toward the gate, with Enric close on her heels. She looked them all over with a confused expression, seeing no faces she recognized. When Inezha exuberantly greeted her, Cameni gave her an astonished look, then smiled and waved at the guards to open the gate.

"My dear Inezha!" she exclaimed. "I hadn't thought to find you at my father's gate. You look so—"

"So lovely," Enric broke in. "Quite the surprise to see you like this."

Both Enric and Cameni glanced at Namid, Aahmes and Mehratar, and of course, saw three other people they did not know. Namid smiled to herself. With the glamour effectively concealing her identity, and Aahmes', Cameni and Enric were in for a surprise beyond Inezha.

"Welcome!" Cameni said to them and introduced herself and Enric. Then she turned back to Inezha. "Have you any word—"

"Of course I have news for you!" Inezha interrupted

her. "But shall we not take ourselves inside to better converse?"

~*Ouch! That one almost hurt,*~ came Aahmes' voice to Namid in thought-speech.

She stifled a grin.

Shouting and sounds of a scuffle drew everyone's attention to Roivah-neheb's temple complex across the street. At one of the doors a small crowd had gathered and seemed to be fighting with some of Roivah-neheb's people. Namid thought she saw Ilenii's symbol on armbands worn by some of the combatants. Were the followers of the so-called gods now fighting each other, too? After watching the scuffle grow worse, the guards at Cameni's house ushered everyone into the courtyard and closed the gate.

Namid and her companions followed Cameni and Enric into the imposing house through a side door. Cameni led them through a small maze of hallways and rooms to a pleasant room that opened on a small, lush garden. She waved everyone to seats by the open doors and sent a servant for refreshments.

While Inezha chatted about inconsequential things, Aahmes paced to the open doors and studied the area nearby and the garden.

~*Looks clear out here,*~ he told Namid using thought-speech then unobtrusively placed a shell of Power around the room before he took the seat next to Namid.

Namid's attention was drawn back to the conversation when Inezha told Cameni and Enric that she had brought another surprise. With a grin, she waved dramatically at Aahmes and Namid. Both Cameni and Enric gave them quizzical looks, and at that moment two servants entered with food and drink.

So everyone busied themselves with getting cups of wine and small plates of good things to nibble until the servants left.

"Can we be heard in here?" Inezha said.

Cameni and Enric exchanged looks and both shook their heads.

Mehratar sent out a small wave of Power then gave Namid a nod. "No one nearby," he said.

~*Please drop my glamour just a breath-of-time,*~ Namid told Aahmes.

Cameni squeaked when Namid's features became her own and Enric exclaimed aloud.

"Namid!"

Namid made shushing motions as she felt her glamour return, then endured Cameni's impulsive hug. "Please, I'm Saina while I'm here."

"But, why?" Cameni said. "And how…." She peered at Mehratar and Aahmes.

"Quietly, please," Namid said. "And there's one more thing for you to see before I get into the why…."

She nodded to Aahmes, who briefly dropped his own glamour.

Enric gasped and Cameni staggered back with a stunned expression. Then they swarmed Aahmes, making sure he was really there and demanding explanations.

Mehratar just sat back and watched everyone with an amused smile, turning his intent gaze from one to another. Inezha grinned with delight. Aahmes gave Namid an entreating look and a pained smile. She just grinned back.

"Such a grand surprise I brought, don't you agree?" Inezha said.

"Please, quietly," Namid said. "And we'll explain."

"I just can't believe it!" Cameni said, her gaze still on Aahmes, even with his glamour restored, as she returned to her seat. "We looked for you—"

"Na— Saina blasted a huge hole in the debris to try to find you—" Enric said.

Aahmes nodded. "She's told me—"

"How long have you known?" Cameni demanded of Namid.

"Why the disguise?" Enric said.

"And who are you?" Cameni said to Mehratar. "Someone else in disguise?"

Aahmes momentarily dropped Mehratar's glamour so Cameni and Enric could meet the real him.

"If you'll settle a bit, we'll tell you," Namid said and took a large gulp of her wine as everyone settled back into their chairs.

She and Aahmes told Cameni and Enric about happenings since they had last seen each other. They kept the explanations as succinct as possible while trying to have the tale make sense. Still, the telling took them late into the afternoon and they still had not come to their reason for seeking out Cameni.

"It's getting late," Cameni said after the tale had reached their visit to Lady Estaevi and the tragedy there. "Will you take the evening meal with us?"

Namid glanced at the darkening sky. "We'd prefer to remain as inconspicuous as possible," she said. "Your father—"

"Nothing to worry about there," Cameni said. "Father is dining with several of his nobles this evening, to discuss some business or other. And mother is away, visiting my aunts. So, the rest of us are free to do as we wish. We can dine in my private dining room. Bide a breath-of-time…."

She hurried to the door to the hall and spoke with the guard outside. While she was occupied, Enric leaned closer and spoke in a quiet voice.

"Is your reason for coming here connected to the events of last autumn? I had hoped all that was resolved…." He glanced over his shoulder at Cameni. "I believe her father is starting to look favorably on me. But, of course, whatever help you need."

"We're not here to yank you away from all this," Namid said, with a wave at the opulent room. "But we'll speak more."

She poured herself her second cup of wine for the afternoon and sipped it while staring out into the garden.

Against the background of light chatter from the others, she contemplated the situation. She did not doubt Enric sincerely meant his offer to help, but she did not see dragging anyone else further into this. It would be bad enough if they took Haeith from Cameni.

And she worried what the so-called gods were doing. While she would like to believe that Aahmes' glamour was truly keeping them hidden from their attention, she feared that they had that much more knowledge and experience with the Power that they only toyed with them... giving her and Aahmes the impression that they were safe. Were they just playing with them while they prepared some devastating attack?

Cameni returned and led them all into the depths of the house to a lovely small dining room, where servants brought a variety of foods for them to choose from. After everyone had filled their plates, the servants left the rest of the food on a side table and filed out the door.

A few bites into the meal, Cameni fixed Namid with a stern look. "Time again to tell the rest," she said and smiled at the reminder of past discussions that her words invoked.

Namid nodded and swallowed the food suddenly gone tasteless in her mouth.

"The message Wesh left for me said to seek the survivor," Namid said. "I think that's the survivor of the attack that devastated the group my brothers traveled with. I need to speak with Haeith. He might be able to help—"

"Haeith?" Cameni broke in. "How can—"

"Because I used to be a Flame Warrior," came Haeith's voice from the doorway to the hall.

Cameni looked astonished. "Wha— You're supposed to be in the north...."

Namid studied the warrior as he closed the door behind him. He looked much the same as last autumn except he wore only a simple black tunic and trousers, instead of his habergeon. And he did not have his great-sword with him. He looked over everyone at the table, and Namid saw his hands tremble. Then his eyes widened as his gaze came to Aahmes.

With his experience with illusions and semblances, he must have seen right through Aahmes' glamour, Namid thought.

Haeith took a step toward them and uncharacteristically stumbled. Extreme fatigue flashed across his features and was gone again.

Both Cameni and Mehratar jumped up and hurried to help him to a seat at the table. Cameni poured him some wine and filled a plate for him. Mehratar studied Haeith with that intent gaze of his while Cameni got the food and he placed a hand lightly on Haeith's forehead.

Cameni looked at Mehratar in surprise, then narrowed her eyes. Namid sensed she used her Power to watch what Mehratar was doing.

"You do know how dangerous it is to deplete yourself so much," Mehratar said as he returned to his seat.

Haeith looked better, now merely exhausted rather than ready to crumple to the ground. He nodded and began to eat. After several bites and a good long drink of wine he gave Aahmes a slight nod.

"Your glamour is well done," he said.

Aahmes nodded acknowledgement of the compliment.

"You're a Healer," Cameni said to Mehratar.

"And still she states the obvious so well," Aahmes said with a grin. Inezha chuckled.

"*Now* I believe he's back with us," Enric said.

Cameni just continued to eat but glared at both Enric and Aahmes.

"Yes," Mehratar responded to Cameni's comment. "I finished my studies some years before you studied at Jelth's temple complex."

Namid groaned. "Right, the temple...."

"What?" Cameni demanded.

"You haven't heard?" Aahmes said.

Cameni looked from one of them to the other. "No…."

"All right," Enric said with a slight grin. "Just tell us the rest. Whatever it is you're so reluctant to share."

Aahmes and Namid exchanged looks.

"I have to warn you, it's not good," Namid said. "Jelth's temple complex was destroyed a few weeks ago. We think the attack came from Belaraketh's temple complex—"

"Theomachy," Haeith said in a quiet voice.

"What?" Cameni said.

"The battles among the gods," Haeith said. "They begin again. Because of Sesaisyd's death?"

"Not exactly…" Namid said.

"When we fought the Dark Priests in Corentris," Aahmes said, "Sesaisyd showed Saina the gods' history…. They're not really gods. Just extremely Powerful mages who thought to take the gods' places but couldn't find them to oust them. They fought each other for Power for many long years, leaving us with the ones who survived, the ones we have right now. They declared themselves gods – there was no one with nearly their amount of Power to gainsay them."

"Not gods?" Cameni said, her eyes wide and her expression doubtful. "That can't be!"

"They're no more gods than Aah— Fathir and I are," Namid said.

"And you *believe* Sesaisyd?" Enric said.

"We recently heard words directly from a couple of them that support what he showed her," Aahmes said.

"And some of them are trying to eliminate Aahmes and Namid," Inezha said.

"Fathir and Saina," Namid said, emphasizing the names for their noble guise.

"That explains the glamour," Haeith said.

"You're fighting the gods?" Enric said.

"We're trying very hard *not* to fight them," Namid said.

"But if they come after us again, we *will* fight back. And they're not gods."

Enric shook his head, his expression one of disbelief. Namid also saw a hint of fear lurking in his eyes. She did not blame him for either.

Cameni stared at the table for some time, then refilled her cup and drank, giving Namid an odd look.

"So, you two could be gods…" she said.

"Yes!" Inezha said. "You see it too. So much they could make right, make people do right."

"No!" Aahmes said, and Namid seconded him.

"I'm not going to *make* people do anything, right or not. I just need to find out what happened to my brother," Namid said.

Cameni stared at Namid then turned to Haeith with a stern expression.

"You haven't yet explained yourself," she said. "You were supposed to be in the north for another couple of weeks."

He inclined his head to her. "Yes, I was. But my task there was all but complete. Only the bickering over wording, and the writing and signing were left, which the others would do better anyway. And then I knew that I was needed elsewhere." At their astonished looks, he smiled slightly. "It's a specialty of the Flame Warriors, one of the things that makes them so valuable, this ability to feel where they are needed."

"You knew we were coming here?" Inezha said. "Are you a Seer?"

Haeith looked alarmed at her question and shook his head sharply. "No, not at all. Flame Warriors are just trained to be able to notice through Power when they are needed. They can tell who and get a sense of how urgently. Then they have to figure out how to get to whomever has the need." He looked at Namid. "I recognized that it was you and that it had to do with me having been a Flame Warrior. Through the Power I knew that you traveled south, so I came here, hoping to meet you here. If I hadn't, I would've begun to search for you."

"When did you sense this need?" Mehratar said.

"About a week ago. I used various swift-travel spells to get here. Mainly yours." He nodded at Aahmes.

Cameni gave him a surprised look, and he almost smiled at her.

"Fathir's spell is most effective," he said.

"Technique," Aahmes muttered and grinned when Namid caught his eye.

Cameni waved off Aahmes' comment and again fixed her gaze on Namid. "What is it you need from Haeith? He's still in my father's service."

Namid nodded and looked at Haeith. "You might be able to just tell me what I need, if you know it." She pulled the drawing of her brother from a pocket in her gown and smoothed it out on the table in front of Haeith.

"Do you recognize him?" she said.

Haeith studied the drawing, and the others crowded around to look as well. After a several long breaths-of-time, Haeith nodded slowly. When he looked at Namid she saw the pain in his expression.

"I remember…. And I suspect you've guessed."

Namid nodded. "You were one of the Flame Warriors who guarded the group of nobles."

He nodded and tapped the drawing. "This is your brother?"

After Namid's nod, he continued. "We guards did not know their names. And we failed them. So many killed. He was one of the missing, I later learned. I was almost counted among the dead. I don't know what I can tell you to help."

"I was told to seek the survivor to find the path to my brother," Namid said. "Maybe some small thing you remember that doesn't seem important?"

Haeith fell into thought as he continued with his meal. When he finished eating, he just shook his head.

Cameni rose. "Perhaps after you've rested and recovered more completely from your journey," she said. She looked around at the others. "You're most welcome to stay here."

"We have rooms at an inn," Namid said. "We're fine there."

Cameni nodded. "I'll have a carriage take you back then and return for you in the morning."

Chapter 26

After they returned to the inn, Namid slept poorly, more often awake than asleep, for no reason she could think of. She sent out a wisp of Power to see if something in the city was the cause of her restlessness but found nothing. Finally, still a few candle-marks before dawn, she got up to stay. Inezha looked peaceful in the bed next to hers. Namid dressed in one of her gray tunics and trousers and slipped out into the sitting room.

And barely stifled a squeak when Aahmes spoke.

"Trouble sleeping, too?" he said from a chair across the room. He rose and approached her.

"Something's disturbing me, but I can't seem to figure out what it is," she said.

He took her hands in his and gave a slight tug, pulling her closer. "I can think of a few things," he said. "Being too close to one of the temples… concerns about dragging everyone along, probably into more danger. How we've not been alone…."

He raised her hands to his lips and kissed the back of each one, while holding her gaze with his own.

She smiled, pleased at the attention, and stepped closer still. "So, you meant what you shouted at me a couple of weeks ago…."

"Which part?" Aahmes said, with a mischievous expression.

Namid gave him a mock glare, and he grinned.

"Oh, *that* part," he said. "Without question."

Namid leaned closer and playfully brushed his lips with hers. Then she stepped back with a grin. "So, does that mean you apologize for all the annoyances, all the tormenting?"

He gave her a wicked look. "Well… some of it was rather fun…."

She chuckled and leaned in for a longer, proper kiss.

And a familiar Power washed over them, interrupting.

"Was that—"

"That felt like in Kilaadi," Aahmes said at the same time.

"I still see our glamours," Namid said after a quick check.

Aahmes nodded. "It didn't take them down, anyway. But I wonder—"

They both felt the surge of Power coming from the northwest. Their gazes met and together they threw together a massive shell of blended Power, attempting to blanket the whole city.

A bolt of Power slammed into their shell. They felt it crack, but it held… until a bolt from within the city flew out and shattered the whole thing.

Both Namid and Aahmes staggered and the doors to the bedrooms flew open.

"What was *that*?" Inezha said.

Mehratar hurried to Aahmes and Namid and helped them to the closest chairs.

"Another temple attack, I think," Namid whispered. Her head throbbed and even that small effort made it feel worse.

"And the counter-attack from Roivah-neheb's temple," Aahmes said as he rubbed his forehead, then leaned back against his chair with a groan.

Mehratar's light touch on Namid's forehead sent pain pounding through her head. Then his Power flowed over her and the pain eased. With a quick nod for her, he moved to Aahmes.

"And I think we just told them we're here," Namid said. She watched as Aahmes' anguished expression smoothed under Mehratar's Power. "Maybe even exactly where we are," she added

Aahmes cursed and struggled to his feet with a wince, then headed toward his packs.

"Agreed," Namid said. She stood, pleased to discover that the remaining pain got no worse. She headed to her own things and threw her stuff in her pack.

"We have to get out of here, as fast as we can," she told Inezha over one shoulder.

Inezha looked confused. "Why?" she said.

"Whoever hit their Power shell, either time, might have been able to tell they were the ones who made it," Mehratar explained from the other room.

"And if either was one of the 'gods', they'll probably be coming for us," Aahmes said.

Inezha cursed, then. Namid agreed.

After they had everything gathered, they made their way as quietly as possible down the stairs. As they passed the bar in the common room, Namid reached behind it and tucked one of the cornelian gemstones on a shelf for the innkeeper to find. It was worth several times the cost of their rooms and the boarding for the horses, so should give the innkeeper no reason to think ill of their abrupt departure.

Then the four were out in the stables, where they saddled their horses and loaded their packs. A sleepy stablehand peered out at them but returned to her bed at a murmured word of reassurance from Mehratar.

They headed toward the gate, but when they got to one of the wide main streets, odd lights from behind caught their attention, green-yellow, but otherwise flickering like flames.

"That's near Cameni's house," Inezha said.

"Yes," Namid said. "Probably the temple…."

"But it might be Cameni's house," Inezha said.

Namid gave Aahmes an anguished look, torn between returning to make sure their friends were all right and the need to get away, to draw any attacks against them away from the city.

"I know," Aahmes said.

Namid nodded. "Aahmes and I need to get out of the city, in case they can find us, in case they come after us."

"Go!" Mehratar urged her. "I can check on that." He waved a hand in the general direction of the odd lights. "I'll be able to find you after."

Inezha glanced between them with an uncertain expression. "I'll go with Mehratar," she said after a breath-of-time and took the lead of one of their packhorses.

Namid nodded and grabbed the leads of the other two packhorses. With a wave to Inezha and Mehratar, she followed Aahmes down the street toward the gate. They were forced to dodge a number of people running both directions in the street. As they rode, Namid tried to raise that semblance of nothing around them that she had learned from Haeith the previous autumn. She was not entirely successful. The horses' hooves still sounded on the hard street, but at least no one gave them a second look.

Aahmes slowed to ride next to her.

"What about the gate?" he said.

Namid considered that. "I think we have to be noisy and obvious. If anyone's paying attention or looking for us, that should tell them we've left. Then we disappear outside the city."

Aahmes nodded. "Noisy and obvious, I can do," he said. He rubbed his forehead, but then grinned at her.

Namid laughed.

They urged the horses faster and soon approached the

gate, closed, of course. Aahmes threw some kind of glamour around them that replaced Namid's semblance and directed a bolt of Power at the bar that held the gate shut, scattering the guards. Namid threw one also, and the bar disintegrated, shooting pieces high in the air, along with bright bits of Power. Aahmes threw the gate wide open with Power and they galloped through. Namid twisted to look back over one shoulder and slammed the gate shut again with the Power, making sure a bright splash of Power shot skyward.

Aahmes moved close. "Should be noisy enough. Take my hand," he said.

"What?"

"I'm starting the swift travel, but I think it'll be smoother if we're all connected by something. You have the leads, so…."

Namid clasped his hand and hoped she could hold on while staying on her speeding horse. Aahmes, of course, seemed to be having no trouble. "And now you have me," she said.

"Yes." He winked at her and wrapped them in the swift travel.

~ ~ ~

Roughly a candle-mark later, Aahmes dropped the swift travel and pulled his horse to a halt, requiring that Namid halt hers also, since he still held her hand. He gave her a weary smile, which she returned, and let go to dismount.

"Did that make it easier?" she said, also dismounting.

He nodded and plopped down in the grass on the side of the road. "Can you show me how you and Haeith formed those semblances you used last autumn? I think it's worth trying – send a semblance of us one way, while we go elsewhere under that semblance of nothingness."

Namid sat next to him. "I'll show you as well as I can," she said and took his hand again. He wrapped his other arm around her shoulders and she leaned against him. When she felt he was ready, she showed him in his thoughts—much like using the thought-speech—everything about how the semblances were set up and how they worked.

When she finished, he nodded. "I think I can duplicate what Haeith did, if you want to control the semblances of us traveling away, like you did before."

Namid nodded. "Should the semblances look like the real us, or the disguised us?"

Aahmes gave that some thought. "Disguised, I think, since we were seen in the city looking like this. In fact, I'm going to drop the glamour right now, to give any watchers the impression we have exhausted ourselves. We'll put it up again when we move. But once the semblance splits off, I'll make us new guises. We can't be 'not-there' all the time."

So he dropped their glamours and worked on creating the semblance of them not there. Namid built the semblances of them where they would not be based on the old guises he had created. They tied a joint tendril of Power to both semblances—so they both could keep track of them and work with them, if needed—and set them up, ready to go when they came to the next crossroads.

After a long kiss that promised so much more, Aahmes said, "We should go."

"I know," Namid said. "But I think you still need to redeem yourself for Foroughi, like you tried to say back at Tower Hold." With a smile, she stole one more kiss.

Aahmes chuckled, then placed their glamours on them again, but sloppily, as if still wearied, and they mounted and continued away from the city.

More than a quarter candle-mark later, when they came to a crossroads, Namid felt the semblances come alive, ready for their final direction.

Aahmes leaned close. "Which way do *we* go?"

Namid looked down each road that led from the

crossroads.

"We came from that way," she said, pointing down one road. "So I think not there. Let's send the semblances that direction." She yawned. "But I don't know which way for us. We need to talk more with Haeith…." She stifled another yawn, then started as a wave of Power washed over them.

"What was that?" she said.

They both looked back the way they had come, back toward Kezenae.

Namid squinted, trying to see better. What were those yellow sparkles in the dark? Widely scattered, they all seemed to come from the same direction.

"Let's move," Aahmes said.

Namid heard tension in his voice as he grabbed the packhorses' leads and headed off the road, toward a depression a short distance away. Namid urged her horse to a trot to stay at his side. The horses caught their sudden tension and seemed eager to move.

"I have no idea," he answered her earlier question and glanced at the sparkles that continued to come closer. "But I don't get a good sense of them…."

Namid reached out with a tiny bit of her Power. She did not recognize the feel of the Power coming toward them. The sparkles advanced faster when her bit of Power drew close to them.

"Hurry!" She urged her horse faster.

They galloped to the low spot in the grasslands. Aahmes slowed to ride into the depression, Namid right behind. She glanced toward the sparkles and saw one pass right through her horse. The animal did not react at all. And Namid saw the sparkle continue on away as if it had encountered nothing.

Before she could say anything, something hit the side of her thigh, a little above her knee. A fiery sting tore through the spot and she gasped at the pain. Aahmes turned toward her and cursed as one of the sparkles hit his upper arm. Namid slid off her horse after they all reached the deepest part of the depression. She watched the yellow sparkles whiz by overhead. They looked like narrow crystalline arrowheads, about half the length of her smallest finger.

Shooting agony in her leg took all her attention then and dropped her to the ground a short distance from the trembling animals.

"One of them hit me," Namid gasped. She tried to grab the end of the thing where it stuck out of her skin, but it just stretched out in her fingers and seemed to burrow further into her leg. She stifled a cry at the increased pain.

"Me too," Aahmes said. "What *are* these things?"

"We have to stop them," Namid said. She threw a shell around herself, tight to her skin, much as Mehratar had used to survive the attack back in his village. Then she opened the shell only at the spot the thing was buried in her leg and slid the shell within her skin until it lay beyond the point of the Power arrowhead. She sealed the shell there and hardened it as much as she could manage. When the Power arrowhead again burrowed further, it hit the shell… and stopped. She felt it pressing inward, but it went no further.

When she looked to see how Aahmes fared, she saw that he had done something similar to the spot in his arm where he had been hit.

Namid laid back, trembling. The thing could not get further into her leg, but the agony had only eased a little. She tried to force the arrowhead back out by moving the shell, but that did not work. Neither did trying to grasp it with Power to pull it out. She looked up but saw no more of the things overhead. She studied the blood that seeped through her trousers. At least *that* didn't look too bad. And when she tried to stand, she found she could, with difficulty, and even hobble around.

His injured arm hanging limply, Aahmes worked to pull the packs off the packhorses. Namid joined him, wincing at every step. Together they managed to unsaddle their mounts and get their packs, cursing softly at the stabbing pain. Namid briefly wobbled in place, then helped drag their packs off to the side.

One-handed, Aahmes helped her prop herself against the packs, then he plopped down next to her. He winced at the pain from moving but gathered her close with his good arm. She twisted so she lay slightly on one side, facing him and tucked up at his side, to keep from pressing the exposed end of the arrowhead in her leg against the ground.

"What do you say we wait to decide which direction to go?" he said, with a catch in his voice as he inadvertently moved his arm. "I'd like to see Mehratar before we try to travel further."

Namid nodded against his shoulder. "These things came from Kezenae," she said. "Or at least that direction. I suspect Roivah-neheb might have just joined in the theomachy."

Aahmes nodded and jostled them both as he reached around to dig something out of one of the packs. He handed Namid a jug of Karinthe.

"I remember that you like this," he said. "And enough might help with the pain, too."

Namid nodded then opened the jug and took a good long drink. "I hope it'll help." She passed the jug to Aahmes, then tried again to grab the Power arrowhead and pull it out. It would not budge, and the pain was too great to continue. Aahmes passed the jug back to her.

He brushed her ear with his lips. "Not what I would have wanted for time alone," he whispered.

She laughed. "True. And it's not like we haven't shared a jug before." She twisted around to look at him. "But I'll take what I can get." Her lips met his for an intoxicating kiss.

Then she gasped as a slight movement sent agony tearing through her leg.

"Drink," he said with a smile.

~ ~ ~

They finished the Karinthe and managed to doze some between waves of pain. Sometime before dawn, Namid woke suddenly from nightmares to excruciating pain in her wrists. She discovered the palms of her hands were both dark with blood that seeped from beneath her armguards. With a cry, Aahmes woke, too. He put a hand to his throat, where Namid now saw an open wound, as if someone had sliced across his throat. Blood ran into his shirt at the neck.

A breath-of-time they stared at each other in horror, then both twisted to dig in the packs they leaned against. Namid gasped at the renewed pain the motion created and grabbed the first cloth her fingers found and pulled it out. A shirt. Good enough. She turned back to Aahmes with the cloth ready to staunch the blood and froze. The gaping wound on his neck had closed and was now just an angry-looking mark with some scabbing. Blood still stained his shirt but looked old now.

Aahmes grabbed her wrist and held it up. Her hand was no longer bloody, but the edge of her armguard looked stained, much like Aahmes' shirt.

"What is this?" she said and unlaced both armguards. After she pulled them off, they both inspected the inside of her arms. Slashes crossed both her wrists, looking like the slice on Aahmes' neck.

Aahmes gingerly touched his neck and locked gazes with her.

"No one is here," he said. "Or even was, I think. Look at the horses."

Namid looked where he indicated. Their horses all stood placidly dozing, not at all disturbed, which they would have been had someone else come into the depression.

"Something similar happened to me right after we left Rhadanthus," Namid said. "After horrible nightmares. I had those again tonight."

Aahmes nodded. "Nightmares for me, too, tonight."

They shared a look, but Namid had no ideas to share.

It seemed the same for Aahmes. He looked thoughtful, then shrugged and shifted his position with a wince. He grabbed a second jug of Karinthe from his pack, took a long drink and passed the jug to her.

"Try to get some more sleep, if you can," he told her. "I'll keep watch for what's left of the night."

~ ~ ~

At dawn, Namid checked the semblance and sent their illusionary selves traveling further down the road. She winced at the headache she had. Her wrists ached and looked no better healed from whatever it was. Aahmes' neck was the same.

Trying to move as little as possible, she and Aahmes dug some food and a waterskin out of the packs.

Almost every movement sent pain shooting through Namid's leg. And the Power arrowhead had increased its pressure on her shell. She had to bolster the shell periodically to keep the arrowhead from slicing deeper.

When they compared notes, Aahmes described much the same thing.

They spent the morning in their little hollow and rested as much as they could. Their animals stayed close, so keeping an eye on them required little extra effort. As the midday sun warmed them and her headache finally eased, Namid wondered how long it would take Mehratar and Inezha to get to them. She hoped Mehratar would be able to remove the arrowheads.

"Think we should start riding back toward Kezenae?" Aahmes said with a look toward the sun. "Try to meet Mehratar on the way?"

Namid considered it. "Probably should. I think the sooner we can get rid of these things…." She waved a hand at the Power arrowhead in her leg.

"Yeah," Aahmes said.

So, they laboriously loaded the packhorses and tacked up their mounts. Namid needed Aahmes' help to mount. The pain from the Power arrowhead limited her motion.

After they both mounted their horses, they sat waiting for the pain to subside some. Then they headed back to the road and rode back toward the city.

"At least this direction should be an unlikely one for anyone looking for us," Aahmes said.

Namid nodded. "And both semblances are working just fine. I hope to keep them up as long as possible."

~ ~ ~

Toward evening, when both Namid and Aahmes had begun to flag from the additional pain of riding, Aahmes spotted what looked like dust on the road some distance ahead of them. They guided their horses off the side of the road to wait to see who rode toward them.

"You've got the new guise ready?" Namid murmured.

Aahmes nodded. "Am I releasing the semblance on us?"

"Not unless it looks like you have to. Or if that's Mehratar and Inezha." She waved a hand at the approaching dust cloud.

"Looks like four horses," Aahmes said after they had waited about a quarter candle-mark. "Coming pretty fast."

Namid nodded and sent out the thinnest tendril of Power.

"It's them. And Haeith's with them," she told Aahmes, with a smile.

"Good," he said and dismounted. "Nice to have something go our way."

Namid also dismounted and they unloaded their

horses, setting up a rough camp a short distance off the road.

As the riders approached, they slowed to a walk and Haeith moved out in front of the others, dressed once more in his familiar habergeon and carrying his great-sword. Namid noticed both Mehratar and Inezha looked like themselves. Aahmes' glamour apparently didn't hold at too great a distance. Nothing to be done about that now.

"If you will allow," Haeith said in a hushed voice. "I can bring us into your semblance, so you needn't drop it and start all over."

Aahmes and Namid exchanged startled looks. And so did Mehratar and Inezha.

"Who are you talking to?" Inezha said.

"Bide," Haeith said to her.

Aahmes walked up to Haeith's horse. "How do we do that?" he said.

Haeith looked at him and stopped his horse. His companions stopped behind him and exchanged confused looks. Haeith held out his hand.

"Much as before when I showed Namid how to make the semblances."

So Aahmes clasped his hand and Namid felt him share the semblances with Haeith. Only a few breaths-of-time later, Inezha gasped.

"Aahmes! Namid!" she said with a delighted smile. "Oh, right... I mean Fathir and Saina."

Haeith released Aahmes' hand and turned his horse toward the rough camp.

"Cameni and Enric?" Namid said, looking up at him from her seat on the ground against one of the packs.

"Unharmed," Haeith said. "Only the temple was damaged."

"Destroyed, really. Everyone inside killed when the last attack dropped on it," Inezha said as she followed, marveling at all that she saw that had previously been hidden from her. Mehratar slid off his horse and hurried to

Namid's side.

"What happened?" he said.

Haeith took Mehratar's reins from him. "I've got the horses."

Aahmes dropped down next to Namid and they told Mehratar about the Power arrowheads, what little they knew. While he listened, Mehratar crouched by them and extended the slits in their clothes to be able to bare their limbs from the arrowheads down. He studied the arrowheads without touching them. After Aahmes and Namid had shared what they knew and what they had tried, Mehratar reached out to the arrowheads with his Power. And pulled right back with an alarmed expression. Then he noticed their other wounds.

"What of these? What happened?"

Aahmes and Namid shared a look. "Something related to nightmares, I think," Aahmes said. "Something going on with our Power."

Namid felt Mehratar's Power wrap around her, and Aahmes, too. Then Mehratar shook his head. "Nothing like what I Healed for you earlier," he told her. He looked from one to the other, then. "And they resist Healing."

He glanced at Haeith, who had nearly finished with the horses, and Inezha who was pulling out food and drink.

"What is it?" Namid said.

Mehratar sat fully on the ground before he answered. "A couple of things. First, no one should touch these arrowheads, as you've been calling them, with bare hands. They seem designed to want to burrow into flesh, of someone with Power, I suspect."

Namid winced.

"The color's changed," Aahmes said.

"Blood Power somehow, drawing on your blood. Another reason for no one else to touch them."

"Can you get them out?" Namid said.

Mehratar nodded. "You've already said you couldn't pull them back. So, we'll need them to continue forward –

with a hard push, to force them all the way through and out, so they don't lodge themselves within your limbs."

Aahmes and Namid exchanged looks.

"We'll have to keep them from coming right back at us," Aahmes said. "Or someone else."

Mehratar studied them both. "You'll need to make something to hold each arrowhead."

Aahmes stared into the distance while he considered that. Inezha brought over a bit of cold food and a waterskin.

"Can we have a fire?" she said looking from Namid to Haeith and Aahmes.

"Best not," Haeith said with a glance at her over his shoulder while he finished brushing down his horse. "So close to the road—"

"The smoke," Inezha said with a nod. She handed Aahmes the last bit of food she carried then leaned against a pack nearby while she ate.

Aahmes took a bite of food and returned his attention to Mehratar.

"*We'll* need to make something?" Aahmes said.

The Healer nodded. "I'll show you how. You and Namid already know how to create a sort of shell – this is similar, just smaller and not around yourself."

"And that'll give us time to figure out what to do with the things, how to destroy them," Namid said.

"What *are* they?" Inezha said.

Mehratar shrugged. "I'm not sure. I only sense hints. One is that they are something to help one Powerful person locate another. They seem able to use blood Power to maintain themselves. I don't sense any connection to anyone, though."

Namid winced as the arrowhead in her leg increased its pressure against her Power shell. "Think they'll burn?"

Aahmes grinned at her.

Mehratar shrugged. "Let's get them out of you first."

Haeith joined them. "What do we need to do?"

"It'll take one person to push the arrowhead out, a second with the container to catch and contain the arrowhead, then me to Heal," Mehratar said. He looked at Aahmes and Namid. "Each of you will need to push against your own arrowhead – you'll best be able to feel how it reacts and adjust. Also, use the Wild Power for that."

"You can still use that Power?" Haeith said.

Namid gave him a quick nod.

"And who'll make the containers?" Inezha said.

"That must also be Aahmes and Namid," Mehratar said. "Again using the Wild Power. Because any container made using one's own Power will be vulnerable to the arrowhead drawing on the Power as it's drawing on each of them right now. Not any difference to these things. So they'll need to alternate pushing out arrowheads and catching them."

Mehratar reached toward Aahmes and Namid, inviting contact to show them how to form the containers. A quarter candle-mark later, after he had shown them how to create small hollow spheres with a hole in the side and then close the hole quickly, he set them to practicing.

Namid and Aahmes each formed several hollow Power spheres, one at a time, between cupped hands, with only a short struggle to pull the Wild Power. The spheres were roughly a handspan across and clear, with faint green swirls that moved across the surface and helped define the edges. Namid's spheres had swirls a bit darker in color than those Aahmes made. They formed each sphere with a large hole in the side, then worked to close the hole as quickly as they could. Nearly a candle-mark later, Mehratar was satisfied with their work.

"How do you even know about making these spheres?" Namid said as she and Aahmes rested before they removed the arrowheads. "It doesn't seem like a Healing use of Power."

Mehratar shrugged. "Something I read about in another

book of Jelth's. He had books on all sorts of topics tucked away at the temple complex."

He turned to Haeith and Inezha. "Do we have some scrap cloths? I'll have to wait until the arrowhead is completely out to Heal, so this will be messy."

Inezha dug some cloths out of her pack and brought them over. Haeith held out a full waterskin and handed Namid a small, parchment packet that she recognized: his herbal concoction that helped relieve pain. He gave Aahmes one, too. When Namid opened the packet, Mehratar leaned close and gave it a quick look.

He nodded. "Might help some," he said and watched her and Aahmes both swallow the concoction with a drink of water.

Mehratar nodded then to Inezha and Haeith. "Please stay close with those." He grabbed a couple of cloths from Inezha and dampened them, holding one in each hand. Then he looked from Aahmes to Namid.

"Namid first," Aahmes said. He drew Wild Power and formed a sphere, then told Mehratar that he was ready.

Mehratar showed him where to hold it so that the arrowhead would go straight into it.

"Don't actually touch the arrowhead," he then told Namid. "Form a finger of Wild Power and use that to propel the arrowhead out of your leg. Good thing it went in at an angle."

Namid studied the arrowhead and pictured its path. It seemed to have continued to stretch as it moved further into her thigh. The point was in deeper than before. She shuddered at the damage it would likely do along the rest of its path as she pushed it out.

She took a deep breath to try to steady herself. She reached out for the Wild Power, then fought to bring it to her. Before too long, she was able to form the finger of Wild Power. She held it poised over the end of the arrowhead that still poked out of her leg.

With a look, she judged that everyone was ready. She

dropped her protective shell and drove the Wild Power against the arrowhead. For a breath-of-time the arrowhead seemed to try to anchor itself in her flesh, but she threw more Wild Power against it and it shot out into the sphere Aahmes held, compressing back into its original length. And Namid cursed at the line of searing pain that sliced through her leg from one side to the other in spite of Haeith's herbs. Mehratar immediately pressed the damp cloths to both the entry and exit wounds.

Aahmes closed his hands around the sphere, closing the hole in the sphere with Power, and sealed the arrowhead inside.

Namid closed her eyes and reminded herself to breathe as another wave of pain sliced through her. Then the touch of Mehratar's Power eased the pain. Someone gently touched her cheek.

"Namid?" Aahmes, of course.

She opened her eyes just enough to peer at him.

"That… was bad," she whispered.

Aahmes nodded. "Not looking forward to it," he said with a slight grin.

She tried to smile back, but it felt more like a grimace. Then Mehratar drew her attention.

"You did fine," he said. "I've Healed the immediate needs, but like Aahmes' injury when we first met, this will need more than just the one Healing."

Namid nodded. "At least the pain is bearable now. More an ache really."

"Good. After you help with the other arrowhead, you need to rest. Both of you will. And no walking about on that leg without someone to help support you until I Heal it again in the morning."

Then it was Aahmes' turn, which went much as Namid's had, right down to similar instructions from Mehratar after he had Healed Aahmes' wounds. After cleaning up, Mehratar studied the arrowheads within their spheres while Haeith finished settling the horses for the night.

Then they all gathered around Aahmes and Namid and passed around a wineskin.

"I've still remembered nothing further that will help to find the path to your brother," Haeith said after the skin had gone around once.

"Maybe share your memories of what happened?" Namid said. "Perhaps we'll notice something."

Haeith frowned. "There's not much to tell. We followed a trail through the edge of the Arinsk Mountains. Our scouts reported no concerns and our charges were in a fine mood, laughing and joking with each other. One breath-of-time, fine. The next, we were under attack, perhaps twice as many of them as us guards, all of them in that dark green-gray that I now know means they belonged to Sesaisyd's Dark Priests. I hadn't seen their like before."

He took a long drink from the wineskin and passed it to Namid. "They combined Power with combat in a way that foiled our training," he said. "They cut us down. Some of our charges fought too and fared the same. The last I saw before I fell was the last of the Flame Warriors drop—except for me—and the attackers surround the few of our charges who were left."

Haeith stared at his hands. "Our attackers didn't say anything."

He looked at Namid, then. "Thinking back with what I know now, I do know that your brothers, all three, were in that last small group I saw as I fell. When I recovered enough from my wounds to take note of where I was, I found I was nowhere near the place. And many days had passed. Everything else I know about the ambush is only what I heard from others."

"Where are the Arinsk Mountains?" Aahmes said.

"Some distance east," Haeith said. "They form Navele's eastern border. Much of Luag's too, as they run far north."

"Would you be able to take us to the ambush site. Or

tell us how to get there?" Namid said.

"I wouldn't want to wager that there'd be anything there after so many years," Inezha said.

"True enough," Namid said. "But that message came to me after all these years. Perhaps there's something for us there." She shrugged. "I don't know what else to try."

"I can take you there," Haeith said. "It's over a week's travel from here."

Namid nodded and yawned. "How soon?" she asked Mehratar.

He shook his head. "Not tomorrow. Perhaps you'll be ready for travel the next day. I'll see how your wounds are tomorrow."

CHAPTER 27

Mehratar Healed Aahmes and Namid early the next morning and told them to rest as much as possible for the day. He also checked their other wounds and told them they looked improved. Namid and Aahmes checked the spheres holding the Power arrowheads. During the night, the spheres had weakened some, so they bolstered them with more Wild Power.

Everyone else then straightened the makeshift camp and settled things better for another day spent there. Haeith took control of the distant semblances so that Namid could rest better. Aahmes settled new glamours on her and himself. The others refused any glamour, reasoning that anyone they encountered was unlikely to link their presence to Aahmes and Namid. Aahmes then dropped the semblance of no one there.

The day was frosty so Inezha happily started and tended a small fire. Namid and Aahmes spent the morning lazing about and dozing near the fire in the sunshine. But by mid-afternoon, Namid felt ready to crawl out of her skin from tedium. Aahmes grinned at her as she formed small whorls in the fire.

"I see your control has improved even more," Haeith

said as he watched.

"We've been working with our Power," Namid said.

"Aren't Cameni and Enric concerned that you have come with us?" Inezha asked Haeith.

He shook his head. "They both have many responsibilities they must see to after that attack on the temple. My last task for them was finished and I convinced them that this needed me more than any other tasks looming right now."

"Can you make anything with the fire," Inezha said to Namid.

Namid shrugged. "I've only played with knots and these twists."

Mehratar looked up, having been in his meditative state until then. "Tired of the inactivity?" he said with a smile.

Namid nodded. "And eager to get going. Another week…."

"Maybe less, if Aahmes… I mean *Fathir* can do that travel spell," Inezha said.

"Technique," Aahmes said.

Mehratar studied Aahmes with that intent look of his and shook his head. "Not for a couple of days, at least," he said. "I want you well-healed before doing something that involved with Power."

"And what of these things?" Inezha said and tapped her boot against the side of one of the Power spheres holding a Power arrowhead.

Namid grabbed the one containing her arrowhead and peered into it. "I don't want to carry them with us. But I'm leery of leaving them somewhere, even hidden, with our blood on them." She looked at Mehratar. "Any objections to us seeing if we can destroy them?"

Now he gave her the intent look and she felt a hint of his Power brush over her.

He shook his head. "No objections. But if anything starts to go wrong…."

"She'll jump right in to fix it," Aahmes said with a grin

for Namid.

She frowned at him, then studied her arrowhead. It floated in the middle of the sphere as if suspended there. The color had lightened somewhat but otherwise it looked much as before. But when she tentatively extended a tendril of Power toward the sphere, the arrowhead jumped toward her, hitting the side of the sphere.

With a small shriek, she lurched back and dropped the sphere, which rolled across the ground until Haeith grabbed it.

"Well, that was unexpected," Aahmes said in a sedate voice. But Namid saw he held a dagger in one hand.

"I don't like it," Mehratar said.

"Me neither," Namid said. "But even more than before, I think we have to destroy them. I think Wild Power, like when we got them out of us."

"I have a feeling this is going to get interesting," Aahmes muttered and built a Power shell around their camp. "Just in case," he said to Mehratar's questioning look.

Namid poked at Aahmes' shell with a finger of Wild Power and nodded. "I like the combination of concealment from without and protection for us inside," she said.

Aahmes gave her a mock bow. "Only the best for my lady," he said with an impudent grin. He still held the unsheathed dagger, and he held some Power ready, too.

With another nod, she turned her attention to her Power arrowhead. She left the sphere sitting on the ground this time and drew Wild Power to herself, having an easier time of it than the last time. She extended a tendril of Wild Power toward the sphere. When the arrowhead did not react, she touched the sphere with the tendril and slid it through without disturbing the integrity of the sphere. Still no reaction from the arrowhead. Namid glanced at the others and siphoned more Wild Power into the sphere.

"Everyone ready?" she said.

Nods all around, and the others backed away to the edge of Aahmes' protective shell. Except for Aahmes, who stepped up behind Namid and placed a hand on her shoulder.

Namid looked up at him and gave him a brief smile. She took a deep, steadying breath.

She called fire with the Wild Power within the sphere.

The sphere flashed a brilliant blue-white, bright enough to hurt to look at. Then a wave of scorching air burst out from it and knocked them all back to Aahmes' shell.

With a groan, Namid hauled herself back to her feet and looked to see what damage she had done.

The others were struggling to their feet but seemed unharmed otherwise. Aahmes' shell still held, and both spheres still lay where they had been before on the ground. Namid hurried to hers to look inside. Within, the arrowhead still floated, now looking stripped of the blood Power but otherwise unchanged. Namid dropped wearily to her knees beside it with a sigh.

The others joined her.

"Nothing?" Inezha sounded incredulous.

Namid shook her head and picked up the sphere. "That should have at least damaged it," she said.

"Look here," Aahmes said, holding out the sphere that held his arrowhead. Within, his arrowhead looked chipped around its edges, its glow much diminished.

He set the sphere on the ground in front of Namid and took hers.

"Try that on mine," he said and stepped back behind her, waving the others back toward the edges of the shell.

Namid nodded and repeated what she had done to her arrowhead. This time the Power within the sphere grew brighter after the initial blue-white flash, with no wave of scorching air, and changed to yellow, then pure white. Namid closed her eyes against the glare, but still maintained the fire within the sphere. With a final flash, it went dark.

Namid tentatively peered through slit eyes at the sphere in front of her. Its green swirls had lightened almost to invisibility and within was a small pile of fine, light-gray ash. The others crowded around to see.

Aahmes extended a thin tendril of Power toward the sphere, and finally touched it, with no response from the ashes within. He grinned at Namid. "Got it!" he said.

Namid returned his grin and headed to the packs to dig out a waterskin. "Your turn, then," she said to Aahmes over her shoulder.

"Bide," he replied. He set the sphere he held on the ground and picked up the one with the ashes.

"What are you going to do with that, then?" Inezha said.

Aahmes gave her a wide grin. "This," he said.

He cupped his hands around the sphere and squeezed, making it smaller and smaller, while weaving a new tendril of Wild Power into its structure. A nudge and the new tendril burst into flames that promptly engulfed the sphere, including the ash within. Then the whole thing was gone.

Inezha grabbed one of his hands and studied the unmarked palm. "Remarkable," she said. She dropped Aahmes' hand when she met Namid's gaze then grinned at Namid.

Mehratar placed a hand on Namid's forehead as she drank some more water and a wave of his Power washed over her. "Good," he said and removed his hand. "No harm done."

Then he nodded at Aahmes. "Go ahead."

With a repeat of what Namid had done, Aahmes reduced her arrowhead within its sphere to a pile of ash. Then Namid followed his example and scorched the remnants into oblivion. After that, Mehratar ordered them both to rest the remainder of the day. Neither argued.

~ ~ ~

After the evening meal, Mehratar insisted on Healing Aahmes and Namid once more, then agreed that they would be able to ride in the morning. "But still no swift travel for another day or two," he said.

Everyone settled around the low fire, wrapped up against the still chilly air, and passed around a wineskin that Inezha had warmed by the fire.

"Something about your brothers' journey seems odd," Aahmes said as Namid passed the wine to him. "Why would they go to the Arinsk Mountains? The Lady Royal said they were visiting other nobles in the land, but the map that Estaevi gave us shows no cities or towns in the mountains. Not even close to them, really."

"Might some trick have lured them into going there?" Inezha said.

Haeith seemed lost in thought. After several breaths-of-time he met Namid's gaze. "I remember nothing that makes me think someone tricked them," he said. "Of course, the nobles' conversations and decisions did not include the guards. I do remember hearing them speak of the hidden valleys."

The others exchanged looks.

"The hidden valleys?" Inezha said.

Haeith nodded and took a long drink from the skin, then passed it to Mehratar. "Within the Arinsk Mountains, so the tales say, are hidden valleys that are pockets of Power. Wild Power I suspect, from the description. When I crossed the mountains to Navele many years ago, I encountered no such valley nor felt any Power like that. Of course, if it *is* Wild Power, I wouldn't have sensed it. I remember the Navelean nobles sharing tales in the evenings with their guests. And soon after, they had us headed to the Arinsk Mountains."

"Hidden valleys," Namid murmured.

"Perhaps one has hidden your brother these many years!" Inezha said.

"Perhaps," Namid said. "If they even exist." She shrugged and shook her head. "It gives us a possibility to look into, anyway."

She stared into the fire, wondering about such a thing. If they did exist, and *were* pockets of Wild Power, probably she and Aahmes would have little trouble finding them. Or so she hoped. She had no idea what else to look for.

~ ~ ~

A little less than a week later, they entered the foothills of the Arinsk Mountains. Haeith and Aahmes had alternated setting the swift travel for them, so they managed to shorten the time to get there by a couple of days. Haeith took the lead when it was clear they were close, and they rode without the swift travel.

Another day of travel brought them to an area that Haeith remembered. They camped that night off the faint path that he pointed out to them, then the next morning followed it further into the mountains.

The trees and bushes grew more thickly here and provided some welcome shade from the day's mid-spring warmth. Namid saw small flowers on many of the bushes, an assortment of colors and shapes. As they climbed higher into the foothills a breeze sometimes helped cool them, but the day grew noticeably warmer anyway.

At midday, they stopped at a somewhat level spot that looked like it had been used before for a stop for other travelers. A small meadow with a thin stream nearby provided grazing for the horses and water for all of them. Piling their tack and packs nearby, Namid and the others settled into some shady spots to eat and rest before they moved on.

"Another couple of candle-marks from here, we should reach the ambush site," Haeith said.

"Did the group stop here all those years ago?" Inezha said as she looked around as if she expected to find something from that time.

Haeith shrugged. "Probably, although I don't remember specifically. My memory of times surrounding the ambush is still unclear, even now."

Inezha frowned, then leaned back and closed her eyes. "This is nice, anyway," she said. "Wake me when it's time to leave."

Mehratar also settled back and closed his eyes. While Haeith leaned against a tree, he remained alert and watchful. Aahmes leaned toward Namid.

"Walk with me?"

Hand in hand, they strolled toward the meadow where the horses grazed, giving Haeith a wave as they passed.

"I've been trying to sense anything odd with the Wild Power," Aahmes said and stopped at the edge of the meadow. "So far nothing really…."

"But we should try it together," Namid said.

Aahmes smiled and nodded.

Namid leaned toward him for a quick kiss that went on much longer than planned and left her breathless.

When they parted again, Aahmes grinned and shook his head at her. "Not what we're supposed to be doing…."

Namid gave him a wide-eyed look. "You object?"

"Not at all." He leaned in close and rested his forehead against hers. "In spite of my best efforts otherwise," he said in a quiet voice. "I find I *do* care greatly for you."

Namid gazed back at him, noticing how dark his eyes looked at that moment. "Good thing I feel the same," she said. "In spite of your best efforts otherwise."

Aahmes chuckled and gave her a quick kiss. They found a comfortable spot in the shade under some small trees and settled there. Aahmes tucked one arm around her shoulders and pulled her close to his side. His other hand he held palm-to-palm with her hand. As they had been practicing, they pulled Power together, Wild Power this time, with the struggle they had both grown accustomed to. They sank into the Power they found and reached out through the nearby mountains to see what they could sense.

And discovered more Wild Power than they had expected, extending all through the mountains.

They spent more than a candle-mark sifting through the Power looking for the hidden valleys with pockets of Power. When they returned to themselves, they shared astonished looks.

"The stories are true," Namid said.

Aahmes nodded. "I sensed perhaps a dozen of those pockets nearby," he said. "But most of them seemed very small."

Namid nodded, too. "But there were a couple of larger ones in the direction this path seems headed," she said.

"And so much Wild Power here," Aahmes said in a quiet voice.

Namid grinned at him. "As if we need even more Power," she said.

"On the other hand, more of this…." He gathered her close for another kiss.

And they both jumped when someone cleared their throat.

"With most sincere apologies for the interruption," Inezha said and gave them both a wicked grin. "Shouldn't we be heading out?"

Namid and Aahmes exchanged exasperated looks, but Namid nodded.

"We even think we've found some of those pockets of Wild Power that Haeith spoke of. A couple seem to be the direction the path is headed," she told Inezha.

She and Aahmes rose and helped Inezha collect the horses. They led them back to the others and everyone helped tack and pack them and they rode out again.

As they rode, Aahmes and Namid described as well as they could where they thought the nearest pockets of Wild Power might be. Haeith nodded, but it was clear that the trail claimed most of his attention.

After close to two candle-marks, he called a halt and dismounted. He looked at Namid.

"Here?" she said.

At his nod, she also dismounted and looked around. After so long, she doubted she would see evidence of the ambush, but still she looked.

And the area seemed somehow familiar.

The others also dismounted and wandered around looking at the ground, poking through the grasses and in the brush.

Haeith moved a pace further down the path and stopped. "Best I remember, this is where I went down," he said. He pointed back toward Namid and the others. "And our charges were there, last I saw."

Namid felt Aahmes reach out to the Wild Power. She drew some to herself, too, but could not tell what he was doing. He staggered, then sank to his knees. She hurried to his side but only lightly touched his shoulder when she saw he was still wrapped in the Power. The others sent concerned looks Aahmes' direction but did not approach.

After several long breaths-of-time, Aahmes shook his head and groaned, rubbing his forehead. Then he met her gaze.

"I thought I was supposed to be the one doing the crazy things," she teased.

He smiled and shook his head. "Not sure anything I saw will be helpful."

The others gathered close.

"What *did* you see?" Inezha said.

"Disjointed images," he said. "Flashes of fighting, a glimpse, I think of Namid's brothers, others in noble attire, blood, Haeith falling. I tried to see what happened after Haeith fell. But the images were too jumbled and unclear."

Namid looked around again. And she remembered seeing this spot before, remembered seeing Haeith fall, more than a season ago, when they had been caught in similar images in Nazextas.

Aahmes clasped her hand. "I'm sorry, I couldn't see what happened to Tal after Haeith fell."

The others reported that they had found nothing. When Mehratar approached Aahmes, probably to see if he was all right, he waved him off. They all poked around the area a little longer, then met at their horses.

"I've been no further along this particular track," Haeith said. "And, since Corentris, I no longer sense the Wild Power."

Aahmes glanced ahead. "The pockets Namid and I sensed are somewhat further that way," he said and waved a hand that general direction.

Namid touched the Wild Power. "Can't seem to tell their exact location," she said.

"Maybe if we're closer?" Inezha said.

With a shrug, Namid mounted her horse. "I'd like to look further along the track anyway. Maybe we can find something." She turned to Haeith. "Think of anything else that might help?"

He shook his head. "Unfortunately not."

"There's something about these mountains," Inezha said. "I feel twitchy…."

Namid nodded. And the others did, too.

They headed out with their hands near their weapons.

CHAPTER 28

As they followed the faint track, Namid kept a light contact with the Wild Power, trying to determine the direction to the nearest pocket, and the distance, too. She sensed Aahmes doing something similar.

After another candle-mark had passed, Namid pulled up and gave Aahmes a questioning look. He nodded.

"One is close," he said.

"But it feels like it's changing, sort of," Namid said. "But I can't tell why, or even what it's doing."

"Doesn't feel like anyone's deliberately using it, though," Aahmes said.

"Where?" Mehratar said. "Can you tell how to get to the pocket now?"

Namid turned around, then turned to an area of dense growth to the left of the track. "That way, I think."

Aahmes nodded. "Feels like it to me, too."

Inezha gave the area a dubious look. "And we'll get the horses through there how?" she said.

Haeith dismounted, his gaze intent on the dense growth that Namid had indicated. When he was close enough, he reached out into the closely growing plants. "Incredible."

"What is?" Inezha said as she dismounted and joined him, leading her horse as Haeith had. She fingered a leaf and gave him a puzzled look.

Haeith looked over his shoulder at Namid and Aahmes with a hint of challenge in his expression. "Do you see it?"

Aahmes and Namid exchanged puzzled looks and joined Haeith. Mehratar watched them from a pace back.

Namid slowly reached toward some leaves, uncertain what to expect. But they were just leaves. They looked like leaves and felt like leaves.

"Odd," Aahmes said. "There's a hint of Wild Power here. Doing something. But it doesn't feel like someone is controlling it… exactly."

Namid closed her eyes to help block out distractions and sank into the Wild Power. She sensed what Aahmes was talking about. But she also sensed that some sort of purpose lay within the Wild Power somehow. She drew Wild Power to herself and discovered what Haeith had probably been referring to.

"Illusion," she muttered. "A unique kind of semblance."

"Yes," Haeith said.

"But… how can that be?" Inezha said. "I can feel the leaves, the branches."

Namid opened her eyes, but still kept the Wild Power close. "A fantastic way to conceal a way to a hidden valley, wouldn't you say?" she said.

Inezha's eyes widened and she grinned. "So, we just need to go through here." She gave the plants an intent look and brushed her hands across them. Then she stepped forward and tried to ease her way through, between and among the branches. But only two steps in, she got tangled in the dense growth and could go no further.

After they freed her, they all stepped back and studied the area.

"So trying to slip through my way isn't the way,"

Inezha said.

"It's an incredible semblance," Mehratar said. "I even sense the plant life in the Power."

"Can you sense any people nearby?" Aahmes said.

Mehratar concentrated, then shook his head.

"Try to take it down?" Aahmes said.

"I'm not sure we can," Namid said. "And it might not be a good idea, anyway. I'd rather figure out how to get through while disturbing things as little as possible."

"Perhaps try to slip through a different way. Maybe using something like those shells you two create," Inezha said to Namid and Aahmes.

Aahmes gave her a thoughtful look and a quick nod. He pulled Wild Power and formed a thin shell close around himself then strolled to the edge of the dense growth. After studying it, he changed something about his shell of Power. Then he stepped into the plants.

At first, it looked like he would get entangled as Inezha had. But then the plants seemed to each move slightly and slide around his faintly visible shell, letting him advance. He took only one more step then returned to the others. The plants closed again behind him, looking undisturbed.

"I hope that you'll be doing that for all of us," Inezha said with a grin.

"Namid and I can," Aahmes said.

"Don't you mean Saina?" Inezha gave him a teasing grin.

Aahmes sighed. "Of course."

"I also can make a similar shell, at least for myself," Mehratar said.

Aahmes nodded. "Like back in your village. But I used Wild Power for this one."

"Still, it's worth trying," Mehratar said. "Perhaps one less thing you two will have to hold."

He stepped up to the plants much as Aahmes had done and formed his own shell. When he attempted to move into the foliage, it first slid a little around his shell, but then he could advance no further. He backed out with a rueful grin.

"The burden's on you two," he told Aahmes and Namid. "But if you need to pull any additional Power…" he offered.

"Have you noticed how much Power they've got?" Inezha muttered. "Why you don't just make things the way they should be…."

"I think we should link for this," Namid said to Aahmes. "And you can show me exactly how you set it up, too."

He nodded and held a hand out to her. Haeith dismounted and began tying leads to all of their horses, hooking them together in a single line, with the packhorses in the middle of the line.

Namid took Aahmes' hand and they slipped into the familiar Power link. Following Aahmes' lead, Namid gathered only Wild Power and they constructed a shell around each of their companions and around each of the horses, making sure the horses' shells also wrapped the lead ropes. Within the Power, it seemed to take little time. But when Namid again became aware of the others, she found them finishing a small meal.

Mehratar handed her and Aahmes each some food and a waterskin and urged them to eat and drink. Then they all packed the little they had pulled out and lined up to attempt the passage, each of them taking a place at one of their horses' heads.

"I've got the tail end," Aahmes said and moved into position at the last horse's head.

With a nod, Namid took the lead and moved toward the plants. When she first stepped among them, she felt a slight resistance to her passage, then they slid around her shell and she was able to continue forward, albeit slowly.

Within the plants, they found the air cooler than it had been, but the light level stayed much the same, not shaded as might be expected amid so much foliage. Namid kept thin tendrils of Wild Power out around them to help guide her and give her an idea of the direction to the closest pocket of Wild Power.

They traveled this way more than a candle-mark, then Namid called a halt in a clearing in front of a huge rock outcropping right in their path.

"Something different," she told the others. While they gathered in the small cleared area, she touched the rock and attempted to push through it, without success.

"Haeith, would you please take a look?" she said. She stepped to one side and sank her awareness into the Wild Power to see if she could discover anything.

"Of course."

Haeith handed off the untying of the horses' leads to Mehratar and moved closer to study the rocks.

Namid sensed nothing useful from the Wild Power and turned to watch Haeith's expression change from concentration to mild confusion.

"I *think* it's also a semblance, but much more involved, more complex than what we've been walking through," Namid said when he turned his attention to her.

"I agree. Although I can't definitively confirm that." He glanced at the others, then the horses. "I think your Wild Power can get us past or through this, whatever is applicable. But the horses will likely be a problem."

Namid nodded. She could see that. While they had seemed unconcerned with walking through plants that moved only a little—an experience not too foreign to them—the horses would probably balk at any attempt to walk into or through what looked like solid rock.

The others dismounted and moved closer to study the rocks. Inezha placed both hands on them and pushed, then backed up with a rueful grin and brushed her hands together.

"It even feels like rock," she said.

"Are we certain the semblance is in this location?" Mehratar said.

Namid felt Aahmes touch the Wild Power much as she had. "It's near, at least," he said. "But might not be directly along the path we've followed so far."

Haeith nodded. "It's even more enmeshed with the reality here than what we've already seen," he said.

"Will the same thing work here?" Inezha said. "Using these Power shells to slip through?"

"Need to find it first," Aahmes muttered. He paced along the rocks away from the others, trailing tendrils of Wild Power across the rocks from the ground to twice his height. After she watched him a breath-of-time, Namid copied his actions on her side, while Haeith moved slower between them, doing whatever he was doing with the Power.

Close to a half candle-mark later, they all met back where they had first stopped by the rocks. Namid saw that Mehratar and Inezha had unloaded all the packs and let the horses graze.

At questioning looks from Inezha and Mehratar, Namid, Aahmes and Haeith all shook their heads.

"Does that mean the Power shells won't get us through?" Inezha said.

"Not necessarily," Namid said. "Just can't determine *where* we need to even try to go through."

Aahmes gave her shoulder a squeeze. "We should try linking and looking again," he said.

"That might be what it takes," Haeith said.

"I can feel that twitchiness on my skin," Inezha said. "That sort of feeling of Power nearby."

Mehratar gave her a thoughtful look. "Does it intensify when you are anywhere in particular?"

Inezha gave him a wide-eyed look. "I hadn't thought of that." So she paced the length of the rocks while the others dug out a couple of skins for drinks.

When she returned, she shook her head, too, with a downcast expression.

"I couldn't tell any difference in the areas that I feel it," she said. "But it feels like it's within an area about five paces long."

"That helps," Aahmes said. "If you're just becoming sensitive to Power, you might not yet be able to feel anything more specific. That might come in time."

She gave him a bright smile. "Certainly, that's what it is." She took the skin Haeith offered her and took a long drink.

"I have no real experience with semblances, but I can offer raw Power, if you want," Mehratar said.

Haeith nodded. "Best to make use of all we can," he said.

"I've got the horses and will keep watch," Inezha said.

The others settled themselves in a tight circle near the center of the five paces of Power that Inezha had pointed out.

"Link in a chain or a clump?" Namid said.

"Who's controlling the link?" Mehratar said at the same time.

They exchanged quick smiles.

"Haeith needs the control," Aahmes said. "He's best at spotting this sort of thing."

Haeith gave him a nod of acknowledgement. "I think a clump, as you put it," he answered Namid. "Everyone clasp hands in the center. Namid and Aahmes, would you please bring in the Wild Power, too, but hold tight control on it. As I remember, it and I didn't get along well."

Namid heard Inezha settle nearby, then lost track of anything but the Power.

At first, their link wobbled, uneven, since they had not all linked like this before. Before too long, Haeith was able to smooth out the link and channel the Power toward the rocks. He shared with them that he was seeing—but not sensing—ever-shifting swirls and eddies of the Wild Power in dusty-blues and grays, extending the length that Inezha had identified. When he extended their Power to it, it swirled around their Power and absorbed it into the whorls.

They tried several ways to slip through the Power with their own, even switching around the control, but nothing seemed to let them through it or even let them glimpse the reality there.

When they finally dissolved the link, Namid saw that it was much darker. She felt stiff from sitting motionless for so long.

"I think the whole area Inezha paced is the semblance," Aahmes said, voicing what Namid had begun to suspect.

Haeith nodded. "But I don't see a way to take us through it."

Mehratar shook his head wearily. "That took more than I expected. I don't think I'll be much further help until I've rested."

"Shall we make our camp here?" Inezha said. "Revisit this in the morning?"

Namid glanced around at the arrangements Inezha had made while they were occupied. Inezha had the horses all free of gear, which she had stacked neatly nearby, their packs sorted out, and a fire ring set up, but no fire burning yet. She smiled at the Prazny. "You've done all the hard work," she said. "Our thanks."

Namid felt a wisp of Mehratar's Power brush past her, then he turned to dig out some food. "I don't sense anyone as far away as I can sense right now," he said.

"As good a place as any," Haeith said and stretched out, propped against the base of a tree. He munched on some dried meat he had pulled from his pack.

After grabbing food themselves, the others followed suit. Inezha first got a small fire going and checked on the horses.

They decided on watches for the night and settled in.

~ ~ ~

After she passed the watch off to Inezha and settled

back to sleep for another couple of candle-marks or so, Namid's dreams filled first with a jumble of images that seemed inspired by what Aahmes had seen at the ambush site. Then slowly the Wild Power seeped in and connected her to the barrier semblance that they had examined earlier through the link. Something shifted in the Wild Power, some change in the way it felt to her. And she woke to the sound of her name to find herself standing in the pre-dawn murk in front of the rock outcropping at the spot where they had linked the night before. Inezha's hand rested lightly on her forearm.

She gave Inezha a questioning look.

"I hadn't known that you are a sleepwalker," Inezha said.

Namid frowned. "I'm not. Someone's coming."

"What? Who? How do you know?"

Namid shrugged. "I don't know who. How? Somehow through the Wild Power…." Namid shook her head, trying to get rid of the groggy sensation. "Better wake the others."

They both jumped as Aahmes suddenly lurched to his feet and stared at them, like he could not quite focus on them. Then he blinked and came fully awake.

"You felt it, too," he said to Namid. He grabbed his daggers and stepped back to the edge of the surrounding foliage.

Namid woke Haeith while Inezha woke Mehratar.

"Someone's coming," Aahmes told the other men.

Everyone grabbed their preferred weapons, Mehratar even grabbed a dagger, and backed away from the rocks to the edge of the surrounding plants as Aahmes had done. Namid felt the light touch of Mehratar's Power as it swept out around them.

"I still don't sense anyone," he said in a quiet voice.

Aahmes just pointed to the rock outcrop. A section of it gradually luminesced, giving a glimpse of the swirls of Wild Power. Then four people stepped into the small clearing and ranged themselves a pace or so apart. They each held a short, powerful-looking bow with an arrow nocked, but not pointed at Namid and her companions. Both groups studied each other in silence.

The newcomers, two women and two men, were dressed similar to each other in long, sleeveless tunics that reached below their knees, with trousers underneath and low leather shoes. Intricate, embroidered designs decorated their brightly colored clothes. All of them wore several bracelets, circling both their upper arms and forearms. The bracelets looked to be made of silver, except for one gold one worn by one of the women. They all had long hair worn pulled back in tails and braids. One of the men had streaks of white in his brown hair. The others in the group looked younger than him, but Namid guessed they were all probably older than her. Both men had closely trimmed beards.

After each group had time to look the other over, the woman with the gold bracelet stepped forward. She was the shorter of the two women, and had auburn hair and light brown, freckled skin.

"Ladies and lords," she said and inclined her head slightly. "You seem to have lost your way. Mayhap we can help."

Namid stepped forward, squelching the somewhat silly feeling that washed over her at being clad only in her shirt and trousers. At least they were some of the quality ones, not her tattered Shadower clothes. She gave the newcomers a nod of greeting.

"Your offer is kind," she said. "But our way isn't so much lost as obscured, we think."

The woman glanced at her companions and turned back to Namid.

"There is nothing here of concern or benefit to Navelean nobility," the woman said.

"We aren't Navelean nobility, nor here on behalf of any Navelean nobility," Namid said. "We seek someone who was lost years ago in these mountains, perhaps injured. His name is Tal Shartov."

Namid saw the woman's eyes widen before she turned away. The man with the white in his hair stepped up to her and they conferred in voices too low for Namid to understand what they said. She glanced at Aahmes, but he only shrugged.

"Do you know of him?" Namid said. "I have a drawing of what he looked like those years ago." She handed both her daggers to Aahmes and took a step toward her pack but stopped when the other two strangers lifted their bows at her movement.

"I have the drawing in my pack," Namid said.

The auburn-haired woman turned back. "Show me." She gestured at her companions to lower their weapons and joined Namid at her pack, crouching down next to her.

Namid dug the drawing out of the pocket of one of her dresses. She unrolled it and handed it to the woman, noting her expression of surprise as she looked at it. The man with the white-streaked hair stepped closer to peer over her shoulder. He dropped a hand on her shoulder and she patted it absently. She gave the drawing back to Namid.

"You aren't Navelean," she said as she rose.

"No," Namid tucked the drawing away again.

The woman handed off her weapon to the older man and faced Namid. "I am Rannvei," she said. She extended her right arm, fingers outstretched toward Namid. After a breath-of-time, Namid mirrored her actions. The woman touched her fingertips to Namid's, then brought that hand up, touching her own chest at her heart. Again, Namid mimicked her.

"This is Geir." Rannvei gestured to the man with the white streaked hair, then introduced the other woman as Kyerla and the other man as Beithr.

As each one was introduced, they exchanged the same

gestures of greeting with Namid that Rannvei had used.

"I'm Saina," Namid told them, then gestured to each of her companions in turn. "My companions... Inezha, Mehratar, Haeith, and Fathir."

The newcomers each repeated their gestures of greeting with each of Namid's companions.

"What can you tell us about Tal?" Namid said when all the greetings had been exchanged.

"Perhaps better to show you," Rannvei said. "Will you come with us?" She waved a hand back at the rock outcrop, which again looked impenetrable.

"You can take us through?" Inezha said.

"If you are with us, you can walk the path," Geir said. "Even your horses."

Namid exchanged a glance with Aahmes and began to gather her bedding. "Do we have time to eat first?"

"The journey will not be long," Kyerla said.

"We can promise a meal at the end of it," Beithr added.

So while the newcomers waited, Namid and her companions put on boots, tunics and otherwise prepared to travel, and Namid pulled the drawing from her pack and tucked it into a pocket of her tunic. She and the others broke their camp and tacked and loaded the horses.

"It'll be best to lead them," Geir said as Inezha began to mount her horse. "Also blindfold them for this first part. Horses don't usually like trying to walk through what looks like rocks to them."

With Rannvei and Geir in the lead, and Beithr and Kyerla bringing up the rear, they all headed to the rock outcrop, leading the blindfolded horses. They passed within the semblance with no problem at all.

~ ~ ~

Less than a quarter candle-mark later, they stepped out of the faint twilight swirls of Wild Power onto a wide dirt road that led down into a large valley. Namid saw a good-sized town situated slightly below their vantage point, with cultivated fields around it, nearly filling the valley from one side to the other. And one large meadow that held sheep and cattle. Beyond the fields lay a forest that looked like the one they had seen on the other side of the rock outcrop.

Rannvei waved a hand toward the town. "We can provide you with breakfast in the council hall," she said. "The council members will likely wish to meet with you at some point. This way."

She led them along the road and into the town. Although the coming dawn now lit the sky, shadows still shrouded the town, and few people were about. Those who were wore attire similar to their guides. They gave Namid and her companions curious looks. Most followed them, while a few hurried away. By the time they arrived at the building that Rannvei identified as the council hall, they had acquired a good-sized following.

Beithr and Kyerla took their horses, assuring them that they would be just down the street, and led them off. Rannvei led them inside the hall, while Geir spoke with the crowd who had followed them.

Inside the hall, they found several long tables scattered about most of the floor, each surrounded by chairs. One shorter table sat at the far end, with chairs only along the back.

"Please wait here while I make arrangements for some food," Rannvei said and left by a side door to their left.

"How did they get us through the rocks?" Inezha said as she plopped down in a chair.

"They're connected somehow to the Wild Power here," Aahmes said. "Or rather, it's connected to them."

"From what little I sensed," Namid added, "they don't consciously use it like Fathir and I do. More it responds to them. To their needs, perhaps."

She wandered around the room looking out the windows as she passed. A knot of anticipation tied up with uneasiness had settled in her stomach and resisted her efforts to ease it. She was no longer certain she wanted any food just then. She hoped that they might finally have found word of Tal, but feared that word would only be of his death.

Aahmes caught up to her pacing and wrapped an arm around her shoulders. "Nervous?"

She stopped pacing and leaned against him. "Some. They seemed to recognize Tal, but what if—after all this— he's died?"

"Wait and see," Aahmes said. "I think we'll know soon enough."

Less than a quarter candle-mark later Rannvei returned. "They'll bring the food shortly," she told them. Then she smiled. "We had not planned to have guests this morn. Please, sit."

As they headed toward a table roughly in the center of the room, the side door opened and a man entered. "Vei, what's this I hear about visitors?" he said.

Namid froze and turned slowly to look at him, almost afraid to look. The voice sounded close to what she remembered. Could it be her hopes were answered rather than her fears?

The man who had just entered stood a little taller than Namid, with the same red-brown skin but much darker brown eyes. He wore his dark hair long and pulled back in a tail. Like the townsfolk they had seen, he wore a bright, long, decorated tunic over trousers, with leather shoes. One of the bracelets on his arms was gold and resembled Rannvei's in design. A second bracelet, in silver, exactly matched one of Rannvei's silver ones.

Aahmes leaned close. "Is it Tal?"

Namid watched as the man gave Rannvei a quick kiss, then studied the newcomers to his town. She realized that she had been staring when he gave her a questioning look followed by a half smile that she knew. She returned the smile, then remembered he saw only her glamour, not her.

"Shall I drop your glamour?" Aahmes said in a whisper, keeping his eyes on the man and Rannvei.

Namid shook her head. "I'd prefer if he were alone for it, at least at first, if it can be managed," she whispered.

Aahmes nodded and took a place at the table. Namid sat next to him and watched as Rannvei and the man she believed was Tal spoke together. When they finished, they came to the table and Rannvei took a seat. The man wordlessly greeted Namid and her companions with their greeting gestures, then took a seat next to Rannvei. He looked them all over again and his gaze lingered on Inezha.

"Do I know you?" he said.

Inezha's eyes widened and she shook her head. "I don't see how."

He frowned and studied the rest of them one by one. When he came to Haeith, this time he looked certain. "I think I remember you. Something about the attack…."

Haeith nodded. "Yes. I was there, too."

The man winced. "So much of it is hazy. You were sorely wounded? You went down?"

Again, Haeith nodded.

"I remember fighting…." The man's expression darkened, and he looked pained. Rannvei put a hand on his arm and he covered it with his own. Namid tried to stop staring at the man but her gaze was drawn back to him every time she looked elsewhere.

After a breath-of-time of this, Rannvei cleared her throat. "May we see the drawing again?" she said.

Namid nodded and pulled it out, passing it across the table.

The man took it and studied it for a long time.

"This is familiar," he said.

At that moment the side door banged open and several people poured into the room, led by a young boy and an older girl who had to be his sister. And looking at them, Namid felt certain they were the man's children.

"We brought the food, Papa," the girl said to the man

seated across from Namid, confirming her supposition.

Everyone set the food they carried on the table closest to the door and most of them filed right back out. The two children lingered.

"Can we stay, Mama? Papa?" the little boy said as he looked from Rannvei to the man and back. The girl grabbed his hand and led him toward the door.

"Not now, Byartal," she told him. "Looks like councilor business."

He nodded wisely as she pulled him through the door. He waved at everyone before she shut it behind them.

"Please, get some food," Rannvei said and filled a plate herself.

Everyone else followed her example, then returned to the table, where they ate in silence. Namid kept sneaking looks at the man as he continued to study the drawing.

After everyone had their fill and pushed aside their plates, the man slid the drawing back to Namid.

"I'm Tal Shartov," he said. "And like I said, the drawing seems familiar. It's certainly me when I was younger. Where did you get it? You've been seeking me?"

Namid concentrated on rolling the drawing and avoided meeting his gaze. Now that the time had come, she was uncertain what to say. A sudden reluctance had her hesitating to speak. And she had never thought to find him with a family. Should she even say anything? She had to say something. But once she said something, everything would change, especially for Tal. She felt a touch on her arm and glanced at Aahmes, who urged her to go ahead with a tilt of his head toward Tal.

"I'm not sure where to begin—" Namid said. And that was as far as she got.

When she spoke, when he heard her voice, Tal stiffened in his chair, his eyes going wide.

"Tal?" Rannvei clutched his arm but he remained motionless.

"Mehratar!" Namid shouted, but the Healer was already

out of his chair and headed for the stricken man. Rannvei ran to the door and yelled for someone to get a Healer.

"Mehratar's a Healer," Aahmes told her when she returned.

"An assistant doesn't hurt," Mehratar murmured and sent his Power out and around Tal.

Namid felt a faint surge of Wild Power from around them. A glance exchanged with Aahmes confirmed that he felt it too.

And Tal suddenly slumped in his chair, seemingly unconscious.

"What did you do?" Rannvei demanded of Mehratar as another man ran into the hall.

"Nothing," Mehratar said and backed away to give the other man room. "I had just begun to try to see what was wrong."

"He speaks truth, Councilor," the stranger said to Rannvei. "This doesn't feel that it's of their doing. It seems related to his injuries when he came to us. Let's get him to his own house and I can see what's to be done."

He looked at Mehratar. "I'd welcome your help, if you would."

Mehratar nodded. "Of course."

While the others stood back, Mehratar and the other Healer lifted Tal and carried him from the room, following Rannvei.

Before she closed the door behind them, Rannvei called back. "Wait here."

Then they were gone.

CHAPTER 29

"Like with Stefe," Namid murmured. She sank back in her chair and covered her face with her hands.

"We don't know that," Inezha said.

"You heard their Healer," Namid snapped. "It's tied to his injuries when he came here. It's got to be blood Power. And he was fine until he heard my voice."

With gentle hands, Aahmes tugged her to her feet and wrapped his arms around her. She leaned into his embrace for a long while before she pulled away with a small smile for him and a nod of thanks.

"And I hate waiting like this," she said.

"Now you sound more like yourself," Aahmes said.

Namid paced with a pause at each window to look through. After more than a quarter candle-mark of this, the side door opened and the girl they had seen before entered. She walked up to Aahmes, who was closest to the door, and offered the greeting gesture to him, with a slight frown, like she was concentrating to make the gestures exactly right.

"I'm Hildevei," she said.

Aahmes returned the greeting gesture. "Fathir," he said, then introduced the others.

The girl greeted them all in turn, then moved back near the door to a spot from which she could see them all at once.

"Mama said to tell you that Papa is resting. He's awake and wants to speak with you. But both Healers say that he should wait some candle-marks before doing that. So Mama sent me to take you to a guesthouse for your use while you are here."

She opened the side door. "Please come with me."

They exchanged glances and followed Hildevei down the street. As they passed, she pointed to a small corral, with a stable at the far end.

"Your horses are here," she said. "They're well cared for, but you can check on them any time, of course. Your packs are in the guesthouse."

Several paces further down the street, she stopped outside a house that was a little larger than the others they had seen so far.

"Here is your house while you are with us. The other councilors are spreading word that we have guests so anyone should be able to help you if you need anything." She turned to go, then turned back.

"I almost forgot. Mama said you won't want to venture outside town without at least one of us with you. Since you're strangers to the area, it might not be safe for you. Oh, and there's a bathing house for your use out behind the guesthouse."

She gave them a slight smile and hurried off.

They stepped into the house, into a central room with several chairs and small tables scattered about and a fireplace at one end. Their packs sat in a neat stack near the door they had entered by. Two other doors led off the room to either side, and one straight ahead. A quick exploration revealed that one of the side doors led to a small kitchen area and the other to a room with several beds. The door across from the first one opened on a short path that led to a small building, presumably the bathing house.

They hauled their packs into the bedroom and each chose a bed, setting Mehratar's pack by one of the others. Haeith then stretched out on his and seemed to go right to sleep. Namid, Aahmes and Inezha returned to the middle room.

"I'm for the bathing house," Inezha declared. "Anyone care to join me?" She gave both Namid and Aahmes a wicked grin, which grew wider when they declined.

"Your loss," she said and ducked into the bedroom to get some things from her pack. Then she was gone out the back door.

After she had gone, Aahmes dropped into a chair. "It's a nice town, from what we've seen," he said with a bland expression.

Namid nodded. "Very." She began to pace. "I never thought that he might have a family. But he doesn't seem to remember his past. How can I tell him now? I can't take him from his home."

She plopped down on a chair. "I can't make him take the throne."

"Do you want it, then?"

"No!"

"But you'd take it to spare him…."

Namid made a rude noise. "I don't know."

"Just tell him everything. You'll not be *making* him do anything. Let him make up his own mind."

Namid sighed. "I feel like I'm about to ruin his life."

Aahmes shook his head. "You're giving him information that rightly should be his. I imagine he can decide for himself."

"Part of me wants to convince him to go back and take his place as the heir…" Namid muttered.

Aahmes shrugged. "Not surprising. Will you?"

Namid shook her head. And hoped that she was being truthful. Some of what Inezha had been saying seemed to mock her in her thoughts. It would be so easy to use the

Power…. She shook her head again. She would *not* do that!

Aahmes rose and stretched. "I think Haeith's got the right idea," he said and headed toward the bedroom. "Maybe more rest will help you, too. It was interrupted last night and it's a good way to make waiting seem shorter."

Namid gave him a thoughtful look. "I suppose." But she stayed in her chair. With a shrug, Aahmes went into the bedroom.

Namid sat for over a quarter candle-mark and stared at the floor, trying to get her thoughts in order. When that did not help, she left the house and randomly picked a direction to walk down the street. Her direction took her further into the town.

She spent the rest of the morning wandering about the town, sometimes stopping to watch the various townsfolk. They all seemed hard at work at their various tasks, even the children. Those people who caught her gaze gave her friendly nods but did not approach to talk or introduce themselves. The children stared at her, but their gazes were only curious.

All of the buildings she saw, whether shops or houses, were made of the same reddish stones tightly fitted together, with wood-shingled roofs. She spotted what looked like two other guesthouses, empty right then. The streets she walked were dirt, but with a lot of small rocks ground into them.

Probably wouldn't get too muddy in the rain or snowmelt, she thought.

From the edge of the town, Namid spotted what seemed like a lot of people working out in the fields. For a time, she stood watching them and a shepherd to her right, as the sun warmed her. As she turned back to the town, she spotted Inezha near a small building some distance away at the edge of one of the fields. Inezha stood with one hand resting on her chest near her throat.

The gesture seemed familiar somehow, but Namid could not remember where she had seen it before.

Inezha seemed to be talking to someone. But Namid could not see who it was from her vantage.

Then Inezha stepped around the building and was lost to Namid's sight.

Probably charming some of the townsfolk, Namid mused as she turned back into town. She took a different street back in the general direction of the guesthouse, thinking she would get something to eat, then check on Tal.

For the most part, Namid found the town surprisingly clean, certainly cleaner than Rhadanthus had been before its destruction the past autumn. Namid saw some variations in the quality of people's clothes, but no one looked destitute. She saw no beggars such as she had grown used to seeing in nearly every city she had ever been in. The town was anything but quiet. She heard children laughing and people calling to each other, and several different voices raised in discussions or arguments.

Spotting what looked like a tavern, she decided to stop.

Inside, she found the expected tables and chairs, looking well used, but clean. A few patrons sat scattered around the room, eating and drinking. At one end, near what she presumed was the door to the kitchen area, two men engaged in a heated discussion.

Her entrance sent a wave of silence flowing out around her, until even the arguing men fell silent. She was the object of nearly a dozen gazes, not hostile, but almost as intense as Mehratar's. In some ways it reminded her of Rhadanthus.

She gave everyone a broad smile.

"Greetings," she said. "I was hoping to get something to eat?" She looked at one of the two men who had been arguing, thinking that he seemed like he might be the owner.

He gave her a smile and a nod. "Good eye," he said. "I'm the one to talk to. And yes, you can get a bite to eat here." He knocked twice on the door next to him but kept his attention on her. "You're one of our visitors, aren't you?"

She stepped closer, aware that she was still the center of attention. "I am."

The man clapped her on the shoulder, hard enough to knock her forward a couple of steps. "Good. Then you can settle up Magnor here. He says you and your friends are here to talk our Council into letting Navele absorb our town into their realm. But I say you're not even from Navele at all. So, which is it?"

Namid grinned. "You have the right of it," she said. "I'm from considerably further west, and not here representing any of Navele's possible interests in this area. In fact, this is the first time I've ever even been in Navele."

"Well, and you're not in Navele here now, anyway," the second man said with a grin. He handed the first one some coins. "And you got the best of me this time," he said. "But I'll call the next one, Reinulf."

He and Reinulf clasped hands and embraced. "I'll see you back home later," Magnor said. With a nod to Namid, he walked past her and out the door.

"Just pick a chair," Reinulf told her. "I'll bring your food out. What'll you have to drink?"

Namid looked at the other patrons, noticing most of their glasses held drinks of a clear golden-brown color.

"Pick me out something good," she said.

He gave a laugh at that. "That I will."

When he returned, he set before her a bowl of what looked like a hearty stew and a glass mug of the golden-brown drink.

Namid reached for her pouch. "What do I owe you?"

"Before we'd even talk of what's owed, you should taste your meal and drink," he said with a smile. "And for this, you owe nothing anyway. You're a guest of the town."

He waited until she had tried the stew and a sip of the drink. The stew she found delicious, with some seasoning that had a bite to it. As for the drink….

The man's smile widened when he saw her surprised, pleased reaction to the drink. The subtle sweetness, with a hint of some fruit, was unlike anything she had ever tried before. She gave him a wide smile and took a second drink.

"Thought you might like it," he said and left her to her food and drink.

When Namid finished her excellent meal, she again offered to pay and was again refused. Reinulf, the tavern owner she learned, told her to just bring her friends by soon.

"You'll find my place's the best in town," he said. Then he immediately took up an argument with one of his patrons who claimed that a place on the other side of the town was just as good, but different.

With a wave—that many of the patrons returned—Namid headed back out into the town.

A few paces from the tavern, she encountered Hildevei.

"Oh, there you are," the girl said. "Mama and the Healers think that Papa is well enough now to talk with you and the others. I'll show you the way."

Namid nodded and walked with the girl.

"Are you here to make us part of Navele?" Hildevei said as they walked.

"Not at all."

"Good. We're good just as we are."

Namid smiled. "Earlier you said something about councilor business—"

"Oh, yes," Hildevei said with an enthusiastic nod. "Both Mama and Papa are councilors right now. Papa's been a councilor as long as I can remember, and this is my tenth spring."

"So the councilors aren't councilors all their lives?"

Hildevei shook her head. "Not here in Draeivon. But I've heard that the other towns don't do things the same way."

Namid gave her a surprised look. "The other towns?"

Hildevei nodded. "We trade with them and meet for festivals and such. And we pick our life-partners from another town."

Namid glanced at her. "Oh?"

"Except for Mama. But then Papa came from further away to stay with us. So that's like coming from one of the other towns." She stopped in front of a house not too far from the guesthouse. "Here we are. Mama said you'd meet your friends here, too."

Hildevei turned to go.

"You're not coming in, too?" Namid said.

"Mama said to let you grownups talk. Besides, I'm supposed to be at the shop for the afternoon." She gave Namid a half-wave and ran down the street.

When Namid went inside, her first impression was that the house was too small. Everyone seemed crowded into the front room, all standing quietly. Most of the people were townsfolk, people she had not met. She spotted her companions in a corner near a door in the back wall. Everyone in the room turned to look at her. She had a sudden desire to turn around and leave, run and find someplace to hole up.

Aahmes gave her a questioning look.

~*Thoughts of running?*~ came his voice in thought-speech.

~*A few,*~ she admitted. ~*This'll change everything for them.*~

He grinned. ~*True. If it was me, I'd still want to know, though.*~

"She's here," Rannvei said from somewhere to her left.

A space opened in front of her leaving a path between her and Rannvei.

Rannvei turned toward the door near Namid's companions. "I'll just get Tal," she said.

"Wait," Namid said. She glanced at the others in the room, only then noticing their matching gold bracelets.

More of the town's councilors, perhaps?

Namid stepped closer to Rannvei and lowered her voice. "This initially concerns your family more than anyone else," she said. "I suggest just family hear first what I have to say."

Rannvei looked around the room and nodded to Namid.

"This way, then," she said.

Namid turned to Aahmes and held out her hand. With a nod, he took it and joined them.

Rannvei gave Namid a curious look, then led the way into the next room.

Within, Tal sat in a chair next to a wide bed, his expression weary and worried, but otherwise alert. He gave Namid a piercing look, though.

"You have something to tell me, I believe," he said. His voice was softer than earlier but sounded strong enough.

Namid glanced at the two Healers who hovered at Tal's shoulders.

"Is it like with Stefe?" she asked Mehratar.

He shook his head. "Only in that the sound of your voice began the unravelling of the spell. Tal here is perfectly healthy, and his life isn't Powerfully sustained. He's safe."

Namid nodded and looked back at Tal. The town's Healer clapped Mehratar on the shoulder and left the room. Namid reached back to make sure the door closed behind him.

"This first part will be easier to show you," she said and nodded to Aahmes.

"Just yours?" he said.

"Both."

When Aahmes dropped their glamours, Tal started out of his chair in astonishment and Rannvei gasped. Tal's gaze jumped between Aahmes and Namid, then settled on Namid.

"Tanya? Is it possible?"

Namid gave him a slight smile. "Yeah, it's me. Though I go by Namid now."

She winced as he crushed her in a tight embrace, exclaiming how good it was to see her and asking about the rest of the family all in a rush of words. When she finally freed herself, she pushed him back to his chair even as he explained to Rannvei that Namid was his younger sister.

"Oh!" he turned back to her. "I see it now. 'Saina'. And 'Namid'. Parts of your middle name. But why this guise? What about the others? And who is this?" He gestured to Aahmes at that last.

Namid spotted a second chair in the room and pulled it close. "This might take a while," she told Rannvei as she took a seat.

With a nod, Rannvei darted into the outer room and brought back two more chairs. Mehratar excused himself and went into the outer room.

"I can't believe I didn't remember all this time," Tal said as they all settled into their seats. "But your friend, Mehratar is it? He said it was some kind of magic laid on me. Although my memory is still hazy around the attack and a while afterward."

Namid and Aahmes exchanged looks and Namid nodded.

"Yes, a kind of *Power* spell," she said. She then related what had happened since Tal had disappeared, trying to keep from being too long-winded without leaving out anything important. She deliberately spoke vaguely of her time as a captive of the Dark Priests and what she had seen and experienced there. And her voice broke when she spoke of their siblings' deaths, their two older brothers and the sister who had been between them in age.

For the most part Tal listened in silence, only sometimes asking for some clarification. As Namid spoke of the events of the past autumn and everything since, both Tal and Rannvei first looked astonished, then a bit worried. And when she told them the truth about the gods, they shook their heads, expressions full of doubt touched by fear. The fear grew when she told them why she and Aahmes wore the glamours.

When Namid finished, neither Tal nor Rannvei met her gaze. She exchanged a worried look with Aahmes.

~A lot to think about,~ he said in thought-speech.

Tal finally looked at her. "I-I'm not sure what to make of all this," he said.

Namid nodded and asked Aahmes to bring back their glamours.

"You really need to do this?" Rannvei said as she waved a hand in their general direction. "We're safe here."

"I don't want to take any more chances than I have to," Namid said. "Those people have shown that they are completely ruthless."

Tal and Rannvei exchanged looks. "We'll need to decide how much the other councilors need to know," Tal said.

"I just ask, if at all possible, you keep Aahmes' and my identities secret," Namid said. "Please. I'm just a cousin traveling with some of my friends who brought you news and a way to return your memories to you. Oh, and these."

She pulled Tal's signet ring off her thumb and handed it to him. She swallowed a couple of times, from nervousness at his reaction and trying to ease her dry throat.

He took it and turned it over in his hands, studying it, his expression closed.

When she handed him his stylized hawk brooch, he smiled and pinned it to his tunic at the shoulder.

Then he nodded. "Rannvei and I need to talk," he said. "You're welcome to continue using the guesthouse, or if you prefer, we have a couple of houses in town that aren't in use, if you want to move to them."

Namid glanced at Aahmes, who shrugged.

"The guesthouse is fine," Namid said and rose. "We'll

leave you to your talk."

Rannvei stood too, and clasped Namid's hand. "You're family," she said, and embraced Namid, kissing her once on each cheek. "I'm delighted to have a svaina, a sister by marriage."

Namid tried to hide her surprise and gave what she hoped was a sincere smile as the import of Rannvei's words struck her... sister by marriage... and a niece and nephew.

Namid and Aahmes left Tal and Rannvei to their talk. Namid did not pause in the outer room but headed straight outside. She was aware of a few people who lingered in the room, and of her companions joining her, but did not want to talk.

Tal and Rannvei had seemed to take all that she said well enough... upset, of course at the parts that were bad news. Namid was unsure that *she* was taking it all as well. Telling the whole tale had revived and fed some of her worries, with a new concern added about the changes to Tal's life that she could see in his future. And a faint sense of dread had begun to eat at her. Something was coming....

Namid realized she had been hearing her assumed name repeated. She stopped walking and turned her attention to her companions.

Inezha placed a light hand on her arm. "Saina? Are you all right?"

Namid shrugged. "It was rough telling them. And I fear the changes it will bring to them, maybe to this town." She felt a light touch of Mehratar's Power and looked into his intent gaze.

"I'm all right," she said. "Really. Just need to sort out some of this for myself, too."

Inezha gave her arm a squeeze and turned to look around. "I'd wager a drink or two would do you good," she said.

"Food, perhaps, as well," Haeith said.

Namid gave him a surprised look. He returned one of his slight smiles. "You were speaking with them most of the afternoon."

Namid glanced around and saw that it really was late afternoon.

"I know a place that has food and drink, both good," she said, and led the way to the tavern she had visited candle-marks earlier.

The proprietor greeted her like an old friend and after introductions were made all around, pushed two small tables together for them. He brought them tasty meat pies and warm dark bread. And, of course, the drink that Namid had enjoyed earlier. He told them it was called Melomel, a specialty of the town, and if they wanted this type, they should ask for Zeltakra. Then he recommended they also try the other types at the other two taverns in the town and left them to their meal.

They lingered long over their food and more than one glass of Zeltakra, keeping to light topics of conversation. More than once Namid lost the thread of the conversation as her worried thoughts plagued her, but she managed to enjoy the meal, even so distracted. As they finished, her companions took their leave and soon only she and Aahmes sat at the table.

Namid realized she had been staring absently at the table's surface when Aahmes' hand entered her field of vision and waved at her. She looked up at him with a grin.

"Worrying won't change it, or make it better," he said.

"I know. But right now, I can't actually do anything, so...."

"What would you do?"

Namid shrugged and finished her drink. She glanced at the table next to theirs, where several townsfolk sat dicing, but that did not appeal to her. She looked back to find Aahmes watching her with a small smile.

"What?" she said.

"Just liking what I see," he said and grinned.

She laughed, then looked away feeling suddenly shy.

"It's dark now," Aahmes said. "Our time of day. Unless you want another drink."

Namid pondered her glass, then shook her head. "It *is* good, but not now." She caught Reinulf's eye and lifted her coin pouch, giving him a questioning look.

He shook his head with a grin, so she headed to the door, Aahmes a step behind.

Outside, he pulled her close, her hand clasped in his. They sauntered down the street heading away from the guesthouse.

"Do I need to coerce you into sparring with me again?" Aahmes said after several paces.

Namid chuckled. "No. I'm not angry… I just don't want to become Monarch. I want anything but that. But I don't like the feeling that I've made Tal take that path…."

"I didn't notice you making him do anything," Aahmes said. "Just giving him information."

"I suppose."

They walked in silence for a time then, sometimes meeting others and exchanging short greetings. When they reached the edge of town, at a spot different from the one Namid had visited earlier, they stopped and looked out over the moonlit fields.

"Quite the change from Rhadanthus," Aahmes murmured.

"That it is," Namid said. "It's nice here."

Aahmes nodded. She leaned against his side, finally letting go of her worries, at least for a time, and just enjoyed his nearness, the feel of his hand in hers.

"Would you like to live someplace like this?" Aahmes said after a time.

Namid gave it some thought. "Perhaps…."

She felt him laugh. "Might miss the excitement of Rhadanthus?"

"Maybe. I think I'd like to try it sometime… try having the chance to miss it, though."

Faint laugher and shouting came to them in the darkness. They both turned toward the sound, an area of town they had not visited yet. Bright lights came from that direction and the noise increased.

"Shall we see what that is?" Aahmes said.

Namid nodded. "Sure. Sounds like it might be a bit of excitement, anyway."

And so they spent a good portion of the night at one of the other taverns with an unruly group of townsfolk who kept trying to top each other with crazy wagers and contests.

CHAPTER 30

Namid woke the next morning with a slight headache, but a welcome overall sense of well-being that felt foreign to her. When she rolled over on her bed, stretching, she found Aahmes watching her with a smile from where he lounged on his own bed. He lay stretched out on one side with his head propped on one hand. He wore only an old pair of snug trousers and one of his thin, worn shirts, unlaced at the neck and down the front.

"What? Did I snore?" she said.

"Not much. Anyway, they're cute little snores."

Namid threw her pillow at him. He caught it and threw it right back. His expression turned mischievous. "Liking what I see," he said.

Namid realized that her stretching had dislodged her sleeping shift, baring a shoulder and letting the neckline plunge dangerously low. She held his gaze for a breath-of-time, then deliberately let her own gaze rove over his muscular legs, his wiry forearms and his bared chest where she could see it through the open front of his shirt.

"I think I see your point," she said with a wicked grin.

He chuckled.

She laughed too, then winced as the motion made her

headache flare.

"Headache?" He swung his feet over the edge of his bed and sat up. "The townsfolk swear that a glass of Zeltakra will cure that."

Namid sat up too and tugged up the neck of her shift as it threatened to slide even further. "So, you were looking to cure a headache this morning?" she said. "Your own, perhaps?"

He only grinned.

"Does it work?" she said.

"Come out to the main room when you're ready and find out. The townsfolk have brought us quite the variety of food to sample."

He disappeared through the door to the other room and Inezha stuck her head through to give Namid a mock glare.

"About time you were up," she said. "Although considering how late it was—or rather how early—when you two finally stumbled in…."

At Namid's glower, she retreated, laughing.

Namid muttered to herself, with a grin, at how cheerful everyone was. She grabbed the simple servant's gown she still had from Kilaadi and dressed. She dropped the sleeping shift atop her pack, with the passing thought that she should probably soon see to some washing and mending. She checked her daggers in her armguards, out of habit rather than any thought of needing them, then joined the others in the central room.

Both the food and the one glass of Zeltakra that she drank helped Namid's headache. She learned from Inezha that Haeith and Mehratar had left earlier, the former to find a smithy and the latter to visit with the town's Healer. Inezha finished her own meal and announced that she hoped to spend the day with a couple of rather nice men she had met. She left with a grin.

Aahmes ate a little, to keep Namid company as he had already eaten earlier, and joined her for a glass of Zeltakra.

"Do you think they're deliberately leaving us alone?" Namid said with a grin.

"Finally?" Aahmes said. "Could be. So whatever shall we do with ourselves?"

Namid tilted her head slightly and gave him a sidelong look. "Well, let's see… what could two Shadowers possibly come up with?"

"So, you're thinking of thievery?" Aahmes said in mock horror.

Namid gave him an innocent look. "So, you're thinking of something else?" she teased.

He gave her a solemn nod. "Definitely." He held her gaze, the corners of his mouth quirking up just a little.

"Clothes," he said.

"Clothes?"

He nodded. "If you're wearing that, you must be down to the bottom of your pack," he said. "So, much as I hate to say it, I guess that means it's time to wash and mend."

Namid stared at him, then as he slowly grinned, she laughed.

"What did you think I meant?" he said.

She just shook her head with a grin. "Unfortunately, I think you're right. Do you remember where we stashed the mending kit?"

"No, but I'll find it." Aahmes headed into the other room and looked through the packs holding things for everyone's use.

Namid stole a couple more bites of the little bit of food that was left and carried all the dishes and cups to the kitchen area. There she found a large washing basin, complete with a chain pump. She gave everything a good rinse and stacked it all on a table next to the basin. She'd look for soap later.

As she stepped back into the middle room, she heard a knock on the door. With a hand on a sheathed dagger, Aahmes stepped out of the bedroom and closed the door behind him.

"Habit," he said at her look.

With a grin, she showed him the hand she held behind her back, with her stiletto from that armguard. Then she opened the door.

Hildevei and Byartal stood there, looking disheveled and breathing as if they had run a distance.

"See," Hildevei said. "They *are* here."

"Then race you back," Byartal said and ran off.

Hildevei shook her head and sighed. "Boys," she said and shared a look with Namid, who sensed Aahmes' mirth from next to her.

"You were looking for us?" Namid said, trying not to be infected by Aahmes' amusement.

"Oh, yes. Well, Papa is. Well, not exactly looking. Yet. He'd like to talk with you, if you can come over now?"

Namid glanced at Aahmes, who shrugged.

"All right," Namid said.

"Both of us?" Aahmes said.

Hildevei looked at her feet. "Uh, I think just Saina, if that's all right."

"Of course," Aahmes said. Then to Namid, "I'll just keep looking for that kit."

Namid nodded and ducked back inside to get her boots and sheath her stiletto. Then she followed the girl down the street.

"Thank you for coming," Hildevei said as they walked. "Papa and Mama look worried. Maybe you can help?"

Namid wondered at the girl's trust in her. "Have they said what's bothering them?"

"No. Are you a councilor where you're from?"

Namid gave her a surprised look. "Uh, no."

"Oh. I just thought it was because of that. Why he wants to talk with you, I mean."

Byartal ran up to them. "Papa says to go get the spices," he told his sister. "Both of us. We were supposed to pick them up yesterday."

"You go on," Namid said. "I remember the way."

She watched the two children run off and continued to Tal's home. He met her at the door and showed her inside.

He led her to a small table with a couple of chairs in the corner of the room and they took places on either side of the table. Namid shifted at the uncomfortable silence but waited for him to speak first.

"This is rather strange," Tal said finally. "I know you, Tanya. I now remember our childhood again, and you've told me what's happened since the ambush. But it's been so long. I almost feel that we're strangers."

Namid nodded. "Me too. I was still a child when you left... I remember you as you were then."

"The annoying big brother?"

"Yeah."

They sat in silence again for a breath-of-time.

"Is there anything you left out of what you told us yesterday?" Tal said.

"Well, a few details that weren't directly pertinent," Namid said.

"And where does your friend fit in? Fathir. Aahmes. Whatever his name is."

Namid peered at her brother. "Why do you ask?"

Tal chuckled nervously and rubbed his chin. "Well, speaking as your annoying big brother—"

She swatted him on his arm. "Oh, stop!" And laughed at his sheepish grin.

"That's more like it," he said. He studied her. "This... glamour you called it? It's weird talking to an unfamiliar face but hearing your voice and knowing it's really you."

Namid gave an uncomfortable shrug. "Sorry about that. But we feel we need to—"

"I'm not condemning it," Tal broke in. "I understand why. I just wish I could do more directly to help...."

"Keeping the truth of our identities to yourself is an immense help," Namid said.

Tal nodded, but his expression soured.

"Tal?"

He sighed. "I could almost wish you hadn't told me about everything, that I could go on in contented ignorance," he said. "I know my responsibility. I feel drawn to return to Kilaadi, to help mother and father. But this is a good life here. And it wasn't supposed to be me. Being the heir, I mean. With Kalon and Jiro both older than me, it seemed impossible that I'd ever be called on to rule after father and mother. I don't think I can be a good Monarch."

"But you had the same training that Jiro and Kalon had," Namid said. "All of us did really, although I missed out on some things."

Tal slumped down to drop his head on his arms. "I can't take them from here," he said. "Rannvei's family is here—"

"You should talk with Rannvei about that," Rannvei said from the doorway.

Tal lifted his head and looked at his wife with an expression of such torment that Namid felt embarrassed to witness it. After glancing between the two, she rose. "I'll just... I'd better go... see how my friends are faring," she said and hurried past Rannvei and out the door.

Namid paced the streets of the town, lost in thought and not caring where she walked. How could she think to send Tal and his family to the intrigues of the Monarch's court? But she did not want to take his place. The more she tried to picture herself there, taking up the role of heir even—with Andrin and his schemes soundly thwarted of course—the more she wanted to run as fast as she could the other direction. Screaming, even. Maybe she shouldn't have said anything to Tal.

Her wandering eventually brought her back to the guesthouse door, where she stood an interminable time and wrestled with her churning thoughts. When the door opened, she did not even register right away that it had.

Then Aahmes clasped her hand and drew her inside.

"You need to get out of your thoughts, I think," he

said. "Here."

He led her to a chair by a window with a table next to it that held the mending kit. He dumped some of her clothes in her lap and set a full mug of Zeltakra on the table.

He pointed at the clothes, with a stern look. "Mend."

He filled another mug with Zeltakra, from a jug on another table, and sat tailor style on the floor at her feet. He pulled his damaged clothes from a nearby chair and began to work on a torn shirt.

Namid pondered the clothes in her lap, then reached for a needle and thread. "I don't see that this is going to help," she muttered. "I don't really need to think about mending, which means I'll just stay trapped in the same whirl of thoughts."

"Ah," Aahmes said and raised one hand dramatically, the one in which he held his needle. "You have clearly never mended to tavern songs."

"What?"

He looked back over his shoulder at her with a grin.

"How well do you remember the words to 'I'm Done, Go Home'?" he said, naming a song the Shadowers had loved to sing when they gathered in Shadow Keep, making up many silly new verses as the song went on.

Namid stared at him. "Really?"

He nodded. "Really." He sang the first verse as he continued mending his shirt's sleeve.

When he reached the second verse, Namid joined in, soon laughing her way through many of the silly verses.

And so they were just finishing the last of the forty 'official' verses of the song when Inezha returned. She stood in the doorway to the guesthouse and stared at them.

"Well isn't this the homey scene. You two look far too settled here," she said finally and poured herself some of the Zeltakra. "I'd never pictured you knowing how to sew," she said to Aahmes, who just shrugged.

"Can you believe these two?" she tossed over her

shoulder to Haeith, who entered behind her.

"Something I might need to do, too," he said.

Inezha snorted. "Are you all going domestic here?" She drank her Zeltakra and poured the last into her mug. "Need to get out of here before it gets to me, too," she muttered.

She plopped down on a chair and took a sip of her drink. "So, when are we leaving? We're taking Tal back to Kilaadi, right?"

"None of that's been decided," Namid said.

"He's the rightful heir," Inezha said. "He needs to take up those duties. Just make him see that—"

"No," Namid said. "He knows what's at stake."

Inezha waved a hand in a cutting gesture, her expression one of disgust. "I know, I know. You won't use your Power to make anyone do what they should, even though it would make it so much better for so many. And easier for us, too."

She stomped out the door and let it swing behind her. Haeith closed it.

"Wonder why she's so insistent on that," Namid muttered.

The three stared at the closed door without finding any answer there.

With a shrug for that topic, Haeith grabbed Inezha's unfinished mug and drained it. "The smithy here is good," he said. "If any of your blades need attention."

Namid nodded acknowledgement of the information. "Did you see Mehratar when you were out?"

Haeith nodded. "He's going around with the town Healer, seeing to whomever needs them. He looked… content."

"He used to ride circuit Healing, probably mostly villages much like this town, if smaller," Aahmes said. "This must feel a bit like home." With a flourish, he cut his thread with a dagger. "There, all done."

"Me too," Namid said as she tied off her last stitches

and cut the thread.

With little discussion, the three decided to visit one of the other taverns in town for the midday meal and to sample one of the other Melomels.

And afterward, they spent the afternoon cleaning their clothes, checking their gear for any needed repairs, and generally getting ready to depart again, when the time came.

Mehratar and Inezha returned in time for the evening meal, which they took at the third town tavern. There everyone sampled the last two Melomels the town boasted, finding both sweeter than the Zeltakra but tasty in their own way. They left the tavern together as the sun was setting, giving everything an orange glow, but planned to go their own ways for the evening.

Once outside, they paused and sniffed the air.

"That smells like smoke," Mehratar said.

They spun around but saw no signs of anything wrong. The townsfolk they could see were calmly going about their business.

"Must be all the evening cookfires," Inezha said.

After a few breaths-of-time, the others agreed.

They stepped away from the tavern entrance and met Tal coming toward them.

He greeted them warmly and they all chatted about the tasty food to be had at the taverns.

"I'm glad I found you," Tal said after the exchange of pleasantries. "Can we talk?"

He ambled down the street, Namid at his side and the others following along, but within earshot.

"First, I never thanked you," he said. "For bringing my memory of myself back to me and telling me what's been happening."

Namid nodded. "No thanks are needed," she said.

"You've seen much of town these past couple of days. What do you think of it?"

"You've got a good place here," Namid said. "Good

people."

"The other towns in these hills are the same," Tal said.

"Others?" Aahmes said from behind them.

"Yes. I'm sure you've heard tales of the hidden valleys in these mountains. Well, they're real. Within them we have a web of towns, all much like this one, that trade with one another and exist peacefully. Without all the turmoil that's so common in the Six Lands."

Namid nodded.

"So, you see why Rannvei and I don't want to leave," he said. "I hope you don't hate me for deciding to stay… for leaving you as the heir."

Namid stopped dead in the street as dread wrapped tight around her. While not unexpected, she had hoped….

"No, I don't hate you," she said. "I couldn't hate you, of course."

She stared at her feet for a time. "Couldn't you at least come see mother and father?"

"I'd like—"

"Tal!" Rannvei's shout interrupted him.

They all turned toward her as she ran up to them. "Fire!" She waved an arm toward the fields Namid had seen her first day.

Tal and Rannvei ran that direction. Namid exchanged a look with Aahmes and tried to reach out to the Wild Power as they followed, the others keeping pace with them.

"In the fields?" Tal said as they ran.

"Beyond," Rannvei said. "But headed this way. I'll spread the word." She turned down the next side street they came to.

Namid glanced at the orange sky as they ran and realized that the color was not to their west. The odor of smoke grew stronger as they ran.

They halted at the edge of the town overlooking the fields. Beyond the fields, in amongst the still-verdant trees flickered the devouring tongues of flame. They saw the fire advancing their direction.

"We might be able to do something," Aahmes said and clasped hands with Namid. Together they reached out to the Wild Power, seeking, trying to draw it to them.

Trying to concentrate on the Power and the immediate danger both, Namid said, "Haeith, Inezha—"

"I've got the horses," Haeith broke in and turned back toward town.

"Packs," Inezha said.

"Spread the word on the way. Get people moving," Aahmes shouted before they got out of earshot.

"I'm to the Healer's," Mehratar said. "Meet you at the guesthouse or far edge of town." And he was gone.

"What are you going to do?" Tal said.

"See if we can stop it," Namid said as she worked to pull Wild Power. "But if we can't…."

Tal nodded and shouted instructions to others who had come to look. Soon everyone had run back into the town, except for Tal, Aahmes and Namid.

In just those few moments, the fire had reached the edge of the forest and now hungrily clawed at the far ends of the fields. It stretched as high as the treetops and they could hear the roar of the flames. Smoke billowed across the fields toward them, making them cough.

Still trying to draw on Wild Power, Aahmes diverted a little of his own Power to make a shell around them to keep out the smoke.

"I can't draw on any Wild Power!" Namid yelled.

"Me, neither. Just use ours."

So they twined their Power together—it blended almost immediately—and Namid showed Aahmes how she had tried to use Power against the inn fire the past autumn. Together they sent their Power against the flames that raced toward them through the fields, laying their combined Power over the fire, willing it to subside.

The fire paused and writhed at that point, halfway across the fields. Aahmes and Namid poured their Power out against the flames. And slowly, so very slowly, the fire shrank, shorter than the tree-tops, then only as tall as a man, then shorter....

Then it flared again and surged toward the three. Aahmes adjusted his shell, pushed it out away from them to send the fire flowing back. For a breath-of-time it rolled the flames back away from them.

Then they rolled right back toward them, faster than before, towering paces into the air. One section of the fire flared and stretched toward them faster than the rest, headed straight for Tal.

Namid tried to take control of the flames as she had done with various campfires, but these slipped away from her. Her dread from earlier took hold of her. She looked around for the reason.

Namid caught a hint of a sickly-sweet stench on the fire-driven wind. She spotted, mixed in with the conflagration, a greenish-black fog that moved with the fire. Swirls of the green-black fog twisted around and through the bright flames and gave the appearance of pushing the flames forward against their Power.

Namid shuddered as a shock of horror sliced through her. She recognized the fog!

The memory of the fog engulfing Dar, killing him right in front of her, threatened to overwhelm her.

"Look!" Namid pointed toward the fire while she fought to free herself from Aahmes' grasp and run.

"Sy'shythys? How?" Aahmes yelled.

Terror gripped Namid and she lost control of her Power. Aahmes still gripped her hand but her need to run had her pulling him back from the edge of the fields.

Without her Power helping thwart them, the flames shot across the fields toward them, one part bulging far ahead and reaching toward Tal. Aahmes lost control of his Power, too, as the killing fog surged toward them. His Power shell disintegrated, and they all coughed in the smoke that quickly engulfed them, burning their eyes and throats.

Then Tal grabbed Aahmes' and Namid's arms and hauled them back from the approaching conflagration.

"Run!" he shouted.

As they fled, Namid looked back. The flames surged after them still, clearly attempting to reach Tal.

Chapter 31

All was confusion in the small clearing and surrounding forest along the rock outcropping. Townsfolk milled about as they looked for family and friends and tried to sort themselves out. In the mix were all the animals they had been able to rescue, the sheep and cows, dogs and the town's few horses.

Tal, Namid and Aahmes stumbled out of the Wild Power semblance of rocks into the chaos. The last ones out.

Aahmes and Namid dropped to the ground, unable to move another step. Tal took a step away from them, calling for his family and the Healer. Excruciating pain sliced across her tongue and Namid tasted blood. She wiped her mouth with the back of one hand and stared at the blood there. When she lifted her gaze to meet Aahmes', she saw him cradling his left hand obviously in pain. Fresh blood ringed his fingernails and dripped from his fingertips.

~Something to do with blending our Power, I think,~ he said using thought-speech. *~With throwing around so much Power, maybe.~*

Namid only nodded.

Rannvei, Hildevei and Byartal ran to Tal, assuring him they were all right. Mehratar, Haeith and Inezha converged on Namid and Aahmes.

Mehratar reached them first and sent a surge of Healing Power flowing through them, and Tal, to ease their racking coughs and sooth the burning in their throats and chests. With a nod of thanks for Mehratar, Tal moved into the chaos and called in a raspy voice for various townsfolk.

Mehratar's Power did nothing for the bleeding. He gave Aahmes and Namid a concerned look, which Namid waved away. But he still grabbed some cloths and wrapped Aahmes' hand, then handed Namid a waterskin so she could at least rinse the blood from her mouth.

Namid let herself fall back on the ground, feeling she could not even sit up any longer. She spat some blood to one side, then assured her companions that nothing else was wrong with her, aside from a raw throat. Mehratar used Power again to ease that more.

"How could that be possible?" Aahmes muttered.

"What?" Inezha said.

"Looked like Sy'shythys was blended in with the flames," Namid said, with some difficulty as her tongue seemed swollen now. But the bleeding seemed less. "All the townsfolk make it?"

Inezha's eyes went wide at the mention of Sy'shythys and she shrugged in answer to Namid's question. "Don't know yet. They're still figuring it out."

Namid propped herself on her elbows to look around.

"What a disaster," she murmured. She flinched as someone ran by, their feet hitting too close to her fingers.

"We're off to the side," Haeith said. "If you feel up to getting out of the middle of the tumult here."

Namid struggled to her feet and looked for Tal. She spotted him not too far away in earnest conversation with some of the other townsfolk who wore the gold bracelets.

"He'll be able to find us if he needs us," Aahmes

murmured in her ear.

"I feel I should help—" she broke off as a deep cough shook her.

"Later," Mehratar said in a firm voice and led the way to where their horses and packs were.

While Aahmes and Namid rested, still coughing from time to time, the others set up a quick camp, then spread out to help where they could.

Aahmes rolled over to grab a pack, then scooted over next to Namid. He wrapped an arm around her and she leaned against him. They sipped a warm tea that Mehratar had made for them. It helped sooth their throats even more. And the bleeding finally stopped.

As they reached the bottoms of their mugs, the others straggled back and plopped down on the ground.

"They've found everyone, it sounds like," Mehratar said.

"And now they're arguing about staying here, or going to another town, or trying to go back," Inezha said.

"Go back?" Namid repeated. "I doubt the fire would've burned itself out so quickly."

"And we don't know how long Sy'shythys lingers," Aahmes muttered. "If it *was* Sy'shythys."

"If it was, does that mean someone deliberately sent the fire on the town?" Mehratar said.

"Not sure," Namid said. " I just know we couldn't stop it."

"But why not?" Inezha said. "Aren't you two Powerful enough—"

"Sure," Aahmes said. "If it was just the fire, we could probably have beaten it."

Namid stared at the ground. "But when I smelled the killing fog… saw it again…." Namid shook her head.

"Understandable," Haeith said. "After Rhadanthus…."

"There's nothing to say our Power would stop that fog anyway," Aahmes said. "And finding out might well have killed us. And Tal."

Namid nodded. They were right, of course. She looked around at the townsfolk still milling about. They seemed to have decided to stay put for the night, anyway, as it looked like they were making camp the best they could.

The others followed her gaze.

"It'd be foolishness for them to try to go back any time soon," Inezha said after watching the townsfolk. "Fire, fog, or both, they must needs go somewhere else, I think. Reclaim their town later. But be sure to reclaim it…."

Namid peered at her, hearing an odd tone in her voice. But Inezha turned to her with a bright smile.

"Of course," she said. "That's what anyone would do, right?"

Namid nodded and looked up as Tal approached. He gave Aahmes what Namid was coming to think of as the older-brother appraisal, then turned his attention to them all.

"Thank you," he said. "Your help was invaluable. Everyone escaped, and with only a few minor injuries." Then he looked at Namid.

"When you said you had magic… uh, Power, I didn't really think it was—"

Namid gave him a mischievous grin. "You were always the skeptical older brother when I told you things."

He shrugged, with a sheepish expression. "At times, your tales were rather unbelievable."

"But not untrue," Namid said.

Tal shook his head. "No, not untrue, as it turned out."

"I'll have to hear about some of these tales sometimes," Aahmes murmured in Namid's ear, making her smile.

"But after seeing what you did. What the two of you can do," Tal continued, with a gesture that included Aahmes. "I… I certainly can't do anything like that magic!" He shook his head, his expression one of wonderment. "That fire was coming for me, wasn't it? Certainly, the whole town, too, but specifically after me?"

Namid nodded. "That's what it looked like."

Tal sighed and frowned. "I thought so. That's what it looked like to me, too."

Shaking his head, he left them to return to his family.

~ ~ ~

In the morning, while the townsfolk organized themselves in preparation for returning back home, Tal again sought out Namid and her companions.

"Rannvei and I have decided that I'd better take my place as heir," he told them. "That fire didn't just happen to be coming for me. What's to say it won't happen again? I have a duty to the townsfolk, too, as well as to the Six Realms. As long as I stay with the town, I'm a danger to them, much as I wish it could be otherwise. And we'd have no one who could oppose anything like that fire."

His gaze touched on each of Namid's companions, meeting nods of acknowledgement and a smile from Inezha.

"Are you sure of this?" Namid said. "You know what you'll be walking into."

Tal nodded. "It's been good living here. But it's time to return to Kilaadi." He gave Namid and Aahmes a mischievous grin. "As my first official act as heir, I think I'll name the two of you my court mages. That should take care of most of the problems, yes?"

Namid glanced at Aahmes and they grinned at this echo of Thes' words so many weeks earlier.

After more than a candle-mark of getting themselves organized, the first of the townsfolk headed to the rock outcropping to go through the Power-concealed path. But when they tried, they were no more able to pass through than Namid and her companions had been earlier.

This generated more confusion and a lot of arguing, which Namid and the others were careful to avoid. They leisurely packed their own camp while they kept an eye on the townsfolk.

Namid's tongue still ached, but no longer felt swollen. Aahmes unwrapped his hand and studied it, then rinsed most of the dried blood away. A little still circled his fingernails and Namid saw him wince when he moved the fingers.

After close to a candle-mark, the townsfolk reached a decision and by midday had set off to travel to the next town, wherever that was. They gave vague replies regarding the location when Inezha asked.

Tal and his family said their farewells to their friends and handed their gold bracelets to one of the other councilors. Hildevei and Byartal alternated between excitement over going somewhere new and sadness over leaving their friends.

The town councilors gave Tal and Hildevei two of the town's horses and what provisions they could to help with the journey. Namid assured them that she and her companions had plenty and the councilors need not deplete their stores, but they insisted. With secretive smiles, they assured her they would be fine on their journey to the next town.

After the last of the townsfolk disappeared into the trees, Namid and her companions set out the opposite direction. They found their way easily back to the path and headed back the way they had come just days before. Hildevei and Byartal each rode double with one of their parents and the entire family had numerous questions about the realms of Navele and Paronia and the rest of the Six Realms, and the capital Kilaadi. Namid and her companions answered the best they could.

Since the children in particular, but also Tal and Rannvei, were unaccustomed to this kind of journey, the group traveled at a slower pace than usual and decided to stop while the sun still sat above the horizon. But not until after they had passed the ambush site. There both Haeith's and Tal's expressions turned bleak, but no one wanted to pause, so they rode on.

When they stopped further along the path, Mehratar tended to Tal's family's aches from riding while the others set up camp. The children were delighted at eating outside around a fire and after the meal, chased each other through and around the camp.

Inezha hauled out a skin filled with Zeltakra and passed it around.

"How long did it take you to get to the town from Kilaadi?" Tal said as the skin started around a second time.

Namid gave that some thought, her head titled slightly. "About six weeks, I think," she said. "Although we didn't come directly here. Still, it's probably about that long of a journey."

"About that," Aahmes concurred.

"Six weeks?" Rannvei said. She looked at the children. "How are we going to manage six weeks of traveling?"

"We'll be able to shorten that a bit," Aahmes said, and explained about the swift travel technique that he used.

"Since I've learned it too," Haeith added, "we can alternate holding the swift travel and so might be able to make the journey in about half the time."

"Wonderful!" Inezha said.

"You're coming to Kilaadi with us?" Namid said to Haeith.

"I'd thought to," he said. "I might be of some help."

Namid frowned at the thought of what awaited in Kilaadi, but then nodded. Tal patted her shoulder.

"We'll be able to take care of it," he said.

She gave him a smile. "Of course," she said.

But then she met Aahmes' eyes and the concern she saw in his expression matched her own.

"Why didn't you start the swift travel today?" Inezha said. "We could've been well on our way into Navele, I'd think."

"This path," Aahmes said. "Too rough, winds too much, for the swift travel to be much use. We've had to pick our way over the various rocks and roots. If we were trying to swift-travel, those likely would knock us out of it when we ran into them."

Inezha looked at the path, studying it in the twilight, and nodded.

"But as soon as we're done with this mountain path…" Inezha said.

Aahmes and Haeith both nodded.

"Now that we're really going," Tal said, "I *am* eager to get there."

"There might be a problem in Navele. These four don't have those pendants that we got at the border," Mehratar said.

"Oh, I'd forgotten about that," Namid said.

"Pendants?" Rannvei said.

Mehratar pulled his pendant from the neck of his shirt and showed it to her. "The border guards gave us these," he said. "Something they all seem to wear in Navele to identify by sight whether the person is a noble or a commoner."

"They made a bit of a fuss about them," Inezha said.

"Right…" Tal said and dug in his pack. He pulled out one of the pendants, one for a noble. "I remember now, they gave us these at the border all those years ago."

And Namid remembered the pendants for commoners that she had never returned. She dug them out of the bottom of her pack.

"I do still have these," she said, holding them up for everyone to see. "So we have enough pendants. It's just that these four are for the 'free commoners from out-land' as those guards described them."

"While it's been amusing playing the noble," Mehratar said, "I'm happy to be one of our free commoners." He pulled off his pendant and handed it to Rannvei, who gave it a dubious look before she put it on.

"Me too," Namid said as she handed Mehratar one of the commoner's pendants. "I'm much more comfortable traveling in my Shadower clothing."

"And I'll make the third," Aahmes said. "With our guises different from those we used when we crossed the border, this will work out better anyway. I doubt they'll pay as much attention to free commoners."

He and Namid handed their pendants for nobles to Tal for his children and slipped the commoner pendants over their heads. Namid tucked the last pendant back in the bottom of her pack.

"I'm glad to still play the part of a noble," Inezha said with a wide smile. "Although I would have taken a commoner's pendant if needed. But I'm having too much fun being Lady Inezha Nazextas."

She grinned at Namid. "Now you can be *my* handmaiden."

Namid shrugged and gave her a slight smile. Inezha looked crestfallen at Namid's lack of a stronger reaction.

"You'll need to leave the pendants visible while we're in Navele," Haeith said as he pulled his pendant from under his shirt. It was unlike the two kinds Namid had seen so far.

Haeith noticed Namid's interest. "One unique to such as I in service to the Earl Navele," he said.

"Won't there be trouble for you for leaving Navele with us?" Inezha said.

"I have a great degree of discretion in the terms of my service," Haeith said. "There will be no trouble."

Rannvei called the children to her and gave them their pendants, to their delight. Then she took them aside to try to settle them for the night. Tal gave them a fond look and leaned close to Namid.

"I'm impressed at how my little sister has become such an accomplished woman," he said for her ears only. "Who'd have thought you'd be so comfortable taking charge and dealing with all these unusual difficulties." He gave her shoulder a pat, then joined Rannvei.

The others decided on watches and everyone settled in

for the night.

~ ~ ~

The group traveled slowly along the path, taking only an extra day longer than the trip into the mountains had. Late afternoon they rode through thinning trees as they discussed the merits of stopping or riding on a bit further. Namid studied the greenery around them. It looked peaceful.

Something felt off.

She reached out with tendrils of Power and still felt that something was wrong but could not sense even a hint of what it might be. She started the struggle to pull Wild Power, just in case, as she urged her horse up next to Mehratar. He gave her a questioning look.

"Would you please see if you sense anybody nearby?" she said in a hushed voice.

Aahmes caught her attention. *Problem?* he asked using the Shadowers' hand-talk.

Not sure, she replied the same way.

"I don't sense anyone other than us," Mehratar said. "But there's a strange Power, near where the path finally comes out of the foothills. Near where we camped that night before we headed into these mountains."

"Not the Wild Power of these mountains?"

Mehratar shook his head. "I can't sense that. And I haven't sensed this one before. I don't like the feel of it."

Namid sent out the thinnest tendril of Power to that spot and recoiled instantly.

"Dark Priests," she said.

That got everyone's attention.

"How?" Inezha said.

"Maybe they escaped with Randoq," Namid said. "Some probably did. They're down near the bottom of the path."

"Waiting for us," Aahmes said.

"It seems so," Namid said.

"Can we go around them?" Mehratar said.

Haeith shook his head and drew his sword. "Not through this foliage. So let's end this," he said.

"No, we're not staying back," Rannvei's voice rose from her discussion with Tal. "They could sneak around and come from behind. We're better together." She slid off her horse to string her bow, then put both children together on her horse and prepared to lead it. The children looked around with wide eyes and stayed quiet.

Haeith positioned himself next to the children's horse and nodded to Aahmes and Namid.

Namid studied the children, then her gaze was drawn to Tal.

"I haven't fought anyone in earnest since the ambush," he told her. "Although I've attempted to keep in practice."

Namid met Rannvei's stern but worried gaze.

Rannvei shook her head.

Namid turned back to Aahmes. "I'd say to try to use the swift travel right past them—"

"We can't yet start it," Aahmes said. "Too many obstacles."

"I thought that might be so," Namid said. "Haeith, if three of us work together to hold a semblance of nothingness around us, will that make it stronger? Harder to discern?"

With a thoughtful expression, Haeith sheathed his sword. "Your reasoning is sound."

"Then you set it up and draw Aahmes and me in to strengthen it. And let's sneak right past these Priests."

Haeith nodded and began to weave his Power into the nothingness semblance.

"Will this work?" Rannvei said.

"I think it will," Namid said. "But hold yourself ready in case they do discover us."

Rannvei nodded

Haeith held out his hands to clasp Aahmes' and

Namid's, then drew them into the working. Less than a quarter candle-mark later, they came out of the Power.

"Is it done?" Mehratar said.

Haeith nodded. "And the strongest I've ever seen." He gave Aahmes and Namid one of his rare smiles. "A delight to work with so much Power."

"Then let's get going," Inezha said. "I, for one, wish to be well past them as soon as we can."

Aahmes and Namid led and rode side by side when they could. Haeith took the rear. The others followed close behind Aahmes and Namid and kept the children's horse in the middle of the group. Rannvei continued to lead their horse.

They traveled in silence, to avoid straining the Power that held nothingness around them. After about a quarter candle-mark, they emerged from the last copse of trees and saw the expected group of people near the path. Although not dressed in the distinctive dark green-gray the Dark Priests used to favor, the sense of their Power that Namid felt clearly identified them as such. Namid counted twelve of them and wondered if they were all of the Dark Priests who had escaped Corentris, not counting Randoq.

Slowing slightly to lessen the sounds the Power needed to cover, they started past the Priests.

Namid felt a sudden surge of unfamiliar Power that wrapped around them and the Priests. As she felt the semblance disintegrate beneath the Power, both she and Aahmes threw defensive Power shells around their group.

"Can you grasp any Wild Power?" Namid said to Aahmes.

"Not yet. The Wild Power in these hills is not particularly cooperative," he said.

Namid chuckled. "As opposed to the Wild Power we've wrestled with everywhere else."

He chuckled with her. "True."

When the group's semblance vanished, the Dark Priests moved to surround Namid and her companions.

Then a shimmer a short distance away attracted everyone's attention. Fading into view from the shimmer, a tall woman strode toward the two groups. She wore simple clothes, trousers with a plain short tunic that wrapped to one side and tied there, both of a dark green color that matched the pine needles Namid had seen in the mountains behind them. Her low boots were the brown of the tree trunks.

Namid studied the woman as she approached. The woman wore her black hair woven into many thin braids that hugged her head, then flowed down her back, not quite as long as Namid's single braid. The woman's skin was dark brown, a shade or so lighter than Inezha's, and her eyes a pale green-gray. Namid judged she stood about Aahmes' height. She stopped a pace or so away and looked them over with a stern expression, hands on her hips. Her gaze lingered first on Mehratar, then on Haeith.

"Narqir," Haeith said.

"The war god?" Hildevei said, awe clear in her voice.

The woman nodded.

At this, the Priests surrounding the group backed away from the woman, muttering. Namid saw fear in the expressions of many of them. A couple of them dropped to their knees.

Narqir peered at Haeith.

"I greet you, Flame Warrior," she said.

Haeith bowed in his saddle. "Flame Warrior no longer," he said.

She studied him and a slight smile touched her lips. "Whoever has told you that is sorely mistaken," she said. Then her gaze ran across everyone else there. "But I'm not here for that. Explain what you've been doing in my mountains." Her gaze touched on Aahmes and Namid, then the Dark Priests... then snapped back to Aahmes and Namid.

"Ilenii spoke true, for once," she muttered. "The resemblance is remarkable."

Both Aahmes and Namid drew Power to themselves in preparation. Narqir laughed.

"I take no part in their enmity against you," she said. "But you are among the ones who used Power in my mountains. Explain yourselves."

~Think these Priests started the fires?~ Aahmes said to Namid using thought-speech.

Narqir whipped around to glare at the shrinking Priests. "You started the fires that have brought such hardship to the people who shelter in my mountains?"

~She heard you,~ Namid said to Aahmes, then flinched when Narqir glanced at her and smiled.

One of the Priests, greatly daring, stepped toward Narqir and bowed deeply.

"We knew not that these are your mountains, oh war god," the Priest said, her voice trembling. "We simply sought to drive these royal miscreants and their lackeys away from the good townsfolk and out into the open, so we could take them to Kilaadi. *They* fanned the flames with their Power and drove them out of control, destroying the valley to stop us."

"Miscreants and lackeys? I think we've been insulted," Aahmes murmured to Namid.

Namid grinned at him and turned to glare at the Priest. "And what of Sy'shythys?"

Narqir looked from her to the Priest. "You would bring that vile creation to my territory?"

The Priest trembled so hard she could barely speak and several more of her fellows dropped to their knees. "It was but an illusion."

"An illusion?!" Namid shouted at the Priest. "We could have stopped the fires if not for your *illusion*!"

Narqir's Power swept across them all, stilling Namid's anger and the Priest's trembling. Then the Power wrapped around the Priest in a way Namid had never seen before.

"Tell me," Narqir said in a soft voice.

Staring straight ahead, the Priest spoke in a toneless

voice. "We couldn't find a way into the valley. We started the fires as close as we could and sent them that direction, to fulfill our mandate to kill the heir, so only one would be left."

"What?" Inezha exclaimed, sounding indignant. Mehratar laid a calming hand on her arm, but she still looked outraged.

Narqir nodded and her Power slid away from the Priest. "I've heard what I needed," Narqir said.

With a growl, the Priest sent a bolt of Power directly at Tal and his family.

And Namid laughed as it bounced off the double Power shells that she and Aahmes still held.

"Short memory," Aahmes murmured.

"I think they missed the finale at Corentris," Namid said.

"Ah, right. They were already running away."

A faint glowing aura around her, Narqir flowed into a pose that resembled those the Shadowers used in their unarmed combat and she leapt at the woman. Faster than Namid would have thought possible, with leaps and kicks, Narqir spun through all the Priests, dropping them to the ground. When she turned toward Namid and her companions, her eyes glowed faintly.

The group held themselves still and waited to see what Narqir would do then.

She only took a deep breath and closed her eyes for a breath-of-time. When she opened them again, the glow had vanished, and she looked as she had before her attack.

"Are they..." Tal ventured.

"No, young prince," Narqir said. "Merely rendered easier to transport. They have much to do to correct the damage they have done."

"What will happen to them after?" Rannvei dared to ask.

With a gentle smile, Narqir shrugged. "That will depend at least in part on what they are like after they complete the tasks I have for them. But know that, either way, they will not come again after you and yours."

Rannvei nodded.

"I wish you a much more pleasant journey from here," Narqir said. She sent out a wave of Power that gathered the Priests all together in a pile—like so many sticks bundled up for carrying—and lifted them to float behind her.

When she turned back, she seemed surprised to still see the group there. She gave them a questioning look.

"No need to linger here," she said. "I know you have things to do."

Aahmes and Namid glanced at each other.

"About the theomachy—"

Narqir interrupted Namid. "We both know that you know I'm no more a god than you," she said. "True, I once felt as the others did and joined in on all the Power-grabbing and scrambling. But I'm no longer of that mind. Surprisingly, Sesaisyd was the one who helped me see that it didn't have to be that way. He was the first of us who tried to leave that life. For me, he gathered the Wild Power into the pockets to protect the valleys in these mountains."

She grinned at their stunned expressions. "I see that surprises you. Now is not the time but seek me out sometime and we can talk more. Just know that what is commonly told about the gods is not always reliable. And know that I'm staying out of the current conflict. I cannot speak for any of the others."

With a wave, she gathered up her pile of Priests and started walking toward the mountains, right through the Power shells as if they did not exist. She stopped next to Haeith and rested a hand on his knee. For a time, they looked at each other.

Talking with thought-speech, Namid assumed.

Haeith shook his head once, then Narqir raised one hand, palm facing him. He stared at her until she nodded, then touched his fingertips to hers.

Namid saw a faint, golden glow where their fingers touched. Then the glow vanished.

Haeith inclined his head to Narqir and she gave his knee a friendly pat. With a glance back at Namid, the war god took her pile of Priests into a shimmer of air like the one that had brought her.

For a stunned breath-of-time, the group stared after her. Then with a quick exchange of looks, they headed away from the mountains.

CHAPTER 32

They used the swift travel as much as they could and tried to avoid cities and towns along the way, only pausing near any when they needed more provisions. At those times, Haeith got what they needed while the others remained hidden beneath a nothingness semblance. They fell into a pattern of several candle-marks of swift travel in the mornings and afternoons, separated by a couple of candle-marks of rest, with long evening breaks from travel, too.

Roughly a week into their journey, in the evenings, Aahmes began to teach Hildevei and Byartal some basic dagger techniques, under Rannvei's watchful eye. Tal and Haeith frequently sparred and Tal's sword-work improved quickly as he remembered previous teachings. Namid and Aahmes worked together with the Power mostly to strengthen their linking and coordination. Otherwise, they tried to keep the Power use minimal to avoid attracting unwanted attention. And Namid, Inezha and Aahmes sparred from time to time in three-way dagger mock battles. Those usually ended with Mehratar Healing a few slices and cuts. Rannvei practiced with her bow, when Aahmes was not teaching her children, and began to teach both Namid and Hildevei, who were the only ones who expressed interest. Although Haeith once borrowed Rannvei's bow and released all his arrows directly into the targets he picked.

"Haven't forgotten," he said in a quiet voice as he returned the bow with a slight bow.

And so the days and leagues passed. They bypassed the border posts that lined Navele's border with Paronia by crossing at night and as far away as they could manage from any border post. Even using the swift travel, they still took longer than three weeks to reach a point from which they could get to Kilaadi the next day.

The evening before they planned to enter Kilaadi, Namid sat with her back against a tree and watched Aahmes with Tal's children. He seemed comfortable with them and they both seemed to like him. They listened intently to what he told them, then they backed away and he demonstrated several techniques all strung together into a deadly dance at breathtaking speed.

"Impressive," a voice said from Namid's left. Rannvei settled to the ground next to her and also leaned against the tree. "And your man is good with the children."

Namid just smiled and nodded, still watching him, feeling a rush of pleasure at the thought of 'her man'. After Aahmes set the children to practicing some simple unarmed moves, he glanced at her with a grin and bowed to her with a dramatic flourish.

Both Namid and Rannvei chuckled at the sight.

"I have some concerns about the morrow," Rannvei said after Aahmes returned his attention to the children.

Namid nodded. "We should all discuss how we want to do this."

"Do you think we'll be fighting our way in?" Rannvei said.

Namid shrugged. "It's certainly a possibility. After Aahmes is done, let's all talk."

Rannvei left her to join Tal where he stood watching their children with their mock battles. Namid thought Tal's expression looked resigned. He and Rannvei spoke briefly, then he met Namid's gaze and gave her a nod.

After the children finished with their lesson and everyone had eaten, they all gathered around the fire, the children included. Although with the number of times they yawned, Namid doubted Hildevei and Byartal would stay awake much longer.

"How do you want to do this tomorrow?" Inezha asked Namid. "March in the front door and toss Andrin out on his—"

"What do you think?" Namid broke in, looking to Tal.

"I don't know," he said. "I'm fine following—"

"Tal!" Namid interrupted.

He grinned. "Well, I thought I'd try. You *do* seem to have more experience at this sort of thing than I do."

Aahmes leaned close to Namid's ear. "He's got you there," he said.

Namid made a shooing motion at Aahmes and gave Tal a pointed look.

He sighed, then straightened his shoulders and looked around at everyone.

"What do we know? What do we guess? And what's going to trip us up?" he said.

"We might know a less obvious way in," Inezha said. "Up to a point." She looked at Namid.

"Uh, yeah," Namid said. "I might have blocked the citadel side of the one hidden way in that Inezha and I know."

Aahmes chuckled. "I did discover a couple other places those secret passages come out," he said. "Didn't have time to explore them all. But none of them are near or outside the walls. So, we'll likely have to cross areas that at least servants frequent, before we can get into those passages."

"We have secret passages?" Tal asked Namid.

A laugh went around the group. Namid nodded. "Mother showed me an entrance from the heir's rooms."

Tal looked thoughtful.

"More of what we know is that Andrin controls father," Namid said. "We don't know if that control can be removed without hurting father. And we're not sure what else that might do to him."

"I'll be of help there," Mehratar said. "But I'll need to see what ails the Monarch before I can say for sure."

"How close do you need to be to him to find out?" Haeith said.

Mehratar thought about that. "Inside the outer walls of the citadel, for certain. Maybe no closer than that, but the closer I am the easier it will be and the less likely that my Power will be noticed."

"Did you find a passage running to mother and father's rooms?" Namid asked Aahmes.

He shook his head. "But then I wasn't looking for any, either. I think there *was* a passage that headed that direction."

"What else?" Tal said.

"I have a way to temporarily incapacitate people by getting them to fall asleep for a brief time," Mehratar said. "That can help us sneak in."

"I also have something that will work similarly," Namid said as she remembered the poison that Aahmes had given her.

"So we should be able to sneak in and get into these secret passages," Rannvei said.

"On the guessing side, we might have a problem holding glamours and semblances," Namid said. "Last time, a Power lying over the city broke the glamours Aahmes held on us at the time. Don't know if that Power's still there."

Tal nodded. "Good to know ahead of time, in case it is. Is it this Andrin's work?"

Namid shrugged.

"Can those of you with Power contain this Andrin once we get inside?" Tal said. "Keep him from doing anything else so we can imprison him?"

Aahmes and Namid shared a look.

"We should over-Power him enough to be able to do that," Aahmes said.

"Such a thing is not something I know," Mehratar said. "But I can lend even more Power, if you need."

"I also," Haeith said.

Tal looked around at everyone, his gaze lingering on his son and daughter, then sighed.

"All right. I see two possibilities for getting in, but don't know which is better, if either one is. We can try to enter the city tomorrow during the day, maybe mix with others who are entering, and hope that the glamours hold. Then find an inn in which to wait until nightfall to sneak into the citadel. Or we can just remain here until nightfall tomorrow and have a much greater distance to cover to get to the citadel."

"With the likelihood of closed and guarded city gates to get past," Inezha said.

"That, too," Tal said.

They all considered the options.

"Both have risks," Mehratar said finally. "Some of which we can't know until we've committed to one. I'd favor getting closer to the citadel during the day. That will also let us more easily leave most of our things and the horses."

"And those of us with knowledge of creating semblances and glamours will just need to be prepared to throw new ones on everyone if this Power is still there," Aahmes added. "If we can."

"We should only really need them anyway to get to rooms in the inn," Namid said.

"We need not make a final decision this night," Haeith said. "A look at the people entering the gate tomorrow and the alertness of the guards could tell us much and might help decide." He looked at Tal.

Tal glanced at Namid and, when she remained silent

and gave no indication of her thoughts, sighed. "All right, then. I agree. I also favor getting closer first, but let's see what more we can learn from a look at the gate after it's open."

"I'll approach the gate in the morning," Haeith said. "I should be able to sense any Power blanketing the city from that close and can assess the guards' alertness."

"I'll follow to watch your back," Inezha said.

Tal nodded.

"So, a preliminary plan…. Assuming then that we'll be finding an inn tomorrow, we'll just leave from there after full dark. Then, expecting problems of course, we'll sneak into the citadel, incapacitating anyone only if we must but preferably bypassing them altogether, and hide in the passages. We find the closest egress near mother and father's rooms, free father from this Andrin's Power, and neutralize and capture Andrin."

He looked around at the others. "Anything to add for now?"

"Will the youngsters stay at the inn?" Inezha said, with a wave of her hand at the two children who slept at Rannvei's sides.

Tal and Rannvei exchanged looks. "We can find a place for you and them to hole up in these secret passages," Tal told Rannvei. "Keep them hidden and safe until it's all straightened out."

"It won't be comfortable, but I'm sure we'll find a good spot," Aahmes assured her.

Rannvei nodded to Aahmes and gave Tal a look that Namid recognized, one that said they would talk about it more. Later.

~ ~ ~

The next day, midmorning, they moved as close as they dared to Kilaadi, and settled in a hollow not too far from one of the gates, concealed among the trees.

Haeith and Inezha slipped through the trees to the road to see what they could learn at the gate. Everyone else tried to wait patiently in their hollow, mostly settled on the ground among their packs. But Namid saw she was not the only one who periodically strained to look the direction Haeith and Inezha had gone.

After she had paced around the hollow enough to begin wearing a path in the grass, she finally settled at Aahmes' side. With a smile for her, he wrapped an arm around her shoulders.

"I've been thinking we should try to use Wild Power as much as we can for this," Namid said.

Aahmes nodded. "Should make it that much less likely that Andrin will sense it or recognize that it's us."

So, they together sought nearby Wild Power and painstakingly drew it to them and linked to it, so they could call on it at need.

Inezha and Haeith returned after nearly two candle-marks.

"There are four guards at the gate," Inezha said.

"Two flank the gate on the outside, and two more on the inside," Haeith said. "They're not as attentive as they should be. And I sensed no Power blanketing the city."

Aahmes nodded. "Good. Glamours and semblances will make this much easier."

"Were there many people entering the city?" Tal said.

"Not as many as you'd see on a market day, but a steady stream nonetheless," Haeith said. "No group as large as ours, however."

"We'll split up then, but stay near each other," Tal said. Then he asked Namid, "Should we all have glamours?"

Namid glanced at Aahmes, asking his thoughts with a look. He shrugged. "Namid and I, of course. The rest of you… probably. At this point we can't say who might have descriptions, or even drawings of any of us."

"Can you hold that many glamours?" Inezha said.

Aahmes grinned. "But I'd prefer we waste no time

finding an inn. I want to have as much Power available as I can later, just in case."

So Aahmes crafted new glamours for each of them while everyone else packed up the horses. It took him longer than usual because he used Wild Power to construct them, something he had not done before. He warned everyone the glamours might not hold as long because of using Wild Power, but no one else would be likely to sense the glamours either.

They decided to divide into three groups. Rannvei, Namid and Inezha would travel with the children. Aahmes and Mehratar would be slightly ahead of them, while Haeith and Tal would follow.

They backtracked a little through the trees, then made their way to the road. After they watched for just a quarter candle-mark, they spotted a large gap between groups that let them slip right in as if they had been there all along.

At the gate, Namid kept an eye on the guards, looking for any sign that they planned to raise an alarm, but as Haeith had said, they were inattentive. Their gazes only rested on Namid's group for a breath-of-time, then slid away, dismissing them. They did study the two pairs of men longer, but then returned to their conversations.

Namid and her companions all waited until they got further into the city, out of sight of the gate, to regroup and begin the hunt for an inn. This area they found themselves in was clearly a poorer section of the town, and the people they saw showed no interest in them, but it was further from the citadel than they wanted to be. So they ventured further inward.

Namid saw more guards in the streets than when they had arrived in Kilaadi the last time. Many of the guards took some interest in the group, but not enough to stop them or talk to them. After close to a candle-mark of making their way through the streets, their pace no faster than the others around them, they came within sight of the citadel.

"How rich of an inn do we want?" Aahmes said, leaning close to Namid so he could keep his voice low.

"Rich enough to ensure privacy and a measure of security for the horses," Namid said. "But not so rich that we really stand out as wealthy. Although we do have enough to cover whatever we might find."

Aahmes nodded and peered at the nearby structures.

"How about that one?" he titled his head toward a large inn near the end of the street. As Namid studied it, a small, merchant's caravan stopped outside it.

"Should be good," she said. She glanced back toward the citadel. "And we're good and close for later."

They rode to the inn and dismounted, hauling their packs off the horses before they turned them over to the care of three stablehands who came running. The merchant they had seen gave them a friendly nod as they passed him headed for the main door.

Inside, the main room was well lit, with several patrons at the tables taking their midday meals. The room smelled pleasantly of baking bread and spiced meat. When they paused inside the door, a server hurried up to them.

"Accommodations, or just a meal?" she said.

"Accommodations," Tal said.

She nodded. "Just head over there and I'll tell Orth to come on out." She pointed toward the bar at the side of the room and hurried through a door opposite.

Before they reached the bar, a large man came out from behind the door and headed toward them, wiping floury hands on a towel. He met them at the bar and pulled a book out from behind it.

He looked them over quickly. "If you don't mind sharing, I've got two rooms that between them have enough beds for all of you, with a common room between," he said. "Otherwise you'll need to split into rooms for twos and threes scattered on the two upper floors."

With a quick look at the others, Namid stepped

forward. "The two rooms with the common room will do just fine," she said. "And feed and stabling for our horses, of course."

"Of course." He nodded and pulled a pen and ink out from behind the bar and made some tick marks on two of the lines in his book. "How many nights?"

Namid glanced at the others. They had not talked about that.

"Two," Tal said. "With an option to add some more, I hope."

The innkeeper nodded again. "My pleasure." Then he named the price for everything for the two nights.

Namid pulled out two of the smallest of the cornelian gemstones she still carried and handed them over. Orth examined them closely and even took them into the sunshine from a window. Then he pulled out two keys and handed them to Namid.

"Entry to the bedrooms is through their common room," he told them. "The second key's so you don't have to find me if you decide to go out in more than one group. Take the stairs to the third floor and go to the end of the hall on your right. Evening meals and breakfasts are included for what you've paid me. You can buy your midday meals here or anywhere you like."

"I'm hungry," Byartal spoke up.

The man smiled at the boy and looked around at the adults, deftly picking out Rannvei. "If you wish, I can send up a midday meal for all of you. We're quiet today, so the servers have the time."

Rannvei glanced at Namid and Tal, who both nodded. "My thanks," Rannvei said. "We accept your kind offer."

Aahmes passed over two navns to pay for the meal and the service.

The innkeeper smiled and nodded. He promised that someone would bring their meal in less than a quarter candle-mark, then returned to the kitchen.

Following his directions, they found the rooms with no

trouble.

Namid felt relieved when they were all inside and had locked the door behind them. A slight sensation like water flowing off her tickled her skin. She gave Aahmes a questioning look.

"Trying something a little different," he said. "I'm hoping that will let me bring back the glamours easier and quicker, even using Wild Power for them."

Namid nodded and placed a shell around their rooms to keep anyone from hearing anything they might say within.

"You took them off?" Inezha said to Aahmes.

"For now." He tossed his pack through the door into one of the bedrooms and plopped down in one of the chairs in the common room. Haeith and Mehratar also dropped their packs in that room, with Inezha following their example. Tal and Rannvei took the children and their few belongings into the other bedroom. Namid just dropped her pack near the outer door and looked around.

"Should do just fine," she said.

"And we need to stay hidden until tonight?" Inezha said with a hint of complaint in her voice. "Dull."

"My children will likely agree with you," Tal said as he returned to the common room.

"I know some games that help pass the time," Haeith said. "Perhaps they will amuse the children after our meal."

Tal gave him an absent nod as he looked around the common room. Then he rearranged the chairs and the two tables so they could all find a place at a table. The server brought their food just as he finished. Aahmes slipped the glamours back on everyone and answered the knock at the door. He released the glamours again after the server left. On her way out, she told them to just leave the dishes outside the door when they were finished.

After they finished their meal, Haeith pulled out some dice and taught the children a few of the games that warriors used to pass the time while they waited, or so he told them. Namid recognized a couple of them as similar to games the Shadowers had played in Shadow Keep, although Haeith left out the wagering part. She even joined in for a while, as did the others at various times throughout the afternoon.

When Hildevei and Byartal tired of the dice games, Mehratar engaged them in some riddle guessing games for over a candle-mark, with the others again sometimes joining in. Then Haeith pulled out several small carved wooden pieces with numbers on them and a rolled piece of leather that had been marked into checkered squares and began teaching the children a complex game he called "Numbers Battle". This drew everyone's attention, and soon they became engrossed in learning the game and trying to help Byartal and Hildevei play against each other.

And so the afternoon passed.

For the evening meal, they ate in the inn's common room, with their glamours active again, then returned to their rooms. A few more games to pass the time, then everyone prepared for the evening's excursion, choosing what to take and what to leave behind in the rooms.

They planned to travel as lightly as possible. And everyone dressed pragmatically, in tunics and trousers. No gowns, not even servant's clothes, for this excursion.

When they judged it dark enough, and the inn had quieted, indicating most everyone had retired for the night, Haeith put the nothingness semblance around the group and they made their way through the inn and outside. They encountered no one on the way.

It was late enough that they saw few people about in the city. Taking their time, they made their way to one of the side gates that Namid remembered in the citadel walls, deliberately avoiding the one they had used weeks earlier when Namid, Aahmes and Inezha left so precipitously.

They paused among the buildings nearest the gate and looked across the paces-wide cleared area that extended from the city buildings to the citadel wall. A couple of the moons gave dim light and they watched two guards at the gate pacing and chatting with each other.

Namid looked at Mehratar. "Can you tell if there are guards inside the gate, too?" she whispered.

He let his Power waft out into the night and shook his head.

"There's a Power shell similar to yours covering the citadel," he whispered back. "I can't sense anything through it."

"Andrin?" Aahmes said.

Namid reached out with a tendril of Wild Power and just brushed the shell. She nodded. "Andrin."

"Let's ease up next to the wall," Mehratar said. "And I can send both guards to sleep while staying under the nothingness semblance."

After the guards were safely asleep, Aahmes picked the lock. They propped the guards against the wall out of direct sight through the gate, locked the gate behind them to make their entry less obvious and hurried through the garden in which they found themselves.

~Is this the garden that you found that has the entrance to the passages?~ Namid asked Aahmes using thought-speech.

~I think so. We'll know in a breath-of-time.~

When they reached the wall of the citadel, Aahmes poked around, then shook his head at Namid.

"I don't see a way in to the passages here," he whispered.

"There's another garden next to this one," Inezha whispered. "I saw a gate to it as we passed."

So they followed Inezha to the gate to the next garden—unlocked—then headed back to the citadel.

"This looks right," Aahmes said as they walked.

At the citadel, he led them almost directly to the hidden door. He sent a sliver of Power through the wall to pull the lever on the other side and they all slipped into the darkness of the hidden passages. Aahmes closed the door behind them.

Namid tried to create a light orb but could not using Wild Power. When she told the others the problem, Mehratar managed to create a small, dim light orb and set it to hover a couple of handspans above the ground.

"Can you try to sense father now?" Namid then asked the Healer.

Again he sent his Power out, and this time concentrated much longer than when they were outside the gate.

"Things are still somewhat obscured," he said. "Like looking through fog. I think I sense the Monarch. Someone extremely ill, anyway…." His voice trailed off as he concentrated more.

"What is it?" Tal said.

"He was poisoned," Mehratar said. "This Andrin is preventing the poison from killing him, but it has hurt him badly. I get the sense that this Andrin is very familiar with this poison."

"Probably gave it to him himself," Namid muttered angrily.

"I can't say for certain," Mehratar continued. "But I think I'll be able to help the Monarch, to save his life. But not at a distance."

"Where is the Monarch?" Inezha said.

"I can't say where in the citadel," Mehratar said. "I don't know the rooms. But he's that way." He pointed ahead and to their left.

"Is he asleep?" Namid said.

Mehratar nodded as he pulled back his Power.

"His chamber, then," Tal said. He looked at Aahmes. "Can you guide us there?"

"Perhaps not directly," Aahmes said. "But we'll get there. Follow me." He led them further into the passage, the light orb keeping pace with him.

They worked their way through the passages at a slower pace than Namid would have liked, sometimes having to turn back at wrong turns. Namid lost any sense of their direction and hoped Aahmes knew what he was doing. She sensed him reaching out through the Wild Power from time to time but could not tell what he was doing with it.

When they paused at one crossing of passages, they all sank down on the floor for a brief rest. The children looked exhausted. Rannvei gave Namid a look of concern when she noticed her studying the children.

"We need to find someplace better to rest," she told Namid. "They won't last much longer."

"How long have we been in here anyway?" Inezha said.

"Close to two candle-marks, I think," Namid said.

All of a sudden, Aahmes cursed.

"What?" Namid said.

"Look." He gestured to the floor of the passage crossing the one they sat in.

Mehratar moved the light orb closer to Aahmes. Then Namid saw what had him upset.

The dust on the floor of that other passage was clearly disturbed. Recently. By a group that included two people with much smaller feet.

"But how?" Mehratar said.

"Some kind of semblance, maybe," Namid said. "To hide that we've been through this way. Sort of."

Aahmes shook his head but said nothing.

"More than that, I think," Haeith said. "Something more like a veneer. That in this case has us inclined to think we are traveling new paths within these passages."

Now Namid cursed, but softly.

"Does that mean they know we're here?" Rannvei said.

"Not necessarily," Haeith said. "I'd say it's certain Andrin knows of these passages though."

"And knew that we'd return to the citadel," Namid said. "And likely use them."

"He might have set this veneer as part of that Power he's got overlying the citadel," Haeith said.

"Does that mean we must take to the regular

hallways?" Tal said.

Everyone exchanged glances.

"Are the glamours still an option?" Inezha said. We can grab some servants' clothes…."

Aahmes shook his head. "Whatever took the glamours down before is active again," he said. "No glamours for us."

"But the semblance is holding," Haeith said.

"So if we're very careful about being quiet, no one should know we're here?" Rannvei said.

"That's the idea," Aahmes said.

"Then it's become even more important to find a spot for Rannvei and the children to hide," Tal said.

"We're staying with you," Rannvei said.

Tal shook his head. "I don't want to risk you—"

"If you'll permit," Haeith broke in, looking from one of them to the other. "I'll help guard the children. I pledge my life to their safety."

Tal studied him, then looked at Rannvei, who nodded.

"Very well," Tal said. He turned to Aahmes.

"Find us someplace less-frequented to come out, then a good place to rest a bit."

Aahmes nodded and led the way, this time extending tendrils of Wild Power before him to help find the way.

CHAPTER 33

The longer they traveled through the passages, the more Namid fought a growing sense of something horribly wrong. While nothing she could put her finger on, she had an impression that more was going on in the hidden passages than only a veneer of having not traveled that way. By the time Aahmes stopped them at a door and said they would leave that way, her head ached from tension.

She gathered Wild Power to her through the links she and Aahmes had set up in preparation, and also drew two daggers. As Mehratar released his small light orb, Aahmes opened the door the smallest crack to peer through.

After several long breaths-of-time, he opened the door wide and led them through, closing the door behind them.

Namid looked around at what she guessed must be one of the guest rooms, a smaller one for guests of lesser stature and more brightly lit than she expected. Judging by the dust everywhere, the room had not been used in a long time.

Aahmes strode to the single window and drew the curtain aside a finger-width. "How?" he said.

Namid peered out around him to an overgrown garden clearly visible in the light of early morning. "Dawn already?" she said.

Haeith joined them. "Must be something like what we experienced in Nazextas," he muttered.

Having settled the children on the room's single bed, Rannvei sat next to them and gave the others a puzzled look. "How can it be dawn already? We weren't in those passages that long."

"It didn't *feel* that long," Inezha said.

"Something with that Power you've said blankets the citadel?" Tal said.

"Probably," Aahmes said. "Maybe part of the veneer that led us to think we hadn't been in certain passages already."

"Wait until tonight, then?" Tal said. "Or go now and hope we catch father and Andrin with few others around?"

Everyone exchanged looks.

"Or go back and return another time," Mehratar said.

"I don't trust any of the options," Namid said.

Haeith opened the outer door a crack to check outside, then closed it. "No one about right now," he said. He unsheathed his sword and leaned his back against the door.

Namid put a thin shell of Wild Power around the room to prevent anyone outside from hearing them. And Aahmes sealed the outer door with Wild Power.

"No one but one of us can open it now," he said.

With a nod for him, Haeith slid down to sit against the door, sword still out.

"It seems that being stealthy isn't going to work," Tal said after silently studying his family. "So, I think we should take the direct approach. In a few candle-marks, father will hold morning court."

He looked at Namid. "Assuming he still follows the pattern I knew?"

"As far as I know," Namid said.

"So, we bring this before the full court. Expose this Andrin to everyone at once."

Namid plopped down in one of the three chairs in the

room as she considered this. It certainly appealed, but she feared that so much could go wrong. "I don't trust Andrin to be civil," Namid said after some thought.

Aahmes snorted. "I'd expect the exact opposite."

"Surprise should help?" Inezha said.

"Not sure he'll be surprised to see us," Aahmes said.

Namid felt a wisp of Mehratar's Power flow past her and gave him a quizzical look.

"The man I sense—the Monarch, we believe—has little time left," he said. "Even with Andrin's Power bolstering him. I'll have to get to him soon. Every day that passes lessens the chance that I'll be successful."

"Do we really know how much time we've lost wandering here?" Inezha said.

Namid frowned at the thought that it could have been more than only most of the night.

"I'd prefer the stealthy approach," Namid muttered.

Aahmes settled himself next to her on the floor and leaned against her leg. "Me too," he said. Then grinned at her. "Because it worked so well in Corentris."

She chuckled. "Well, yeah…."

"So we get a few short candle-marks' rest—we're in no shape for a confrontation right now—then we'll head to morning court," Tal said and settled on the floor near the bed. Rannvei stretched out next to him.

The others settled in as well as they were able.

"I'll watch," Haeith said in a quiet voice when Namid glanced at him.

With a nod, Namid tried to settle back in her chair to doze but found the chair too uncomfortable. She slid to the floor next to Aahmes and dozed with his arm around her shoulders.

~ ~ ~

Too soon it seemed, Haeith woke Namid and Aahmes, then moved on to the others. A glance out the window told Namid it was midmorning. She pulled a bit of dried meat from a pouch and chewed on it to hopefully keep her stomach from growling.

As the others readied themselves, Namid saw Tal and Rannvei in a heated discussion. It ended with Tal turning away with a wave of his arm and a frown on his face.

"I'll set a faint veneer around us to give others the sense that we belong here as we travel the halls," Haeith said as everyone gathered at the door. "I'll hold it underlying our semblance of nothingness, in case that fails us."

Namid nodded and looked to Tal. He took a deep breath and sighed, then looked over the others.

"We'll go straight to the great hall," he said. "But I want to use the family's entrance. That should put us closest to father and away from most other people. Give us time to do what we need to, I think, before anyone can interfere or get caught up in it."

He looked to Rannvei. "You're determined on this?"

She nodded and beckoned the children closer to join the rest of them at the door. "We all go together. Best that way."

Tal gave Haeith a look that he answered with a bow.

They encountered few people in the hallways leading to the great hall. The people they did encounter wore the dazed expressions that Namid remembered from towns where the Dark Priests had controlled the townsfolk. Andrin must have done something similar here. She suspected he had probably drawn blood Power from the citadel's people, too.

She clasped Aahmes' hand and shared her observations with him using thought-speech. He nodded and linked with her so they could share Power, if needed.

In the hallway that led to the family's entrance to the great hall, the group paused a couple of paces from the door to study the guards that flanked it. Namid recognized neither guard. Both looked slightly dazed, but more alert that the rest of the people they had seen.

Mehratar pointed to himself and inclined his head toward the guards. Namid looked to Tal, who nodded.

They watched as Mehratar slipped up between the guards and paused, a hand poised beside each of their faces. He closed his eyes and simultaneously touched both guards on their temples. Their eyes widened momentarily, then closed and they began to slump. Mehratar caught their collars and helped ease them to the floor, keeping the noise to a minimum. Namid looked around to see if anyone noticed the noise they made. But no one came.

The group stepped up and crowded around the door.

"This opens into a small alcove behind a tapestry," Tal told them in a quiet voice. "Beyond that is the dais where the Monarch, and often the Lady Royal and some nobles, sit for the court."

Namid felt Mehratar reach out with his Power. "He's there," he said. "But I still can't do anything even this close. I'll have to be able to touch him to work on countering the poison and its effects."

They all exchanged glances, and everyone nodded to indicate their readiness. Then Aahmes eased open the door.

He, Namid and Tal stepped into the alcove. With only the slightest movement of the tapestry, Aahmes peeked out.

"Andrin's to our left, across the dais," he whispered. "The Monarch and Lady Royal are almost right in front of us, just a little to the right."

Tal reached back and clasped Mehratar's arm. "We'll go right."

Aahmes nodded. "Left for us," he said, indicating Namid, who nodded agreement.

After a pause to tell the others, they slipped out from behind the tapestry.

Namid saw that the hall was more than half full of courtiers and guards, who all looked as dazed as the other people they had seen in the citadel. She dismissed them from her attention and focused on Andrin.

And felt something tear the veneer and semblance from the group, revealing them to everyone in the room.

Only vaguely aware of mild exclamations of surprise from the courtiers and guards, Namid sent a wave of Wild Power toward Andrin, intending to wrap it around him and confine his Power. Aahmes followed up with one of his own. But something caught at their feet, just the slightest sense of slowing, and they both stumbled, sending their Power off to the sides and missing Andrin completely.

Rannvei shot an arrow at Andrin. He raised a hand and the arrow shattered in the air a handspan from his chest.

And most of the people in the room stopped moving.

Andrin's spell that held people frozen in place, Namid felt certain.

Andrin frowned. "Almost had you," he said.

He sent a bolt of Power across the dais. Namid and Aahmes slammed Power shells around themselves, then Namid realized he was not aiming at them. She turned, too slowly it felt.

Might Andrin's Power still be dragging at her?

She glimpsed Tal between their mother and father, all three held frozen by Andrin's Power. Rannvei and the children stood not far from them, also frozen. Odasoro was held frozen just beyond Yokana, hands poised as if prepared to play his lute. The guard Ordra stood frozen behind him.

Andrin's attack was aimed at Tal and his family!

Then Haeith stood between them and Andrin's attack, his sword out and emanating a faint fiery glow. The fiery aura spread out from the sword to form a shield that blocked Andrin's Power.

Andrin threw more Power, also blocked by the fiery aura from Haeith's sword. Andrin threw another bolt of Power, larger, this time toward Namid.

As she strengthened the Power shell around herself, Namid saw movement from the corner of her eye. Then her father darted out around her, out from within the protective Power shell. He lunged at Andrin, a long dagger raised to strike. Namid frantically threw Power toward him to try to wrap him in protection.

Too late.

Multiple bolts of Power from Andrin flew across the dais. Most struck the Monarch of the Six Realms. He crumpled without a sound.

"No!"

Namid was uncertain who else shouted that with her as she dropped to her knees at her father's side.

Inezha hurried by, snatching the Monarch's dagger as she passed. Her newfound ability to feel Power must also have kept her from being caught in Andrin's spell. Numb, Namid watched her kneel next to Odasoro, who also lay sprawled on the dais. She touched his face, then gave Namid a sorrowful look.

Namid closed her eyes against the sight. Not him too!

She looked again at her father. Mehratar joined her at the Monarch's side. She thought she saw her father move slightly and she clasped his hand. It was so very cold. Slowly, she became aware again of happenings around her.

Aahmes had strengthened and expanded the defense shell around them and stood between her and Andrin, throwing bolt after bolt of Wild Power at the former Dark Priest. Namid rose to her feet and added her Power to Aahmes'. But Andrin's defensive shell held.

"Blood Power again," Aahmes murmured.

As she and Aahmes pounded Andrin, Namid noticed Inezha making her way across the dais again. Inezha gave Namid a feral smile and slipped behind Andrin, who was drawing more Power to himself.

Then the former Dark Priest gasped and jerked several times. He seemed to be struggling to breathe. He coughed and red foam caked his lips. He sank to his knees, revealing Inezha standing behind him clasping the Monarch's dagger, now dripping blood. She leaned forward to stab the dagger into Andrin's neck then yanked the blade sideways and out. Andrin collapsed.

Dropping the dagger in the blood next to Andrin's body, Inezha inclined her head to Namid. She placed her empty hand on her chest near her throat. And vanished.

And Namid remembered where she had seen that gesture before…. Myung, who was Chendrukhar, who was Wesh the Dark Priest, had done the very same thing.

With the collapse of Andrin's Power, the people he had held began to move again. Namid looked from her father to Odasoro, torn. Aahmes gave her shoulder a squeeze and walked over to kneel next to the fallen troubadour. A breath-of-time later he looked at Namid and shook his head.

Namid closed her eyes against the tears, but they came anyway. She turned her attention to her father's plight. Tal and Yokana joined her and Yokana clasped her hand tightly.

Mehratar glanced up and said only, "Give me time." He sank deeper into his Power, working to save the Monarch.

Still clasping Namid's hand, Yokana grabbed Tal in a tight embrace. "I'm so glad you're back," she murmured and buried her face in his shoulder.

He said nothing but wrapped both arms around her, watching Mehratar with an anguished expression.

Namid stared at her father as Mehratar's Power flowed through and around him. She was marginally aware that Aahmes spoke with Ordra, and the guard gathered others to keep everyone else back. Namid pulled her hand from her mother's grip and knelt again next to the Monarch. She saw that he still breathed, but each breath was a struggle and he looked bad. She glanced at Aahmes when he knelt next to her and placed a hand on her shoulder. She blinked against the tears and he wrapped his arm around her shoulders.

After nearly a quarter candle-mark, Mehratar sat back and met Namid's gaze. He slowly shook his head, his anguish clear in his expression.

Namid looked back to her father. To her surprise, his eyes were open and focused on her. He spoke. She had to lean close to hear the faint whisper.

"Sorry…" he said. "Had to send you…. Seer said—" The Monarch lifted a weak hand toward Yokana who knelt down and clasped it, her cheeks wet with her tears. She turned to Namid.

"A Seer had told us that when you showed signs of having Power, you needed to be sent away from us," Yokana said. "When you returned with Power, after leaving the Dark Priests' horrid stronghold, we knew that the Seer had spoken truth, that we must send you from us."

Yokana's attention returned to the Monarch and a sob caught in her throat. She gently placed his hand on his motionless chest. Mehratar closed the Monarch's eyes. Namid just sat looking at him as her tears fell.

After a few breaths-of-time, Yokana straightened her shoulders and picked up the crown that had slipped from the Monarch's head when he fell. Rising, she turned to the motionless guards and courtiers in the rest of the room.

"The Monarch is dead," Yokana told the assemblage and held the crown aloft.

She then gave Namid a questioning look and slightly extended the crown toward her. Namid shook her head then tilted it toward Tal, who stood slightly behind Yokana, tears streaming down his cheeks. Yokana gave Namid a slight nod, then turned to her son. She held the crown out to him.

"Long live the Monarch," the assemblage voiced the traditional response as Tal reached for the ornate crown.

~

Notes and Pronunciations

A week is eight days long.

A "candle-mark" is roughly equivalent to an hour.

A "breath-of-time" is an indeterminate short amount of time, roughly seconds to a few minutes.

A "pace" is the length of a double step (roughly five feet).

Aahmes -- AH mehz
Aahmestharq -- AH mehz thahrk
Akavos -- ah kah VOHSS
Andrin -- AN drihn
Anya -- AHN yuh
Arinsk -- AHR ihnsk
Arndu -- AHRN doo

Beithr -- B-EYE thuhr
Belaraketh -- bel AHR uh kehth
Breln -- BRELN
Byartal -- BYAHR tahl

Cahodre -- kah HOH dreh
Cameni -- KAM uh nee
Chall -- CHAL
Charov -- CHAHR uhv
Chendrukhar -- CHEHN droo kahr
Chimirya -- chih MEER yuh
Corentris -- kohr EHN trihss

Dar -- DAHR
Das -- DAHSS
Desmon -- DEHZ muhn
Draeivon -- DRAY ih von

Elnathan -- EL nuh thuhn
Enric -- EN rihk
Eisunal -- EYE suh nuhl
Estaevi -- ehss TAYV ee
Etha -- Eh thuh

Fabor -- FAY bohr
Fathir -- fah THEER
Finor -- fih NOHR
Foroughi -- FOHR oh ee

Garai -- guh RAY
Geir -- G-EYE-R

Haeith -- HAY ihth
Harunsson -- HAHR uhn suhn
Hildevei -- HIHL duh v-eye

Ilenii -- ihl EHN ee
Ina -- EE nuh
Inezha -- ihn EH zhuh

Jiang -- jee ANG
Jiro -- JEER oh
Jelth -- JELTH

Kalon -- KAL uhn
Karinthe -- KAH rihnth uh
Keizha -- KAY zhuh
Kezenae -- keh ZEHN ay
Kilaadi -- kih LAH dee
Krendl -- KREHN duhl
Kyerla -- KYER luh

Lazarn -- luh ZAHRN
Levil -- LEH vuhl

Luag -- LOO ahg

Magnor -- MAG nohr
Mehratar -- MEH ruh tahr
Melomel -- MEL uh mel
Mezeft -- meh ZEHFT
Mira -- MEER uh
Myung -- mee UHNG

Naalin -- NAH leen
Namid -- NAH meed
Narqir -- nahr KEER
Navele -- nuh VEEL
Nazextas -- naz EHKSS tuhss
navn -- NAH vuhn
Nolan -- NOH luhn

Odasoro -- oh DAHSS oh roh
Ordra -- OHR druh

Padrag -- PAH druhg
Paronia -- puh ROHN yuh
Prazny -- PRAHZ nee

Randoq -- RAN dok
Rannvei -- RAHN v-eye
Reinulf -- R-EYE nuhlff
Rhadanthus -- ruh DAN thuhss
Roivah-neheb -- ROI vuh NEH hehb

Sainamid -- sah EE nah meed
Saina -- sah EE nah
Sesaisyd -- seh SAY sihd
Shartov -- SHAHR toff
Staehw -- STAY oo
Stefe -- STEHF uh
svaina -- SVAH ee nuh

Sy'shythys -- sih SHIH thihss

Taakha -- tah AH kuh
Talorisin -- tal OHR ih sihn
Tal -- TAL
Tanyala -- tahn YAH lah
Tanya -- TAHN yah
Tarn -- TAHRN
Thalace -- thuh LAYSS
Thes -- THEHSS

Urel -- oo REL

Vayaza -- vuh YAY zuh
Vei -- V-EYE

Wesh -- WEHSH

Yala -- YAH lah
Yokana -- yoh KAH nuh

Zeltakra -- zel TAH kruh
Zianya -- zee AHN yuh

~

TITLES BY S. LYNN HELTON

Wild Heritage fantasy series

Duplicity of Power
Power Awry
Power Redeemed

Trial Run (prequel novella)
Trial and Tribulation (prequel novella)

The Deliberia Chronicles fantasy trilogy

Crystalborne Sigils
Songborne Gates
A Galeborne Resolve

AUTHOR'S NOTE

Thank you for reading my book. I hope you enjoyed it!

Please consider leaving an honest review on the book's
product page at your favorite online bookstore
and on Goodreads. Reviews from readers like you are
powerful and greatly help other readers
discover books they might enjoy.

-Lynn

ABOUT THE AUTHOR

S. Lynn Helton lives in the foothills of the Rocky
Mountains, U.S.A., with her family and a couple of crazy
cats. Lynn enjoys camping and hiking, playing games,
crafting, reading (a lot) and, of course, writing.

Read more about her books on her website:
www.slynnhelton.com

www.ingramcontent.com/pod-product-compliance
Lightning Source LLC
Chambersburg PA
CBHW072259020726
47501CB00002B/320